PENGUIN BOOKS

WHO MOVED MY BLACKBERRY™?

'Quite possibly the best book ever written on any subject ever'
Boris Johnson

'Like all good comic creations, this Alan Partridge of the corporate
world is instantly recognizable' *Daily Telegraph*

'A funny, acute take on ambition, hypocrisy, chance couplings – the
usual office fare' *GQ*

'Read this and you will never be able to mention "blue-sky thinking"
again without blushing' *Metro*

'Acutely and hilariously observed. The very best satire. If there's one
book every ambitious manager should read it's this one'
Evening Standard

'Enormously funny, touching . . . should become an instant classic'
Financial Times

'Hilarious. Will astound any reader not familiar with the current
mores of white-collar corporate life' *Sunday Times*

'The funniest book I've read about management . . . really is hilarious.
Management clichés and fads are ruthlessly ridiculed, and the book's
brilliant ending turns it from a clever satire into a Dantean vision of
corporate hell. Bridget Jones for the middle manager, only better'
Sunday Telegraph

MARTIN LUKES is Director of Special Projects at a-b glôbâl (UK), the London branch of a Fortune 500 company. Martin's career progression has been exponential in the last few years, rising from Marketing Director (UK) to Chief of Staff, Office of the CEO, making him at one point the most senior British executive on the US business scene. Born in Basingstoke in 1961, Martin is married to Jens, an a-b glôbâl director in her own right, and they have two sons, Jake (16) and Max (14).

For the last six years Martin has been writing a weekly column about his life, his loves and his management philosophy in the *Financial Times* on Thursdays. The column is eagerly read by captains of industry, among whom Martin Lukes has established an unrivalled track record as an iconic leader and trendsetter. This is his first book, which he plans to use as a platform to launch his career in the 'literary world'.

Martin has won countless awards, including 'BT Outstanding Individual Contribution to Work Life Balance 2004' (runner-up) and 'Best Change of DNA in Outsourced Space 2003' (sponsored by Hyatt Regency). His hobbies are golf, theatre, opera and reading 'the Classics'.

LUCY KELLAWAY is the *Financial Times'* management columnist. She lives in London and is married with four children. Her second novel, *In Office Hours*, is available in Penguin now.

MARTIN LUKES

Who Moved My BlackBerry™?

WITH LUCY KELLAWAY

PENGUIN BOOKS

PENGUIN BOOKS

Published by the Penguin Group
Penguin Books Ltd, 80 Strand, London WC2R ORL, England
Penguin Group (USA), Inc., 375 Hudson Street, New York, New York 10014, USA
Penguin Group (Canada), 90 Eglinton Avenue East, Suite 700, Toronto, Ontario, Canada M4P 2Y3
(a division of Pearson Penguin Canada Inc.)
Penguin Ireland, 25 St Stephen's Green, Dublin 2, Ireland (a division of Penguin Books Ltd)
Penguin Group (Australia), 250 Camberwell Road, Camberwell, Victoria 3124, Australia
(a division of Pearson Australia Group Pty Ltd)
Penguin Books India Pvt Ltd, 11 Community Centre, Panchsheel Park, New Delhi – 110 017, India
Penguin Group (NZ), 67 Apollo Drive, Rosedale, Auckland 0632, New Zealand
(a division of Pearson New Zealand Ltd)
Penguin Books (South Africa) (Pty) Ltd, 24 Sturdee Avenue, Rosebank, Johannesburg 2196, South Africa

Penguin Books Ltd, Registered Offices: 80 Strand, London WC2R ORL, England

www.penguin.com

First published by Viking 2005
Published in Penguin Books 2006
Reissued in this edition 2011

1

Set in Monotype Dante
Typeset by Palimpsest Book Production Limited, Falkirk, Stirlingshire
Printed in Great Britain by Clays Ltd, St Ives plc

A CIP catalogue record for this book is available from the British Library

ISBN: 978-0-241-95220-7

www.greenpenguin.co.uk

To dearest Mum, my #1 fan

Prologue

December

December 2

From: Martin Lukes
To: Sylvia Woods

Hi Sylvia
What's this message to call Sebastian Fforbes Hever? Did he say what it was about? I'm going out now for a spot of lunch. If he calls back, I've got my mobile, pager and BlackBerry with me.
Martin

From: Martin Lukes
To: Jenny Lukes

Darling –
Sorry about last night . . . had a few too many. Will try to get back early tonite to make amends.
    btw one of the top headhunters at Heidrick Ferry has been trying to get hold of me(!) . . . dunno what it's about
Love you, M xx

From: Martin Lukes
To: SebastianFforbesHever@HeidrickFerry

Hi Sebastian
Thanks for your most intriguing email. Yes, indeed, I could find a window to meet up with you tomorrow. I'll have to juggle a couple of meetings, but should be do-able – could see you at your offices in Buckingham Palace Road at around 3ish.
Bestest
Martin Lukes
Marketing Director, A&B (UK)

From: Martin Lukes
To: Jenny Lukes

Darling –
Guess what?? I've been approached to be director of marketing and strategy at a major FTSE 100 company!! All very hush hush . . . the headhunter wouldn't say which one over the phone, but I'm going to meet him tomorrow.
   I know you're really up against it this pm but wld be v grateful if you'd pick up my grey Hugo Boss suit from the cleaners. Love you M xx

December 3

From: Martin Lukes
To: Sylvia Woods

Hi Sylvia, I'm popping out now. If anyone wants to know where I am, say I'm at a forward planning meeting with Tim at BGF. Will be back 5ish.
Martin

From: Martin Lukes
To: Jenny Lukes

Darling – FANTASTIC meeting with Sebastian just now. The job is marketing director of Sainsbury's!! The role's heaven made for yours truly – I'd be in charge of 350 people globally, $1bn annual budget. Very high profile.

Sebastian didn't mention the package at this stage, but said it wouldn't be an obstacle to finding the right person. I assume at least twice what I'm on now . . . It's got my name all over it – what they want are unrivalled communications skills, out of the box thinking, results-driven mentality and an outstanding track record in driving performance . . . I've got ticks in all the boxes. Coming straight home now.

Love you M xx
Sent from my BlackBerry Wireless Handheld

December 4

From: Martin Lukes
To: SebastianFforbesHever@HeidrickFerry

Hi Sebastian
Great to meet with you yesterday – I felt we were very much singing from the same hymn sheet. I just wanted to reiterate how positive I am about this position, and how much I have to bring to the party.

Just to re-cap: I'm very can-do, very get-up-and-go – I operate very well within a large company – but have a pronounced entrepreneurial streak, that keeps me thinking outside the box.
Look forward to hearing from you.
All my very bestest
Martin

From: Martin Lukes
To: Jenny Lukes

Darling –
I'm on the shortlist!!! I'm going to meet all the top bods at Sainsbury's on Monday. I've got to prepare a presentation on how I would transition the marketing strategy onto a higher

plane. Should be no problem, though I'm a bit out of the loop on food shopping – you've deskilled me on that one! As a shopper, have you got any pointers on supermarkets – from the consumer's perspective? Debrief tonite?

Love you, M xx

PS I'll be working flat out all weekend . . . so don't think I'll be able to make it to yr parents on Sunday.

From: Martin Lukes
To: Jenny Lukes

Darling – don't think you understand this is the biggest inflexion point in my career to date. I'm sure your parents won't mind – they don't like me anyway . . .

December 9

From: Martin Lukes
To: Jenny Lukes

Darling – total triumph!! The chief executive of Sainsbury's has the IDENTICAL take on the future of marketing to yours truly. I gave them my spiel on how we have gone beyond traditional marketing into a new age of synchronicity across functionalities. The interview was meant to last an hour, but I got the feeling they had made up their mind after 15 minutes, and after that it was more like a relaxed friendly chat than your bog-standard interview.

   My presentation on their marketing strategy was 110 per cent on the button. I decided not to pull my punches, and I was pretty critical – though obviously in a very positive sort of way. Basically I said that in the past they've relied too heavily on Jamie Oliver – they need to have a more flexible approach to winning hearts and minds of today's shoppers. See you later.

M xx

From: Martin Lukes
To: SebastianFforbesHever@HeidrickFerry

Hi Sebastian
Just wanted to touch base to find out how you think that went?
Have you had any feedback from your client? From my point of
view it was very positive indeed . . .
Bestest
Martin

From: Martin Lukes
To: Jenny Lukes

Darling – Just had a brief chat with Sebastian – and he says they
are 'very interested' in me. Re package, we're talking of something in the region of 350k, plus bonus which could be same
again. Obviously share options, pension, health insurance, gym
club membership. Car allowance would be double so that we
could trade in the Mitsubishi Shogun and get a Porsche Cayenne
V8 Turbo S.
    We could also think of moving. I could see us in one of those
8-bed detached jobs on the common itself – near where George
and Stacey live. I just called the estate agent, and there's one on
the market for 3.2mil, which would be do-able.
Love you M xx

From: Martin Lukes
To: Jenny Lukes

Darling – Yes, I know I shouldn't count my chickens. And I'm
not. I'm simply repeating what I've been told. In any case in this
market milieu if you don't have a positive headset you don't get
anywhere.
M

December 10

From: Martin Lukes
To: Graham Wallace

Hi Graham
Did you notice that I wasn't firing on all cylinders in the board meeting just now? Between you and me and the gatepost, that could be the last one I'm ever going to attend. I'm up for a big job. It's as good as in the bag, though can't tell you what at this juncture. But put it this way. Think supermarket. Think Jamie Oliver. Think Chief Marketing Officer . . .
Mart

From: Martin Lukes
To: Graham Wallace

Cheers, Graham. Yes obviously I am totally over the moon. I had started feeling very stuck here – but I suppose I've been in denial about it. At the end of the day, being marketing director has been a load of fun, but I've outgrown it.
Mart
PS Keep this under your hat till it's greenlighted. Then monster drinks in order.

From: Martin Lukes
To: Sylvia Woods

Hi Sylvia
I think I should let you into a little secret. I'm afraid our ways are about to part. I've been headhunted for a very senior job, so looks like this might be my last week here. If anyone from Sainsbury's or Heidrick Ferry calls in the next hour when I'm in the budget meeting come and get me out.
M

From: Martin Lukes
To: Sylvia Woods

Anyone called?

December 11

From: Martin Lukes
To: SebastianFforbesHever@HeidrickFerry

Hi Sebastian
I don't want to hassle you, but I just wondered if there was any news?
Bestest, Martin

From: Martin Lukes
To: SebastianFforbesHever@HeidrickFerry

I don't understand. That wasn't what you implied earlier. I thought the Sainsbury's board loved me. Is this a joke, or what?

From: Martin Lukes
To: Jenny Lukes

I don't fucking believe it. They've gone and fucking given it to someone fucking else. Sebastian is a fucking lying sod. He said they LOVED my presentation – practically said the job was in the bag. And now he's saying I didn't have the right skillsets, fit not quite right blah, better qualified candidates . . . blah blah. I think the guy who got it is head of marketing at Tesco or Asda, so I suppose that means the idiots have gone for the safe candidate rather than the best candidate. I still just can't fucking believe it. It's so unfair.
My dream job.
M

From: Martin Lukes
To: Sylvia Wood

Sylvia I'm feeling very unwell. I think I'm coming down with the flu. I'm going home now.

December 15

From: Martin Lukes
To: Graham Wallace

Just to check – you haven't told anyone about that job, have you? As it happens I've decided against.

Basically, I've always believed that work is all about the people. And although it was very flattering to be offered such a mega job at Sainsbury's, at the end of the day, I didn't want to work with them. Apart from anything else fun wasn't part of their DNA at all. Feeling a bit rough this am. Hair of the dog later?
M

Chapter One

January
Myself – The Basics

January 1

From: Martin Lukes
To: Pandora@CoachworX

Hi Pandora
I'm jotting down a few key facts re myself, so that we'll be able to hit the ground running when we have our first CoachworX session on Wednesday.

But first I'm going to be upfront about the key learnings I want to take out from the coaching experience. For me, it's about achieving peak performance. At the end of the day, it's about winning. And that's what I want to do – to win.

So, with that out of the way, who am I?

Basically, I'm a board director of A&B (UK). Our parent company is based in Atlanta – and I'm Director of Marketing here in London. It's an exciting and challenging leadership role, and I feel I play a critical role in shaping the business going forward. I have always seen myself as a high-octane player. I'm very results driven, very can-do. However, over the last year I feel I have hit a plateau careerwise. Last month I was headhunted for the position of Marketing Director at Sainsbury's. I was way out in front of the field in terms of skillsets, but at the end of the day they went for the safe choice – someone less talented but who had retail experience.

Frankly, following this set-back, I am faced with a choice. Do

I hunker down here, or do I play the field? I've thought deeply about this and have decided to stay at A&B for now, as my values are well aligned with the company – and at 43 I feel I still have a huge amount to contribute.

You have probably read in the media about Barry Malone, our new CEO. He's an incredibly energetic, charismatic guy – one of the most revered business leaders globally.

However under him the company is becoming more political, and personally, I think that's a pity. Barry's also very much into business jargon, it's all a bit too 'American' for my taste. People who know me will tell you that I always call a spade a spade! I think you wanted to know a few key facts re my home life? I've been married for 17 years to Jenny and we have two smashing boys. Jake is 15, and Max is 12. Jake is highly creative, though has some issues around behaviour – which makes him typical for a youngster of his age. Max is a highflyer across the board – a chip off the old block, if you will. He's doing Common Entrance this year – we've put him down for Eton, and according to his head teacher, he's expected to walk it.

I'd say the marriage is definitely a happy one, albeit with the usual ups and downs. The only thing I'd flag up is that in the last couple of years Jens has been getting stressed about her career – she works part time for a pr agency. Frankly I sometimes wonder if there are time of life issues at play too – I mentioned it to her the other day, but she didn't see the funny side! She's a year older than me, but she takes good care of herself, and is still a perfect size 8!

Home is in Wimbledon in a six-bed villa we bought back in 1993 for £250,000, and has just been valued (conservatively for insurance purposes) at £1.9 mil.

You ask about my personal health and fitness, exercise regime, diet and alcohol levels. Basically I'm in reasonable health – if you push yourself as hard as I do, your immune system has to work 24/7! I try to get to the gym as often as possible – I'm in between personal trainers at the moment, but obviously would like to start again asap, time permitting. I've put on a bit of weight recently, and for Christmas Jens gave me Atkins Made Easy – The First Two Weeks. I've tried Atkins before but not stuck to it. This year it's going to be different, and today is Day One!

Drink? I'm a great believer in the value of alcohol as a stress buster, but I don't drink to excess. Probably in the region of 14–17 units a week, or thereabouts.

Smoking – no way. I'm very anti smoking. In fact this is something I'm totally passionate about. I've told both my boys that if they get to 18 without smoking I'll give them both £1,000 cash in hand. At the end of the day, getting the incentive right is key. What do I get up to in my spare time? I don't have any! Joking aside, I'd say it's divided in three.
1. Golf – though I don't get to play nearly as much as I'd like. Currently got a handicap of 14, which I'm not at all happy about.
2. My family. Of course they are mission critical in every sense of the word.
3. The culture scene. Theatre, opera, cinema, reading. Words mean a lot to me. I sometimes think I would have liked to be a writer, and have got lots of book ideas. But at the end of the day there are only so many hours available.

Hope that's enough for now. I'm eagerly anticipating speaking with you on Monday at 3.30.
All my very bestest,
Martin Lukes

January 2

From: Pandora@CoachworX
To: Martin Lukes

Thank you for that Martin! It is always good to know as much about my clients as possible! We are embarking on an exciting life-changing journey together and I have the highest expectations of you. I'll be your number one fan and I believe in your phenomenal potential to do, to have and to

be whatever and whoever you want. Look forward to talking to you on Monday.
Strive and thrive!
Pandora

From: Martin Lukes
To: Sylvia Woods

WHERE THE HELL IS MY TIGER WOODS MUG? IT'S BLOODY TYPICAL – YOU GO ON HOLIDAY FOR A COUPLE OF DAYS, AND COME BACK TO FIND SOME-ONE HAS TAKEN YOUR SODDING MUG.

From: Martin Lukes
To: Sylvia Woods

Hi Sylvia
False alarm – mug found. Happy New Year, hope you had a good one. Would appreciate if you could get my expenses done this am, as Christmas cost me an arm and a leg. There's a pile of receipts on your desk – some of which are blank – please make sure the total comes out slightly higher than this time last year, though not out of the ball park.
Ta muchly, M
PS When you've got a mo, could you get me a latte and a bar of Green and Blacks white chocolate. Alas, no more almond croissants for me, as this is day two of Atkins!

From: Barry S. Malone, CEO
To: All Staff

Howdy!
First up, Happy New Year! This is a particularly joyous occasion as it is my first at the helm of this fine company.

New Year is a time for a new beginning, not just for us as individual leaders but for us together, as a global family

Over the festive holiday I met up with Chuck P. Stallone, the best coach basketball has ever seen. We got talking about what he had done to keep his team at the top for nearly two decades. Chuck said something to me that made a whole lot of sense. He said it wasn't about getting to the top – but staying at the top. The name of his game is not 'peak performance', but Peak Performance – Permanently. And that is my dream for us. That we will peak perform not just this year, but every year going forward.

This is going to involve one of the greatest change programs this company has ever undertaken. We are going to transition hearts and minds into a whole new ball park. Step one is to rebrand our company. We will be looking for a new name and a new identity that will reflect our new PPP culture.

I want to share with you the image of stonemasons building a cathedral. Their task is no different to ours here at A&B. Why did they chisel that stone? Because their bodies and their souls bought into the idea.

I am asking you to be like the stonemasons. If you have faith in our great company, if you buy into the idea of PPP, we can build our cathedral together.

Have a joyful New Year. One of the things that makes me proudest about this company is you all. This company would not exist without the passion and the sweat of every one of you. So if any of you have any ideas, or feelings you would like to share, please email. Or just email to say HI! That sustains me.
I love you all
Barry

From: Martin Lukes
To: Graham Wallace

Hi Graham – how goes it? Our Christmas was a classic of peace and harmony. Jake got pissed on Christmas day and threw up on the in-laws' new Axminster.

Have you read BM's seasonal twaddle? I'm hacked off at this rebranding thing – I've been going on about rebranding for yonks, and how much credit do I get for this? Zero. Btw, can't remember

if I mentioned to you that I've signed up with a top life coach? I've got Pandora Barry – she was trained up by the guy who did Chelsea Clinton, Nelson Mandela and Bill Gates. First session this pm – watch this space!!
Mart
PS Fancy a drink later?

January 5

From: Martin Lukes
To: Sylvia Woods

Sylvia – what the hell is this budget meeting in my diary for 3 pm? I've blocked out that hour to talk to my coach on the phone. Email Roger I can't come.
Can you get me two litres of mineral water and a latte?
M

From: Martin Lukes
To: Pandora@CoachworX

Hi Pandora!
Great to talk to you just now. I was impressed at how quickly you got my number – I can actually be quite awkward at times, and certainly don't tolerate fools gladly – but when I click with someone then the sky's the limit! I think we're going to make an unbeatable team!

As we discussed, the top-of-the-range CoachworX Platinum Service would be most appropriate. As I understand it, you would be available on a 24/7 basis on the telephone and by email and face 2 face to coach me through ongoing issues as they surface, and would bill A&B @ £300 per hour.

I need to get our finance director Roger Wright to greenlight the expenditure, but I anticipate that as a formality.
All my very bestest,
Martin

From: Martin Lukes
To: Jenny Lukes

Darling – First coaching session was SENSATIONAL! Pandora
clearly thinks I'm destined for the very top.

   She's a fascinating woman – used to be a ballet dancer but
then had a breakdown and got ME and cancer – was given six
months to live, but basically coached herself into remission.

   She says I have this amazing power inside myself. I just have
to learn how to unlock it! Only issue was that I ate four bour-
bon biscuits while talking to her – which was very bad news
with the Atkins. Will tell all tonight.
Love you, M

From: Martin Lukes
To: Jenny Lukes

Actually, darling, I think you've got it arse around tit. Coaches
aren't 'untrained shrinks' – they're experts in lifting performance.
Pandora says lots of the people she's coached have increased their
income ten times as a result of the programme!!! Do you have
any IDEA what that would mean for you? You could chuck in
your job and become a Lady Who Lunches! And we could have
our garden relandscaped with the Chatsworth style water feature
that you admired at Chelsea last year – only ours could be bigger.
See you 9ish –
Love M
PS Big juicy steak would be nice . . . quite fancy a slab of
dolcelatte for afters and that lovely chocolate cake of Nigella's
that doesn't have any flour in it . . .

From: Martin Lukes
To: Roger Wright

Hi Roger
Yesterday I had the first complimentary coaching session with
Pandora Barry of CoachworX, and would like to proceed with
the Platinum Executive Coaching Programme. I am attaching
the fee schedule.
Bestest, Martin

From: Martin Lukes
To: Roger Wright

Hi Roger
You ask: why do I need a coach? You're probably thinking that
as I'm highly successful already, I don't need one. But look at it
this way – Tiger Woods has a coach. Wayne Rooney has a coach.
They don't need a coach, but they have one because they feel
more comfortable with the career success that a coach can
provide. Even Pandora herself has a coach because she is committed to consistently beating her best, month by month.

   I realize she charges a premium price, but in this business
there is no point in having anything less than the best.
Martin

From: Martin Lukes
To: Pandora@CoachworX

Hi Pandora
Some bad news, I'm afraid. I have been informed by Roger
Wright, our autistic finance director that due to ongoing restric-
tions to our operating budget, he's only prepared to greenlight
the Bronze Programme, which I understand is coaching by
monthly emails.

This is obviously a blow. And it's bloody typical of this place, if you'll excuse my French. Spends a fortune on moronic diversity training programmes, and then as soon as you suggest something good, there's no money. Also typical of Roger – who thinks blue sky is what you can see on a sunny day.
Bestest, Martin

From: Pandora@CoachworX
To: Martin Lukes

Hi Martin!
One of the things I will teach you on this journey is that everything is possible. I'm going to teach you to say goodbye to negative feelings and get back to your childlike optimism. The Executive Bronze Life Coaching Program is going to help you get there!

Now a lesson for you. Where we at CoachworX differ from other coaches is that they teach you to be the very best you can be. We think you can go further. This program is about being *better* than your very best. I'd like you to meditate on that, and think of a quantifiable target that you think is achievable. We will then assess your progress against this target every month. I think it is fair to say that I have never had a coachee that did not finish the year ahead of their targets!
Pandora

From: Martin Lukes
To: Pandora@CoachworX

Hi Pandora
What you say makes a lot of sense to me – in the kind of hyper-competitive field I operate in, the best is an entry ticket, if you like. I've always said to the people who have worked under me: keep pushing the envelope until it falls off the table!
So, this is the goal I am signing up to.

By year end I will achieve performance levels that are 5 per cent better than the very best I can be.

Certainly this journey will take me way outside my comfort zone, but I'm ready for that.

Bestest
Martin

From: Martin Lukes
To: Sylvia Wood

Hi Sylvia – when you've got a window can you make me a big laminated sign for my wall that says:

BY YEAR END I WILL ACHIEVE PERFORMANCE LEVELS THAT ARE 5 PER CENT BETTER THAN THE VERY BEST I CAN BE.

Also plse cancel Christo – I was meant to be having my first session mentoring him, but I'm too busy. See if you can diarize something for next week or the week after.

Ta muchly
Martin

From: Pandora@CoachworX
To: Martin Lukes

Hi Martin!
You are starting to think big – but not BIG enough! I am going to help you make a quantum leap in your self-belief. I, your greatest fan, sincerely believe you can beat your best by 50 per cent by year end. What is stopping you?
Strive and thrive!
Pandora

From: Martin Lukes
To: Pandora@CoachworX

Hi Pandora
It's energizing to realize how much you believe in me, but I wonder if your metrics are a bit high. Can we compromise and say that I'm going to aim to be 22.5 per cent better than the very best I can be? I think that's probably scaleable!
22.5 per cent better than my bestest!
Martin

From: Martin Lukes
To: Keith Buxton

Hi Keith
I have just visited the staff canteen and found that there was not a single menu choice consistent with the Atkins diet.

Today there was toad in the hole, or mushroom risotto, or chicken pie. All of the above combine carbohydrates and protein.

Many of the more senior members of the staff follow Atkins and we should be encouraging them to use the canteen. It is only by the mingling of staff that knowledge is shared.
All my very bestest
Martin

January 7

From: Keith Buxton
To: All Staff

Dear all – I am delighted to inform you that Cindy Czarnikow, Global Head of Strategic Marketing, is to join us in London on a two-month assignment. Cindy will be spearheading Project Rebrand, a global drive to reinvigorate the A&B corporate personality. She will be working closely with Barry Malone and the top team in Atlanta, and I know you'll give her every support in this exciting initiative.

Additionally, Martin Lukes has been tasked with leading a brainstorming group on how to improve the staff canteen. Any thoughts about delivering uplift to the current service should be addressed to him. Keith

From: Martin Lukes
To: Graham Wallace

Fucketyfuckingfuck. I didn't opt for a high-flying career in order to discuss toad in the sodding hole.

What do you know about Cindy Czarnikow?? My sources in Atlanta say she's shagged her way to the top – possibly having a scene with Barry Malone . . .
Drink later?
M

From: Martin Lukes
To: Jenny Lukes

Darling – fraid I won't be back in time to talk to Jake about his behaviour tonight. Will send him a motivational email when I get a window.
Love you, M.

January 8

From: Martin Lukes
To: Jake Lukes

Jake, old man. Sorry I didn't touch base with you yesterday. I just wanted to reinforce the ground rules we agreed before Christmas. This term is make or break for your GCSEs but also for your future, and I'd like to share some advice with you. In this life, you get out what you put in – and you are not putting enough in.

Set yourself a stretch goal and then stick to it. I'm not asking you to be your best – think BIG Jake! Push the envelope! Be BETTER than your best! Agreed?

C u later!

Love Dad

From: Martin Lukes
To: Jake Lukes

J – No I haven't lost the plot, as you so charmingly put it. I was merely passing on to you some advice my coach has given me. I suppose it was asking too much to expect you to buy into the philosophy behind it.

Dad

From: Martin Lukes
To: Sylvia Woods

Thanks for making me the poster – very nice. Unfortunately there's been a slight change. Can you do it again, putting 22.5 per cent instead of the 5? Keep this one for yourself if you like.

Martin

PS I've got about 400 emails complaining about the canteen food. Can you reply to all, saying thanks for feedback, I'm looking into it.

January 12

From: Martin Lukes
To: Sylvia Woods

WHAT'S ALL THAT BANGING?? I CAN'T HEAR MYSELF THINK. PLSE CALL BUILDING SERVICES AND TELL THEM TO STOP IT.

From: Martin Lukes
To: Graham Wallace

Hi Graham – Cindy's taken the partition walls down and has commandeered twice as much space as my office. I've just sent Sylvia out to count the ceiling tiles. I've got 49 and she's got 63!! She's got no desk, just squashy sofas – perfect for her favourite pastime. Though, without walls she's not going to be able to get up to much!

Have you clapped eyes on her yet? Check out the teeth and smile – she's got the classic American look – a ton of make-up, perfect grooming, really skinny with a massive arse.

Not my scene at all.
Cheers, Mart

From: Cindy Czarnikow
To: All Staff

Hi everyone!

It's phenomenally exciting to be with you here in London town! I am humbled to be heading up such an exciting project as Project Rebrand. We are taking the A&B footprint and we are going to re-dream it! Task One is to draw a road map. This is going to be an inclusive bottom-up rebrand, and I want to hear from you! I want each of you to come up with five unbeatable words that you think describe the A&B corporate DNA going forward! These will form the building blocks for the new identity.

Please email me, or come see me! I'm right by Martin Lukes' office on the fifth floor. You'll find it looks a bit different up here. I've taken down the walls, chucked out the desk, and put in two white leather couches! This is going to be a space where we can hit ideas around and make it happen!

I'm smiling at you
Cindy

From: Martin Lukes
To: Cindy Czarnikow

Hi Cindy
Welcome to London Town! I'm sure we are going to enjoy working together. A word of advice, if I might make so bold. While I, more than anyone, believe in open lines of communication, I find that at the end of the day one does need to get some work done. And for that I find that a door which closes and a desk have their uses!

As I'm sure you appreciate, I am presently snowed under with work. However, I will do some blue sky thinking on the five traits as soon as I've got a window.
Martin

From: Martin Lukes
To: Cindy Czarnikow

Graham – Five traits of a certain person: Dumb. Big bum. Phony. Devious. Dangerous.
I'm leering at you!
M

From: Martin Lukes
To: Cindy Czarnikow

Hi Cindy – I think I may have sent you something in error. It was meant for Graham . . . Plse ignore. Martin

From: Martin Lukes
To: Graham Wallace

Fucketyfucketyfucketyfuckingfuck. Just done something that would be funny if it weren't so awful. Will fill you in over a large one . . . M

From: Pandora@CoachworX
To: Martin Lukes

Hi Martin!
I just wanted to check that you are doing what we agreed.
Keeping it professional.
Staying proactive. Thinking positive.
Strive and thrive!
Pandora

From: Martin Lukes
To: Pandora@CoachworX

Just seen your message. Yes, I was doing really well until this morning. Unfortunately I now seem to have got into a spot of hot water due to a technical problem. I sent a message to Graham Wallace, who's my opposite number in sales. I can have a good laugh with him – he's no rocket scientist but after a jar or two he's a lot of fun. Basically, I sent him an email which I believe may have been read and misinterpreted by Cindy Czarnikow, a seriously humourless colleague from the US of A.
Martin

From: Martin Lukes
To: Sylvia Woods

Can you check and see if Cindy's on her sofa – I need to pop out for a second, and would rather not bump into her just now.

From: Martin Lukes
To: Jenny Lukes

Hi Jens – Just seen your message re Jake's phone bill. How the bloody hell did the little bugger manage to run up £495 in three months????
M

January 13

From: Martin Lukes
To: Sylvia Woods

Morning Sylvia! Why does Keith want to see me urgently? Any idea what it's about? Large latte would be nice. M

From: Martin Lukes
To: Graham Wallace

Hi Graham
Just had the biggest bollocking of my life from Keith. Now I've got to grovel to Cindy, and Faith is threatening me with a gender awareness course called Sex@Work which sounds rather fun, though have a very nasty feeling it's going to be anything but.
Martin

From: Martin Lukes
To: Cindy Czarnikow

Hi Cindy –
First let me apologize for any embarrassment I might have caused you by my misdirected email, which was far more innocent than it may have seemed!

I realize there are large cultural differences between us people on either side of the pond, and we all need to be congnizant of these 24/7!!

I also wanted to point out that you seem to have got the wrong end of the stick re myself having issues around women. In fact I'm one of their keenest champions, as any of the girls here will tell you. Far from trying to undermine you, I have actively supported your Rebrand work, and it goes without saying, I think you're doing a terrific job.

Would be delighted to give you any advice going forward,

on matters marketing or otherwise. You suggest a breakfast –
I can do next Tuesday, though could we make it 8 am rather
than 6.30?
All my bestest, Martin

January 16

From: Cindy Czarnikow
To: All Staff

Hi everyone!
Project Rebrand is a total blast! First up, the personality trait that most
of you mentioned as being associated with the new brand was joy! Our
new corporate personality is going to be like a joyful smile! The smile
is the strongest form of human communication we have, and we are
going to harness its power!
    I am also phenomenally excited to say that we have hired Beyond the
Box presently which has a team of 12 rebranding consultants dedicated to
our assignment, and have come up with in excess of 1,000 corporate names.
They are assisting our search to find a new name that will create brand
empathy and position us as a company that peak performs – permanently!
I'm smiling at you,
Cindy

From: Martin Lukes
To: Jake Lukes

Jake – I've just seen the itemized bill for your mobile. Your mother
is on a total bender.
EXPLANATION PLEASE.
Dad

From: Martin Lukes
To: Graham Wallace

Hi Graham – You are bloody lucky that you've got daughters.

Jake seems to have been doing phone sex on his mobile. When we were his age Penthouse was good enough for us.
Drink? I need a large one.
Mart

Text message to Jenny. Sent 18:43

What do u mean, where am I?? Am having v quick drink w Graham, and then on my way home pronto. Is that a prob? M x

Text message to Jenny. Sent 18:46

How was I supposed to know that? It wasn't in my diary. M x

From: Martin Lukes
To: Sylvia Wood

WHY WASN'T MY SON'S SCHOOL PLAY IN MY DIARY???
I was meant to be there this evening seeing him star in Romeo and Juliet, and am now in a lot of trouble with the lady wife. I gave you a list with all his school fixtures on it. What did you do with it? Frankly it isn't good enough.
Martin
Sent from my BlackBerry Wireless Handheld

January 19

From: Pandora@CoachworX
To: Martin Lukes

Hi Martin
One of the most important things I am going to teach you on this course is how to turn your stumbling blocks into stepping stones.

I will show you how to stop thinking about obstacles and problems, and start seeing them as opportunities to improve

yourself. Let's start today. Tell me about a stumbling block, and I'll show you how to transform it!
Strive and Thrive!
Pandora

From: Martin Lukes
To: Pandora@CoachworX

Hi Pandora
Frankly, it's occurred to me that one of my biggest stumbling blocks may be my PA Sylvia. She's been with me for two years, but simply doesn't see the point of going the extra mile. Instead she loses things, has cocked up my diary arrangements and had the nerve to say that I never gave her the dates. I've given her a bit of a pep talk, but no effect.
Martin

From: Pandora@CoachworX
To: Martin Lukes

Hi Martin
You are a great leader. Great leaders have great followers, and it may be that Sylvia isn't a great follower. But you need to ask yourself: Is she ready to change? Is she ready to get rid of her limiting beliefs? You need to take the time and work through these issues with her.
Strive and Thrive!
Pandora

From: Martin Lukes
To: Sylvia Woods

Hi Sylvia
I've been mulling over what happened on Friday and I suggest we turn it into a stepping stone. I believe that you need to ask yourself some pretty big questions: Do I want to change? Am I

ready to get rid of my limiting beliefs? Shall we discuss over breakfast tomorrow?
Martin

January 20

From: Zach Smart at Beyond the Box
To: Everyone@A&B.com

Hi!
Let me introduce myself. I'm Zach from Beyond the Box and I, co-jointly with my partners, have been working on the rebranding of A&B.

At Beyond the Box we have no hierarchies and we believe all partners are equally valid. It is not our mindset to think in terms of leaders, but if you do need to talk to someone in authority, then I'm a good place to start. Thanks to the unique flexibility of our structure we have been able to road-test literally thousands of names in record time and have come up with four uniquely exciting possibilities for a rejuvenated A&B.

a and b This represents a path-breaking image revitalization. It retains the best of the tradition but by using lower case lettering has also taken on much of the energy and buzz of the new economy. Replacing & with 'and' lends an honesty and freshness that is closely aligned with A&B's personality.

qwerky! This is exhilarating, modern, and shows the company to be proactive, zany, and above all youthful. However it does represent something of a break with the past, which may take some of you out of your personal comfort zone.

abba This highly innovative name was arrived at by taking the two initials of A and B and then repeating them backwards. It proves conclusively that A&B are lateral thinkers who will go to any lengths to deliver value to their entire community of stakeholders.

<Wednesday> Neither the start of the week, nor the end, the name embodies the best of all worlds. It is a mixture between work and home, in the thick of things. The Chevrons at either end enhance its inclusiveness.

Please email either Cindy or me, and tell us what you think of these sensational names!
Zach Smart

From: Martin Lukes
To: Cindy Czarnikow

Cindy –
There's no contest is there? The clear winner among the names they suggest is <Wednesday> – the others are frankly disappointing. <Wednesday> is just what were're looking for – it's got integrity, buy-in, universal appeal while being a bit unexpected.

Do you want me to lobby for it?
Best, Martin

From: Pandora@CoachworX
To: Martin Lukes

Hi Martin
Good to talk to you just now. Can I recap? You must focus, focus, focus on your self-belief Martin. You must love yourself, because if you don't, no one else will. If you have a good idea, market it! If you don't like the way the rebrand project is going, step in! Shape it! You have great talents, Martin! Show them to the world!
Strive and thrive!
Pandora

From: Martin Lukes
To: Sylvia Woods

What did you want to see me about? Can't it wait? I'm writing what is arguably the most important email of my life.

From: Martin Lukes
To: Barry S. Malone

Hi Barry

Let me introduce myself. I'm Martin Lukes and I'm Marketing Director in London. I just wanted to touch base, first of all to say hi, and also to say how very inspirational I find our new PPP culture. It has always struck me that what matters is winning – not just now but going forward. You may be interested to know that I am actually going through something similar with my coach on an individual level. The best, I passionately believe is only an entry ticket!

I also wanted to say that a body of support is building in London behind <Wednesday>. I feel that this name alone conveys how seriously committed we are to a peak performance as a journey that has started, but not yet finished! From a marketing standpoint, <Wednesday> will secure buy-in from all our stakeholders. The chevron signs will keep our customers coming back to the brand forever!

All my very bestest
Martin

From: Martin Lukes
To: Sylvia Woods

You want to QUIT? But you can't when there's so much on! I'll get you a pay rise.
Martin

From: Martin Lukes
To: Faith Preston

Faith,
Sylvia's threatening to resign, which is obviously highly inconvenient. I think she's on 20k – can you up it to 20.5k effective at once?
Martin

From: Martin Lukes
To: Faith Preston

I see. So what did she say about me? Sylvia and I had our differences at first but recently we've had an excellent working relationship. And I'm always very appreciative whenever she makes a special effort – which, to be perfectly honest, doesn't happen every day. I've already given her a massive coaching pep talk. Maybe a box of chocs would do the trick.
All my very bestest
Martin

January 21

From: Martin Lukes
To: Phyllis Lukes

Dear Mum
Many thanks for your message which I got yesterday – in fact I got six of them!! You only need to press the send button once! Still, not to worry, we'll make a silver surfer of you yet! How are you? Have you been getting out in this cold weather at all?

Boys are both really well. Max was brilliant as Juliet in the school play – looked quite convincing as a girl! Jake beavering away at his GCSEs. Otherwise not much is happening on the family front, Jens is a bit tired and hacked off with her job – but has decided to re-do the kitchen (again!). She's fed up with the stainless steel and we're getting something more authentic. But for now it means total chaos chez nous!

Mum, I wanted to iron out a little misunderstanding we had on the phone last week. When I told you about my coach, you seemed to think I was off somewhere! I didn't mean that sort of coach – a coach is someone who helps people like your loving son become more successful. I know you think I'm already the most successful man on earth, mummy, but according to Pandora – she's my coach – I could climb a lot higher!

Fraid we're not going to be able to get up to see you at the weekend. Hope you don't mind. I've been invited to play golf at Wentworth, which is too good to turn down!

Sorry to hear that the shelves I put up last time have come down. As I said to you at the time, you didn't have the right rawl plugs, and that wall isn't really suitable. I'll sort something next time I come.

Your loving son

Martie

From: Martin Lukes
To: Barry S. Malone

Hi Barry

On reflection, I must say I empathize with your reservations about <Wednesday>. I too feel that its chief weakness as a new identity for us is that it is totally irrelevant to our history, culture and product.

I also strongly agree that the list from Beyond the Box has been very disappointing, and would be the first to support your idea of proceeding via an internal naming competition. I have every confidence that inside this organization we have the energy and the brilliant minds to unlock solutions ourselves.

All my very bestest,

Martin

January 22

From: Cindy Czarnikow
To: All Staff

Hi everyone!
I am phenomenally excited to announce that today we are inviting all of you, the people of our global family, to choose A&B's new name via an online jamming session, led by Christo Weinberg, our brilliant UK brand ambassador. This is going to be a high-engagement, high-energy,

all-employee process. We have chosen a competition because we want to make sure our new name is not just best of breed but uniquely fits our culture.

Does this mean that the work with Beyond the Box has been wasted? Far from it. We have extracted some key learnings from the process, but now feel it is time to move on.

Some co-colleagues have asked me what the winning name will be like? That's up to you!! But I hope it will be global, pro-active, hyper-creative and caring.

There are some phenomenally exciting prizes including a workshop in circus skills, and a free feng shui makeover of your master bedroom. I'm smiling at you
Cindy

From: Martin Lukes
To: Cindy Czarnikow

Cindy – Can I just correct something in your message? Christo is not our brand ambassador. As director of marketing that role falls to me. As you know, from a hierarchical point of view, I don't mind about these things – I only mention it because it is best to avoid confusion where possible. I've been mentoring Christo since the beginning of the year, and would be delighted to help keep him on track with this new assignment!
All my very bestest
Martin

January 23

From: Christo Weinberg
To: All Staff

Hi!
There are unbelievable riffs coming out of this process! I'm forwarding to you some of the online jamming session. Really mellow! Keep it coming!

I'd like to kick things off by suggesting 'a and b global'. It is a win-win name. Modern, traditional and global . . . (Keith Buxton, UK chairman)

Sounds fab to me! It's really can-do. (Suzanna Elliott, Marketing Manager)

I'm comfortable with it. It clears my two hurdles – it underlines our commitment to diversity, and is passionately caring. (Faith Preston, Director for People)

Re: a and b global it takes a long time to say (5 syllables), it involves too many key strokes. (Roger Wright, Finance Director)

How's about 'a.b global'? It's funkier than Keith's suggestion and shorter, authoritative, and has instant impact. (Christo Weinberg, Marketing Manager)

Thank you Christo! I buy into that! That sure has made my pulse race. (Cindy Czarnikow, Leader of Rebrand)

Fine by me. Shorter is better. (Keith Buxton)

I feel this debate goes to the very heart of what we are trying to do as a company. Let me suggest an alternative: a-b global. The hyphen has more heart than a full stop. It shows that we can move quickly and that we are unerring in our attention to detail. (Martin Lukes)

Very radical. Very out of the box. I really like it! (Suzanna Elliott)

The hyphen has no place in the company history. (Roger Wright)

This discussion is ongoing. Please continue to add riffs of your own. Keep it mellow! Christo Weinberg

From: Martin Lukes
To: Suzanna Elliott

Hi Suzanna – I'd like to congratulate you on your perceptive contributions to the rebranding jamming session. Well done!
Martin

January 26

From: Martin Lukes
To: Pandora@CoachworX

Hi Pandora
Sorry I haven't been in touch. This rebrand project is seriously eating into my time! I had a near disaster with my email to Barry recommending <Wednesday>. My suggestion was too blue sky for him – but he sent me a nice email back saying how much he loves to hear from people, so I think it was good I touched base.

Things are getting better with Cindy – she is now very impressed with my professionalism, and I feel that I am regaining the initiative on the rebrand. Christo is getting a bit big for his boots. As his mentor, I should probably try to gently take him down a peg or two . . .
22.5 per cent better than my very bestest
Martin
PS Thanks for sending me audiotape of Why Men Lie and Women Cry, started listening in the car, though Jens objected!

From: Martin Lukes
To: Sylvia Woods

Sylvia – If you are determined to leave us, I can't stop you. What are you going to do?
Martin

From: Martin Lukes
To: Sylvia Woods

You're going to be a PARTNER at Beyond the Box?
Congratulations!
Martin
PS I found that list of school dates at the bottom of my brief-
case. All forgiven! Mea culpa!!!

January 27

From: Cindy Czarnikow
To: All Staff

Hi!
This is an exciting day! The Rebrand Steering Committee, in conjunc-
tion with Barry have considered two sensational options: a.b global,
and a-b global, and I would like to give you a heads up that we have
decided the name best aligned with our PPP values is a-b global. When
the designers have worked on a livery we will be ready to start rolling
it out!
I'm smiling at you!
Cindy

From: Martin Lukes
To: Barry Malone

Hi Barry
I'm delighted that you like a-b global – you may not be aware
that I am actually the man behind the hyphen! As my coach says,
sweat the small stuff – the devil's in the detail!
All my very bestest
Martin

January 29

From: Martin Lukes
To: Rebrand Steering Committee

I've seen the roughs of our new logo from the design team and the designers have put the name under a square root sign, which, though innovative, represents a cultural dissonance with our core values.

I suggest that we build on the success of the hypen by having an umlaut over the o and a circumflex over the a, so that the name would appear: a-b glöbâl. This is an exhilarating option that would provide a feelgood factor for our stakeholders globally. All my very bestest
Martin

From: Roger Wright
To: Rebrand Steering Committee

Hi! Although I am not myself a student of modern languages, I under-stand that the umlaut suggested by Martin Lukes would make the word pronounced 'gloerbal', which does not work in any language. The circumflex is now obsolete in France and as a forward-looking company, we are not seeking association with the past.
Roger Wright
Finance Director

From: Cindy Czarnikow
To: Rebrand Steering Committee

I love Martin's solution! I think it's really cool! I think these accents will encourage our global stakeholders to want to love, and live our brand!
Cindy

From: Martin Lukes
To: Pandora@CoachworX

Hi Pandora!
I am radiating self-belief and even Cindy is buying into my charisma!

I've had some enormous wins on Rebrand – and now looks like the final name will have three vital components supplied by yours truly – a hyphen and two accents. Must dash – will email at greater length when (if) things aren't so hectic!!
22.5 per cent better than my very bestest
Martin

January 30

From: Barry S. Malone
To: All Staff

Hi everyone!
A & B is starting the New Year way ahead of the curve. We have chosen a sensational new name for ourselves – a-b glöbâl – we have harnessed our own dreams and sustained and renewed ourselves from within.

Our rebranding process has been a case study in how to make it happen. It demonstrates how a close-knit team – led by Cindy Czarnikow, ably assisted by Christo Weinberg – has brought about a best-of-breed outcome. It has shown just what can be done within our community when we are all aligned and reading from the same roadmap.

I would like to offer heartfelt thanks to Cindy, who will be coming back to Atlanta a month early in new role of Chief Morale Evangelist! Have a phenomenal week,
I love you all
Barry

From: Martin Lukes
To: Graham Wallace

IT'S FUCKING BRILLIANT . . . I DO ALL THE WORK AND DON'T EVEN GET A MENTION . . .

From: Martin Lukes
To: Keith Buxton

Hi Keith
Just seen your message re the progress on Project Eat Well! I
have done some interesting preliminary work on this project,
though due to my increasing interest in Project Rebrand I have
not had the resources to devote to it. However, Eat Well! will
become top of mind for me going forward.
Bestest, Martin

From: Martin Lukes
To: Pandora@CoachworX

Hi Pandora!
Here is my first report card for the month of January.
MY WINS!
1. Basically I have taken control of the rebranding platform. I
contributed the bulk of the winning name.
2. I have put myself on the map with Barry Malone.
3. I have managed to get rid of a PA who was blocking my
energy, leaving the path open to a better partnership going
forward.
4. I have seen Cindy off to Atlanta. We had our ups and downs
but I think she has a greater respect for myself.
5. There have been some ongoing issues at home with my son
Jake. I have made a good start with applying coaching techniques
to him, but there is some way to go.
LEARNING OPPORTUNITIES
1. I should market my personal brand harder if I want to get the
recognition I deserve with the powers that be.
2. I am prepared to attend the Sex@Work seminar, as a sign that
I am always open to new learnings.
3. Project Eat Well! has been a tough learning experience. My
strategy is to assume that Keith will eventually forget about it

. . . In future I'll think twice before mentioning the canteen's offering again!

22.5 per cent better than my bestest

Martin Lukes

From: Pandora@CoachworX
To: Martin Lukes

Hi Martin

Congratulations on completing the first month! You've had some great wins. Before we wrap up for January, can we just take a minute to make a commitment to each other? I find this really helps build trust between us. Can you sign your commitment, date it, and return it to me?

COACHING CONTRACT

I, Pandora Barry will

1. Believe in you totally, and be your # 1 Fan!
2. Consistently feed your self-belief so that it will grow and flourish.
3. Help you define a plan of action to achieve your goals and desires, and keep you on track to achieve them.

I, Martin Lukes, agree to demonstrate my commitment to myself and to the coaching relationship by

1) Carrying out the challenges and assignments that my coach sets for me – without delay.
2) Choosing to adopt a more enthusiastic optimistic perception on my life from this moment onwards.
3) Spending a minimum of 35 minutes a day in silent contemplation of the day's goals and learnings.

Signed
Pandora Barry   Martin Lukes

Chapter Two

February

My DNA

February 2

From: Pandora@CoachworX
To: Martin Lukes

Welcome to month two of the CoachworX Executive Bronze Program. Last month you thought long and hard about where you are now. And that's not a bad place, is it Martin? This month we are going to dig a little deeper. We are going to find out about your values and your essential DNA. Let's start with an exercise! I want you to imagine that you are a number, a building and an animal. Which animal, building and number would you be? Don't think too profoundly about this, Martin. I want to know what first comes into your head.
Strive and thrive!
Pandora

From: Martin Lukes
To: Pandora@CoachworX

Fascinating questions, Pandora. I will answer as soon as I get a window.

I'm actually feeling a bit rough this morning – had a couple of drinks last night as today is my first day on the wagon.

Did I tell you I always go on the wagon in February? It's an interesting fact to flag up about myself – as it speaks volumes both for my self-control, and for my desire to stand out from the crowd. I know a lot of people do it in January, but I believe that if you can find your own niche in life, you get noticed. February is also the shortest month!!

22.5 per cent better than my very bestest

Martin

From: Martin Lukes
To: Sylvia Woods

Hi – I see Cindy has left all her clobber outside my office. Call building services and tell them to remove it. I'll keep the sofas, but tell them to take away that awful picture of the eagle with DARE TO SOAR written underneath.

Also see if you can get the partition wall of my office shifted out to include some of Cindy's old area. Also, when you've got a mo I'd like a double espresso, a bacon sandwich and some Alka Seltzer.

Martin

PS You don't know anything about modern buildings do you?

From: Barry S. Malone
To: All Staff

Howdy!
Today is the happiest day of my life – with the exception of that sunny day 31 years ago when I made love for the first time. This morning we committed our company to a migration path that will sustain and renew us going forward. I feel proud and humble to announce this historic, momentous change in our corporate mark from A&B to a-b glöbâl.

I am delighted also to be able to share our first ever global family of slogans that will go with our new global identity. The campaign will kick off Monday 16th and will be rolled out globally over the next two weeks.
'a-b glöbâl – FEARLESS in our CARING'
'a-b glöbâl – RELENTLESS in our SHARING'
'a-b glöbâl – PEERLESS in our DARING'.

Every day each and every one of us should look at our actions and ask: did I live these values? If we all strive together, this company will peak perform – permanently.
I love you all
Barry

From: Martin Lukes
To: Graham Wallace

Hi Graham – Terrifying to think of the first shag of BM's life . . . rather more information than one strictly needs.

Feeling a bit rough this am – went for a few jars last nite to escape Jens' women's reading group. When I got home they were all going on about this book written by a 15-year-old autistic boy about a dog at night – or something. Whatever turns you on . . . I'm reading something brilliant at the moment How We Won the Ryder Cup – The Caddies' Stories. Have u read it?
M
PS No can do drink tonight. Am on the wagon for the month of Feb.

From: Martin Lukes
To: Sylvia Woods

Sylvia – thanks for the tip, though when I googled Mease van de Rower just now, I couldn't find any matches. He's obviously too modern by half – can you think of any other architects?
Martin

From: Martin Lukes
To: Jenny Lukes

Darling – Sorry about last night. Got the feeling that you and your girlfriends didn't appreciate my comments re autism . . .

I know you're hard up against it today, but could you help me with something? I'm trying to dig down to the bottom of my

essence, and I wondered if you can think of any leading-edge modern buildings that remind you of yours truly?
Love you,
M

From: Martin Lukes
To: Jenny Lukes

It's an exercise of Pandora's. Actually quite interesting . . . It's a long time since I've had to think on such a philosophical level re myself, and I'm struggling a bit.

I've got a lot on today – having to sort out a new PA, and being nagged by Rog for new metrics for this year's operating plan. See you late tonight.
Love M x
PS It's Sylvia's last day tomorrow. I haven't got time to get anything. Would be eternally grateful if you could find a minute to sort some flowers or something?

February 3

From: Martin Lukes
To: Faith Preston

Hi Faith
Attached is the revised text for the ad for my new PA. I've made some changes and taken out 'sense of humour required' as that sounds as if working for myself might be frustrating! Can you get it into Crème de la Crème section of The Times soonest?

PA to DYNAMIC LEADER Culturally diverse! Ever-changing and Evolving DNA! Ours is a fast-moving innovative culture. Can you keep up with us? In this high-profile Personal Assistant position you will provide a range of support and administrative functions to a dynamic leader on the board of a-b glöbâl (UK). Do you have phenomenal interpersonal, communication and diary management skillsets? A can-do headset? Unrivalled problem-solving skills? £££ Highly competitive + perks!! YOUTHFUL ENERGY A MUST!!

From: Martin Lukes
To: Faith Preston

Faith – What do you mean, it's illegal to say youthful?? All I am saying is that I have very high levels of energy. And anyone who is going to be working for me must be able to take the pace. Best, Martin

February 4

From: Martin Lukes
To: JakeLukes@MillgateSchool

Hi Jake – No, you can't go to Amsterdam with Tarquin at half term. You are meant to be revising. Remember?

If you want to make yourself useful – you could answer a question. Can you think of an animal that reminds you of yours truly? Love Dad

From: Martin Lukes
To: Pandora@CoachworX

Hi Pandora

Here you go – the answers to your questions. Sorry it took a while – I'm someone who likes to get things right first time!

1. If I was a number, I would definitely be the number one. Partly because that is the only position I'm comfortable with, but also because the number is straight and upright and has a kind of understated simplicity.

2. re buildings – I've being thinking outside the square on this and can see some interesting parallels between myself and the more innovative modern structures. My first thought was the twin towers. Although they are very tall (which I'm not!!)

and there are two of them, and, obviously, they were blown up by Osama Bin Laden (which I haven't been – as yet!!) there are some revealing areas of overlap. They were very competitive. They wanted to be the tallest in the world. They wanted to be noticed and stand out from the crowd. Again, there was this understated simplicity about them, that is very much my style too.

But after some research I found a building that captures my essence exactly. It is Farnsworth House, built by one of my favourite architects, Mise Van der Rohe. At the time it was controversial, and was way ahead of the curve. It wasn't frightened to offend. Simple yet revolutionary. It's also stood the test of time, and is still as relevant as when it was built!

3. As for animals – I've been doing some 360-degree brainstorming on this. My son Jake suggested some parasite that gets into your bowel, and makes you flatulent!!! Jake's got a great sense of humour – a brilliant mind, he just has issues with harnessing his natural talent to his school work!

Seriously, though, if I was an animal I'd be a sheep dog. They are intelligent and are catalytic, they are natural leaders and they know how to drive a team to achieve peak performance.

Hope that helps

22.5 per cent more than my very bestest

Martin

February 6

From: Keith Buxton
To: All Staff

Hallo everyone
Many of you will have seen hostile articles in the media over the weekend, accusing us of having squandered $38m of shareholders' money and wasting valuable senior management time on our new corporate name, a-b glöbâl. As you know, this is far from the truth – the global figure on our rebranding bill is coming in south of $20m

and the management time expended on the project has enabled us to think deeply and strategically about the nature of the business we are in.

The key learning we should take out from this is to examine the interface between us and the press. Until now most of our PR has been handled out of Atlanta. I believe we must now strengthen our capability in London.
Bestest, Keith

From: Martin Lukes
To: Jenny Lukes

Sorry, darling – now isn't the best time to discuss this. I'm totally snowed under on something mission critical.

But basically – yes – I do think you should tell PR Palace to stuff their stupid job. You're never going to be able to work with Rowena as a boss. She's got issues with you because you are smarter than her – and a lot sexier. And, obviously, because you have such an eligible husband and enviable life.

There's no problem moneywise if you do decide to quit – we could save on the cleaner and the au pair? If we got rid of Svetlana I wouldn't have to pay extortionate rates for her phone calls to her boy friends in the Ukraine. That'd be a big win!
Love, M xxx

From: Martin Lukes
To: Jenny Lukes

No, of course I don't have an issue with you as a career woman. I'm just saying that if you are not comfortable with where you are – change it! As Pandora would say, the only person who can re-dream your life is you! Anyway, let's discuss later.
M xx

From: Pandora@CoachworX
To: Martin Lukes

Hi Martin
How are you? The last exercise you did for me obviously got your creative juices flowing! Now I'd like you to try something a bit harder. I want you to tell me about the six brilliant characteristics that you think define yourself – and the six brilliant characteristics others would say defined you.
Strive and thrive!
Pandora

From: Martin Lukes
To: Pandora@CoachworX

Hi Pandora
Interestingly, I don't think there's a gap between others' perception of myself and my own perception. I've always been realistic about myself – maybe it's in my DNA, or maybe it's because my family keep me down to earth!
1. The most noticeable thing about yours truly is my sense of humour. Ask anyone around here, and they'd say I was someone who lives, eats and breathes the fun message!
2. The next is creativity. This is a very important part of myself, and has driven my success in the marketing space.
3. Communication skills. My style is very easy, very natural, very empowering.
4. I see myself as a hub. I am a born networker, and like nothing more than getting people together.
5. Emotional intelligence. As I said earlier, I've got a very high EQ – self-knowledge and empathy are both big things for me.
6. Last but not least, passion. I believe that if you don't bring your passion to work every day, you're a round peg in a square hole!
   Hope that helps.
22.5 per cent better than my bestest
Martin

From: Pandora@CoachworX
To: Martin Lukes

That's great Martin! Well done! Now what I want you to do
is to Live your DNA! Each time you have had a major win
using your key skills, send me an email, telling me which skill
you are using and rank it with 1 to 4 stars. That way we can
monitor your progress!
Strive and thrive!
Pandora

February 10

From: Martin Lukes
To: Keith Buxton

Hi Keith
I've been doing a little blue-sky thinking, and have come up with
a phenomenal idea about how we can win back hearts and minds,
and prove that we care about the communities we serve. I suggest
we give away all the old A&B merchandizing to charity. If the
public can see us handing out goods free to the homeless it could
go a long way to reversing the brand damage suffered because
of the name change.
All my very bestest
Martin

From: Martin Lukes
To: Sylvia Wood

Hi Sylvia – One last task! Can you go through Yellow Pages and
find a list of all the homeless charities in London?
   Really sorry we're not going to have time for a drink before
you depart for pastures new. But I wish you all the best of British.
We'll all miss you here, and hope things really work out well for
you at Beyond the Box. You and I have been an unbeatable team,

and I want to thank you for your unstinting passion and contribution. I have no doubt that you'll teach that Zach Smart a thing or two!!
Keep in touch and all the best
Cheers, Martin
PS Can you leave details for your unlucky successor sharing your ancient wisdom on how to get along with yours truly?

February 11

From: Martin Lukes
To: Pandora@CoachworX

*Creativity **** Communication **** Fun ***
Hi Pandora
I'm really motoring now! I have come up with a scheme that builds on my success last month with the hyphen, umlaut and circumflex. I am now spearheading Project Boxer Shorts. Although the title is deliberately humorous, it actually could be the tipping point of my career. I'm really starting to feel the power of self-belief coursing through my veins. It is unbelievably energizing!
22.5 per cent more than my very bestest
Martin

From: Martin Lukes
To: Jenny Lukes

Darling –
Just had a brainwave. Here's evidence of how much I support your career: why not come back here? Following the debacle of our media coverage, we've decided to beef up the PR department. We're in the market for two or three extra bods, some of whom will be at a fairly junior level. There's bound to be something part-time. As Pandora says: Dream it! Plan it! Do it!
Love M

PS May be a bit late tonight – Can you get me something nice for supper – chicken korma with pilau rice would go down nicely.
M x

From: Martin Lukes
To: Jenny Lukes

Glad you like the idea. And I know that's not Atkins, but I can't do that and the booze. In any case booze is so fattening that the pounds will fall away. I'd also like some nan bread and an aloo gobi.
Love you, M xx

From: Martin Lukes
To: Pandora@CoachworX

The Hub ***
Hi Pandora
Today I have had a big networking win. I have brought together my wife, who hates her job, with Lucinda, who needs extra help in PR. For both of them, this is win–win. Although there is nothing in it for me, often I find with networking your payback comes later.
22.5 per cent better than my bestest
Martin

From: Martin Lukes
To: Keith Buxton

Hi Keith –
My God, the lady wife moves quickly! I only mentioned the job to her half an hour ago! Yes, she used to work here, long before your time . . . in fact we met here – I thought you knew that. For the last few years she's been working two days a week for a small company called PR Palace but wants to quit as she doesn't get on with her boss. Something relatively unstressful

and part-time may suit her. Obviously I think she's a great girl, but then I'm partial!
All my very bestest
Martin

From: Martin Lukes
To: Jenny Lukes

Jens – Frankly I was a bit taken aback to get a message from Keith saying you had contacted him already. If we're to work together, we can't have you dashing off emails to my boss without me being in the loop . . . Will be very late as I'm interviewing new PAs.
M

February 12

From: Martin Lukes
To: Faith Preston

Hi Faith – Feedback on the PA interviews: yesterday I met Keri Tartt and Preetha Patel. Both girls were aligned with our values though I have a preference for Keri who has a can-do headset and seems very results-driven. I felt Preetha, though clearly stronger on paper, didn't have the requisite passion quotient. Can we get Keri to start asap? I've attached her CV for your files.
Martin

> *Keri Tartt CV*
> *Age 29*
> *An energetic, fun-loving PA with loads of get up and go!!!*
> *Place of Birth: Wellington, New Zealand*
> *Education: Wellington Girls High School*
> *Trained: Physiotherapist Module I*
> *WORK*
> *PA to Marketing Director Esquire Magazine*
> *Ticket sales Glastonbury*

Hobbies: Wind surfing, Crystals, Life saving, Holistic healing, Travel

From: Martin Lukes
To: Pandora@CoachworX

Emotional intelligence****
Hi Pandora
I have today deployed my EQ in the selection process for my new PA. The successful candidate has few of the necessary qualifications on paper yet I trusted my emotional skills to intuit from the interview that she'll be the best fit in the job. I often get this powerful feeling about people in the first two minutes. I can tell if the fit is there or not. This time I went with my gut and am expecting results.
22.5 per cent better than my bestest
Martin

From: Martin Lukes
To: Graham Wallace

Graham – eat your heart out . . . I'm getting a gorgeous new PA. She looks a bit like Goldie Horn, trained as a physio, tall, slim . . . very tasty. Mart

February 16

From: Martin Lukes
To: Jenny Lukes

Darling –
I've been doing some detective work re your schedule for this pm. You'll be seen first by Lucinda Mogg Watson, our PR girl.
   She's sweet, in a Sloany sort of way. She's no rocket scientist – I think you'll like her. Then you're being interviewed by Faith Preston, Director for People. She's hell on wheels – aggressive,

humourless, seriously PC – and has me down as some sexist, racist bastard. Let me know how you get on. Fingers crossed! Love you, M xx

From: Martin Lukes
To: Graham Wallace

Graham – No yr eyes didn't deceive you. It was Jenny – being interviewed to work for Lucinda in PR. If she gets the job, she'll only be part-time, so I doubt that our paths will cross much. In fact, it might make things better between us. At least she'll be able to see for herself how hard we all work and how much pressure we're under.
Cheers, Martin
PS I've done two weeks without a drink!! Am feeling pretty good – or would be if I could get rid of this flu.

From: Martin Lukes
To: Lucinda Mogg Watson

Hi, Lucinda
How are you getting along fixing up media interest for our drop of obsolete A&B boxer shorts and sweatshirts to homeless charities? I personally will be taking a parcel to Arlington House in Camden Town on Feb. 26 arriving 3 pm.

I gather you are interviewing my wife this pm. She's quite something – though I would say that, wouldn't I?
Martin

From: Martin Lukes
To: Jenny Lukes

Darling – glad it went so well – extraordinary that Keith wanted to see you, as he normally only interviews people of department head level and above. Did he mention me? I should have warned you about him in advance. He's intensely ambitious and political. Your best mate one minute then stabbing you in the back the next. Btw, you're also way off beam on Faith. She's neither intelligent nor well-meaning.

M xxx

From: Martin Lukes
To: Graham Wallace

Graham, am having second thoughts about the virtues of working alongside the wife. She informs me that Faith is a fine, intelligent woman. She also had an hour-long session with Keith! He never gives me more than 10 minutes. I sometimes think that if we were women we wouldn't have to work our arses off.

Martin

February 17

From: Keith Buxton
To: All Staff

Hallo everyone!
I am delighted to announce that Jenny Withers has been appointed to our rapidly growing External Relations team. Jenny joins us from PR Palace where she has built up an unrivalled track record in delivering exceptional pr solutions. She will be reporting to Lucinda Mogg Watson, and will be helping on all aspects of our press strategy.
Bestest, Keith

From: Martin Lukes
To: Jenny Lukes

Jenny – I've just seen Keith's message – and so far so good! You're honoured that he's making such a big deal of this. But why are you using your maiden name? Before you say anything, I don't have a problem with it – you can call yourself whatever you like. But I don't understand the rationale. As a matter of courtesy you might have discussed it with me first. M

From: Martin Lukes
To: Jenny Lukes

That's ridiculous!! Why wouldn't people take you seriously as my wife? Is being married to me so bad? They know you're my wife anyway, so I don't see where you're coming from.

From: Martin Lukes
To: Keith Buxton

Hi Keith
Thanks for your message! Dinner would be great!! What sort of time?
Bestest, Martin

From: Martin Lukes
To: Jenny Lukes

Darling – We've been invited to dinner with Keith and his wife on Monday – just the four of us at his place!! He said it'd be v informal, v low key. We're honoured!
Love you, M xx

February 18

From: Martin Lukes
To: Lucinda Mogg Watson

Hi, Luce
Wow! The six o clock news and all the broadsheets?? I thought they weren't supposed to be interested in reporting good news?!

I've decided the occasion calls for a speech – which I'll write tonight and send you for the press pack. I think it should also include a copy of my CV. Do we need a mug shot, or will the papers all be sending their own photographers? Might be worth getting a pic done just in case. Can you contact a good portrait photographer?
Martin

From: Martin Lukes
To: Jenny Lukes

Lucinda says there's massive media interest in Project Boxer Shorts!

What do you think I should wear? I think suits work best on TV, but might not strike the right note with the drunks and nutters at the shelter. I thought my new Paul Smith polo shirt – the pink one with Serenity written on it would be just right. Casual, informal but with a hint of difference? What do you think?
M xx

February 19

From: Martin Lukes
To: Barry Malone

Hi Barry
I wanted to touch base with a charitable initiative I am heading up in London, under which we are giving away our old merchandizing to the homeless. I believe this is 110 per cent aligned with our slogans.

It is *fearless in our caring* – we are showing we CARE by clothing the homeless.

It is *relentless in our sharing* – because we are not just keeping the old caps for ourselves, but are – literally – sharing them with those less fortunate than ourselves.

It is *peerless in our daring* – we are sticking our heads above the globalization parapet, and saying: here we are! We are proud of where we're going!

All my very bestest

Martin Lukes

From: Martin Lukes
To: Pandora@CoachworX

Communication**** Humour**** The Hub ****

Hi Pandora

I've had two huge wins since I last emailed.

Jens and myself have been invited to dinner with Keith. This reflects partly his excitement at Project Boxer Shorts. It may also be because his radar has picked up on the New High Achieving Me.

Even more exciting is the head of steam behind Project Boxer Shorts. Half the nation's press is going to be there – which makes it the perfect opportunity to position myself as a national thought leader. I'm attaching my speech – wld be v grateful for feedback. I made it humorous but with a serious message – I'm pretty chuffed with the tone and content. Hope you like it.

22.5 per cent better than my bestest

Martin

SPEECH TO HOMELESS *(ML mounts the podium)*

Ladies and Gentlemen of the media, homeless persons, social workers.

First let me introduce myself – I'm Martin Lukes and, for my sins, I'm Marketing Director of a-b glöbâl uk. I've been fortunate enough to be one of the team working on the rebranding project that has seen our famous brand A&B transitioned into a-b glöbâl.

In your press packs you will find details of the new logo, a story about the journey that took us there and a brief biog of myself.

But while the glamour of our rebranding gets the headlines, underneath we are tirelessly thinking: what can we give back? Here at a-b glöbâl, this duty is always front of mind. So what we are doing today is giving back to you, the homeless. We are providing hi-quality merchandise, free of charge, with no strings attached.

What's in it for us, you may be thinking? Nothing, except that it gives us the opportunity to show that we are here for you. I know you sometimes read biased reports in the press (and I shouldn't say this with so many journos here!) about fat cats and big companies riding roughshod over the lives of decent ordinary people. But at a-b glöbâl we are here for all members of the community that we serve.

Today isn't just about merchandizing. Remember the saying 'Give a man a fish and you feed him for a day. Teach him to fish and you feed him for life?' Well, today I'll be sharing knowledge – not on how to fish!!! – but on how to rebrand yourselves. I will be challenging your mindsets to rethink the homeless brand, if you will. There is a lot of negative baggage around the term 'homeless', which I hope I will help you leave behind. There is a need for a root-and-branch rebrand, and I hope today will be a first step on that exciting journey.

Thank you for coming today, and I hope you'll stay behind to ask me further questions over tea and biscuits.

(applause – (I hope!). ML gets down off the podium)

February 24

From: Martin Lukes
To: Keith Buxton

Good morning Keith! Many thanks for a great dinner last night. You really are the chef! Much enjoyed meeting your wife . . . didn't realize what a successful woman she is in her own right.

Had a very interesting intellectual discussion with her, please onpass thanks.
All my very bestest
Martin
PS Hope we didn't outstay our welcome!

From: Martin Lukes
To: Pandora@CoachworX

*Fun **** Communication *** The Hub *****
Dinner was a huge hit. I thought about my values in advance. I feel I was dynamic and humorous. I did waive my February alcohol ban, but under the circs it was quite justifiable and helped break the ice. Definitely cemented relations.
22.5 per cent better than my bestest
Martin

From: Martin Lukes
To: Graham Wallace

Graham – Did I tell you that I supped with the boss last night? It was a great evening . . . only slight blight was that Keith was all over Jens – I wonder if he fancies her?? – they talked about books half the night. I really liked Mrs B – she's something big at Channel Five. I said how much I liked topless darts – obviously in an ironic sort of way – I think she found me a breath of fresh air after all the PC idiots she has to put up with.
Cheers, Mart

From: Martin Lukes
To: Jenny Lukes

Darling – just had a nice message back from Keith. You were quite wrong to say that I disgraced myself by being pissed. He said they enjoyed it, and he's now thinking of starting a men's book club!

We should have them back soon. Might be an idea to invite someone from the 'arts world' with them. Did you mention meeting Ian McEwan's agent's wife at a school thing of Max's? Love you, M xx

From: Martin Lukes
To: Jenny Lukes

Oh, she's his agent in her own right? Good for her!! All the more reason to ask her. What does the husband do?

February 25

From Martin Lukes
To Keri Tartt

Hi Keri – welcome to a-b glöbâl! I hope Sylvia has left you a list of tasks . . . fraid I'm not going to have a window to show you the ropes.

You'll have to excuse us today because everything is going to be totally crazy – though if I'm frank, every day in marketing is crazy, as we like to push ourselves to the limit and beyond. Tomorrow afternoon I'm doing a major media event – might be a good learning experience for you if you'd like to come along. M

PS Have you changed your hairstyle? Very fetching, if I might make so bold.

From: Lucinda Mogg Watson
To: All Staff

Calling all square eyes!!!! Programme your videos for tomorrow night! Our own Martin Lukes will be on the Six O'Clock News giving away our old A&B boxers and tops to poor people!
Luce (Mogg Watson)

From: Martin Lukes
To: Jenny Lukes

Darling – Thanks for the pearls of wisdom, but frankly you're getting a bit ahead of yourself. You haven't even started the job yet, and you're not up to speed on the background, so I really wish you'd stand back, and leave Project Boxer Shorts to myself and Lucinda.

In any case, your concerns are totally off piste – we've sold the story to the media as a colourful example of how big business really cares at the grassroots level – and they've bought into that. In fact they can't get enough of it. Don't forget to watch – I've sent Jake a text too. He'd probably be quite chuffed in front of his mates to see the old man on the box.
M x

From: Martin Lukes
To: Graham Wallace

The wife is really getting on my tits. She's already started telling me how to do my job!! I bet Lynne doesn't give you a hard time about your sales figures . . . (though the way they are going, maybe she should!!)
M

From: Martin Lukes
To: Phyllis Lukes

Dearest Mum
Thanks for your email. Sorry your knee's playing up. Do you want me to hassle the hospital to get you bumped up the waiting list a bit? I could get my new PA onto the job . . . she's this nice New Zealand girl. Very capable.

Don't forget to watch the six o'clock news tonight. I am going to be on helping the homeless how to improve their lives. I know your views about the homeless, mum, and up to a point I totally agree. A lot of them are just wasters and spongers – but you need to understand that the media doesn't see them like that, and we need to reflect public opinion.

Boys both doing fine. Did I tell you Jens has finally quit her job and is going to work here? I know you don't approve of her working, but at the end of the day it's her call. In any case it's going to be very part time. I swung it for her – it was really getting to me how miserable she was.

Will try to get down at the weekend. Jake's going to be back for half term, and I've been banned by Jens from playing golf. Not sure I'll be able to fix the tap, but I'll have a go, if you've got the right tools.

Yr loving son
Martin

February 26

From: Martin Lukes
To: Keri Tartt

Keri – Can you pop in here and help me? Can't get the new email to work. It's not recognizing our new email address.
Martin

From: Help Desk
To: All Staff

We have been experiencing difficulties with our messaging infrastructure. Currently we are conducting consolidation efforts to measure network traffic and coordinate tasks with regional hardware availability. We are investigating remote procedure call (RPC) transaction latency, WAN traffic per mailbox store, WAN traffic per public folder store, and percentage of failed RPC requests. We realize that the consolidation will have knock-on effects on the consolidation's effects on the WAN and WAN-dependent applications.
Brian Morris
Team leader, Help Desk

From: Martin Lukes
To: Brian Morris

FRANKLY I DON'T GIVE A DAMN ABOUT WAN-DEPENDENT WHATSITS!! GET THIS BLOODY NEW EMAIL WORKING NOW!!!!!!!!!
Martin Lukes

From: Martin Lukes
To: Pandora@CoachworX

Passion **
Hi Pandora
Feeling a bit nervous about this afternoon, but had one minor win this am. I told some home truths to the idiots in IT. Really let my passion show!

Thanks for sending me your book Take Yourself Beyond the Top, looks a great read!
22.5 per cent better than my bestest
Martin

From: Martin Lukes
To: Keith Buxton

Hi Keith
Re your message, I am most surprised that Brian has complained. I was simply voicing the frustrations felt by everyone. I'm working flat out going the extra mile on Project Boxer Shorts which is going live this pm. And if other departments are not giving 110 per cent, I strongly believe that they should be given negative feedback.
All my very bestest
Martin

From: Martin Lukes
To Keri Tartt

Hi Keri – Trust all set for later today. Can u call a cab for 3.30?
M

From: Martin Lukes
To: Jenny Lukes

I'm off now – should be back home by 6, in time to see myself on the news! Wish me luck.
Love you M xx

Text message to Jenny. Sent 16:17

ohgodgodgodgod . . . run the bath. pour me a large whisky . . . i'm on my way home.

February 27

From: Keith Buxton
To: All Staff

Hallo everyone! Last night, as many of you will be aware, A&B was the victim of a concerted attempt to damage our reputation as a global company that cares passionately for the local community. Martin Lukes was ejected from a hostel and set upon by the homeless and by anti-globalization protesters. One hostel resident put a pair of A&B boxer shorts on his head and jostled him in front of the camera. Another set fire to a bundle of our A&B sweatshirts. These are attacks that we cannot tolerate.

The key learning that I, personally, take out of this is that our mission has not been universally understood by the public at large. We must think clearly about our target audience and how best to connect with them emotionally.
Bestest, Keith

From: Martin Lukes
To: Pandora@CoachworX

Hi Pandora – Basically, long story short, it was the most humiliating day of my life. When I got there, no one seemed to know I was coming. Eventually this news reporter turned up – looked really young and cute, but then started asking me all these really cynical and ignorant questions. I feel I gave some pretty good answers, but they were all cut out.

She insisted on filming me with this homeless woman – probably a crack addict with multiple body piercings who picked up our fleecy sweatshirt and said 'I'm not wearin that, innit?' I told her that she was being ungrateful, and then a riot started.

And the tragedy was that I didn't get the chance to give the rebranding seminar. Keith isn't being at all supportive – he's going through the motions but when I saw him just now he was pretty standoffish.

22.5 per cent worse than my bestest (!)
Martin

From: Pandora@CoachworX
To: Martin Lukes

Hi Martin
Can I say one thing to you? NO FAILURE ONLY FEEDBACK. Repeat this mantra. It's really important. Failure has no place in your life. There is no such thing as failure. Only feedback. Yesterday was a positive for you. There were some big key learnings there. What do you think they were, Martin?
Strive and thrive!
Pandora

From: Martin Lukes
To: Pandora@CoachworX

Hi Pandora – Frankly it's hard to feel positive when drug addicts are pelting you with rotten eggs. But you're right that this wasn't a failure of mine, and you're right about the key learnings. I can think of at least four.

1. The homeless don't give a shit about anything apart from themselves.
2. Frankly it is no surprise to me at all that they are homeless. There wasn't a can-do headset between them.
3. I also feel really angry about having been forced to this by Lucinda and Keith. It was always obvious to me that there were going to be serious risks associated with this project, but they were insistent on getting the publicity at all costs.
4. Giving back isn't all it's cracked up to be.

22.5 per cent better than my best
Martin

Chapter Three

March
My Dream

March 1

From: Pandora@CoachworX
To: Martin Lukes

Hi Martin!
Give yourself a big pat on the back for reaching month three!
This is one of the most vital months of the whole Executive
Bronze Program. You have your DNA under your belt and
now its time to dream! So what is your dream?
   You may not believe this, Martin, but many people do not
actually know what their dream is! They need a little help to
reach out and touch it.
   The first exercise should be great fun. I want you to get a
big piece of paper. Place it landscape and then get some felt
pens. I want you to draw your dream. You need to let your
conscious mind go blank and let your subconscious mind get
to work!
Strive and thrive!
Pandora

From: Martin Lukes
To: Keri Tartt

Hi Keri
How are you this morning? Great outfit! If you've got a mo, a

large latte and a pain au chocolat would go down nicely. Also a big bag of felt pens – I'd like some thin ones and some of those big chunky highlighters and some A3 paper.
Tx Martin

From: Jenny Withers
To: All Staff

Hi

I should introduce myself – I'm Jenny Withers, and this is my first week working in external relations with Lucinda Mogg Watson.

Over the coming weeks I shall be looking at ways of promoting our ethically and socially responsible strategies.

Already this morning people have told me about ways in which they are generously giving their time to worthwhile causes. What I want to do is to bring all this good stuff together in a way that we can promote, and show the outside world what we are doing. After the events of last month, there is a public perception that we are not entirely committed to the Corporate Social Responsibility agenda. We need to prove that we are. I shall be holding a Lunch and Learn session on Friday. Please bring your sandwiches and your ideas!
Jenny Withers

From: Martin Lukes
To: Jenny Withers

Darling –

Brilliant memo, well done! A couple of tiny points. First, not sure you've got the tone and the vocab quite right. You sound a bit – how should I put it? – downbeat.

I'm also concerned that you misunderstood what I was going on about last night. When I said that in order to get noticed in this place you have to be very visible, I meant within reason. I didn't mean that you start cluttering up people's inboxes on Day One. There's a lot of resistance here to creating company spam. I have a rule which I find quite helpful: before I send out an email, I always think: does this pass the need-to-know test? And then, and only then, do I press send.

If I were you I'd concentrate on getting my feet under the desk before you start in with any more initiatives! Obviously it's too late to take this morning's missive back. But worry not, everyone will be very forgiving on your first day!
M xx
PS Could do lunch later if you like?

From: Keith Buxton
To: All Staff

Hallo everyone
I would like to congratulate Jenny on a best-of-breed memo. It is always a pleasure when individuals who have just joined the company buy into our values from Day One!

Being seen as a socially responsible company is top of our agenda going forward.
All the best,
Keith

From: Martin Lukes
To: Graham Wallace

Hi Graham
Just called a chum in the headhunting community who says Keith's in line for the number one job at Boots!! Which would be win-win – he'd stop ogling my ladywife . . . and his job'd be up for grabs. You heard anything?

I just went up to talk to Keith about cuts to the marketing spend, and found him shut in his office with Rog. Asked Mary what was up, and she did her mine-is-not-to-reason-why routine.
Mart
PS Was that Lucinda you were sneaking out of the office with last nite??

From: Martin Lukes
To: Keri Tartt

Hi Keri
Oh dear, sorry that Faith has had a go at you. Her bark's worse than her bite . . . actually I take that back. Her bite's pretty lethal too. But don't worry about her, I'll sort it.
Martin

From: Martin Lukes
To: Faith Preston

Hi Faith
I understand that you have reprimanded my PA for having a visible stud in her belly button. Can I remind you that she is not in a client-facing role, and that therefore our 'business appropriate attire' dress code does not apply to her. It is also highly sexist to make personal comments about her appearance. If Keri had been a man, I don't think you would have said anything.
Martin

From: Christo Weinberg
To: All Staff

Hi – Following on from Jenny Withers' memo, I'd like to tell you about some voluntary work that I'm passionate about. For the last couple of years I've been helping produce sensational musicals in London prisons – this year we're putting on an all-male Chicago at Pentonville, which should be a mind-blowing event. It's all about jamming, improvisation, resolving paradoxes. It's structure versus freedom, inside versus outside, the summing up of all the vectors.
Keep it mellow,
Christo

From: Martin Lukes
To: Christo Weinberg

Hi Christo
I'm afraid I'm going to cancel our mentoring session for this pm, as I've got rather a lot on. Can we do same time, next week?

Re your memo, can I just say how great it is that you are developing your creative talents outside the office. However, don't forget that you should be bringing those same talents to work every day!
Best, Martin

From: Martin Lukes
To: Keri Tartt

Hi Keri
Can you bring me some more A3 paper? Drawing my dream is actually much more challenging than you'd think. I'm meant to let my mind go blank – which is particularly hard when idiot co-colleagues like Christo Weinberg are bragging about what they get up to in their spare time. The trouble is that when your mind is as full as mine, it's very hard to empty it. Have you got any tips of what I could draw?
Martin

From: Martin Lukes
To: Keri Tartt

Wow! Thanks for that, but I'll stick with the basics!!!

Can you keep everyone out of my office for the next half an hour? If my wife comes round, tell her to wait. I'm having lunch with her later . . . maybe you'd like to join us?? The two of you will need to bond. I should warn you she likes to keep a close eye on my diary! There were issues with Sylvia over communication

. . . dates went missing, yours truly in deep trouble. Sure that won't happen with you!
Martin

From: Martin Lukes
To: Pandora@CoachworX

Hi Pandora
Just sent you the picture. I did spend a tiny bit more than five minutes on it, but I think in the end I got pretty close to something. Though I'm no Picasso, I'm actually quite chuffed with the end result!
22.5 per cent better than my bestest
Martin

From: Martin Lukes
To: Jenny Withers

Darling – How's your first day been? Shall we leave together? I could go home early for once – see you downstairs 6ish.
    What did you think of Keri? She is a bit flaky, but willing. She lost me at lunchtime when she was going on about chakra gemstone kits. But she's much nicer to work with than Sylvia. And, no, I don't fancy her.
Love you M xx

March 3

From: Martin Lukes
To: Graham Wallace

Really????????????????????
    I was only joking the other day when I said that about Lucinda. Wouldn't have thought posh totty was yr style . . .
Mart

From: Martin Lukes
To: Graham Wallace

Graham – are you asking me to lie for you? If Lynne calls, am
I supposed to say that you're with me but can't come to the
phone??? I'm not entirely comfortable with this – I've always
believed truth is the best option.

Another rule of mine is never to mix work and pleasure –
which rather cramps my style as Suzanna Elliott would otherwise be v appealing. She's one of my most junior brand managers
– Kylie with a bit more between the ears. Blushes charmingly
when I talk to her – could be partly a power thing, but I think
she's got a bit of a thing for yours truly. So what's Lucinda like,
then?
Mart

From: Martin Lukes
To: Graham Wallace

Yes, that was a 'yes'. I will cover for you – but just this once.
And no, I won't tell anyone, not even Jens. I don't do gossip of
that sort.
Have a good one (!)
Mart
PS Not sure it's a brilliant idea you discussing this on work email
. . . though on second thoughts our IT department is so retarded
they can't bloody get our email to function normally let alone
manage any surveillance activities.
M

From: Pandora@CoachworX
To: Martin Lukes

Hi Martin
Thank you for sharing your dream with me. It is always
fascinating watching coachees' dreams take shape, and yours

is a uniquely special one. Your road symbolizes your journey, the castle is your home life – those walls are very thick and solid, which is a great sign! However, this may also be a reflection of you as a defensive adult, with a vulnerable child within. The tree shows your personal growth – that strong root structure you've drawn is going to be absolutely key when you start to live your dream.

The white circle in the corner is your true North. This is your guiding star. It shows that whatever you do, you want it to be for a bigger purpose. Yes you want success – but you want it because it helps you achieve immortality.

Now Martin, I want you to break your dream down into achievable targets. Tell me your specific dreams. And I will help you make them come true.

Give yourself five minutes and write down as much as you can. Think: what do I really want?
Strive and thrive!
Pandora

From: Martin Lukes
To: Pandora@CoachworX

Hi Pandora
Actually you're spot on re my artwork. The only thing I'd say is that when I drew the white circle I meant it to be a golf ball, but you're right, it works just as well as a guiding star!!

Here are my goals. I don't need to think too hard about these, they are, in no particular order:
1. I'd like to be CEO of a-b glöbâl
2. I'd like to earn some serious money
3. I'd like to have a big villa in Tuscany and another one in the Seychelles
4. I want an Aston Martin DB9
5. I'd like an indoor gym and a jacuzzi
6. I'd like Cindy to be found out for the featherweight she is
7. I want a handicap in single figures

8. I want to spend some quality time with Kylie Minogue
9. I'd like to lose 2 stone, develop a six pack and re-grow a full head of hair

22.5 per cent better than my bestest
Martin

From: Martin Lukes
To: Jenny Withers

Darling – sorry you're finding Lucinda a bit difficult . . . Actually thick isn't her only drawback. I've got something incredible to tell you about her in totally strictest secrecy. It might throw some light on her behaviour – will tell all tonight.
M xx

March 5

From: Barry S. Malone
To: All Staff

Howdy
Everywhere I go in this company I get fired up by how you are living by our five values, Purpose, Practice, Potency, Performance and People.

Of these the most important is People. And that is why I am today announcing a new board level position, Chief Talent Officer. The CTO will focus in on our people globally and ensure we have the very best talent mix we can. I am delighted to tell you that this position will be filled by Keith Buxton who is currently chairman of a-b glöbâl UK. Keith has an unrivalled track record in managing talent. He will add unique leadership and powerful insight to all our talent nurturing initiatives going forward.
I love you all
Barry

From: Martin Lukes
To: Graham Wallace

Talent officer? Is that glorified HR or what? Sounds v flaky to me. So are you going to apply for Keith's job??

From: Martin Lukes
To: Keith Buxton

Hi Keith
Congratulations! Really well-deserved promotion. I've always passionately believed that the talent space is very under-developed. Get the talent pool right and everything else flows from that. When are you off?
　　Any news yet on a successor? I've got some views on this. Could we have some face time soonest?
All my very bestest
Martin

March 8

From: Martin Lukes
To: Pandora@CoachworX

Hi Pandora –
My dreams have been a bit of a moveable feast in the last 24 hours – I've just learnt that Keith is going to Atlanta, so the top UK job is up for grabs.
　　So that's my number one dream – to be chairman of a-b glöbâl (UK). Timing is perfect for me – this time I'm going to come out on top.
22.5 per cent better than my very bestest
Martin

From: Pandora@CoachworX
To: Martin Lukes

Hi Martin
I love your dreams! I love your confidence! What you need is a plan to ensure you succeed. Remember you can have whatever you want. You need to want it enough, and you need to follow the GROW! model.

This is a four-step process. Goals, Reality, Options and Will.

This will chart out a journey that will allow you to achieve your goals. Under each of these titles I want you to tell me how you are going to get this job!
Strive and thrive!
Pandora
PS Can you check with your payments department if there is a problem. In the contract it specifies that payments must be made AT THE BEGINNING of the month.

From: Martin Lukes
To: Pandora@CoachworX

Hi Pandora
Here is the outline of my GROW model. Just a first draft at this stage.
GOAL
To be appointed chairman of a-b glöbâl UK
REALITY
This is how the candidates stack up
Roger – No chance at all. He's just a bean-counter.
Faith – Totally ignorant of everything outside HR, but has got one massive thing going for her – she's a woman. Everyone's freaking out on the diversity ticket so that gives her a head start. Otherwise she'd be useless. At the end of the day, she's not that bright.
Graham – unlikely. If you go down the list of leadership skills,

he's hardly got any ticks. He's a wide boy without bottom, if you will.

Cindy – Assuming that she's having a scene with Barry (which is what my Atlanta sources tell me) he won't want her 4,000 miles away.

Christo – Total outsider, though very much flavour of the month. He's my mentee, so this would be worst case for me. He's smart, but very cocky and very immature. Luckily I think his chances are zilch.

Myself – Well aligned skillsets. The obvious choice!

OPTIONS

I need to lobby relentlessly with both Keith, and Barry. Although Keith won't be making the choice, Barry will certainly listen to what he says. I need to come up with an unbeatable strategy of my vision for the UK subsidiary.

WILL

I have the will to do this. I will turn all stumbling blocks into stepping stones. I believe in myself, and I believe this job will be mine!

22.5 per cent better than my bestest

Martin

March 9

From: Faith Preston
To: All team leaders

Hi!

A reminder that all Work and Development Plans MUST be signed off by the end of the day today and returned to myself. These documents are the most important score card of all co-colleagues' performance. Please ensure that all your team members are committed to making twice-weekly shows of integrity, aligned with company policy.

Faith

From: Martin Lukes
To: Keith Buxton

Keith – That's great! What can I say? I'd be delighted to stand in for you! It's ages since I was last at St Andrews.

On a different matter, could we share some face time soonest? I'd like to talk through my ideas for a-b glöbâl (UK) going forward. Have you got a window to discuss today or tomorrow?
Best, Martin

From: Martin Lukes
To: Jenny Withers

Darling – Keith has just asked me to take his place at the St Andrews Old Course this weekend!! It's a charity do – it's going to be brilliant networking!

The fact he's picked me to replace him on the golf thing strongly suggests that I'm his chosen successor!! Graham and Roger will be FURIOUS!!! Sorry about leaving you in the lurch with Max.
Love you M xx

From: Martin Lukes
To: Max Lukes

Max old man
Sorry I'm afraid I'm not going to be able to take you to Stamford Bridge for your birthday on Sat. But worry not, Svetlana will go instead. Will make it up to you next weekend. Promise.
Dad xx

From: Keith Buxton
To: All Staff

Hallo everyone!
Many thanks to all of you who have offered me congratulations on

my promotion. I am, of course, extremely excited about this opportunity.

Next week our CEO, Barry Malone, will be visiting us from Atlanta on Wed. 17 March. The timeframe is very tight. Barry has requested that this day be highly informal. He is here to listen and to learn. Attached is his schedule.

I know I can count on all of you to make the day a great success.
Keith

07.30 BSM arrives Wharfside. Briefing by KB.
08.00 BSM and CC have working breakfast with department heads.
09.00 Walkabout with KB and JW.
10.00 by BSM '5Ps to achieve PPP'.
12.00 Action meal attended by cross-section of staff.
2.00 CC to all staff on 'Pushing the Morale Envelope in Europe'.
4.30 BSM debriefed by KB.

From: Martin Lukes
To: Jenny Withers

Jens – How come you get to show him around?? This is out-rageous favouritism. You may find life here a bit tougher when KB goes – unless of course they do the decent thing and give the job to your second greatest fan – yr loving husband!
M x

From: Martin Lukes
To: Barry S. Malone

Hi Barry
Delighted to hear that you are crossing the pond next week. I wondered if I could beg a few minutes of your time to tell you about some blue-sky thinking I've been doing re the role of a-b glöbâl UK. As Marketing Director I am uniquely well placed to assess our strengths and weaknesses as a corporate brand. I believe that we are currently at an inflection point – the challenge

is to harness our talent to create a proactive headset that will take us from 'good' to 'great'.

I would be delighted to meet with you when you are in London to discuss these ideas.

All my very bestest

Martin

From: Martin Lukes
To: Graham Wallace

You're way off-beam on that one, Graham. No way I'm interested in Keith's job. Given the demands that Atlanta puts on us, the job's got no upside. You interested by any chance?

And how was it last nite? Jens obviously doesn't think Lucinda's got much on top, but then I don't suppose you are spending your time discussing the general theory of relativity?

Mart

From: Martin Lukes
To: Phyllis Lukes

Dear Mum

Sorry I couldn't get down to see you at the weekend. Happy Birthday for next Tuesday. Great news about the op . . . How long are you going to stay in for?

I've got some very good news too. You know I've been a bit cheesed off at work recently? Well I'm in line for a big job, running the whole outfit in the UK. That means 1,000 people, and your loving son would be in charge of all of them!

We shouldn't cross bridges until we reach them, but I'm pretty optimistic about my chances.

I know you think all this coaching stuff is just mumbo jumbo, and obviously I was pretty sceptical at first, but I actually think Pandora's doing me a lot of good. She's made me push myself forward a lot more. I've got a session with the CEO next week when he's over from Atlanta, so fingers crossed!

Boys are both fine. Max is on the school debating team, and is leading a debate on immigration: 'This house believes immigration has undermined the nature of Britishness.' You'd be right behind him on that!

Don't go on fussing about the shelves, mum. I'll do them next time, but for now can't you get the home help to pile all the stuff into the cupboard, and I'll sort next time I come?
Lots and lots of love
Martin

March 10

From: Keith Buxton
To: All Team Leaders

Hi, Team Leaders
I understand from Faith that some team leaders have still not completed the WDPs. This is not an acceptable situation. These forms are now two weeks late, and must all be in by the end of the day at the very latest.
Best, Keith

From: Martin Lukes
To: Jenny Withers

Darling – Jake's housemaster just left a message saying that Jake and Tarquin have been drinking Bacardi Breezers on the school premises, and they are both suspended. Next time either of them steps one foot out of line, they get expelled. Can you sort it? J needs picking up this pm. M x

From: Martin Lukes
To: Jenny Withers

Jens – No I can't ring Tarquin's mother. I don't have her number, and I'm preparing one of the most important presentations of my life, and I still haven't got these sodding WDPs done for Faith.

I know you've got your Lunch and Learn today, but can't Lucinda do it instead?

The little bugger has picked the worst possible time to do this.
M

From: Martin Lukes
To: Suzanna Elliott

Hi Suzanna,

Attached is your completed Work and Development Plan. I don't think you'll be at all surprised to see that the comments are of a strongly positive nature. Your contribution to the marketing department in the past six months has been better than excellent!

You need to sign the completed form, but I'd like to get some feedback from you re the WDP – I'm tied up until 6.30 – what about a drink after work?
Martin

Suzanna Elliott
Position: Associate Brand Evangelist
Suzanna's performance has been consistently excellent since the last WDP. She delivers high-quality results, handles multiple priorities well. She uses logic and intuition to define problems. She achieves technical mastery and develops it in others. She sets specific stretching objectives and meets or exceeds them. I recommend her for promotion to marketing manager.
   Signed by
   Countersigned by

From: Martin Lukes
To: Christo Weinberg

Christo – Attached is your latest WDP. Let me know if you are in agreement, and I'll sign off on it. Martin

Name: Christo Weinberg.

Position: Assistant Brand Evangelist

Christo has achieved some creative successes over the past six months; he develops own capabilities, and improves business processes. However, there are issues around his ability to work effectively with others. He needs to demonstrate integrity and high personal standards, and needs to support the development of others' creativity. He shows enthusiasm in giving time to non-work activities.

While this is to be encouraged, it is a pity if it is allowed to interfere with his work. I recommend he attends a refresher course in Teamskills and three-day residential seminar on How to Work Effectively with Others. His progress will be reviewed at the next WDP in six months' time.

Signed by

Countersigned by

From: Martin Lukes

To: Christo Weinberg

Hi Christo

I'm sorry that you are not comfortable with the WDP. This is actually a highly balanced assessment, with positives and negatives.

As we discussed in our mentoring session, you need to get better at receiving feedback. It is only by recognizing weaknesses and building self-knowledge that one shifts performance onto the next level.

Martin

From: Martin Lukes

To: Jenny Withers

OK – I'll deal with the headmaster, but frankly, Jens, I think we need to talk about this. Basically, I don't feel you're being at all supportive of me. I sometimes get the idea that you don't care if I become the next UK chairman or not. I also think you're

getting a bit over-intense about your job. I, more than anyone, am totally your champion. But I do think you should remember it's not the be-all-and-end-all. At the end of the day, no one ever said on their deathbed: I wish I had spent more time in the office!
Martin

From: Martin Lukes
To: Headmaster@MillgateSchool

Dear Mr Pitman
Thank you for your message. I'm very sorry to learn about the incident this afternoon, concerning my son, Jake. I would like to take this opportunity to personally thank yourself and the school for taking swift action.

You ask if there is anything wrong at home that might explain the lad's behaviour. As you are probably aware, we are a very tight-knit, supportive family, with traditional values, and place high emphasis on being better than our very best. The only change since last term is that Jake's mother has recently had a career change that has resulted in her being more preoccupied than before.

Rest assured that she and myself will talk to Jake when he gets home. I am certain that this is a one-off and will ensure that this unfortunate type of occurrence does not happen again. Jake, as you know, is an exceedingly talented lad who needs the right sort of motivational programme in order to unleash his true potential, which I am confident is very substantial.
Yours very sincerely
Martin Lukes

From: Martin Lukes
To: Jake Lukes

Jake –
I have just had to grovel to your headmaster on yr behalf which is NOT an experience I enjoy. You are a complete idiot and are

now grounded. You have no allowance, no telephone. You are going to spend the rest of the week at home, working. Svetlana will pick you up at about 4ish.
Dad

From: Martin Lukes
To: Barry S. Malone

Barry – That's great! A 6 am power hour briefing is good for me, too. I've always been an early riser! Looking forward to meeting with you.
Martin

From Martin Lukes
To: Pandora@CoachworX

Hi Pandora
You may wonder why you haven't heard from me recently. This is what I am up against – as well as following the GROW model in preparing for my session with Barry, I am being a coach and mentor to my team, trying to help Jens settle in, getting Keri used to the turbo-charged way I work, and now trying to deal with my son.

There is a cliché that says that only women can multi-task. I am living proof that the opposite is true.
22.5 per cent better than my bestest
Martin

March 15

From: Martin Lukes
To: Graham Wallace

Graham –
Great weekend at St Andrews. The course was in fantastic condition and the weather also came up trumps. Some of the

tee shots are semi-blind which adds to the enjoyment. But my driving was in good nick, and best of all, I birdied the last after hitting a drive and a 9 iron to six feet!!! A small crowd around the 18th will bear witness to my score.

And guess who I bumped into at the 19th hole? Lord Browne! I actually felt pretty sorry for him, BP's obviously got succession problems of its own. He's actually a nice guy, and we really bonded. I gave him some advice on how he should rebrand himself to get back on top. He hinted that if things don't work out for me here, there might be openings at BP . . . though Keith has indicated to me in private, that they have already made up their minds.

M

PS OK, I'll cover for you again tonight with Lucinda. How's it going btw??

From: Martin Lukes
To: Suzanna Elliott

Hi Suzanna – Doing some blue-sky thinking about the role of a-b glöbâl (UK). It's clear to me that we are increasingly a very young, funky company – and I'd like to get a flavour of that into a presentation I'm doing for our CEO. Could we have lunch to discuss?

M

March 16

From: Martin Lukes
To: Keri Tartt

Keri, can you keep everyone off my back today, I'm putting the finishing touches to my presentation for tomorrow?

A large latte and a Bounty would go down a treat.

Martin

March 17

From: Martin Lukes
To: Barry S. Malone

Hi Barry
Just to say how very stimulated I was by our discussion this morning. These are all issues that are very close to my heart – I am highly passionate about a-b glöbâl (UK) – as you may have gathered!

Here in London we are a close-knit high-performing team. All credit to Keith, who has done a better-than-excellent job as chairman. However, as I said to you, I believe there is still plenty of low-hanging fruit that we can use to leverage our performance still more, and I would like to drive that process.
All my very bestest
Martin

March 18

From: Martin Lukes
To: Pandora@CoachworX

Hi Pandora
Had a very interesting pre-breakfast meeting with Barry yesterday. The day started badly – the minicab driver didn't turn up, so I had to drive in, and then I got a bloody wheel clamp. I find it hard to function at 120 per cent at 6 am, but Barry was firing on all cylinders – the man's a human dynamo – having been up since 4 am running and training. Unfortunately there was something wrong with the power supply to my laptop, so I couldn't give him the Power Point presentation I'd spent the whole weekend preparing. Potential disaster, but actually I think it worked out for the best. Barry's so informal that he probably preferred just listening to me kick ideas around. I told him about my concept for repositioning a-b glöbâl (UK) at the heart of

Europe. He kept nodding and saying 'Uh huh! Uh huh! I can feel your passion.'

He didn't ask any questions at all about me, which you might think was a bad sign, but we really bonded on an intellectual level, which was more important than anything. I did exactly what you said and was focused, focused, focused! My creativity came across strongly as did my communication skills. Not sure about my humour. I made a couple of good jokes which he didn't laugh at, but then Americans don't have a sense of humour. I sent Barry a message immediately afterwards saying how much I enjoyed our meeting, but have got nothing back, as yet.

I've now got to go to Jake's school to grovel to his headmaster.
22.5 per cent better than my bestest
Martin

From: Barry S. Malone
To: All Staff/London

Howdy!
Howdy! First up I'd like to say how much of a kick I have gotten out of my visit to London yesterday. There is a load of passionate, diverse human capital in this company and it has been a unique privilege to interact with it. I have taken away one powerful learning from the meetings, which I want to share with you. At a-b glôbâl we know how to play the game. We know how to stay in the game. However, having skin in the game is not enough. To achieve PPP what we must do is shape the game. The UK is one of our most important market spaces and is a springboard to Europe.

I know there is some uncertainty over leadership issues, but I would like to reassure you that we are working on this, and will make an announcement soon!
I love you all
Barry S. Malone

From: Martin Lukes
To: Jenny Withers

Jens – Not sure what to think about that . . . At first I thought
it was a bad sign he didn't send me anything personally. But actually I think he probably needs to tell the people who aren't getting
the job first. So no news may be good news.
M x

March 22

From: Martin Lukes
To: Graham Wallace

Oh dear . . . what makes you think she suspects?
M
PS What are you hearing on the new chairman??

From: Martin Lukes
To: Graham Wallace

No, I have NO IDEA of how Lynne could have got wind of
anything. I certainly haven't told Jens if that's what you're implying. Probably Lucinda let something slip . . . she's not exactly
discreet is she?

From: Martin Lukes
To: Jenny Withers

WHY ON EARTH DID YOU GO AND TELL LYNNE
ABOUT GRAHAM AND LUCINDA??? Thanks to your big
mouth, you have probably wrecked their marriage and you've
landed me in a ton of trouble with Graham.

From: Barry S. Malone
To: All Staff/London

Howdy!
In the coming weeks we will be kicking off root-and-branch reassessment of our talent pool. Ahead of this we believe it would be premature to appoint a permanent successor to the position of chairman of a-b glöbâl (UK). This is one of the pivotal positions outside of Atlanta and it is vital to get this important appointment aligned with the talent pool.

I am today delighted to say that Roger Wright is appointed as acting chairman to a-b glöbâl (UK) until a permanent replacement is found.

I know you will give Roger every support in this function.
I love you all.
Barry

From: Martin Lukes
To: Graham Wallace

AAAAAAAAAAAAAAAAAARRRRRRRRRRRGGGGGGG
GGGHHHHHHHHHH

And I don't suppose you can even have a drink – presumably you need to go home to scrape the shit off the fan as it were. I've lost the will to live.

From: Martin Lukes
To: Suzanna Elliott

S – Fancy a quick drink tonite? Could meet you at All Bar One at 6.30. M

March 23

From: Martin Lukes
To: Suzanna Elliott

Morning, Suzanna. Did you get home all right? The third bottle of champagne was a mistake. Hope I didn't go on too much!
Martin

From: Martin Lukes
To: Jenny Withers

Darling, really sorry about last night. I went out for a drink with Graham to drown my sorrows, and to coach him over his failing marriage. I know I was in no fit state to drive home. Sorry. Hope I cleaned up the mess ok.
Love you M xx

From: Martin Lukes
To: Graham Wallace

No nothing happened. I'm sure she would have been up for it, but I wasn't in the mood.
    As I say, I've lost the will to live.
M
PS Sorry to hear Lynne chucked you out. You might be able to kip down chez nous, but I don't dare ask Jens right now as I'm not flavour of the month after last night.

From: Martin Lukes
To: Pandora@CoachworX

Pandora –
Terrible news. They've given the job to Roger, admittedly only on a temporary basis, before appointing an outsider. I did everything you told me to. I polished up my self-belief. I prepared

some unbeatable ideas. I positioned myself perfectly – and did I get my dream?? No, I got fuck all, if you'll pardon my French. What this proves is that to get anywhere in this place you must either be a box-ticker, or a woman. A man who can think outside the box is going to lose out over and over again. I have been a brilliant coach to members of my team. I have sorted out my son. I am helping my wife with her career. And then I get shat on from a great height.

I am so hacked off. I'm getting in touch with the headhunters today – I'm leaving this company, and frankly, I think I can do that without your help.
Rgds
Martin

From: Pandora@CoachworX
To: Martin Lukes

Hi Martin!
Thank you for sharing that with me. Even negative thoughts are better shared. What you are going through now is a natural part of the SARAH cycle. When you have difficult news you feel shock, anger, resentment, acceptance and hope. I am here to get you into the second part of the cycle as soon as possible.

I think you're forgetting your mantra – NO FAILURE ONLY FEEDBACK. Say it after me.

One learning I've taken out of this is that you don't like yourself enough. People who like themselves are light-hearted and optimistic. They have magnetic personalities. Do you like you? Are you genuinely grateful to be you?
Strive and thrive!
Pandora

From: Martin Lukes
To: Pandora@CoachworX

Of course I bloody like me. That's not the issue. The problem is that no one bloody else seems to. You ask if I'm grateful to be me. With the greatest respect, Pandora, that's about the stupidest thing anyone has ever asked me. I've just been stitched up. I feel that whatever I do goes pear shaped. So am I grateful to be me?? No, surprise, surprise, I'm not at all grateful. And why the fuck should I be??

Frankly, I don't want to go on with this coaching programme. My faith in you, and in your entire philosophy is zilch. You said that I could get this job, and like a complete idiot I believed you.

Please send your closing account to Roger Wright – my new sodding boss.
Rgds
Martin

From: Martin Lukes
To: Phyllis Lukes

Dear Mum
Thanks for your message. Sorry you've been bumped to the back of the list again for the knee op. I've had a terrible blow too. You know that job I told you about? I didn't get it and they've given it to a total idiot. It's so unfair . . .
Your loving son
Martin
PS You were right about Pandora. It's all babble. I've given her the old heave-ho.

Chapter Four

April
My Negative Energy

April 1

From: Martin Lukes
To: Stewart@harleystreetclinic

Dear Dr Stewart,
Over the past few days I have been experiencing the following worrying symptoms: my heart is beating excessively fast, I've got low back pain, and am having trouble digesting my food.

I fear I have bowel cancer. I've looked up the condition on the Internet and I seem to have ticks in all the boxes – though no bleeding rectum, as yet.

Can you fit me in for an urgent appointment at your earliest convenience? I understand that in these cases early detection is vital. The stress of my hi-energy, hi-octane lifestyle is obviously catching up with me.
Yours sincerely
Martin Lukes

From: Pandora@CoachworX
To: Martin Lukes

Hi Martin!
How are you today?

I hope you are rested and are reconnecting with your optimistic, magnetic personality. And that you are ready to start

on month four of our program! This month we will be consolidating the learnings from months one to three, and pushing forward towards even greater success and happiness for you! Strive and thrive!
Pandora

From: Martin Lukes
To: Pandora@CoachworX

Pandora – I think there is some misunderstanding. As far as I am concerned, I terminated this coaching relationship last month. That means that no, I am not ready to start on month four.
Rgds, Martin

From: Pandora@CoachworX
To: Martin Lukes

Hi Martin
It always makes me very sad on the exceedingly rare occasions when coachees fail to complete the Executive Bronze Program. This program has been carefully designed as a holistic package which lasts for 12 months. If you only complete part of the program, you may actually be in a weaker position than when you started.

Remember your six wonderful values, Martin. Be true to them!

I hope and pray that you will continue with the program. In life there are few easy wins. The big wins must be fought for.

However, if you do decide to terminate the contract, I'd like to refer to my contract which states that you will be liable to pay the outstanding full year's fee on termination.
Pandora

From: Martin Lukes
To: Jenny Withers

Jens – Am feeling worse by the minute. I've just googled bowel

cancer again and found that one in 18 men in their mid-40s have it – it's the second biggest killer in men. My athlete's foot has also flared up horribly. Do you think this is connected to the other symptoms?
Love you, M x

From: Martin Lukes
To: Keri Tartt

Hi Keri –
Thank you! That's so sweet of you. Yes, I'm sure you're right. Hi-fibre is the future for me. What is this brown thing you've bought? Am I meant to eat it?

Could you pop out again later on and get me my usual large latte – am I still allowed pain au chocolat? Surely that's got some fibre in it?? Also a tube of Mycil if you're passing a chemist.
Ta muchly, Martin

From: Roger Wright
To: All Staff

Re: weekly HODs meeting
As you know, Barry Malone has invited me to act as Chairman of a-b glöbâl (UK) until further notice. I shall be convening the first in a series of regular weekly meetings for all heads of department to discuss forthcoming issues in Meeting Room 305 at 08.15 hrs tomorrow. There are 39 items on the agenda and it is imperative that everybody attends promptly.
Roger Wright,
Chairman a-b glöbâl (UK) (Acting)

From: Martin Lukes
To: Graham Wallace

Hi Graham – Rog's dictatorial tendencies to the fore . . . would make me feel ill if I wasn't so ill already.

Have spent the past 48 hours trying to come to terms with the fact that I may not have much longer on this planet . . . seems like I've got bowel cancer.

Jens is in denial about it, and says there's no sign whatsoever that I have cancer and it's stupid to go on about it as I haven't even had the colonoscopy yet. Great.

Martin

April 2

From: Barry S. Malone
To: All Staff

Howdy!

This morning I issued an announcement to the SEC that our earnings for the first quarter would show an 18 per cent decline on last year. This is due to adverse exchange rate movements, and to hyper-competitive conditions in our market space. Our underlying position remains strong and I would like to thank each of you for making this happen and for bringing your passion and integrity to work every day.

Today I am delighted to announce the next step on our journey towards achieving Peak Performance – Permanently.

Our number one goal is to raise the talent bar. At a-b glöbâl we should have zero tolerance of low bench strength. We are a home for A players and B players. C players do not belong here.

In alignment with our caring values, we will treat every existing a-b glöbâl co-worker with human dignity. Those of you who stay will be rewarded by working with highly motivated colleagues. Those who do not stay will be free to pursue jobs someplace else where you will feel more passionate and more effective.

I have tasked Keith Buxton, Chief Talent Officer, with implementing the program. He will contact you shortly.

I love you all

Barry S. Malone

From: Martin Lukes
To: Graham Wallace

Graham – Don't like the sound of this ABC thing . . . share price tanking, which means my options are all under water – but as I'll probably be dead by the time I can exercise them, it doesn't make much difference.
Drink later?
Mart
PS Sorry to hear your wife's refusing to let you back . . . Sure she'll come round in time . . . have you actually given Lucinda the push??

From: Martin Lukes
To: Keri Tartt

Hi Keri –
I'm really impressed at how perceptive you are about my illness. I agree this is my body giving me a major wake-up call about the multiple stresses I am under. You can't go on firing 120 per cent on all cylinders indefinitely, can you?
   I'm off to see the doctor in half an hour, so we'll see what he has to say. Can you call me a cab?
M
PS Ta muchly for the crystals . . . really sweet of you.

From: Martin Lukes
To: Jenny Withers

Darling –
I want you to be brave. Just seen Dr Stewart. I'm afraid it's looking very bad indeed. Obviously he couldn't say anything about the bowel cancer at this stage, but he's sending me to a top cancer specialist for a colonoscopy.
   The even more worrying thing is that none of the other symptoms – my back pain, heartbeat or fatigue – is consistent

with the bowel cancer. At some point I'm going to need an ECG, a test for kidney malfunction and a stomach cancer assessment, but he said these tests weren't currently 'indicated', whatever that might mean. Why do these doctors talk in jargon the whole time?

Am feeling very poorly indeed. Would appreciate high-fibre supper and then whisky and bed.

M xx

April 5

From: Martin Lukes
To: Pandora@CoachworX

Hi Pandora

I have had some distressing news, which is making me revisit my decision to terminate the Executive Bronze coaching programme.

I seem to have contracted bowel cancer – which you will be aware is the number one killer in men. I seem not to have bog-standard cancer, but (typically!) some rare form of it. I'm in the process of having tests so we will know more soon.

I remember you telling me that you were diagnosed as having cancer yourself, and that your doctor gave you six months to live but you coached yourself out of it.

Can you help me to do the same? Going forward I would be interested in a programme of coaching targeted specifically at my cancer. I do not believe that you have further useful career advice for myself. And frankly career isn't actually top of mind for me anyway. If I'm being 130 per cent honest I should say that I don't hold out much hope, but at this stage I believe I should try to keep an open headset.

Bestest
Martin

From: Pandora@CoachworX
To: Martin Lukes

Hi Martin!
I am delighted to see that you are working through the SARAH cycle, and have reached the resentment/acceptance stage. Yes, I would be delighted to recommence our program. However it is imperative that you sincerely renew your commitment to me and to the Executive Bronze program. Coaching is not something that you dip in and out of. For it to succeed you must commit now to completing the course, and to striving to being 22.5 per cent better than the best you can be. You have lost a little time, but I still believe this target is very achievable.

The trust between us is an imperative part of the learning process. For my part, I repeat my sincere promise to
1. Believe in you totally and be your Number One Fan!
2. Consistently feed your self-belief so that it will grow and flourish.
3. Help you define a plan of action to achieve your goals and keep you on track to achieve them.

In return you must reconsider your commitment to adopt a more enthusiastic optimistic perception of your life.

You mention your cancer. Yes, I can certainly help here. However, there is not a special cancer coaching module – instead, the principles of self-love and self-belief that I teach strengthen the body both inside and out.
Strive and thrive!
Pandora

From: Martin Lukes
To: Keri Tartt

Hi Keri – I'm working from home today. I feel really awful, so I'd rather that people didn't ring or email. I put the crystal healing thing by my bed last night, but alas no improvement yet!
M

PS Tell Rog to sod off. I don't care if there is yet another of his budget meetings. Christo can go in my place and debrief me later.

From: Roger Wright
To: All Staff

Re: working from home
It has been drawn to my attention that we currently have no binding guidelines covering arrangements for working from home. I would like to remind all members of staff that working from home is only permissible in exceptional circumstances, and then requires written approval from a line manager.
Roger Wright,
Chairman a-b glöbâl (Acting)

From: Martin Lukes
To: Roger Wright

Roger – I am somewhat surprised at your memo. I believe that trust should be the cornerstone of our culture, and we should trust our team members to select the work schedule that suits them best.

You may be interested to know that today I am working from home because I will shortly be having hospital tests of a serious nature. Instead of taking the day off sick, I am actually finding that the quiet headspace offered by the home environment enables me to continue to work as per usual.
Martin

From: Martin Lukes
To: Graham Wallace

Hi Graham – The only consolation of my condition is that I can now say what I like . . . have sent Rog an email making quite clear what I think of him, which was v cathartic.

Re yr msg about kipping down chez nous. Will see what I can

do. I did mention it to Herself but she said you had made your bed. I quipped that was just the trouble, you didn't have a bed to make!! Even when the grim reaper is beckoning, my native wit has not deserted me!
Martin

From: Martin Lukes
To: Jenny Withers

Darling – I know Graham isn't your favourite person in the world. And I know what you think about him shagging Lucinda. I couldn't agree more – she wouldn't be my choice at all, and in any case he's an idiot, this is classic male menopause etc. etc. The problem is that he has nowhere to go and I've said he can kip down with us. He's in a very bad way. It wouldn't be for very long. Just a night or two.
Love you, M

From: Martin Lukes
To: Jenny Withers

I realize this is very hard for you too. They often say that the next of kin find cancer even more frightening than the patient. But I really resent the way that you are channelling your worry over my health into anger against me and men in general. It might be your best coping strategy, but it's not helping me at all.
M

April 6

From: Martin Lukes
To: Keri Tartt

Dear Keri
Did you leave Chicken Soup for the Surviving Soul – 101 Healing Stories to Comfort Cancer Patients and Their Loved

Ones on my desk the other day? If so, many thanks! I'll give it
to Jens. She could certainly use a few tips.
Martin

From: Roger Wright
To: All Staff

Re staff changes
Lucinda Mogg Watson will be leaving us at the end of the month to
pursue other options. I would like to extend thanks to her for the work
she has done with us, and offer her every success with her future career.
   Jenny Withers has been appointed Head of External Relations. The
appointment of a new assistant will be announced shortly.
Roger Wright
Chairman, a-b glöbâl (Acting)

From: Martin Lukes
To: Jenny Withers

I DON'T BELIEVE THIS!! When we discussed it last night I
thought we agreed that it would be a very bad idea for you to
take on additional responsibilities given my cancer issues?? So
what are you thinking of??? M

From: Pandora@CoachworX
To: Martin Lukes

Hi Martin
How are you today?
   At this stage in the program we would normally be look-
ing at your energy levels holistically. However because of your
health issues, I think it would be better if we commenced
with your negative energy, which is obviously a big thing in
your life right now.
   Many of my coachees find this a difficult concept to grasp.
The easiest way of understanding this, Martin, is to think

of yourself like a colander. Energy is poured in, but pours out again through the holes. This is your negative energy. We need to find where those holes are, and find ways of blocking them.

Martin, I would like you to do this exercise for me now. Close your eyes and think of that colander. Can you see where the negative energy is gushing out? Email me between five and ten of these 'holes', and we'll find a way of blocking them!
Strive and thrive!
Pandora

From Martin Lukes
To: Pandora@CoachworX

Hi Pandora. I have been trying to find some holes (as it were!!). I have come up with the following list which is by no means comprehensive, but I hope will be a start.
1. My bowel situation
2. Roger
3. Cindy
4. Christo
5. Jake's issues around work, drugs/alcohol, etc.
6. Jens' issues around my cancer, around her career, and generally her sense of humour failure, etc.
7. When Arsenal beats Chelsea
22.5 per cent better than my very bestest
Martin

From: Pandora@CoachworX
To: Martin Lukes

Hi Martin!
Well done! Can I make a suggestion on how we can take this forward? The first thing that strikes me is that many of your holes are related to other people. This isn't at all unusual.

Many people have very high levels of negative energy and are toxic to people like you, Martin, who are committed to being Better than your Best. There is only one thing to do with toxic people. Ignore them! And if this is difficult, explain to them that they are toxic to you, and that you need to limit your exposure.
Strive and thrive!
Pandora

From: Martin Lukes
To: Jenny Withers

Just seen your message. Just because I'm at home doesn't mean I can be a tutor to Jake. In fact I have to be careful at the moment because Jake is connected to my negative energy, which is making the cancer much worse. What time are you coming home?
M

From: Martin Lukes
To: Jenny Withers

No of COURSE I am not saying Jake's caused my cancer. He's one of the holes in my energy colander, if you will.
M

From: Martin Lukes
To: Jenny Withers

No need to be sarcastic about it . . . it's a useful concept of Pandora's – at the end of the day we're all just colanders, energy goes in and comes out. Jake just happens to be one of my holes.
M

April 7

From: Keith Buxton
To: All Staff

Hallo everyone
You will all by now have seen Barry's memo unveiling our exciting
programme for upgrading our talent pool.

As Chief Talent Officer I shall be overseeing this programme, which
is code-named Project Uplift. Under Project Uplift we shall be sorting
our co-workers into three grades – A, B and C. This sorting will be
done in a scientific, highly objective way that will assess each indi-
vidual against target behaviours. Phase One will commence this week,
and will consist in designing a customized Matrix of Key Behaviours.
I shall be inviting a representative from every geography to help build
our Behaviour Matrix. Further details on the intranet site.
Keith

From: Martin Lukes
To: Keith Buxton

Hi Keith!
Great to hear from you! Yes, I'd be only too delighted. I have
lots of ideas about our target behaviours, but will of course make
the consultative process here as inclusive as possible. Needless
to say, I am 110 per cent behind this initiative.
All my very bestest,
Martin

From: Martin Lukes
To: Jenny Withers

Darling – Keith's asked me to head up the Key Behaviours task
force in London!!!! It's incredibly visible – a huge break for me.
I must have really impressed Malone last month after all. It's
going to be a ton of extra work – I didn't tell him about my

health issues. Unfortunately I'm going to have to go to Atlanta next week which will clash with the colonoscopy.
M xx

From: Martin Lukes
To: Keri Tartt

Hi Keri – I'm feeling a little better. My energy levels have stopped tanking and I'll be back in the office this afternoon. See you then.
Martin

From: Martin Lukes
To: Stewart@harleystreetclinic

Dear Doctor Stewart
I am due to go to the US next week on mission critical business. Is it safe to travel? As you know my colonoscopy is diarized for next Wednesday. Could you arrange for it to be moved forward to the tail end (no pun intended!!) of this week?
Yours sincerely
Martin Lukes

From: Martin Lukes
To: Stewart@harleystreetclinic

Dear Doctor Stewart
Thanks for getting back to me so quickly. Frankly, I'm a little surprised at your answer, but will, as you suggest, go ahead with my trip, and have put May 5 in my diary.
Martin Lukes

From: Martin Lukes
To: Jenny Withers

Darling – Just got v cryptic msg from Stewart. For what it's worth, he says it doesn't matter if I postpone the colonoscopy for three and a half weeks. I suppose he thinks I'm toast anyway. They are unbelievably casual, these doctors. If I was that slack I would have been struck off years ago.

M x

April 8

From: Martin Lukes
To: All Staff

Hi Everyone
I have been tasked by Keith Buxton to represent the UK on the task force that will build our Key Behaviours Matrix. I am today inviting a cross-section of employees to sit on the UK Key Behaviours Focus Group. We will get the ball rolling, and then it will be over to you! This is going to be an inclusive process!

Bestest, Martin

From: Martin Lukes
To: Key Behaviours Focus Group

Hi, Suzanna, Matt, Graham and Nigel
Thank you for agreeing to join me on the Key Behaviours Focus Group. Ahead of the first session in my office tomorrow at 10 am I'd like each of you to think of the six behaviours that you personally think are the key drivers for every individual in the a-b glöbâl family to ensure that we as a company excel at every point in the value chain. It should be a highly stimulating session. See you tomorrow.

Martin

April 9

From: Martin Lukes
To: All Staff

Hi Everybody
The Key Behaviours Focus Group had its first meeting today and surfaced many innovative ideas. So far we have identified the following target Behaviours: Courage, Citizenship, Playfulness, Wisdom, Win-win Headset, and Hi-trust. I think you will agree that this has been an outstanding start. Now it's over to you – we want to hear your views!
My best, Martin

From: Jenny Withers
To: All Staff

With my Communications hat on, I'd like to suggest we present each behaviour as a personal statement: 'I am courageous', 'I am a good citizen', 'I am playful'. That way we align them more closely with the values of each individual co-worker.
Best, Jenny

From: Christo Weinberg
To: All Staff

Hi!
I think we can kick this baby up a notch. What we are doing is creating riffs which we all play together. This isn't about 'I'. It's about 'we'. 'I' is a feeble solo, 'we' is a monster big band jamming session. If we say 'WE are good citizens', 'WE are playful', then that creates an inclusive formula we can all feel passionate about!
Cheers, Christo

From: Suzanna Elliott
To: All Staff

Hi!! What about making the behaviours all begin with the same letter? It would help us create a really powerful behaviours brand. Two of them already begin with C, so we could convert all the others to C words. Instead of 'win-win headset' we could have 'can-do headset'. Instead of 'wisdom', 'cleverness'. And instead of playfulness we could have 'clowning'. I know it's a bit outrageous, but you can't accuse me of thinking inside the box!!!
Suze

From: Martin Lukes
To: Suzanna Elliott

Suze – you're a STAR!! That is brilliant, really creative. Just been thinking about this, and it has given me a breakthrough idea: given the quality of your work, I'd like you to clear your diary and come with me to Atlanta next week for the big presentation.
M

From: Keri Tartt
To: All Staff

Hi!! Doesn't 'clever' discriminate against those of us who have not been to university? What about 'caring' instead???
Keri

From: Martin Lukes
To: Keri Tartt

Thanks for that, Keri. Good point. Could you get me a large latte when you've a mo? M

From: Martin Lukes
To: All Staff

Hi!
I'm delighted this issue has caused so much passionate debate!
It shows that at a-b glöbâl (UK) we are all full of courage and
playfulness! I would like to assure all of you who have shared
your views with us that we will discuss them in full at this week's
committee meeting.
Bestest, Martin

April 12

From: Martin Lukes
To: Pandora@CoachworX

Hi Pandora
Sorry I'm a bit late in sending you my negative energy feedback, but I've been snowed under. I've been invited to lead the
UK's effort on the most important global project so far this
year. Basically this suggests that they are still considering me for
the position of UK Chairman, and this project is a hurdle, if
you will.

On the negative energy front I'm making good progress. Have
had potential conflict with Christo and the ladywife, which I have
ignored completely. However, I am surrounding myself by
people like Suzanna who have very high positive energy
quotients, and I can actually feel that high-energy people are
pouring more energy into my colander. The weird thing is that
the bowel cancer situation feels, if not better, then at least held
at its present position.
22.5 per cent better than my very bestest
Martin

From: Pandora@CoachworX
To: Martin Lukes

Hi Martin

You are learning so quickly! I'm impressed!

You are now ready to start managing your own negative energy. Instead of looking at negative energy outside look at the negative energy inside you. One easy win is to look at the words you use. Obviously words are important to you, but you use words that drain your energy.

Here are some of the disempowering words that you use. Shit. Stressed. Distressed. Killer. Bad. Worse. Life Sentence. Awful.

These words are all about pain. And pain has no place in your life. If you say no to pain, you say no to cancer.

Don't say you're exhausted. Say you're RECHARGING. Don't say you're snowed under – say that you're IN DEMAND or that you're STRETCHING. See the difference? Don't say I hate. Say I PREFER. Don't say failure, say LEARNING. Don't say sick, say CLEANSING. Don't say oh shit! Say OH POO! Don't say angry, say A LITTLE BIT CONCERNED!

When you are dealing with the people who sap your energy it is vital to use these empowering words. Try it for a day or two, and tell me about the difference!

Strive and thrive!

Pandora

From: Roger Wright
To: All Staff

I have two interjections I would wish to contribute re the behaviours matrix.
* I fear inadequate consideration has been given to the metrics of the matrix. These behaviours are intended to be the subject of objective measurement. I cannot see which metrics would be used to measure 'playfulness'. Neither do I see how this is a useful addition to our global behaviours set.
* I am concerned that we are losing sight of the bottom line. I suggest 'Commercially minded' or 'Cost-conscious'.
Roger Wright,
Acting Chairman
a-b glöbâl

From: Martin Lukes
To: Roger Wright

Roger – Thanks for sharing your thoughts with us. Can I make a small point? This behaviours matrix is about change, changing behaviour from the negative to the positive. Negative words like 'fear' and 'cannot' have no place in the debate!
All my very bestest
Martin

April 14

From: Martin Lukes
To: Jenny Withers

Darling – Sorry we were out so late and that we made so much noise when we came in. I will tell Graham that it is not acceptable, and suggest he sorts himself out accommodation-wise asap.

However you are wrong to say that drinking is bad for my negative energy. Drinking in moderation (which is all I did last night) is good for me. The person who was pissed last night was not yours truly but Graham.
Love you M xx

From: Martin Lukes
To: All Staff

Hello everybody
I am delighted to say that the Key Behaviours Focus Group has completed its work and I am now in a position to offer you a preview of the behaviours matrix before I unveil it in Atlanta next week. After much highly inclusive debate we have decided on six positive behaviours that define us at a-b glöbâl UK.
Why CONVERSATION? Because this is how we touch each other's souls.

Why CONNECTIVITY? Because no man is an island. We are teams that connect with each other.

Why CRAZINESS? Because without a bit of craziness we would be the same as everyone else.

Why CARING? Because we are global citizens who love each other and the communities we serve.

Why COACHING? Because this is how we nurture each other and pass on our key learnings.

Why CREATIVITY? Because without this we could never change our DNA.

You will notice that the first behaviours begin with the same letter, which gives them a powerful internal brand. I would like to thank my team for going the extra mile to reach what I am sure you will agree is truly a caring, creative and crazy matrix!

All my very bestest,

Martin

From: Faith Preston
To: All Staff

Hi –
We in co-worker services are surprised the matrix makes no mention of work–life balance. We feel that this is the key to the future of our company and that we cannot endorse any behaviour set that does not have a work–life dimension. We are disappointed that you did not give us the opportunity to affect the outcome of the matrix, and plan to share our views with Keith Buxton.
Cheers, Faith

From: Martin Lukes
To: Faith Preston

Faith – Re your suggestion. First, you had plenty of opportunity to present your views to us last week. Second, work–life balance isn't a behaviour at all. Neither does it begin with C.

By all means voice a protest with Keith. I should warn you though, he's pretty busy at the moment and may not welcome the distraction.
Martin

April 15

From: Martin Lukes
To: Keri Tartt

Hi Keri – Can you get the travel arrangements for Suzanna and myself sorted asap? We need to leave mid-morning Monday. Plse check that BA has beds in Business Class on its 747s – I want the window seat in the bubble. In Atlanta, plse book us into the W. Preferably a suite for myself.
Ta muchly, Martin

From: Martin Lukes
To: Jenny Withers

Jens – I DID tell you I'm leaving on Monday – you weren't listening. Yes, I do realize Jake will still be home for the Easter holidays. What do you expect me to do about it – tell Keith I can't come because I need to make my delinquent 15-year-old son revise for his GCSEs? M

From: Martin Lukes
To: Suzanna Elliott

Hi Suze
I'm trying to wangle business-class tickets for you. Even though you're not senior enough, I've told them we have work to do and must travel together. I'm also insisting on the W which is the nicest hotel in Altanta.

Can you do a drink after work today to discuss strategy . . . also this work–life balance suggestion of Faith looks like it

won't go away. She's complained to Keith, and I think he's keen. Can you think of a word for work–life balance that begins with c?
M

From: Martin Lukes
To: Suzanna Elliott

You're a genius! 'Cradle' is brilliant! It's very subtle, but very powerful. Atlanta is going to love it. All Bar One at 7ish?

From: Martin Lukes
To: Jenny Withers

Jens – Yes, Suzanna is coming with me. The only reason I didn't mention it to you was because you've shown no interest whatsoever in this trip. Suze has done a better than excellent job on the focus group, and I really don't see what yr problem is . . . You're always moaning about the glass ceiling and how women don't get a chance in this company.
Love you
M

April 17

From: Martin Lukes
To: Phyllis Lukes

Dearest Mum
Sorry I haven't been in touch for a bit, but I've had a blow on the health front recently. Long story short, I seem to have bowel cancer.

I didn't want to tell you until I had the colonoscopy, because I knew you'd be sick with worry. But then I thought how upset you'd be if you heard from someone else, so I thought better you learnt about it from the horse's mouth.

Don't know what the prognosis is, my strategy for dealing with it is to be very honest about it, and to keep on absolutely as normal. Did I tell you that Pandora is very knowledgeable on matters cancerous, having had a brush with it herself? She says it's all about balancing the positive and negative energies, which makes a lot of sense when you think about it.

Am off to Atlanta on important business next week so fraid I won't be able to come down at the weekend to help prune the shrubs. Will see you when I'm back.

Try not to worry too much.
Your loving son,
Martin
PS Any news on the knee op?

April 19

From: Martin Lukes
To: Keri Tartt

Keri – travel department has booked us into the HOLIDAY INN!! I am a director of this company and travelling on the most important business. Tell them to upgrade my hotel to the W. This is absolutely bloody typical.
M

April 20

From: Martin Lukes
To: Jenny Withers

Darling – Plane delayed three hours at Heathrow . . . I'm totally shattered. Or, as Pandora would have me say, I'm recharging.

There's been a massive cock-up over hotels – everyone else is staying at the Holiday Inn, and no one told me. Suzanna and I are in the W, miles away from the action. Trust all OK at home. I had an email from Max asking me for help on his algebra paper for Common Entrance – told him I'm a bit up against it. Can't you do it?

M xx

From: Keith Buxton
To: UpBOB

Hello everyone! Let me say how delighted I am to see so many of you from so many different geographies gathered here for the project Uplift Brainstorm on Behaviors (UpBOB).

   Tomorrow we kick off with a pre-breakfast Show and Tell. I'm asking each of you to share with us something personal about what the key behaviours mean to you. You will notice that the walls of the meeting room are draped in brown paper. During all sessions, I'd like you to write any thoughts you may have on the walls. Whatever comes into your minds, write it down! It's going to be a lot of fun!
Keith

April 20

From: Martin Lukes
To: Jenny Withers

Darling – just got yr message. Jake's totally out of order. However, it's a pity that you went apeshit at him – I think it's much more motivational to use more empowering language.

   Will send him an email tonight if I have a mo. Just ran into BSM – he said he was really looking forward to my presentation! K's gone native, acting like a touchy-feely American.

   Ugh.

Love you, M XX

From: Martin Lukes
To: Jake Lukes

Jake – I am a little bit concerned to hear from your mother that you stole some money from Svetlana, which has resulted in her threatening to leave.

I must be honest with you: my initial response was: Oh poo, but I have now reflected on the situation, and feel you need to think about changing your behaviours.

Jake, can you do an exercise for me? Can you think up six key behaviours that will help you going forward, and email them to me? Then I can help you learn to live them.

Let's make a new start!

Love, Dad

From: Martin Lukes
To: UpBOB

Hi everyone!
I'm sorry I'm not at the pre-breakfast Show and Tell. I'm stuck in traffic. I didn't realize it would take so long to get across town! Should be with you in half an hour.

Cheers, Martin Lukes
Sent from my BlackBerry Wireless Handheld

From: Keith Buxton
To: UpBOB

Hallo everyone! Thanks to one and all for a stimulating day's discussion. I have never seen so much passionate graffiti in one place! Thanks also to Martin Lukes for joining us eventually and sharing his personal story with us.

It was energizing to realize how he is using a behaviours matrix to help his son with his GCSE revision! I really believe that Project Uplift behaviours matrices have great potential both in the work and the home arenas! Please be prompt for this evening's networking drinks: 6.30 pm in the Printemps Suite.

Keith

From: Martin Lukes
To: Jenny Withers

Darling – really energizing day. We had a very intellectual discussion today about the link between behaviours and values. Will tell all when I get back. Hope everything's fine at home.

Am forwarding Jake's response to my motivational message. Any idea what he's on about?
Love you, M x

From: Jake Lukes
To: Martin Lukes

Dad, you're gay. J

Text message to Suzanna. Sent 18.02

Suze – BSM's not going to be at the bash tonight, and not sure I can face it either. Do you fancy dinner just the two of us? M

April 21

Text message to Suzanna. Sent 07.32

Suze – TERRIBLY sorry. How are you feeling? Jens tried to call in the middle of the night, got no answer and now smells a rat . . . We need to talk. M

From: Martin Lukes
To: Jenny Lukes

Darling, The reason I wasn't in my hotel room when you called is that I was working. You have no idea how hard Keith is pushing us. The sessions start unbelievably early.
Love you and miss you A LOT. M xxxx
Sent from my BlackBerry Wireless Handheld

From: Martin Lukes
To: Keith Buxton

Hi Keith
Thanks for your message. Sorry I didn't make last night. I had a slight stomach upset. Am enclosing a sneak preview of our values ahead of today's presentation – hope you will like them as much as we do!
My best, Martin.

April 22

From: Martin Lukes
To: Keri Tartt

Hi Keri
Just arrived at Heathrow – am off home to recharge and renew. I've got a couple of key memos I need to write . . . Tell Rog that whatever it is, I can't see him today. M
Sent from my BlackBerry Wireless Handheld

From: Martin Lukes
To: Keri Tartt

Thanks for asking. You are so considerate. No, I don't feel great. But then the travel and the stress are bound to impact negatively on my condition. Will be in the office tomorrow.
Martin
Sent from my BlackBerry Wireless Handheld

From: Martin Lukes
To: Suzanna Elliott

Can we please talk?? M

April 26

From: Martin Lukes
To: All Staff

Hello everyone
I wanted to debrief you on an incredibly exciting few days in Atlanta. There is huge momentum behind UpBOB, and our committee's input went down extremely well. Suzanna gave a better-than-excellent presentation that left all the others standing! We are expecting that the UK contribution will be well represented in the ultimate out-turn!
Best, Martin

From: Martin Lukes
To: Suzanna Elliott

Suze – I really think you are making this into too much of a big deal. These things happen. You avoiding me is not the answer. We need to talk . . . M

From: Martin Lukes
To: Keri Tartt

Hi Keri
Can you put through my Atlanta exes asap? If Rog gives any trouble you might point out Suzanna and I worked 14-hour days while we were in Atlanta. We were putting the UK in the driving seat on our most important global initiative since Project Rebrand.
Martin

From: Barry S. Malone
To: All Staff

Howdy!
First up, I wanted to say thank you to all those who came to Atlanta

last week for UpBOB. There is an amazing amount of passion and love being shown on this project. Over the next few days Keith Buxton and myself will be finalizing the matrix based upon last week's inputs, and then we will be able to commence the global roll-out of Project Uplift! I love you all,
Barry

From: Martin Lukes
To: Graham Wallace

Graham – Delighted that Lynne's taken you back. Meanwhile I've got into a spot of hot water myself. On Tuesday night S and I went out drinking, and I ended up in her hotel room. Between you and me and the gatepost I can't remember exactly what happened. Suffice to say that both the booze and the bowel cancer may have impacted on performance somewhat. Anyway she is refusing to talk to me, which is all v awkward.
M

April 30

From: Pandora@CoachworX
To: Martin Lukes

Hi Martin
When we started the program I said I was going to be your greatest fan. And let me tell you that the way you have got back into the Bronze Program has been exceptional. The Old You is dead. New You is alive and growing!!
  Can I ask you to jot down some of the advances you've made this month, and then give yourself a big round of applause? Strive and thrive!
Pandora

From: Martin Lukes
To: Pandora@CoachworX

Hi Pandora

If you'll excuse a literary reference, April is the cruellest month.

As the poet Philip Larkin predicted, this has been a hyper-challenging month for myself, though I have notched some wins that I am very proud of. I am interacting less with people who impact negatively on my energy levels.

I am also making progress with the words I use. I am avoiding disempowering words and words full of pain. This has been highly successful except possibly with my son, who seems to have decided that I'm a shirtlifter. Which is quite ironic, when you think about it(!).

This month I have made a good start in coming to terms with bowel cancer. To have scored a major career win under these circumstances is no mean feat.

I am distressed that not much progress has been made on the home front. Jens is burying herself in her career in order to avoid confronting various issues. I see this as a growing problem.

Basically, going forward I need to look after number one and take things one day at a time!

22.5 per cent better than my bestest

Martin

From: Martin Lukes
To: Keri Tartt

Keri – you weren't meant to catch me doing that! I was clapping as part of my coaching programme!!

What does Rog want to see me about? Is it expenses? Tell him I can't come – I'm in demand . . . M

From: Roger Wright
To: All Staff

Re: Staff Changes
Suzanna Elliott, currently Marketing Manager has been appointed to the External Relations team. She will report to Jenny Withers. At this

time, we would like to thank Suzanna for her past performance, and look forward to exceptional output from her in the ER function.
Roger Wright
Chairman a-b glöbâl (UK) (Acting)

From: Martin Lukes
To: Suzanna Elliott

Suzanna –

Frankly I'm surprised at you. In working for Jens you are taking a step backwards careerwise. External Relations is basically just a cost centre whereas Marketing is the beating heart of the company. As you did not consult me, I can only assume that your decision was related to what happened in Atlanta. As far as I'm concerned nothing happened between us except that we both had a lot to drink.
Martin

From: Martin Lukes
To: Jenny Withers

WHAT THE FUCKING HELL DO YOU THINK YOU ARE PLAYING AT?? NOT ONLY ARE YOU TOTALLY UNCON-CERNED ABOUT MY HEALTH, YOU POACH MY BEST TALENT, AND DON'T EVEN BOTHER TO CONSULT ME. SINCE YOU GOT YOUR NEW JOB YOU'VE BEEN THROWING YOUR WEIGHT ABOUT LIKE A MINI HITLER. IT DOESN'T SUIT YOU.

NOT COMING TO YOUR PARENTS THIS WEEKEND. AM GOING TO PLAY GOLF AT THE RAC.
M

Chapter Five

May

My Heart and My Head

May 3

From: Pandora@CoachworX
To: Martin Lukes

Hi Martin
Welcome to Month Five!
This month we are going to focus in on your heart. But before we do that I want to revisit New You. Can you do something for me, Martin? Stand in front of a mirror very close, with your nose almost touching the glass so that your reflection is out of focus, and then slowly walk backwards. What do you see? Do you see New Martin? Or do you still see glimpses of Old Martin struggling to hide his low self-image from the world?

I want you to describe the man in front of you, using a fun test of mine called KWYA. It's pronounced choir, because it is like your inner choir singing in harmony about the New You.

K stands for your kindness to yourself. W is your wisdom. Y is your values and being true to them. A is your aims and ambitions.

So look in the mirror, Martin, and tell me about the KWYA you see reflected there. We need to check that your inner choir is singing from the same hymn sheet.
Strive and thrive!
Pandora

From: Martin Lukes
To: Jenny Withers

Jens – Just looked at the hospital letter and seems I'll be practically on nil by mouth for 36 hours before the colonoscopy, and have to take three batches of laxatives. I'll stay home tomorrow and the next day, and probably best if I don't go to Max's debating contest tonight. These doctors may kill me before the cancer does . . .
Martin x

May 4

From: Martin Lukes
To: Pandora@CoachworX

Hi Pandora
I am trying to do your tests, though finding it hard thanks to some of the strongest laxatives on God's earth which I've taken ahead of my colonoscopy tomorrow. I started staring at myself close up in the mirror, but was rudely interrupted by a dash to the toilet.

Then when I resumed, the moment was lost.

Still, to the best of my current ability, here we go on my KWYA thingy.

KINDNESS to myself – Yes, I think I'm doing well on this. I'm learning to like myself much more. I'm broadly speaking pleased with what I see in the mirror – could be a bit thinner (though today alone I must have lost half a stone). I see a decent, funny person, good to have around.

WISDOM – yes, I think the guy in the mirror has it. It's not just wisdom about stuff I know, it's wisdom about what makes me tick, and what makes other tick, too.

YOUR VALUES – Not sure that I can actually see my values in the mirror. As you know, I want to use my creativity, my networking, my sense of fun to make the world a better place. But not quite sure I can pick that up from my reflection.

AMBITION – I can certainly see that – this guy is already successful and is on the way up. It's a look of determination in the chin. He wants to be a leader. He wants recognition. Respect. Money. Status. Basically, all the usual things.

That's about it. Though if I am being 140 per cent honest there is something else I see – I can sense that this guy in the mirror is ill. But we'll find out more about that tomorrow.
22.5 per cent better than my very bestest,
Martin

From: Martin Lukes
To: Keri Tartt

Hi Keri – I'm at home today . . . ahead of the big test tomorrow. Can you look through my diary and cancel all meetings until Thursday? Speak later.
Martin

From: Martin Lukes
To: Phyllis Lukes

Dear Mum
I got your nice email this morning, but you don't seem to have mastered the art of the attachment!! The promised pic of Pebbles curled up on the couch wasn't there, so I'll have to take your word for it that he looked sweet!! If you want to try to re-send, then follow the instructions I wrote down last time. It's really not that hard. Otherwise, I'll show you when I come, which will be as soon as I'm a bit better.

Can't remember if I told you I've got my colonoscopy tomorrow. The good news is that my symptoms don't seem to be deteriorating too rapidly – all things considered I've survived the US trip pretty well. Basically, I'm like you mum – tough as old boots, so no need to worry. My strategy is not to think about it, and to carry on as per normal.

On a happier note, we should be hearing if Max has got into

Eton in a few days. The lad seemed really confident after the exams and his last school report (did I show it to you?) says he's a total all-rounder – he's a very useful spin bowler, on the first eleven rugby team, top set for maths, english, Latin. He's a chip off the old block, though possibly a tad more motivated than I was at that age.

Yesterday he reached the finals of the school debating competition (he's got his mother's argumentative streak!!) arguing basically that the Wogs begin at Calais, though he didn't put it like that. Unfortunately I was too poorly to go, but Jens went and said he was brilliant, even though as a bit of a leftie she was on the other side of the argument. You would have been v proud though.

Keep your fingers crossed for me tomorrow. Will be in touch afterwards.

Much love

Martie

PS I can't believe that your op has been put back again. It's beyond a joke. I've really had it with the NHS. I think you should go private, and I'll pay.

May 5

From: Roger Wright
To: All Staff

Re: a-b glöbâl 1st Q earnings

Today you will have seen the announcement out of Atlanta of our Q1 earnings. These show a continued squeeze on margins. It is imperative in this tough climate that we continue to contain costs. To that end I am today announcing the following measures, effective at once.

1. Cuts to travel budget. All air travel must be in economy class. There will be no exceptions to this.

2. Our contract with Bloomin' Krazy has been terminated. In future we will have a display of imitation flowers in the 1st floor reception space only.

3. Headcount. Although project ABC will reduce headcount by an estimated 15 per cent, in addition I am today announcing a hiring freeze.

4. Vending machines. The 3p subsidy per cup will be rescinded, effective immediately.

I trust all staff will support these measures which will enable a-b glöbâl (UK) to put its cost base onto a firmer footing.

Roger Wright
Acting Chairman, a-b glöbâl (UK)

From: Martin Lukes
To: Graham Wallace

Trust you've seen Rog's memo. Frankly, sometimes dying seems like the easy option.

From: Martin Lukes
To: Roger Wright

Hi Roger

I've just logged on from home in advance of some exploratory surgery I'm having this afternoon.

I am extremely concerned at the hiring freeze. I should not need to remind you that the marketing department is the engine room of this company. If we do not have top talent in this department, we have zero chance of maintaining/enhancing our pole position as one of the creative engines in the a-b glöbâl family.

You will be aware that following Suzanna Elliott's departure to ER we are short of one Associate Brand Evangelist. This is a pivotal position and I am not aware of any internal candidate with the appropriate skillset. I may be in the office on Thursday and would appreciate some face time then.

Best, Martin

From: Martin Lukes
To: Jenny Withers

Darling – I'm back at home feeling very dopey after the sedative.
Dr Gorton may be the top bowel cancer bod in the country, but
even he seems to be totally defeated by my case. He claimed not
to be able to find any cancer in the colon at all – which frankly,
I find very worrying. Can you come home soon – I'm in need
of a little TLC?
M xx

From: Martin Lukes
To: Jenny Withers

Darling –
I've just spent the last hour watching the video of my bowel the
doc gave me to take home, and I'm 280 per cent certain he's
missed something. In fairness, the first couple of times I saw it,
I couldn't see anything either. But now I'm sure there is a nasty
shadow lurking on the bowel wall. I've phoned his office and
spoken to one of his dopey assistants who says that shadows are
'perfectly normal'(!) God knows where they get these people
from. I'm definitely seeking a second opinion.
    Come home quickly and watch it with me.
Love m xx
PS I'm very very hungry after my purge. Can you pick up a large
Indian takeaway on yr way back?

May 6

From: Martin Lukes
To: Pandora@CoachworX

Hi Pandora
I've been trying to reach you on the phone for an urgent debrief,
but no luck. The medical profession are completely baffled by

cancer and tests ongoing. Until I had the test I was coping well, better than well in fact. But the results have left me feeling very low and confused. When your cancer was diagnosed did you come across any medical experts prepared to think out of the box on this? Not 22.5 per cent better than my bestest (if I'm honest!)
Martin

From: Martin Lukes
To: IT Department

ARE WE THE ONLY COMPANY IN THE WORLD WITHOUT A FUNCTIONING SPAM FILTER??? I AM TOTALLY FED UP WITH ALL THIS SPAM. I DON'T NEED VIAGRA, OR PENIS ENLARGEMENT – CAN SOMEONE IN THE IT DEPARTMENT GET THIS SORTED – NOW!

May 7

From: Pandora@CoachworX
To: Martin Lukes

Hi Martin!
How are you? I'm sorry to hear that you are letting some negative energy creep back in. This is dangerous not just for your health but for you as a whole person. As I said, I think the best way forward for your bowel is the best way forward for you holistically.

The great news is that your KWYA is in perfect harmony, and you are now ready for the next module, which is all about your heart.

Like many highly successful men, Martin, you let your head work overtime. You are extremely intelligent, and very logical, but unless you let your heart talk, you will have success without joy. You will achieve your goals, but you won't be fulfilled, and you will have a working style that will veer on the demanding and the bullying. So I am going to show you how to join up the left side of your brain, which is the logical side, to the right side, which controls your feelings. We are going to build a little bridge.

Close your eyes, Martin. Imagine a red rose in the right side of your brain. Imagine a white rose on the left. Can you see those roses, Martin? Now swap them over. The power of this exercise is amazing. If you do it every hour for the next four weeks, you will find the bridge is there and the difference in your decision-making will be amazing.
Strive and thrive!
Pandora

From: Martin Lukes
To: Keri Tartt

Keri – do you mind if I ask you something? I'd really like your honest answer. Do you think my management style can be demanding, or even bullying?
Martin

From: Martin Lukes
To: Keri Tartt

Very kind of you to say so! Thank you! Next odd request. Can you come into my office and help me perform a little trick with roses?! A large latte and an almond Danish would be nice . . . it's something that may require a little sustenance!
M

From: Martin Lukes
To: Pandora@CoachworX

Hi Pandora
For what it's worth, you have got me wrong if you think I'm purely a 'head' person. Certainly logical thought is extremely

important to myself, but I am also a very feeling person, and reject 120 per cent the idea that I am bullying. I've just asked for some honest 360-degree feedback from members of my team, who do not buy into the idea at all! That said, I'll practise the tests and see what happens!

22.5 per cent better than my very bestest

Martin

May 10

From: Martin Lukes
To: Phyllis Lukes

Dearest Mum

Can you send me the name of your knee doctor and I'll investigate the private option?? Really don't worry about the money. Obviously I'll pay for it. I thought I had already said that. Yes, the Eton fees are going to be an arm and a leg (assuming he gets in), but I've only got one mum, and I'm going to walk the extra mile to look after her!

Martie

From: Martin Lukes
To: Keri Tartt

Hi Keri

Great trousers! Very fetching!

Can I ask you to do a little something? Can you find out who is in charge of our health insurance? I want to wangle my mother's op onto my policy. I know it normally only covers wife and kids . . . but I think the wording says something like 'dependent family' . . . which is ambiguous as my mum is obviously family, and is totally dependent on me!

M

From: Martin Lukes
To: Roger Wright

Roger – You suggest Bettina Schmidt as a satisfactory candidate for Senior Brand Evangelist. I know that she has worked on some leading-edge marketing projects for a-b glöbâl (Germany) before her maternity leave, but I understand she will only be working four days a week, which makes her commitment questionable. We are all working 24/7 as it is – and a new member of the team must be able to hit the ground running.
Rgds
Martin

May 12

From: Keith Buxton
To: All Staff

Hi everyone
I wanted to update you on where we are with our behaviours matrix. Following the success of project Uplift Brainstorm on Behaviors last month, we have retained !Eureka!Wow!, a global human capital consultancy to assist in making our talent strategy world class.

We must not lose sight that the purpose of the behaviours matrix is to divide all our family into three streams – A, B and C. The A and B players are part of the a-b glöbâl heritage. The C players do not have a future in this company. We feel it would therefore be inappropriate if our target behaviours are branded around the letter C, as this would not be aligned with the purpose of the matrix.

I am delighted to say that we will unveil the matrix next week. In advance of that time, if any co-colleague would like to feed into the process please feel free to contact me.
Keith

From: Martin Lukes
To: Graham Wallace

Graham – Jesus fucking wept. I despair over this place. Rog is fobbing me off with some German girl as the new Suzanna who has just had a baby and who will have fried brains and be dribbling milk and dashing off home the whole time. Now bloody Keith has decided he doesn't like my matrix after all. Drink later? Or is the wife still refusing to let you off the leash post Lucindagate?
Martin

May 13

From: Martin Lukes
To: Keri Tartt

Keri, can I try something out on you?
When I was in the shower this morning I was thinking about the behaviours matrix, and this word came into my mind. Creovation. Cre-ovation – half creativity and half innovation! I felt exactly as if a light bulb had come on in my head. I'm very excited – I'm sure this is the epicentre of the behaviours matrix. What do you think?
M

From: Martin Lukes
To: Keri Tartt

Thanks, Keri – I thought you'd love it! Jens doesn't get it, or at least she pretends not to. Obviously I'm not going to say anything as clichéd as my-wife-doesn't-understand-me, but quite frankly there's been a change in her since she came to work here. Last night she had the nerve to suggest she is the only one who is doing real work and I'm just faffing around. Keri, you are a massive reality check for me, you remind me that I am just trying to do better than my best under the circs and that my creovative juices are still flowing!
M

From: Martin Lukes
To: Jenny Withers

Jens – I know it's your book club tonight, but I don't think I'll be able to make it back in time to hold the fort. I need to prepare something for Keith and BSM on creovation.

With respect, I don't think you quite grasped the point of it this morning – you were too busy giving orders to Svetlana and looking for Max's cricket jumper.

But basically it marries creativity and innovation, but is better than both! Let's face it, the average co-colleague doesn't have the creativity gene. Innovation is much less scary, but it's too bolt-on to make a difference. Will probably be back 10ish.
Martin

May 14

From: Martin Lukes
To: Barry S. Malone

Hi Barry
Just wanted to say that I strongly agree that it's inappropriate to have all our behaviours start with a C. I should explain how the suggestion came about – it was surfaced by a junior member of my team, and I included it in my presentation as I passionately believe that, in order to get a team to co-create effectively, you have to throw everyone's ideas in the pot and stir them around before you start weeding the weaker ones out.

However, it's important we don't throw out the baby with the proverbial bathwater. The most important C on the list is creativity. This is our tool-kit for changing our DNA, if you will. I've been thinking about what sets the truly creative co-colleagues apart. It isn't simply creativity. Neither is it innovation. What the highest flyers do is combine the two into a single behaviour that I call Creovation. A Creovative idea is both out of the box and

actionable. It is bolt-on and blue-sky. I passionately believe it should form the heart of our matrix.
All my very bestest
Martin

From: Martin Lukes
To: Barry S. Malone

Hi Barry!
Thanks for getting back so quickly! I am totally delighted that you think Creovation is phenomenal. Can I revisit your image of the stonemason? If the stonemasons building the flagship St Paul's cathedral in London had been a bit more creovative, they might have come up with something less of a cliché than a bog standard dome!

I would be delighted to help roll out the concept as a plank of the matrix.
All my very bestest
Martin

From: Martin Lukes
To: Keri Tartt

Hi Keri
I've got a challenging one for you. Can you find out how to register something as a trademark? I want to protect my intellectual capital in creovation, before someone nicks it.
Ta muchly M

May 16

From: Martin Lukes
To: Phyllis Lukes

Dear Mum
How are you? Glad to hear your roses are looking lovely.

I've got some great news re your knee op. It's all sorted, you're going to have it done at the Wellington, they'll ring with a date later today. I'm still pretty hacked off with the medical profession – they still haven't traced the source of my cancer. The only person who is being remotely helpful is Pandora, who is teaching me how to tackle it by exercising the right side of my brain. I know you think all of this is mumbo jumbo, and at one level I do too, but I've decided to give it a try. Let's face it, I haven't got much to lose.

Pandora says I must spend more time feeling and less time analysing, and that I must let my heart guide me more. I know it's early days, but I think it's working. I wonder if the same thing would help with your knee? If you are interested I've got some mental exercises you could do.

Despite all this, everything is going v well workwise. I've come up with this new concept called creovation, which is going down a storm here. Which is ironic in a way given that my back is against the wall healthwise. Or maybe it's not so ironic. Didn't Beethoven write his finest unfinished symphony on his deathbed? I'm sure there are lots of other examples . . . when the chips are down, the tough get going!

Hope to see you at the weekend.
Lots of love
Martie

From: Martin Lukes
To: Phyllis Lukes

Dear Mum,
You're such a one for the Queen's English!! It means part creativity and part innovation. Really mum, I think it's time to wake up and smell the coffee. Times change, and you have to creovate!!
Much love
Martie

From: Martin Lukes
To: Phyllis Lukes

Yes I know you never drink coffee first thing!! But that wasn't what I was driving at. It's a saying. Honestly mum sometimes I wonder if you live on Planet Zog!! Must go now.
Martie

May 17

From: Martin Lukes
To: Keri Tartt

Thanks Keri, you're a star! Question. Does the £125 buy me the trademark in the world or just in the UK? I'm going to need global protection for this, as the market in these ideas doesn't respect national boundaries! Can you do some further digging?
M

From: Martin Lukes
To: Jenny Withers

Jens
Don't forget that we're going to Chelsea Flower Show tomorrow pm with my friend Tim from Boogie Gargle Fink . . . Is my Hugo Boss pale grey pinstripe at the dry cleaners?
Mart

From: Martin Lukes
To: Jenny Withers

I told you about Chelsea MONTHS ago. What is this Eve-o-lution cocktail party? Is it some women's networking thing? If it's networking you want you can't do better than Chelsea . . . all the great and the good from the advertising fraternity are on our table.
M

PS I'm going to ask Keri to send you copies of my schedule each week to stop this happening again.

From: Martin Lukes
To: Keri Tartt

Hi Keri
How do you fancy going to the Chelsea Flower Show with me tomorrow? We'd be guests of BGF, which always pushes the boat out on these occasions . . . bubbly . . . nice eats. Jens has decided that it is more important to plot with other career girls on how to take over the world.
   Hope you can make it. Posh togs the order of the day.
M

May 18

From: Martin Lukes
To: Bettina Schmidt

Hi Bettina,
I understand you're returning from maternity leave next week, joining us in marketing. I'm sure you'll notice the buzz after Germany!
   I believe you have requested Fridays off, but unfortunately I shall be starting a regular weekly team briefing on Fridays, which it would be a shame to miss.
My bestest
Martin
PS Congratulations on the baby. What did you have?

From: Martin Lukes
To: Bettina Schmidt

Bettina – Thanks for getting back to me so quickly. I don't think we're on the same page here. The wrap-up Friday meeting will set the agenda for the week, and will generate some of the department's most creovative™ marketing concepts. Can I suggest a compromise? Make your day off a moveable feast, attending the Friday meetings when the agenda is closely connected to your projects.

Martin

PS Boys are great. I've got two.

From: Martin Lukes
To: Bettina Schmidt

Bettina – As anyone on my team will tell you, I'm a passionate believer in work–life balance, but at the end of the day your childminder's schedule isn't my business. Can I give you some advice? If you want to survive here in the marketing department, you must leave family problems behind you. The winners on my team always give 110 per cent, minimum.

Bestest, Martin

From: Martin Lukes
To: Graham Wallace

Graham – Do you ever wish you were a woman?

From: Martin Lukes
To: Graham Wallace

I didn't mean that, you pervert!!!

I meant we men are a disadvantaged species. On one hand I have Bettina expecting me to arrange team meetings for her childminder's convenience. On the other, there is my ladywife forming a women's networking club to give themselves even more unfair advantages . . . drink later? Or are you still on best behaviour?

M

From: Pandora@CoachworX
To: Martin Lukes

Hi Martin
Great to talk to you on the phone just now. I can see that
'creovation' is the product of head AND heart. I'm
impressed!
So far so good. But you can go much further, Martin. You
are starting to build that bridge between the left and right
chambers but I think you can develop your right side more.
You are still intellectualizing everything. Lead more with your
heart, Martin!
Strive and Thrive!
Pandora

From: Martin Lukes
To: Pandora@CoachworX

Hi Pandora
Small point. I've actually trademarked creovation™, so would
you mind putting the ™ sign on it after you've used it? As you
say, I've got to look after yours truly first!
22.5 per cent better than my bestest
Martin

From: Martin Lukes
To: Keri Tartt

Sensational dress! You look so much like a flower that someone
might pick you!! Can you call a cab downstairs for 6.30??

May 19

From: Martin Lukes
To: Jenny Withers

Darling – what time did you leave the house this morning? You were already gone when I woke up. Sorry I was a bit late back – I had to go for a nightcap with Tim and his team afterwards. You didn't miss much – usual crowd, usual gardens, though there was one sensational garden that was all brushed steel and water. It was very attractive in an elegant, urban way. Food for thought for when we relandscape ours. Love you.
Martin x

From: Martin Lukes
To: Keri Tartt

Keri, thanks for an amazing evening, and I hope you're not feeling as rough as I am this morning!! Hope also you didn't think I was a bit forward in the cab on the way back from Annabel's, or that I make a habit of that sort of thing.

It's a long time since I let my hair down and bopped like that – you're such a great mover!
Martin x (if allowed!)

From: Martin Lukes
To: TimZadek@BoogieGargleFink

Hi Tim
Many thanks for a great bash last night . . . Good crowd of people . . . sorry we had to slip off a bit early. Let's do lunch soon.
Bestest, Martin

From: Martin Lukes
To: Keri Tartt

What was that sideways look meant to mean this morning?? Can I buy you lunch?

From: Martin Lukes
To: Keri Tartt

Great!! Can you book a table for two at L'Auberge – one-ish.
M x

From: Martin Lukes
To: Keri Tartt

Wonderful lunch . . . thank you. You are such a great listener,
Keri – and I've never met anyone before who shares my embarrassing passion for the BeeGees. I'm slightly sloshed . . . and now
I've got to go and explain to Rog why marketing is overspent on
this year's operating plan. Wish me luck. M xx

May 24

From: Keith Buxton
To: All Staff

Hallo everyone!
It is with great pride that I am today unveiling our key behaviours
matrix. I would like to offer sincere thanks to co-workers from all over
the globe who participated in the inclusive process that has created a
matrix that will make a-b glöbâl unbeatable. The six behaviours that
define our essence going forward are INTEGRITY, LOVE, DELIGHT,
DETERMINATION, CREOVATION AND DARING.

To introduce these behaviours I am asking colleagues to choose one
that they feel passionate about, and explain how we can use it to sort
out our A, B and C players. Barry will kick off, then Martin Lukes will
explain his creovation concept, but after that the field is wide open!
All my very bestest,
Keith

From: Barry S. Malone
To: All Staff

Howdy!

First up, I would like to celebrate the work of Keith and his team in delivering this outstanding key behaviors matrix.

Today I'd like to share a very personal thought with you. When I was just starting out, I had a mentor, a guy named Hank S. Marshall. One day, as we were teeing off, Hank said to me: Barry, do you know what is the most powerful thing in the world?

I said no, Hank, I guess I don't. He looked at me long and hard, and said one word – Integrity. I have been thinking about Hank these last few days and I know he is right. Each of our behaviors is a vital part of our DNA, but the one that makes my pulse race is integrity. This is a quality that A workers have hard-wired into them. Their every action is brimful of honesty, openness and trust, which are the three drivers of integrity. B players have learned integrity. C players will struggle. They do not belong here.

I love you all.

Barry S. Malone

From: Martin Lukes
To: All Staff

Hi co-colleagues
A big thank you to Keith for inviting me to describe creovation™. Can I first say that I do not think of the idea as 'mine'. This sort of not-invented-here headset is the enemy of creovation™. Ideas are everywhere. They are free. Creovation™ is about grabbing them, harnessing them. Living them.

Question: What is creovation™? A players won't need to ask this. Deep inside they have always known what it is and recognize it in themselves. Creovation™ takes the best blue-sky element out of creativity. It takes the bolt-on practicality results-driven part of innovation. It's a perfect partnership, if you will.

People often ask me: is creovation™ something learnt, or something you are born with? The answer is both. A players are born creovative™. B players have worked hard to acquire the skill. Some C players can innovate, and some can even create, but they struggle to walk the extra mile to creovate™.

All my very bestest
Martin

From: *Cindy Czarnikow*
To: *All Staff*

Hi!

As Chief Corporate Conscience Steward, I know that Love is the key driver in our actions as a company. We Love the communities that we serve, and it is that Love that supports us in facilitating their empowerment.

As an individual co-colleague, I bring my Love to work every day, and I expect the people on my team to do the same. Often I stop in the middle of a task and say to myself, 'I Love doing this stuff!', or 'I Love this company!!'

I'm smiling at you,
Cindy

From: Martin Lukes
To: Cindy Czarnikow

Hi Cindy! Thanks for your kind message. Glad creovation™ rings your bell! I agree with you about Love btw . . . In fact it's something I'm working on with my coach presently!!
Bestest Martin

From: Martin Lukes
To: Christo Weinberg

Thanks for that! Glad you have always been a creovation™ fan too!

From: Martin Lukes
To: Keri Tartt

Keri –

How about doing something tonight?? Jens has got her book club – they are discussing something called Reading Lolita in Baghdad – which promises to be such a stimulating read they'll be nattering away half the nite. She won't be back til late, so we could make an evening of it . . . M xx

May 25

From: Martin Lukes
To: Keri Tartt

Dearest Keri – It's 3 am and I've just got back. I don't even know if you check emails at home, but I just wanted to say what a GREAT LOVELY FANTASTIC time I had tonight.

Jens is fast asleep, so I didn't have to explain why I only had one sock on and was smelling of your perfume. What is it by the way? Can I buy you some? I'm going to bed now, but I don't know if I'm going to be able to sleep. Goodnight to you, you sexy thing! M xxxxxxx (I wish I could give them to you in person)

May 26

Text message to Keri. Sent 09.30

Oh God . . . Just got a message to call Jens – urgent. Nightmare . . . she can't have found out already?? M xxx

From: Martin Lukes
To: Keri Tartt

Keri – catastrophe averted! She wanted to tell me Max has just got a scholarship to Eton!! Don't know if that means anything to a Kiwi, but it's the best school in the country, ergo in the world! Can you come into my office for a second now . . . xxx
Martin

From: Martin Lukes
To: Jenny Withers

Darling – Of course I'm pleased!! The reason I seemed a tad distracted earlier on is that I've got a lot on my plate. This is the most fantastic news – Max is a total star! How much money do we get off the fees?? M xxx

From: Martin Lukes
To: Keri Tartt

God that was dangerous – but I couldn't resist. You really are the sexiest thing I've ever ever seen. Next time we better stick something over the peep hole in my door . . . or find somewhere safer. M xx

From: Martin Lukes
To: Max Lukes

WELL DONE MAX!!!!!!! You're a chip off the old block! . . . I knew you could make it!! You've learned a really important lesson that I didn't learn till much later in life. You know how to be your own greatest fan and how to be better than your best. If I had worked that stuff out when I was twelve, I'd be running the country by now!!! I've bought you a present – Eminem's CD Encore. I've taken advice from someone in the office who is a bit closer to your age . . . and it's the hottest CD of the moment. Mum and I are going to come home early to take you out. Do you fancy the Hard Rock Café?
See u later. Dad

From: Martin Lukes
To: Max Lukes

For Godssakes Max, Eminem is supposed to be hyper-cool . . .

From: Martin Lukes
To: Keri Tartt

Keri – you might be the perfect being, but I'm afraid you bombed with Eminem. I've just had a lecture from a 13-year-old on how this sort of music shows no respect for women! Can I respect you a bit more later on?
Martin xx

From: Martin Lukes
To: Graham Wallace

Hi Graham – Max won a scholarship to Eton!! Obviously I'm really pleased for him, as he'll be a round peg in a round hole. But personally it wouldn't be my choice . . . I don't really hold with all the elitist nonsense . . . tail coats and royalty and all that malarky. And God knows what they get up to in those houses . . . probably all rogering each other . . . still, it's a great place for super bright super sporty kids. Did Fergus pass common entrance?
Martin

From: Martin Lukes
To: Graham Wallace

Oh dear . . . is that a local school? I'm a great believer in horses for courses . . . I'm sure he'll be v happy. Can't have celebratory drink as it's a three-line whip at home . . .
M

May 27

From: Martin Lukes
To: Faith Preston

Faith – I strongly object to the tone of your message. You imply

that I am discriminating against Bettina as a mother. The facts are: 1. I have been highly supportive about her baby to date. 2. I offered her advice on how to be more successful, and told her she needed to make work her number one priority. I did this in my capacity as coach and mentor.
Martin

From: Martin Lukes
To: Keri Tartt

Keri – let's meet at the fire escape in half an hour. I've checked it out – leave through the fire doors on the fourth floor . . . I'll go first – leave it a minute or two then you come.
M xx

From: Martin Lukes
To: Keri Tartt

Wow! That was amazing . . . do I look a bit sweaty??

From: Martin Lukes
To: Bettina Schmidt

Bettina – I am sorry to hear from Faith that you have some issues surrounding your return from maternity leave.

As I told you last week, work–life balance is very close to my heart. Can I tell you a highly personal story? You may not know that I am married to Jenny Withers who works here in HR and has a career in her own right. Issues on the domestic front crop up from time to time, and we take it in turn to solve them. If I need to go home, or go to one of the boys' schools, then I do that. I quite understand that home life matters. Work hard, play hard – that's my watchword. If Fridays are a problem for you – then let's set up a video conferencing link so that you can participate from home.
Bestest, Martin.

From: Martin Lukes
To: Phyllis Lukes

Dearest Mum
Thanks for your message. Still no attachment, though!! Am somewhat up against it, so this must be brief.

I'm delighted that you are booked into the hospital for June 4th. The Wellington is terribly comfortable – you'll love it. Don't worry about the money. It's all sorted. You ask after my health, and fingers crossed and touch wood and all that, but I am feeling a lot better about it, and I've decided for now not to have any further tests. As Pandora says, the heart is an incredibly powerful organ, and at the moment I feel that through my own inner strength I am keeping the cancer at bay.

Your loving son
Martie
PS Thanks for sending Max the Congratulations card and the book token. Much appreciated. He announced he's going to write to you himself to say thanks.

From: Martin Lukes
To: Keri Tartt

My lovely sexy Keri
Jens has just popped her head around the door and asked me what I'm doing. I've said I'm writing a message to BSM.

I have been thinking about you all evening. I love the way you flick your hair around your ears. I love the butterfly you have tattooed on your left buttock. I want to kiss it right now. I love the way you feel. I love the way you taste. Corporal Cock and Private Pussy are made for each other.

When I'm with you, I feel I can do anything or be anything. These last two weeks have been so fantastic for me, and I wanted you to know that.

Love xxx

May 31

From: Pandora@CoachworX
To: Martin Lukes

Hi Martin
I'm just checking up on you – I haven't heard from you for
a couple of weeks but I get this sense that you are following
two key messages – Love like you've never been hurt. Dance
like no one is watching.

Please share with me your wins – month five is nearly at
an end, and we need to measure how you've done . . .
Strive and thrive!
Pandora

From: Martin
To: Pandora@CoachworX

Hi Pandora
Has someone said something to you??? I thought the deal with
coaching was that it was totally confidential?
Martin

From: Pandora@CoachworX
To: Martin Lukes

Hi Martin!
I'm puzzled . . . yes, confidentiality is the cornerstone of the
Executive Bronze Program. I was simply asking if you were
growing your heart, and doing the exercises I gave you
regularly. Is there something else happening in your life you
would like to share?
Strive and Thrive!
Pandora

From: Martin Lukes
To: Pandora@CoachworX

Hi Pandora
Sorry – total misunderstanding! Yes, I have been doing the red and white roses test a couple of times, and I am very impressed at the power of the right side of the brain as a work tool!

For me this has been a great month for both head and heart. My win with creovation™ was a classic bridging exercise. I have also used my heart to make a very difficult situation with a new employee better. I have shared a personal story with her, to help her shift her performance and team loyalty onto the next level. Above all I have used my heart to make myself more in tune with, and more stimulated by, the working environment. No question.

22.5 per cent better than my bestest
Martin

Chapter Six

June
My Body

June 1

From: Martin Lukes
To: Keri Tartt

Pinky
Meet you on the fire escape in five mins. I'll go first, and text you if the coast is clear.
Perky
PS The corporal is standing to attention already!!

From: Pandora@CoachworX
To: Martin Lukes

Hi Martin
One of the biggest wins we have got out of Executive Bronze so far is your great new attitude towards yourself! This month we are going to focus in on your body, and I am going to teach you how to look and feel marvellous – forever! First, let's draw the baseline – tell me how you feel about your health, your diet, your fitness, about how you look. I want you to use the GROW model again, and you'll see it works just as well with your body as with your dreams.
Strive and thrive!
Pandora

From: Martin Lukes
To: Keri Tartt

Hi Pinky – you've exhausted me! You've got some stamina!
   You'll be glad to hear that Pandora is going to work on my body this month – that spare tyre may soon be consigned to history!!! I may not be your porky Perky for much longer!!
PP xxxxx

From: Barry S. Malone
To: All Staff

Howdy!
When I joined a-b glöbâl 10 months ago I pledged to transition this fine company from good to great by significantly raising our talent bar.
   I am delighted to say that we are ready to achieve that stretch goal with the roll-out of Project Uplift. This will enable us to segment our people into three unique talent pools, A players, who are the shining stars in our firmament, B players who are better-than-excellent knowledge workers, and C players who are phenomenal performers, but whose skills are not aligned with our matrix. I have tasked Keith Buxton with explaining to you the next step of this program, which will set us on the way to achieving Phenomenal Performance – Permanently!
I love you all
Barry

From: Keith Buxton
To: All Staff

Hallo everybody
Following on from Barry's highly inspirational memo this morning, I am proud to be able to announce the first step in the roll-out of Uplift.
   Over the next two weeks all co-colleagues will attend an ABC workshop which will kickstart the segmentation process. In every geography a specially trained facilitator from !Eureka!Wow!, the global motivational consultancy, will be assisting with the roll-outs.

*It is imperative that every co-colleague attends the workshops, which
have been designed to be rich learning experiences as well as a lot of fun!*
Keith Buxton
Chief Talent Officer

June 4

From: Martin Lukes
To: Pandora@CoachworX

Hi Pandora
Sorry about the delay in getting back to you. Everything is going
crazy here on ABC, I'm not only positioning myself to be an A,
I'm also having to deal with all the egos on my team who seem
to think by sucking up to myself they will be As too.

I'm attaching my GROW model for my body. As you'll see
I've attempted to be highly honest about how I see my body
going forward.
GOALS
Physically I'm thinking more Swayze than Schwarzenegger.
I'd like better muscle tone, more energy, and weightwise I think
12 stone would be a good target.
REALITY
I am attaching a picture of myself taken for our annual report.
It's a bit cheesy – I had to stand there laughing into the phone
for yonks while some idiot photographer faffed about. Still, all
things considered I don't think I look too bad for 43 – or 44 as
I'll be in two weeks. On the upside, I've got a very good head
of hair, hardly receding and hardly any grey which is more than
most men of my age can boast, and 20:20 vision.

Weight – I've put on a bit of weight around the middle and
maybe a tiny bit on the face since that pic was taken. Just weighed
myself on Jen's scales and apparently I weigh 14 stone 2 – which
I don't think can be accurate.

I've got an exercise bike and rowing machine in my study at
home which I use as much as I can, though I've never found the

home the right environment for a workout. On my 40th birthday Jens signed me up with her personal trainer – a camp black guy called Darius – Jens adores him, but we didn't really click. So now I work out at the gym on my own, as and when.

I'd say I'm pretty health conscious foodwise. Occasionally I eat a Twix or a Bounty, but that is mainly as a result of my highly pressured lifestyle which means I often need to grab a bite on the run. I'm a total water addict. I aim to drink 5 litres for my daily detox.

OPTIONS – I'd like to start with a personal trainer again, and build up fitness. I'd like to continue to watch what I eat, cutting back on the snacks, where possible.

WINS – If I'm being 110 per cent honest, two big wins would be a stronger golf swing, and more stamina in the sack! Without washing my dirty linen, as it were, I don't think there is cause for concern in that quarter, but one can always improve further! 22.5 per cent better than my bestest
Martin

From: Pandora@CoachworX
To: Martin Lukes

Hi Martin –
The bad news is that I am hearing a lot of double talk from you. You say you want a better body, but then you offer me a lot of excuses.

The good news is that I can help you reprogram your mind. There is a little word that begins with f. We are frightened of the f-word, and we teach our children to be frightened of it too.

I can feel that word undermining your GROW plan and affecting everything you say about your body. I want you to turn your back on the f-word. Once you do that, you will succeed!
Strive and Thrive!
Pandora

From: Martin Lukes
To: Pandora@CoachworX

Pandora – Frankly, I'm confused. That word is quite important to me, especially at the present time, and we certainly haven't taught our kids to be scared of it . . . on the contrary Jake (at nearly 16) seems to think of nothing else. He even tried to jump on our fat Russian au pair the other night. I just don't see how turning my back on sex is going to help my body. Quite the reverse, in fact.

22.5 per cent better than my bestest

Martin

From: Pandora@CoachworX
To: Martin Lukes

Martin – you have a great sense of humour!!!!!!!!!!! I didn't say anything about sex! I have no issues with that at all! Sex is great – it's one of the body's natural ways of reenergizing itself.

My f-word is fear! Listen to yourself talk, Martin. You are afraid of your body, afraid of not getting it into perfect shape. You make excuses for not going to the gym, for eating fatty foods. You are setting yourself up to fail month six out of fear. New You doesn't recognize fear. You are not going to fail to rebuild your body, Martin. You are going to succeed! Strive and Thrive!

Pandora

From: Martin Lukes
To: Phyllis Lukes

Dearest Mum

Thanks for your message. It is nice to think of you sitting up in your hospital bed with your laptop on your knee. I hope those nurses are treating you well. Best of British with the op tomor-

row. Will come and visit in the evening, schedule permitting. I've told them that there's no hurry for you to come out. I want you to enjoy being pampered for a bit. Don't worry about the money, I've implied that Phyllis Lukes is my daughter and now it seems it's all on my health insurance!
Yr loving son
Martie

From: Martin Lukes
To: Phyllis Lukes

Dearest Mum
No, I haven't lied, though maybe a smidgin economical with the truth! In any case, you shouldn't worry about insurance companies. They are all parasites, they don't add value . . . not a creovative™ individual in the entire industry . . .
Your loving son
Martie

June 8

From: Roger Wright
To: All Staff

I would like to remind all staff members that on Wednesday employees of London Underground will be staging a strike. This is not a valid excuse for a-b glôbâl staff to stay at home. Overground trains to Canning Town will be running as normal and I shall expect no working time to be lost. Overcoming obstacles to get to work on time is in keeping with our six key behaviours: Obsession, Love, Detail, Creovation, Daring and Integrity.
Roger Wright, Acting Chairman

From: Martin Lukes
To: Roger Wright

Rog, Hope you won't mind if I point out a small slip in your memo – the third behaviour is not detail, but delight. Of course it goes without saying detail is also imperative in everything we do, but we can take that as read!
Cheers, Martin.

From: Roger Wright
To: All Staff

I would like to inform all staff that Doug Rich, Senior Change Agent from !Eureka!Wow!, will be joining us tomorrow, and I request all staff to fully cooperate with the implementation of Project Uplift, without impacting on productivity targets.

I would also like to draw your attention to an administrative error in my last memo. Value three should have read delight, not detail.
Roger Wright
Acting Chairman

From: Martin Lukes
To: Graham Wallace

BINGO!!!! It's not often one gets the chance to make Rog look an idiot. I fear I may have to pay for it though – I just met him in the toilets and he blanked me completely.
M
PS Can't do drink tonight, I'm off to see my new personal trainer. She's dead gorgeous.

From: Martin Lukes
To: Pandora@CoachworX

Hi Pandora
It went really well at the gym. Donna says my upper body

strength is pretty good for my age! She made me do 10 mins on the cycle machine, 10 mins on the treadmill and 10 mins on the crosstrainer then we did pecs, quads, curls and stretching. Donna says the key thing is for me to learn how to exit my personal comfort zone . . . she's very motivational. I'm going to see her every day, so watch this space!

22.5 per cent better than my bestest

Martin

June 9

From: Martin Lukes
To: Keri Tartt

Pinky – I'm hurting . . . I ache all over . . . can you pop in and give me a little rub . . . also if you are going out I have a craving for a packet of beef Monster Munch.

Perky

From: Pandora@CoachworX
To: Martin Lukes

Hi Martin

Well done, New You! As you work your body on the crosstrainer, I want you to try to make a paradigm shift in your mind. This isn't just about fitness. It's about choosing the path of self-care. It takes determination and discipline, but you are a great person, Martin, and I know you can do it.

I've sent you a book called You Are What You Eat, which will help you on the bowel issues. It's written by a doctor who is a former coachee of mine, Dr Gillian McKeith. That's what fires me up about coaching – it's always a two-way street! You learn from me, and I learn from you!!

Strive and thrive!

Pandora

From: Martin Lukes
To: Stewart@harleystreetclinic

Dear Doctor Stewart
I have recently come across a book by Dr McKeith, a leading expert on diet, and have unearthed some pertinent information re my stools. Frequently I pass greasy stools which will not flush, which Dr McKeith says are a sign of liver imbalance. I also occasionally pass foul-smelling stools, which suggests food is stagnating in my large intestine, and that I have become toxic. These are serious conditions that may require medical treatment. However, at present I am going to seek to resolve the situation through self-care and by making a paradigm shift in my mindset to choose health.
   I simply mention this at this stage so that it can be put on my file.
Yours sincerely
Martin Lukes

From: Martin Lukes
To: Keri Tartt

Dearest Pinky
Do you know what the corporal's favourite food is? RAW SAUERKRAUT!! I've been reading this incredible diet book that Pandora recommended . . . there is a section on foods to improve your sex life. Also some chlorella, dulse and spirulina. Do you have any idea what any of them are? Or where we might get hold of them?? Shall we try???
Your less porky Perky

June 14

From: Cindy Czarnikow
To: All Staff

Hi everyone, As chief morale officer, I have been tasked with ensuring that the knock-on morale implications of Project ABC are phenomenally positive. I know some of you have surfaced some issues with the process, which I hope this FAQ will solve!!

Q: Are the people who are As, better than the Bs and Cs?

A: No way! Everybody in this company is a uniquely talented individual. All we are saying is that the talents of A workers are supremely well aligned with our core purpose. Bs are well aligned, and Cs are not so well aligned.

Q: Are the Cs being fired?

A: I'm glad you asked that! The Cs are NOT being fired! We love them and we are deeply appreciative of all the fine work they have done here. However, we believe that in their own best interests they would be happier working someplace else.

Q: Will the senior people all be As?

A: Uh-uh! All the top people have been appraised like everyone else. As I said, the process has been incredibly fair. If I myself am a B or a C I would have no problem with that because I know I have always given this job my love and my passion.

Q: Is my band going to be made public?

A: It's up to you! Only you and your senior manager will know your band. If you want to cherish your band to yourself then we don't have any problem with that!

I'm smiling at you

Cindy

From: DougRich@!Eureka!Wow!
To: All Staff

Hi, my name is Doug Rich, and I am Senior Change Agent at !Eureka!Wow! It is a great privilege to find myself in partnership with a-b glöbâl (UK).

First a word about us. !Eureka!Wow! is a new consultancy designed to be a one-stop talent shop to leverage solutions that excite clients. We combine technology with insight to assist companies in solving all their talent management issues.

Before we launch the formal part of the ABC roll-out, I would like to take some time to meet with you all individually to build up trust levels.

This is a vital plank to how we work here. Only when the client:consultant trust ratio is at a maximum can we deliver unrivalled results. If you have any questions about how we operate please do not hesitate to contact myself or my Associate Change Agent, Sebastian Wriggley.
Big Wow!
Doug

From: Martin Lukes
To: Graham Wallace

Graham – Have you had the pleasure of building up trust with Doug yet? There's something really creepy about him – not helped by the fact that he likes to work barefoot. He says it is to help him be more grounded. Jesus. I hope we aren't all expected to take our shoes off. I don't want to get athlete's foot again as I've only just got rid of mine.
Cheers, Mart
PS no can do drink tonight – mine's an extract of alfalfa grass . . . Are you happy with the condition of your stools, btw? I've got a book I could lend you that might make you v worried indeed.
M

From: Martin Lukes
To: Phyllis Lukes

Dearest Mum
So sorry not to have seen you last night. I came round a tad late and some mini-Hitler refused to let me in as you were sleeping off the anaesthetic. Will stop by today after work.

I can't believe that they got you out of bed on the first day, and that you're walking already! I told Pandora, and she said it showed that your energy levels are in balance! I'm going to try to get hold of some wild blue green algae for you – which is a complete source of everything your body needs – its got all the nutrients, it reverses Alzheimer's, strengthens immunity and is good for your muscle rebuilding.

See you later

Love Martie

From: Martin Lukes
To: Phyllis Lukes

OK, custard creams it is. And no, I wasn't implying you were getting Alzheimer's. I was just saying that the algae is brilliant for everything. Kids do better at school with it . . . maybe it's what Jake needs for his GCSEs which started today . . .

Martie

June 15

From: Martin Lukes
To: Keri Tartt

Pinky – Can't face the fire escape – it's still pouring with rain. Shall we try the Canning Town Novotel at lunchtime?

Btw you must stop being paranoid about Jens. I went on and on last night about how gorgeous Donna is which puts her off the scent (literally!!) Though actually she's so far from suspecting anything it's almost insulting! It simply hasn't occurred to her that anyone might find her husband devastatingly sexy. One day she's going to get a massive wake-up call . . .

Porky

From: Martin Lukes
To: Keri Tartt

No of course I don't! Donna's got hairy arms, and a minute arse.

From: Martin Lukes
To: Keri Tartt

My kinky pinky
You really need to stop this. No I am not saying you have a big bum. As you may have noticed, I think your bum is absolutely totally the perfect size, and in three hours the corporal and myself will be examining it in a proper bed!!
Porky Perky

From: Martin Lukes
To: Phyllis Lukes

Dear Mum
Lovely to see you yesterday, albeit briefly. I can't believe how mobile you are! You are such a toughie mum, I don't know how you do it. Sorry I forgot the Rosamund Pilcher, will bring later.

Did you notice that I looked in pretty good nick myself? It is partly down to Pandora (who I know you disapprove of, but the results speak for themselves).

The trouble with doctors is that they are experts in sickness. She's an expert in wellness, which, at the end of the day, is the name of the game. And it is through that approach that I'm focusing on self-care and am eating better, and doing 45 minutes at the gym every day!

Don't forget my offer of convalescing chez nous . . .
Your loving son
Martie

From: DougRich@!Eureka!Wow!
To: All Staff

Hi! Next week we will be holding a brainstorming session for directors and senior department heads, to allow your team to meet with our team and ensure we are aligned in the aim, scope and practice of Project Uplift.

We will be kicking off with an ice-breaking exercise – I'd like each of you to come up with something that's surprising about yourself.

We'll follow up with some role-play exercises. I want each individual to think of a famous person that exemplifies one of the behaviours and act in character. I know this is going to be a uniquely rewarding learning experience.
Big wow!
Doug

From: Martin Lukes
To: Graham Wallace

Absolutely no way! These bloody consultants don't seem to realize that we're trying to deliver value here in marketing, (unlike your sales team!!) not putting on amateur theatricals. Suggested surprising fact about you – your handicap is only 16 which given that you play every weekend is downright shocking.
Martin

June 16

From: Martin Lukes
To: Keri Tartt

Sweetest Kinky Pinky. Please don't nag me about this. I want to spend more time with you, too. It's just really hard to get it sorted. We mustn't be silly about this. We've taken a lot of risks . . . it is really important we don't get found out . . . I'll see what I can do, maybe try to get J to go away for a bit.
Porky Perky x

From: Martin Lukes
To: Graham Wallace

What are you doing for this role play? I was going to do Einstein for creovation™, but I think it's too obvious. Instead I've decided

to show that I also have some of the other values, too, so am going to do Gandhi for Integrity.
Mart

From: Martin Lukes
To: Graham Wallace

Yes, I know Gandhi didn't have a beer belly. You obviously haven't noticed that I've lost 4 lbs already this month.

From: Martin Lukes
To: Jenny Withers

Darling, sorry if I was a bit short with you at breakfast. I know you find my relationship with mum difficult, but she'll only be with us for a week or two – she'll keep herself to herself, and she loves the boys.

A thought has occurred to me – why not get away from it all for a weekend to de-stress and detox? I could easily hold the fort, and Svetlana could help me. I'd quite like some quality time with the boys, anyway.
Martin

From: Martin Lukes
To: Jenny Withers

Jens – it saddens me that when I try to support you, you start looking for secret agendas. I simply suggested that you do something that might boost your positive energy flow.

You clearly need to de-stress, but at the end of the day, it's your call.
M xx

From: Martin Lukes
To: All Staff

Pinky – It's proving harder than I thought but I'm still trying. Can't wait till later.
Perky

From: Martin Lukes
To: Keri Tartt

Fucketyfuckingfuck . . . I've just sent an email to you to the whole bloody office . . . oh god oh god, my whole life is flashing before my eyes . . .

From: Martin Lukes
To: All Staff

Hi – co-colleagues may have been as surprised as I was re an email sent out this afternoon under my name to all staff. This message mentioned the children's characters, Pinky and Perky. I'm mystified as to the meaning of this and can only assume that some prankster was at my terminal. If anyone has any light to throw on the matter, please contact myself, or my PA, Keri Tartt.
Best, Martin

From: Martin Lukes
To: IT Director

Hi, can you get one of your team to investigate the issue of security. I have just had someone else sending out emails apparently from me. In this department alone we have much intellectual capital with untold value. It is IMPERATIVE that we have adequate firewalls in place.
Martin

June 21

From: DougRich@!Eureka!Wow!
To: All Staff

Hi! I have two words to say about the first Project Uplift workshop: Big Wow! We all got a lot closer to each other – in the course of the day Roger Wright shared the interesting fact that he collects First World War helmets. Jenny Withers told us that her ambition is to write a novel, and Faith Preston told us about her gold medal in salsa dancing.

From the feedback forms, the power of the role-play exercise to unleash your spirit was phenomenal. It would be invidious to single out the performance of any individual, but Christo Weinberg as Frank Zappa for creovation was inspired. Jenny Withers was a fabulous Pollyanna, and Martin Lukes' Gandhi was unforgettable – as was his Indian accent!

It is now time to move on to the next plank of the project, which is a 360-degree exercise. I would like everybody to ask three colleagues to grade them on a scale of 1 to 10 on the six behaviours, and then email the grades to me. Choose one person who reports to you, one who you report to, and one who is a peer.
Big Wow!
Doug

From: Martin Lukes
To: Faith Preston

Hi Faith – I don't understand your message. I haven't got a daughter, and she hasn't had an accident . . . ???
Cheers Martin

From: Martin Lukes
To: Faith Preston

Ah! Yes, I'm with you now. Phyllis is my mother! It's all a big misunderstanding! No, obviously children don't have arthritic

knee replacements!! Leave it with me, and I'll sort it direct with the insurance company.
Cheers, Martin

From: Martin Lukes
To: Bupa

Dear Sir or Madam
I understand there is a problem with a £19,000 claim submitted last week under my health insurance with yourselves. Phyllis Lukes is indeed 72, which as you correctly point out, makes her unlikely to be my daughter.

However, there is ambiguity in the policy statement. I believe it referred to 'dependent family' which covers my mother who is family and is dependent on myself.
Yours truly
Martin Lukes

From: Martin Lukes
To: Bupa

Dear Mr Scott
I very seriously hope that you are not questioning my integrity. I would like to inform you that integrity is a value that this company has elevated to the highest level, and as a director it is my job to personally ensure that I am an exemplar to members of the a-b glöbâl family.
  Yours truly,
Martin Lukes

June 22

From: Martin Lukes
To: Pandora@CoachworX

I am feeling stressed again. I'm doing the diet and the exercises, it's very hard to practise self-care when your colleagues are winding you up and some idiot from !Eureka!Wow! is getting up one's nostrils.

Partly I'm a bit down because it's my birthday today. At the end of the day, I don't want to be 44. I hate birthdays at the best of times, but this year I got no cards at all. I asked Jens for a juicer, so that I could make celery and fennel pick-me-up, but she got me something that squeezes oranges, which is hopeless, as citrus is much too acidic for me.
Martin

From: Pandora@CoachworX
To: Martin Lukes

Hi Martin
Where's the positive headset?? The passing of another year is a HUGE celebration, not something to be depressed about.
Did you know you have three ages, Martin? Your chronological age, your biological age, and your mental age. Only by the first measure are you getting older. The other two measures are much more important, and if you focus on them you can get younger, as young as you like. By self-care you can roll back your biological age. You can also turn back your psychological age by surrounding yourself with younger people. By re-thinking your wardrobe. Martin you are not 44. You are whatever age you want to be!!
Happy Birthday!
Strive and thrive!
Pandora

From: Martin Lukes
To: Jake Lukes

Hi Jake
Good to get your message, though can I remind you that the traditional way of celebrating someone's birthday is to give them

a present, not to ask them for more money. The answer is no, your allowance must last till the end of the month. But once your exams are out of the way, I may give you a little extra.
Love Dad

From: Martin Lukes
To: Keri Tartt

Dearest Pinky, Thank you so much. I've never worn combat trousers before, but it's going to be my new look – Pandora says that by being with you and wearing younger clothes I am making the clock go backwards. Can't be bad! Don't sulk at me about this evening – Jens has invited friends round for a not very surprising surprise party. Can't we celebrate at lunchtime?
M xx

From: Martin Lukes
To: Jenny Withers

Don't you like them? I nipped out at lunchtime to buy them. Fine if you're too tired to cook, we could go out to eat – though if we go to that new Italian place we might get George and Stacy to go Dutch as it's rather pricey . . .
M xx

From: Martin Lukes
To: Graham Wallace

Graham –
Ha, ha very funny. Actually Keri thinks they look great on me. Just because I'm 41, doesn't mean I have to dress it.
    Am assuming that you and I are doing each other's ABC forms? Let's agree on a marking system: no marks lower than 7 and an average of about 8.5. Are you going to get Rog to do it as your boss? As I've completely blown it with him, I may have to ask Keith.
M

From: Martin Lukes
To: Keith Buxton

Hi Keith
I just wanted to touch base to say what a sensational job we all think you are doing with Project ABC. Btw, I wondered if you could do my behaviours rating for me? I feel that you know my strengths (and weaknesses!!!) better than anyone – I'd be delighted to return the favour.
All my very bestest,
Martin

June 23

From: Martin Lukes
To: Keri Tartt

Pinky – Boring horrible evening, and cost me an arm and a leg. I thought about you all the time. This mate of mine from Goldmans went on and on about how much money he's making, and Jens was tired and bad-tempered.
  I'm filling in your ABC form – can u do mine??
Love you,
Perky

From: Martin Lukes
To: DougRich@!Eureka!Wow!

Hi Doug
I have given some deep thought to these forms and am attaching my appraisals. As you will see, I have graded the behaviours of Graham Wallace as a peer, Keith Buxton as a boss, and Keri Tartt as a direct report.
Best, Martin

The following is my appraisal of Graham Wallace.

Obsession, 7
Love, 7
Creovation, 6
Integrity, 8
Daring, 8
Delight, 7.5

This is my appraisal of Keri Tartt: 9 for everything except for love and delight for which she scores 10.

Keith Buxton: 10 for everything except Love, for which I give him 9.

From: Martin Lukes
To: DougRich@!Eureka!Wow!

Hi Doug
I see – I didn't realize you were intending to make the marks public. In my humble experience these things work better when they are not transparent, as people feel free to be quite honest.

I've been looking over my marks, and have actually decided that I was a bit harsh on Graham. Can you up all his marks by 1 across the board? Many thanks.
Martin

June 24

From: Martin Lukes
To: Jenny Withers

Darling –
That's fantastic! OF COURSE you should go. West Midlands CBI is a fantastic forum for you! Don't worry about me – I can hold the fort and make sure Jake is prepared for his GCSEs. It's only one night. Go and show them what you're made of!
Love you,
Martin

From: Martin Lukes
To: Keri Tartt

Kinky Pinky –
Perky's got some fantastic news! J is off to Birmingham tomorrow night to keynote to some boring Midlands businessmen.

I need to pop into the hospital to see mum, then will meet you at One Aldwych. The au pair knows I'm going to be out . . . so long as I'm back by 2 am, should be ok . . . we can have 7 whole hours together . . . can't wait. Corporal v excited.
Porky Perky xxx

From: Martin Lukes
To: Jake Lukes

Hi Jake
How was your history GCSE today? Hope not too horrendous.

Fraid something has come up at work . . . probably won't be back till late. Svetlana will make supper. Make sure you get to bed at a reasonable time, and are fresh for your maths exam tomorrow.
Dad

June 25

From: Martin Lukes
To: Jake Lukes

WHAT THE BLOODY HELL DID YOU THINK YOU WERE DOING LAST NIGHT????? SVETLANA SAYS YOU WENT OUT DRINKING, GOT HOME DRUNK AFTER MIDNIGHT, THREW UP AND WERE LATE FOR YOUR EXAM THIS MORNING. THIS WAS UNBELIEVABLY STUPID, EVEN BY YOUR RECENT STANDARDS.
DAD

From: Martin Lukes
To: Jenny Withers

Hi Darling – hope your speech went well last night, was keeping my fingers crossed. Sorry I wasn't at home when you called . . . I had to pop out for a swift half with Peter next door. Everything fine this end. See you later.
Love you, M xxx

From: Martin Lukes
To: Jake Lukes

I don't like the tone of your message – it is not your business where I was last night, though if you must know I was out with Graham and some clients, missed the last train so stayed at his place.

Can I suggest a deal? Your mother is going to go absolutely ballistic when she finds out about your GCSE. So I suggest that we do not tell her. In return I would be grateful if you did not mention that I was out all night. Your mother doesn't approve of Graham, so it might make life easier if she didn't know.
Is that a deal?
Dad

From: Martin Lukes
To: Jake Lukes

What do you mean 'whatever'? This matters. Do we have a deal?

Text message to Svetlana. Sent 10:42

Best not to mention anything about yesterday to Jens. I know it wasn't your fault, but she might blame you.
Martin

June 28

From: DougRich@!Eureka!Wow!
To: All Staff

At !Eureka!Wow! we have a long track record of forming agenda-shaping relationships with our clients. But with our work here at a-b glöbâl (UK), we have gone further and have definitively pushed the knowledge envelope.

I am delighted to be able to unveil the parameters of the next stage of Project ABC, which has been tailor-made for a-b glöbâl by !Eureka!Wow! You will today receive a form inviting you to grade your own behaviours and to write a paragraph to explain your thinking behind the marks.
Big Wow!
Doug

From: Martin Lukes
To: Keri Tartt

Pinky – Probably best if we cancel our afternoon assignment. I need to give 260 per cent to my own assessment, and need some headspace. Don't put any calls through to me, and if any team members try to see me, tell them to go away.

From: Martin Lukes
To: Keri Tartt

Kinky Pinky, don't be silly. You of all people should understand how important being an A is to me. The corporal is sulking, but I've told him he'll see some action tomorrow.
Love you
(still) Porky Perky

From: Martin Lukes
To: Jenny Withers

Darling – how are you going to approach this self-assessment thing? If I give myself 10 for everything, do you think they might smell a rat? But if I give less I might lose out to people like Graham and Christo who are so boastful . . . how are you going to play it? M

From: Martin Lukes
To: Jenny Withers

What do you mean: 'just be honest'????? That's no help at all.

From: Martin Lukes
To: DonnaAdonis@bodybuild

Hi, Donna
I'm afraid I'm going to have to cancel tonight. I'm totally snowed under here, but will work out at home tonight.
See you tomorrow. Martin

From: Martin Lukes
To: DougRich@!Eureka!Wow!

Hi Doug
Here is the report on myself, as requested.
OBSESSION – 9 out of 10. When I start on a project I eat, drink and sleep it and do not draw breath until it is finished.
DARING – 10 out of 10. I have always been a risk-taker – it's in my DNA. If the upside is there, I welcome overcoming the obstacles.
LOVE – 10 out of 10. Love, for me, kicks in at different levels. I have a love for the company as a whole, a love for my team, and a profound love for the work that we do. Unbeatable.
CREOVATION™ – 10.5 out of 10. As the father of creovation™, I really can't give myself anything less!
DELIGHT – 9 out of 10. I see this as being about letting out the delight in myself – and helping cause delight in all our stakeholders.

INTEGRITY – 9.5 out of 10. To my mind, there is only one way of doing things, and that is the right way. I have zero tolerance of anyone who seeks to cut ethical corners.

Would be delighted to talk about this to put more flesh on the bones.
Martin

From: Martin Lukes
To: Graham Wallace

Jesus, I've just seen the forms we're meant to fill in for our teams. They are 62 pages long and I've got 38 people to do! Don't these consultants realize we have work to do?? Mart

June 29

From: Martin Lukes
To: DonnaAdonis@bodybuild

Hi Donna – really sorry am going to have to cancel again. Rest assured, I'm working hard on my machines at home. This week I'm concentrating on the isolation, definition, intensity and focus of my abdominals.
Will do Tuesday without fail.
Martin

From: Martin Lukes
To: Bettina Schmidt

Hi Bettina
In reply to your message, yes I shall be doing an assessment of you. I know that you have only been on my team a couple of days, but don't worry about that – I'll talk to your line manager in Dusseldorf . . . and we can build up a behaviour profile of you together. If you want to talk, my door is always open.
Cheers, Martin

From: Martin Lukes
To: Bettina Schmidt

Sorry, can't do now – make an appointment with Keri.

From: Martin Lukes
To: Christo Weinberg

Christo – Thanks for sending me the reminder of all your wins in the last year. I shall of course take them all into account. However, it would be totally out of order for me to show you your assessment before I file it. Rest assured that it will be totally objective.
Martin

From: Martin Lukes
To: All Marketing

Team – Various members of the team have expressed concern at the ABC procedure. I appreciate that this is an uncertain time for everybody. However, I hope I don't need to tell you that I shall be thinking long and hard about each of the forms. I suggest that for the time being you channel your concerns into your work. We don't want to let anyone accuse this team of taking its eye off the ball!
Best, Martin

From: Martin Lukes
To: Keri Tartt

Pinky – What were you talking to Doug about for such a long time just now? He seemed to be standing rather close to you, and laughing . . . I didn't know he had a sense of humour . . . did my name come up??
Perky

From: Pandora@CoachworX
To: Martin Lukes

Martin,
Congratulations! You have reached the half-way mark of Executive Bronze. This is always a moving moment. Half the program in the past, and the other half still in the future! I feel that you have come such a very long way. Your body is stronger, more grounded. You are getting younger. When I first met you, you were someone who used the word can't. I haven't heard you say that in ages. There is a very bright future for you, Martin.

I want you to give yourself a treat or a present. You deserve it, Martin. And when you give it to yourself I want you to say: I love me. I love my body. I look and feel fantastic, over and over.
Strive and Thrive!
Pandora

From: Martin Lukes
To: Keri Tartt

Pinky – I've booked us the bridal suite at the Canning Town Novotel for the afternoon. Champagne, rich chocolate fudge cake, the works. Pandora says I deserve it.
Perky

June 30

From: Martin Lukes
To: Keri Tartt

Pinky – Yes, I am cheesed off with you. It was meant to be a treat for me, and after the grim evening on my birthday I felt I deserved it. Frankly I didn't appreciate you rushing off in a huff. To say that I am 'self-obsessed' was really below the belt. I spend my entire life thinking about others, whether it is you, Jens, mum, the boys, my team, etc. etc. The reason I was whispering that to myself was part of Exec Bronze. Of course I love you, and your body too. You are fantastic. Goes without saying.

Please don't be cross.

See you tomorrow.

I love you.

Perky, who is still, if we are going to be 110 per cent honest, a tiny bit porky

Chapter Seven

July
My Funeral

July 1

From: Pandora@CoachworX
To: Martin Lukes

Hi Martin,
Please find somewhere to read this where you are on your
own. It is imperative that no one interrupts you as you enter
one of the deepest stages of the Executive Bronze Program.
Clear your mind, and focus.

I want you to imagine that you are going to the funeral of
someone you love very much. Now imagine the church or the
crematorium. Look at the faces of the other mourners, the
flowers.

Next I want you to imagine yourself slowly going up to
the front and peeking into the coffin. Inside is . . . yourself!
This is your funeral, Martin. Look again at the people's faces,
Martin. Look at their sorrow and their pain. What sort of
gap have you left in their lives?

Now I want you to imagine that you pick up the program
and see there will be four speakers. The first is a member of
your family. The second is a friend. The third a work colleague,
and the fourth is from your church or any organization where
you have been involved in a giving role. Each one will talk
honestly about the role you have played in their lives.

Take your time to think about this. Your funeral is, after all, the ultimate wake-up call on what you have achieved, both in your relationships and your life.

What would it be like? What would those four people say about you?

I'm really looking forward to seeing what you are going to make of this, Martin. This is probably the most life-changing exercise of the whole program!
Strive and thrive!
Pandora

From: Martin Lukes
To: Jenny Withers

Darling – fraid I can't go to Max's speech day this pm. I've got a big report to write for Atlanta, something v time sensitive that I need to crack on with. Tell him I'm sorry but I promise to come next year when he's at Eton.
Love you, Martin
PS Quick question: what colour would you wear to my funeral?

From: Martin Lukes
To: Jenny Withers

No need to be sarcastic . . . the bowel cancer situation is fine, thanks for asking. It is just an exercise I'm doing for Pandora.
M

From: Martin Lukes
To: Max Lukes

Max – Really sorry not to be with you this afternoon, son. I'll be cheering you on from my desk, and expect to see a whole row of silver cups when I get home!!

Can I ask you something? Just suppose I popped my clogs in

the next year or two . . . and suppose you had to say something about me at my funeral, what would you say?
Love, Dad

From: Martin Lukes
To: Max Lukes

Forget it, doesn't matter. I just wondered if you'd mention the football games I've taken you to or me reading you Fireman Sam when you were little?
Love, Dad

From: Martin Lukes
To: Keri Tartt

Would Pinky cry lots of piggie tears if Perky popped his clogs?

From: Martin Lukes
To: Keri Tartt

Cheeky message! I love it when you talk dirty like that . . . though maybe not a brilliant idea on work email!
    Come into my office now, we can pull the blinds down . . . perfectly safe if we're quick . . .
Perky xxxxxxxxxxx

From: Martin Lukes
To: Graham Wallace

Ooops! What can I say??? That was a bit embarrassing! I suppose I should be pleased that it was you and not anyone else . . . Shagging your secretary is a bit predictable and as you know, I specialize in the unexpected!! But Keri's not your classic secretary . . . she's a really amazing girl, shag of a lifetime etc. But please please . . . NOT A WORD!!!

From: Martin Lukes
To: Pandora@CoachworX

Hi Pandora.

It has taken me a long time to write this. Can I be very honest with you? I've found it a highly emotional exercise. Cathartic, really. In fact thinking about my death made me break down and cry. It has been some time since that happened – last time was when Tiger Woods was beaten by that boring Fijian guy – but that wasn't quite the same.

So, here is how I envision my funeral.

Jens will be led into the church with Jake and Max on either side, holding her up. She won't be wearing black – she will have insisted that the funeral is not to be a sad occasion, but a celebration of my life, so she'll be wearing something bright. She'll be ashen-faced. So will the boys.

My mother will be there looking unbearably sad, but not crying. She is a very strong person, who will do all her grieving in private. I've been trying to work out if my father would put in an appearance or not. He walked out when I was 10. Basically, he was the sort of man who was always looking out for Number One. He was involved in various dodgy businesses, made a lot of money and then lost it again. We've always been chalk and cheese – didn't get on even when I was a kid. Mum's the heart of the family, if you will. On balance, I think he'll stay away – I don't think he'd have the guts to face the music. My sister Katherine will come, though. She and I also haven't spoken for years. Katherine has had serious issues around jealousy, and always complained that I was Mum's favourite. She had a series of breakdowns as a teenager, for which I think she blamed me. These days I don't even know where she lives. She'll arrive late at my funeral, and start crying hysterically. They say death is worse for people when there's unfinished business.

Keri Tartt will have organized the flowers. She will be standing leaning on Mary (Roger's PA) sobbing uncontrollably. Although we haven't worked together long, she not only respects me as a boss but also appreciates me as a human being. She will be in a black trouser suit, tight black T-shirt underneath – full mourning. A little detail that chokes me up: she will have taken the silver stud out of her tongue and put in a black one.

Jake will have made a slide show of all the photos of me – graduating from Durham, the one of me and Jens on holiday in Crete. I was looking very tanned and in very good shape. Jens will choose the music, which will be some of my favourite songs and things that remind her of me. Elton John's 'Rocket Man'. The Rolling Stones' 'I Can't Get No Satisfaction'. That brilliant bit of Wagner from Apocalypse Now. The Kinks' 'Thank You for the Days'. And 'Stairway to Heaven' by Led Zeppelin. When Jens hears that she will start to cry, quietly but inconsolably.

The church will be packed. Standing room only.

Everyone from the UK board will be there. Cindy and Barry won't have been able to make it, but will have sent messages to Jens which will be read out by Keith. Barry's message will say I had one of the finest and most creovative™ mindsets and warmest hearts of anyone he had the privilege of working with. It will be all-American and totally over the top, but there will be a kernel of truth and sincerity in it too.

The odd thing is that I always thought there was something between Keith and Jens, but today she doesn't even look at him.

Max will read out my favourite poem, the one that goes 'If you can keep your head, when all around you are losing theirs . . .' and then will say a few words about me. He's very good at speaking – he is head of the debating society at his prep school. He will talk about myself as a role model. He will tell them how I used to read him Fireman Sam as a child. How I took him to football matches, and how, even though I was often at work, I always had quality time for him.

Graham will stand up and talk as my friend.

He will talk about the fun side of me. How mischievous I am, how I'm not frightened to break the rules. He might tell about how when his wife kicked him out, I invited him to stay with us. On second thoughts, he might not want to mention that . . .

He would talk about how my handicap used to be higher than his, but how it is now lower, and how guilty he feels now about giving me such a hard time about it.

As I'm not a member of a church, and as I'm not really part of any charity thing, I'll have just the three speakers. Though if the funeral can be put forward a year or two I may be a parent governor of Eton by then, so maybe the Provost of the school would give a little talk about my added value in the school, and my attitude to the non-profit sector in general.

Then afterwards everyone will come back to our house. At first the mood will be solemn, stunned. There'll be loads of bubbly and posh eats and people will start to talk, and laugh, and dance. It will be the best bash anyone can remember.

On my gravestone it will say:

MARTIN LUKES

A CREOVATIVE™ MIND AND A LOVING HEART WHO NEVER STOPPED PUSHING THE ENVELOPE.

22.5 per cent better than my very bestest

Martin

July 6

From: Barry S. Malone
To: All Staff

Howdy!
It's been a challenging first half! As you'll see from the attachment, our Q2 earnings are down 21 per cent, as we've been hit by the continued competitive pressures in the economic landscape, by adverse currency fluctuations, and by falling demand in many regions.

However, our underlying performance is strong, and we have a strategy in place to transition us to our goal of Phenomenal Performance – Permanently!

I am thrilled to announce that after three months of obsession, love and determination by Keith Buxton and his team, we are ready to raise the a-b glöbâl talent bar. Tomorrow all co-workers will receive a letter at their home addresses letting them know if they are an A, a B or a C.

Can I just say that the Cs who will be leaving our close-knit family will be in our prayers. I would like to take this opportunity to thank each of them individually for their talents and their dedication and wish them joy in whatever the future brings them!

I love you all.

Barry S. Malone

From: Martin Lukes
To: Jenny Withers

Jens – I suggest you go in to work normal time, and I'll wait for the postman . . .
M x

From: Pandora@CoachworX
To: Martin Lukes

Hi Martin
When I read about your funeral, I was deeply moved. Moved at the incredible distance you have traveled since we embarked on this journey together in January. You have the self-knowledge. You have the vision. You are the loving father, and your position at work goes from strength to strength.

However, there are some issues here. I want you to think about closure with your sister and father. Is this something that you should try to get while you are still alive?

I'm also interested at the way you single out Keri, who as you say hasn't been with you that long. Is there an issue here that we need to visit?

My other concern is that your involvement with the community could be stronger. Martin, in this life to achieve the goal of lifelong success and happiness, it is not what

you take out, but what you put in that counts!!
Strive and thrive!
Pandora

From: Martin Lukes
To: Pandora@CoachworX

Hi, Pandora,
Sorry – can't reply at present. I'm waiting for confirmation that
I'm an A.
22.5 per cent etc.
M

From: Martin Lukes
To: Jenny Withers

No fucking post and it's 9.45. The postal system in this country
has gone down the tubes. The whole bloody lot of them should
be fired. I'm going to give it 20 more minutes, then I'm coming
into the office. M xx

From: Martin Lukes
To: Jenny Withers

HHOOOOOORAYYYYYYYYYYYYYYY!!!!! I'm an A!!!!!!!!!!!!!!!
    Shall I open your envelope or shall I bring it in?
M XXXXX
Sent from my BlackBerry Wireless Handheld

From: Martin Lukes
To: Jenny Withers

Congratulations, darling. You are a B. Let's go out and celebrate
somewhere really nice tonight. The Savoy?
Love you, M
Sent from my BlackBerry Wireless Handheld

From: Martin Lukes
To: Jenny Withers

Darling . . . There's nothing wrong with being a B! It's really good! Bs are high achievers who exit their comfort zone to go the extra mile!! Fine about dinner, if you don't want to. Quite understand. Must get into work now . . . I'll see you later.
M xx
Sent from my BlackBerry Wireless Handheld

From: Martin Lukes
To: Keri Tartt

Pinky – that's so sweet of you. Yes, I'm chuffed, though obviously it's not the be all and end all. There are more important things in this life of ours! I'm glad you're dead chuffed to be a B. One of the many things that I love so much about you is that you're so happy with yourself just as you are. What's that great Barry White song, 'I love you just the way you are . . .' Ambition really screws people up. Just look at Jens – she's sulking about being a B as if it's some huge disaster.

  Let's go out and celebrate – we can make a big nite of it. Why not call the Ivy and get a table for two 8ish? I know it's a bit public there and there's a chance of people recognizing me, but I feel like making a splash. We'll just have to be a bit careful to keep our hands to ourselves during the meal . . .
Perky xxx

From: Martin Lukes
To: Keri Tartt

What do you mean they are fully booked??? Call them back and tell them I'm an A.

From: Martin Lukes
To: Graham Wallace

Graham – Popped by your office just now and nothing doing. Dare I ask, have you had some good news too?? Drink in order later on?

From: Martin Lukes
To: Graham Wallace

Bad luck, but at least you're not a C! Actually, I'm an A – probably a fluke! Have you heard about Rog or Faith??
Mart

From: Martin Lukes
To: Pandora@CoachworX

Hi Pandora
Sorry not to have got back to you sooner, but everything's been going mad here. The powers that be have decided in their wisdom that yours truly is an A. Although I wasn't surprised, I was relieved, because in this place (as I have discovered to my cost!!) reward isn't always aligned with talent. Think Roger.

On the whole, they seem to have done it surprisingly fairly. Lots of senior people are B – so I've been having to very much play the diplomat!

I've been thinking about some of your suggestions. I'm 145 per cent in favour of giving something back to the community. It is a matter of finding the right fit.

RE my family, I've decided against touching base with my father, even if it was possible to find where he is. He's a C if ever there was one, and I can't see any value added coming from a meeting. Re Katherine, I'll mull it over. Closure isn't that important for me, but it might make a big difference to her

And re Keri – you're barking up the wrong tree there! She's a great gal, and a terrific PA, and I genuinely think she'll weep at my funeral! But that's about as far as it goes!!
22.5 per cent better than my very bestest
Martin

**Hi Martin
Just a quick note to congratulate you on being an A. But, as
your most sincere fan, I think you should view it as a base-
line. You can go further. Ask what is the point of being an
A? Is it an end in itself? Think of that eulogy. You are the
creovative™ guy who never stopped pushing the envelope.
Don't rest here. Go push that envelope! Give something back!
Strive and Thrive!
Pandora**

From: Martin Lukes
To: Bettina Schmidt

Bettina,
I understand that you are upset, but I think we need to look at
this calmly. First, any decision to make you a C did not emanate
from myself. It was the output of a highly fair 360-degree
appraisal audited by !Eureka!Wow! As you know, I have the highest respect for you and your work.

Your response is perfectly natural and is the first step of the
SARAH cycle. When you hear difficult news, the first response
is Shock and Anger. In time you may feel a little Resentment
moving on towards Acceptance. The final H is either hope or
happiness, can't remember which!

In the long term, you will discover that being a C is the right
thing for you. It gives you the chance to be redeployed somewhere where the fit is better!

You might not believe this, but I've found the SARAH model
quite useful myself. You probably see me as a natural A but I
want to share a little secret with you. I can be pretty vulnerable
myself, and have had one or two knocks along the way. SARAH
has proved very useful to myself dealing with disappointment
and moving on.

Should you wish to discuss it further, my door is always open, as you know.
Martin

From: Martin Lukes
To: Graham Wallace

Rog is an A???? That is absolutely fucking bonkers. He doesn't possess any of the values at all – except obsession – about saving the marginal 2p.

From: Martin Lukes
To: Graham Wallace

Even more upsetting news. Christo is a bloody A as well. It really is the last straw. If they make idiots like that A, it really devalues the currency.

July 8

From: Martin Lukes
To: Keri Tartt

My darling Pinky
Thank you for last night . . . you are so sexy and funny and lovely. I'm only sorry that the evening ended on a slightly off note. I realize that it is hard on you getting closer and closer to yours truly and then having to put up with the fact that I go home to Jens every night.

But I was speaking the total truth when I said the corporal hasn't been anywhere near her in ages. You are the only one for me (and him!!). The hanky panky side of our relationship ended pretty much some time back.

You have to believe me when I say that I do want to be with you properly, I promise. Cross Porky's heart. But I can't leave her just now when Max hasn't even started at Eton yet. Give me time.

We would be brilliant together. We ARE brilliant together.
Love you very very very much
Porky

July 10

From: Martin Lukes
To: Phyllis Lukes

Dearest Mum
So sorry I haven't been in touch. Everything's been going mad
here. I'm delighted that you've settled in so quickly back home
and that your knee is behaving itself.

It's probably more restful being home than it was staying chez
nous!! Thanks for doing all the mending. As you see it is not
something that is top of mind for Jens right now!!

And sorry not to have seen more of you – I'm working v long
hours at the moment, but you mustn't worry about the stress
on me – I thrive on it!

I know you're concerned about Jake too. Yes, he is drinking
a bit . . . but they all do it after GCSEs these days. Look at Tony
Blair's son! At least last week Jake passed out in the privacy of
his own house!

Did I tell you Max scooped up all the prizes at prize day . . .
rugby, maths, debating, he even got a cup for kindness! Haven't
got any other news except that Pandora has had me planning
my funeral! Don't say anything, mum – it wasn't mumbo jumbo,
it was actually very revealing about myself. It got me thinking
about Katherine and wondering if I should contact her. She probably needs closure – it'd be awful if I died without having offered
her the opportunity of apologizing and healing.

She always had issues with my over-achievement, as she saw
it. Which is ridiculous, really, because she was a bit of a slogger
but always got there in the end, if my memory serves. Do you
have an email address for her?

You'll be proud to hear I've been scooping up some prizes

myself of late . . . I've just found out I'm an A – all a bit awkward as some of the other directors aren't, but I'm trying to handle it sensitively. Jens is a B, which seems pretty fair to me, but she isn't seeing it like that.

I must go now, and earn my salary. We'll come down at the weekend. And if the weather's nice, might nip off for a game of golf at the RAC club as one of my colleagues has just become a member.

Yr loving son

Martie

PS I can't believe that you're gardening again. Actually I can believe it knowing you!

July 12

From: Roger Wright
To: All Staff

IMPORTANT: PLEASE READ

I am very sorry to inform all staff that an incident of a serious nature has occurred re Project ABC. There is evidence that an individual or individuals have gained access to computer files held by Doug Rich and some of the appraisals have been tampered with. This is an exceptionally serious matter and we have decided that we will be getting our IT experts to search the hard disks of every computer in the office. All emails and all files will be examined by myself, and by Jeff Grout, Director of IT.

In the meantime all As, Bs and Cs are considered only provisional.

I know I can count on your assistance in this matter

Roger Wright

Acting Chairman

From: Martin Lukes
To: Graham Wallace

Who do you think it is?? I can think of lots of candidates. Christo for one . . . at least you're off the hook, Graham – unless you bumped yourself up from a C!!

I'm feeling a bit anxious re a few of my emails. There are one or two I might rather were not scrutinized . . . presumably you don't want Lucindagate spread out for all to see either . . .

Drink? We both need one.

M

From: Martin Lukes
To: Max Lukes

Hi Max –

This is Dad again in my role as technical ignoramus!!! Max, you're the computer whizz of the family, and I just wanted to ask your advice on something. We've had a bit of a security breach here, and I'm trying to help the IT guys. Suppose someone had sent a load of messages on email at work, and deleted all of them – would they still be there on the hard drive? And how easy would it be to delete them?

Love, Dad

PS Probably best not to mention this to mum. She doesn't like it when I help out people in other departments. She says I should be more focused on my own priorities, and then come home on time!!!

From: Martin Lukes
To: Keri Tartt

Have set up a hotmail account for you. Kinkypinky@hotmail.com
password: privatepussy.

From: Porky Perky
To: Kinky Pinky

Dearest KK

From now on no more emails on the work system. Maybe it's stupid as the damage has been done, but we can't be too careful. This is a complete fucking catastrophe for me – since my email balls-up last month, I've been really careful about deleting everything, but apparently it makes no difference. It's all on the hard drive anyway.

According to Max there is a way of removing all trace . . . he's got a couple of ideas which I've written down. I need some access codes which must be somewhere in the IT dept.

So what I suggest is we try tomorrow night after everyone has gone home. We could go to the Novotel for a bit after work, and then can come back into the IT department at midnight, and try to hack into the system.

What do you think? PP xx

From: Porky Perky
To: Kinky Pinky

Pinky . . . you haven't got much faith in my IT skills! I'm pretty confident I can do it. The main problem is going to be explaining to J why I'm going out yet again . . .
Perky

From: Martin Lukes
To: Jenny Withers

Darling
Tim Zadek from Boogie Gargle Fink has asked me at the last minute to go to Glyndebourne tonight to see Carmen. You know I love Puccini, so I've said yes. He's only got one ticket . . . so fraid it's just me. Won't be back till v late. Hope you don't mind.
Love you
M xx

From: Martin Lukes
To: Jenny Withers

Bizet, whatever. I'll send a cab home to get my dinner jacket.

From: Porky Perky
To: Kinky Pinky

Pinky,
Sorted for tonite!
Perky

July 13

From: Martin Lukes
To: DougRich@!Eureka!Wow!

Hi Doug!
I just wanted to touch base with you to explain what to you might have looked like odd behaviour last night. I had been out to a concert and had come back to finish off a report, and the quickest way to my desk is through IT!

I'm quite the night bird, me!
Best Martin
PS What were *you* doing there?

From: Porky Perky
To: Kinky Pinky

Disaster. Failed mission – not only did I fail to delete anything, they now suspect me of fiddling the ABCs . . . Thank God you didn't come in the end . . . what shall we do?? Maybe a good idea if we don't see each other for a bit.

From: Porky Perky
To: Kinky Pinky

Sweetie . . . don't be like that . . . please . . . please understand my whole life is flashing before my eyes . . .
Worried Perky x

July 14

From: Martin Lukes
To: Pandora@CoachworX

Hi Pandora –
I need to share something that has been bothering me.
Basically, long story short, what has happened is that a low-key
relationship has developed between myself and my PA Keri. All
very casual, which is why I hadn't mentioned anything. If
anything, my relationship with her has been very much in keeping with your teachings, about being with younger people to
reduce my psychological age, listen to my heart, re-energize my
body, etc.

Unfortunately there are a couple of emails on the system that
might be misinterpreted. Obviously, now that I'm an A player,
it's imperative that I am seen to eat, drink, breathe all six values
24/7. Quite apart from rocking the boat with J.

Anyway we now have a situation where some idiot (I've got
my suspicions) has been fiddling with the appraisals, and now
all emails are being read. So I went in the office late last night
trying to do a bit of deleting on the hard disk. Unfortunately I
was seen by Doug who now suspects me of tampering with the
grades myself.
Help!
Martin

From: Pandora@CoachworX
To: Martin Lukes

**Martin, Most of the time, I just love being a coach. It is one
of the most amazingly exciting jobs in the world, but sometimes it's one of the toughest jobs too. When I read your
email just now I felt my own energy levels depleted. I felt
you had drilled a big hole in my colander, and I was literally
watching the energy drain away.**

Martin, I am saddened. You have not been truthful to me. Or to yourself. You have violated your values. If you lie to yourself, you do not respect yourself, deep down.

And without self-respect you cannot generate self-love.

I can't tell you what to do now. You must feel for the true path yourself.

Let the GROW model help you do the right thing.
Strive and thrive!
Pandora

From: Martin Lukes
To: Pandora@CoachworX

GOALS: to get out of this sticky mess.
REALITY: I am an A and I am (or was) going places. I have unwisely sent some emails to my PA that would not look good if read by others. I am now wrongly suspected of fiddling the ABC grades. My wife may leave me. I may be the laughing stock of the company. I may be fired.
OPTIONS: I come clean, in which case Jens may still leave me, and I will look stupid. I can keep quiet in which case I might get away with it, or I might lose everything.
WINS – no wins here, only some losses more totally horrendous than others.
Not better than my best at all
Martin

From: Pandora@CoachworX
To: Martin Lukes

Martin – I quite disagree! There are HUGE wins here from doing the right thing. Remember NO FAILURE – ONLY FEED-BACK! To get back onto the track of being better than the best you can be takes great courage. And I know you have that!
Strive and Thrive!
Pandora

July 15

From: *Roger Wright*
To: *All Staff*

Subject: *IMPORTANT PLEASE READ*
A meeting will be held this afternoon at 15.00 hrs in the staff restaurant to discuss urgent developments re Project Uplift. It is imperative that every staff member attends promptly.
Roger Wright
Acting Chairman

From: Martin Lukes
To: Jenny Withers

Darling
Could we do lunch today? There is something I wanted to talk to you about quite urgently. All Bar One on Canning Town High Street?
Love you, M xx

From: Porky Perky
To: Kinky Pinky

Pinky – I've got to tell her. I'm going to play it down as much as poss, say you were a one-night stand . . . that it's all over anyway . . . no big deal. Wish me luck. Perky

From: Porky Perky
To: Kinky Pinky

Pinky, you're not being very supportive. Don't you see how hard this is for me?

From: Porky Perky
To: Kinky Pinky

Keri – Jens has taken it very badly. She said I was a cretin, and all sorts of highly hurtful things about you – Tartt by name, tart by nature, moronic new age Antipodean, etc. – I'll spare you the details.

Sweetie, what this means is that we are going to have to stop seeing each other. I'm totally gutted, but I really can't see any alternative. I know you are going to be upset, and I can't bear that, but what can I do? I want you to know that it's been really wonderful. I mean it. I'm going to miss you, but I think there is a time for doing the right thing . . . can't talk about it now . . . Rog's meeting is starting. Better go up separately.
Martin

From: Roger Wright
To: All Staff

I would like to document the proceedings of today's meeting for those staff members unable to attend.

We have discovered that the discrepancies in the Project Uplift rankings were a result of statistical errors inputting data carried out by junior members of the !Eureka!Wow! team. There will be no further investigations into this matter.

Correct letters will be sent out by the end of the week.
Roger Wright

From: Martin Lukes
To: Graham Wallace

I don't fucking believe it . . . I've just come clean to the ladywife (actually, not 110 per cent clean as I said it was just a couple of flirtatious emails, and I had only kissed her once). Jens went nuclear, and I've split with Keri. And all for nothing – great

reward for honesty. If I am now downgraded to a B, I'm going to kill myself.
M

From: Martin Lukes
To: Doug Rich@!Eureka!Wow!

Hi Doug!
So now I know what you were doing in IT at midnight! I hope you won't mind if I give you a little tip garnered from my hard earned experience. I find that when I've made a mistake, it's best to put my hand up at once and say mea culpa. It can save a lot of misunderstandings later!
Bestest, Martin
PS Can you give me a heads up on my grade? Assume no change there?

July 19

From: Keith Buxton
To: All Staff

Hallo everyone!
I would like to thank all co-colleagues for helping make Uplift such a phenomenal success. I understand there have been teething problems in some geographies but that these have now been resolved.

However, I want to clarify one small matter. Some people have asked why they are in the band they are in. I am sorry to say we can't give reasons for our decisions. In the most unlikely event any co-worker still feels uncomfortable, we have undertaken to provide coaching workshops 'Being a C: a beginning not an end'. These workshops will be led by highly trained facilitators and should be hugely stimulating learning experiences.
Keith

From: Martin Lukes
To: Bettina Schmidt

Hi Bettina, Tx for yr message. Can I make a suggestion? Why not try the C workshop? It's being conducted by Dr Gary Copper – there's nothing he doesn't know about the stress of under-achieving!!
Martin

From: Martin Lukes
To: Bettina Schmidt

Hi Bettina!
Well what did I tell you? I'm delighted that you've been upped to a B! So you won't be leaving us after all! No one could be gladder than myself! I told you that the SARAH cycle ended in Hope, and I wasn't wrong, was I?
Best, Martin

July 20

From: Martin Lukes
To: Keri Tartt

Hi Keri
Can you go through my schedule for next week, and get me a large latte. And please don't look like that. This is very hard for myself, too.
Martin

From: Martin Lukes
To: Keri Tartt

Jesus Christ! I would have forgotten altogether . . . Thanks for reminding me! Catastrophe averted!!
M

From: Martin Lukes
To: Jenny Withers

Darling – Don't think for a minute I had forgotten your birthday! What do you want? Would really like to push the boat out for you a bit this year. M XX

From: Martin Lukes
To: Jenny Withers

Listen darling. I know you're a tiny bit cross with me and my brief silliness over Keri. I know the ageing process is hard for you. But I think you should focus on lowering your psychological age – it's worked for me!

   If you won't give me clues about a present, I'll just have to use my imagination!
Love you
M xxx

From: Martin Lukes
To: Keri Tartt

Keri – Think gift. Jens is 43, in mid-career crisis, resentful of my success and never wears the jewellery I usually get her. Any bright ideas? M

From: Martin Lukes
To: Keri Tartt

Please don't you be so stroppy and sulky with me. It's not fair. I've ended this as much for your sake as for my own. I didn't mean to be insensitive asking you about a present for Jens . . . you always used to love that sort of task.
Martin

From: Martin Lukes
To: Jenny Withers

Darling – I've got you a luxury weekend to Champneys!! All the treatments . . . shiatsu, massage, facials, pedicures, you name it. You deserve the break, and I'll take the boys. I'd love to have a bit of quality time with them.

Hope you really enjoy it and de-stress a bit! It will show you that there's more to life than work.
Love you, M xx

From: Martin Lukes
To: Jenny Withers

Darling, that's great, well done! Did you get the letter just now? I must say I'm not at all surprised. I was sure you'd be an A – apart from anything it looks bad if none of the top women are As. And I was sure Keith would look after you!
M xx

From: Martin Lukes
To: Graham Wallace

I'm feeling thirsty all of a sudden. Drink?

July 21

From: Barry S. Malone
To: All Staff

Howdy! Project ABC has been an astounding success! I am humbled by the hundreds of grateful emails I have received from Cs thanking me and telling me how they have been empowered to go forward and use their talents!

At a-b glöbâl we have a passion for integrity. A passion for driving performance. But the greatest of all is a passion for the communities we live in.

We will never achieve Phenomenal Performance – Permanently unless we think of our corporate heart, and of what we are giving back. One of my privileges and joys as your co-equal officer is to travel the globe mingling with people from different geographies. Everywhere I go within this company I meet co-leaders who say: what can I do to contribute? Over the past weeks we have done extensive due diligence to see how we can make the world more closely aligned with our a-b glöbâl vision. And we have decided our value added lies with the global under-16 community. Kids in every geography are our seed corn. They are our future. I have tasked Cindy Czarnikow in Atlanta and Jenny Withers in London with heading up the Project.
I love you all
Barry

From: Jenny Withers
To: All Staff

Hi everyone
As you will have read from our CEO's memo, this week sees the launch of Project Global Seed Corn – our way of giving back to children globally. This is a phenomenally exciting initiative that will enable us to achieve our goal: sustainable triple bottom-line growth. This week I am asking every department to come up with ways of improving the lives of children, not in a one-off way, but as part of a long-term relationship that will grow the seed corn!
Jenny Withers

From: Martin Lukes
To: Jenny Withers

Darling! That was brilliant. Your email sounded really professional, very can-do, as well as a cri de coeur. Well done, you.

And to prove that we are at one on this, I am working on a local CSR project with my team. It's also something that Pandora says I need to work on. Will be home by 7 at the latest.
M xx

July 23

From: Martin Lukes
To: Keri Tartt

Keri – can you get me email addresses of the heads of all the local primary schools?
Ta muchly, M
PS Did I see you going out for lunch with Doug Rich? What's he still doing here?

From: Martin Lukes
To: Katherine Lukes

Hi Katherine
I think you'll be pretty surprised to get this email. It's been a long time.
   Look, I'm not going to beat about the bush – basically, I thought it was time we met up. I think there are issues that you, and for all I know myself too, need closure on. You and I haven't seen each other in a long time, and, frankly, I think it's time to let bygones be bygones! You are my sister, and we do have a shared past. I occasionally hear your news from mum who, btw, was a bit miffed that you didn't help more with the knee op, which I don't know if she mentioned, I paid for so that she wouldn't have to wait. Anyway I'd be very happy to buy you lunch or a drink or something in the foreseeable – it'd be good to catch up!
Best
Martin

From: Martin Lukes
To: head@canningtownprimary

Dear Headmaster
My name is Martin Lukes and I am Director of Marketing at a-b glöbâl. You may not know that we are presently looking

at ways of sowing global seed corn. The future of kids is some-thing that we believe to be integral to our business going forward.

Because of the proximity of Canning Town Primary School to our offices and because of the deprived calibre of some of your pupils we have picked you out for assistance! Could I suggest a breakfast meeting with your top team and my team at our offices on Friday?

All my very bestest
Martin Lukes

From: Martin Lukes
To: Keri Tartt

Hi Keri – I think a John Scott from Bupa is after me. Can't deal with it at the moment. If he calls again, take a message.
Martin

July 26

From: Martin Lukes
To: Pandora@CoachworX

This is going to have to be a quick one, as I am trying to get home on time. Basically I think you should be very pleased with me. I am spearheading a major project to help deprived local school kids – I have contacted my sister, and I am being the model supportive husband.

22.5 per cent better than my very bestest
Martin

From: Pandora@CoachworX
To: Martin Lukes

Hi – Martin
Well done! You have done the really difficult thing! You have told your wife, and are working to heal the damage.

Hang on to that view of your wife in the crematorium – ashen-faced. Integrity is one of the values that make you an A. You are fighting for your integrity, and that is a hard thing to do.

I know that, Martin. I have fought for mine in the past. But that is another story.
Strive and thrive!
Pandora

July 27

From: Martin Lukes
To: head@canningtownprimary

Dear Mrs SenGupta
Thanks for getting back so quickly. Sorry you can't find time for a brainstorming breakfast this week. However, my diary permitting, we could renew the offer next term. I am passionately interested in education – and I believe that business has a duty to share its best practice with schools like yours, which due to situation and budgetary constraints, clearly cannot afford the expertise.
All my very bestest
Martin Lukes

From: Martin Lukes
To: Phyllis Lukes

Dear Mum
Thanks for your message. Got the photo at last!!! Well done – Pebbles looks v nice. Have you heard from Katherine? I sent her a long, very open email, and she hasn't even bothered to reply, which is her all over. I've also volunteered to share my knowhow with a local school fequented by asylum seekers and children of single mothers, and been given the brush off! As you'd say, these people don't know which side of their bread has the butter on

it! It was meant to please Jens, who loves that sort of thing, but she seems to be cross with me at the minute.

Must go now, no rest for the wicked etc.
Love Martie

July 29

From: Porky Perky
To: Kinky Pinky

I can't bear this. It's too painful, especially in the hot weather. The corporal really misses his Private. I'm sure we can carry on if we are really, really careful. Fire escape in five mins?

From: Porky Perky
To: Kinky Pinky

Dearest Pinky . . . do you want me to beg? Look, tell you what. J is away for her de-stress weekend at Champneys. I'm meant to have the boys, but I can always bribe Svetlana to take them. Paris, maybe?
Porky Perky xxxxxxxxxxxxxxxxxxxxxxxxxxxxx

Chapter Eight

August
My Work–Life Balance

August 2

From: Porky Perky
To: Kinky Pinky

Dearest sweetest sexiest loveliest Kinky Pinky
Thank you for the best night ever. Ever since I got home I've been pottering around the house singing 'I believe in miracles/ You sexy thing/Daaah, da, da, da, da, daaaaah . . .'

Max has told me to shut up – no respect at all. Trust Eton will see to that. Must go now, as Jens is due back from Champneys any minute. Just wanted to say you mustn't worry about the future. We will be together one day. Porky promise.
Lots of kisses,
Xxxx

From: Porky Perky
To: Kinky Pinky

Dear Pinky
Jens has just gone off to bed, stress levels not much helped by £700 of healing, palmistry, graphology, herbal medicine etc . . . It really pisses me off that she isn't more grateful seeing as she only gave me an orange squeezer for my b'day.

She went nuclear at me for not unloading the dishwasher and at Max for leaving his cereal bowl on the table. She's still very angry about you – keeps making sarky remarks about 'la Tartt'.

Pinky, don't want you to take this the wrong way, but I've done some blue-sky thinking and decided it'd be better for all and sundry if you stopped being my PA. It'd get Jens off my case, and would make it easier for us to carry on.

The best thing would be for you to work for Graham. Denise is on the verge of dropping her sproglet, and as he's in the loop re us, it'll make it easier. Bed now. I need my beauty sleep.
Love you
Porky

From: Porky Perky
To: Kinky Pinky

Pinky, I understand you're upset, but you really mustn't ring on my mobile – it's far too dangerous.

And I take exception to you saying I'm hen-pecked. It's so far off base that I'm not even going to waste words defending myself. OK, I know you don't like me going on and on about Jens all the time, but I do have to live with her, and I think you should be a bit more understanding of that.

I also think you should adopt a more positive headset towards working for Graham. I know it's demotion for you working for a B rather than an A. But at least those lazy idiots in sales don't know the meaning of hard work, so you'll have more spare time to do little things for me – and the corporal.

Bed now. See you tomorrow.
Perky xxx

August 3

From: Pandora@CoachworX
To: Martin Lukes

Hi Martin
Can I share with you a little story about myself? When I

was in my mid-twenties I was given the role of the Sugar Plum Fairy in the Nutcracker at the London Colleseum. At that time, I had been having headaches but took no notice of them. The day before the first night I was dashed to hospital with a small and inoperable brain tumour.

After I had got over the shock, I intuitively knew it wasn't just my body that needed healing. My life had been so stressful for so long – I had worked and worked to get closer to my goal, but as I did my unhappiness grew stronger.

It was time for a massive reality check. I had put everything into my work. I had neglected my personal relationships. It was time to sit down and re-dream.

Martin, I can see you in a similar situation. You put your heart, your soul and your brain into your work. You never get home before 9.30 pm. Are you going to turn around one day and wish you had put more into the rest of your life?

What we are going to focus in on this month is balance.

Each person travels through their own personal landscape of life to find their path. It is a profound truth, Martin, and that path is the path of balance.

I am forwarding to you the StressBusta! RU Balanced?™ test, which I would like you to do today.
Strive and Thrive!
Pandora

From: Martin Lukes
To: Pandora@CoachworX

Hi Pandora
Will do the stress test when I get a window, though slightly in demand today on challenging personnel matters.

Btw, I didn't realize you had a brain tumour as well as leukaemia! What bad luck – it never rains but it pours!
22.5 per cent better than my bestest
Martin

From: Martin Lukes
To: Faith Preston

Hi Faith,
Following up on our meeting just now, Keri Tartt will not be transferred to Graham in the sales until a suitable replacement can be found for myself. You suggest Thelma Dowd, who clearly has the right experience quotient, but does she have the energy profile? We're a very fast-paced team in marketing, and I wonder if she'd keep up.
Bestest
Martin

August 4

From: Cindy Czarnikow
To: All Staff

Hi!
I am attaching a profile of Barry that appeared in Fortune magazine. I know that all of you will be as proud as I am to have such a uniquely inspirational CEO.
I'm smiling at you
Cindy

PRIEST, POET, PRIZEFIGHTER
By Janine Rozenholtz
It is 5.30 am. Barry Malone is in the gym in his beautiful home in Atlanta going through his morning routine. He has spent an hour on the treadmill, looking out over the manicured golf course in the distance. He has meditated for 15 minutes and now is eating a light breakfast of blueberries and hot water with a twist of lemon.

He turns his tanned face towards me and looks at me with his unbelievably blue eyes. 'Every day I thank God for having given me one of the most challenging and rewarding jobs on

God's earth', he says. 'a-b glöbâl is a fine company, and I am privileged to be leading its journey on the road from good to great.'

Malone has built up a reputation for ruthless integrity, teamed with a passion for execution. Last month, he completed the biggest talent upgrade in corporate history. He divided up the company's talent pool into As, Bs and Cs, retaining only the top two streams.

'We have done this with great compassion. Every year going forward we will off-board 15 to 20 per cent of our family giving them the opportunity to work someplace else where their skills fit better. I am obsessed with talent. What places us ahead of the curve is our humanware. If I lift that bar every year going forward, a-b glöbâl will meet our target of achieving Phenomenal Performance – Permanently.'

Malone certainly faces challenges. In the last two quarters, earnings have fallen by 40 per cent, and the share price by 55 per cent from its peak 18 months ago. Malone shrugs this off. 'We have been knocked back by adverse trends in the global market. This is a long-term game. I am positioning this company to perform not just today, but every day, forever.'

For all his ruthlessness, Malone is a deeply modest man. 'I may look like I walk on water. But that is because I have an incredibly passionate team in the water holding me up. We are all leaders here. I surround myself with people who are never frightened of telling me the truth.'

Malone was raised in Arizona by his grandfather, who was a highly ranked prizefighter. 'When I was a kid, I played a load of sports, and was close to the best kid on the block. I put that down to hours of practice and the hustle I brought to the game. Grandpa taught me to be dedicated, focused, relentless. To put my gut and my heart into the game and to enjoy the ride.'

Malone's top team are certainly enjoying the ride with their charismatic boss. 'Working with Barry is a total blast,' says Cindy Czarnikow, Chief Morale Champion. 'He is driven, dynamic and a load of fun. The followership that he inspires is humbling.'

But Malone, for all his results-driven mindset, is a deeply cultured man. In his beautiful home, which he shares with his fourth wife Randee, he has built up a fine collection of art works.

'I started being interested in art because I am fascinated at what the human soul can achieve. These impressionist painters are working with little dots of paint, and they put it together to make a compelling image. It's the same thing as I am doing here. I am taking the dots – the raw humanware – and putting it together to make something bigger than all of us. That's what gets my pulse racing!'

To understand Malone is also to understand integrity, and the role it plays shaping all he does. When he talks about the CEO scandals of recent years, those searching eyes take on an angry glint.

'Sure there are some rotten apples in the CEO cart. But this is not an issue for us. It is an opportunity. We are being given the chance to prove that we do things right. That example comes from the top. It starts here, with Barry Sylvester Malone.'

Barry points at a plaque that is on the wall above his running machine displaying a list of 'Barry's Big Beliefs' chiseled into granite.

'Barry's Big Beliefs
1. Eat and breathe integrity every day.
2. Be an outrageous champion.
3. Can't. Impossible. Never – These words inspire me.
4. Imagine.
5. Exceed expectations.'

So is this what it takes to be a truly great CEO? 'I'm so glad you asked me that,' Malone smiles, revealing perfect white teeth. 'One of my early mentors, the great Lou D. Feiner, always said the outstanding CEO must be priest, poet and prizefighter. Priest, because we believe in the sacredness of every individual within this company. Poet, because storytelling and learning are two of humankind's greatest passions. And prizefighter, because, as my granddad taught me, he who fears failure will never succeed.'

From: Martin Lukes
To: Graham Wallace

Graham – hard to know who had their tongue further up BSM's arse – Cindy or that Fortune journalist . . . Barry talks such a load of crap sometimes. Makes me wish I worked for a British company.

Btw have you spoken to Faith about Keri? I hope you're very grateful. You get a gorgeous 29-year-old New Zealand physiotherapist. I'm getting Thelma Dowd – fat, 55.
Can't wait.
M

August 5

From: Martin Lukes
To: Barry S. Malone

Hi Barry
Apologies for not touching base earlier – I just wanted to put on record how much I enjoyed the article in Fortune. In my experience, journalists usually get everything wrong – but this Janine Rozenholtz sounds one smart cookie!

I also wanted to say what incredibly good sense your tips made to me. I particularly relate to 'Be an Outrageous Champion' – I long ago realized that the sky's the limit when championing my team and my company.

I hope you won't be offended if I suggest a 6th tip – Play Golf! I've thought deeply about this, and concluded that golf isn't just a game – it's a whole philosophy of life. As Jack Welch once told me, golf is about two things – people and competition – which is the same as being a CEO!

My bestest, and once again, congratulations on an excellent article!
Martin Lukes

From: Martin Lukes
To: Barry S. Malone

Hi Barry
Thanks for getting back to me so quickly. Delighted you buy into my golf idea! And yes, I'd be honoured to come and play at Augusta!

My handicap's 15 – would be lower if I took my own advice and played a bit more. But what with the pressures of work and family, we none of us get to play as much as we would like!!
Martin

From: Martin Lukes
To: Graham Wallace

Eat yr heart out Graham – BSM has asked me to go and play in the US company tournament at Augusta!! M

From: Martin Lukes
To: Jenny Withers

Darling – BSM has just asked me to go play golf in Augusta in two weeks. I hope you don't mind – it'll mean cutting our holiday short by a couple of days, but Florida is quite close . . .
Love you, M XXX

From: Martin Lukes
To: Jenny Withers

Jens darling. I know we've got our pact on spending more time together as a family – I'm 120 per cent committed to that . . . But please understand, this is a massive big deal for me.
M x

From: Martin Lukes
To: Pandora@CoachworX

Hi Pandora
I've finally done the StressBusta test and sent it off. It was very long, and I'm not sure how relevant some of the questions were. Actually I'm not feeling at all stressed at the moment. Energized would be a better word. My relationship with Barry is getting stronger, and I've been asked to play at the company tournament in Augusta, which I sense will prove the tipping point in my career!

Very bizarrely I think the person who is having more difficulty with stress levels and balance is Jens, who keeps on taking on additional responsibilities, and has recently been put in charge of work–life balance for the UK company.
22.5 per cent better than my bestest
Martin

From: Martin Lukes
To: Thelma Dowd

Hi Thelma
Welcome to the marketing family! I think Keri has left you a list of tasks so that you can hit the ground running. As you see, we're a very young department – until now I've been the oldest by a wide margin, so I'm grateful to you for raising the average! A latte would be nice, if you're popping out later.
Martin

From: Martin Lukes
To: Thelma Dowd

Quite possibly they did brew up their own Nescafé in finance. But here in marketing we go for authenticity – so it's Starbucks' lattes for us! Strictly speaking it may not be your job to get me coffee, but I always discourage my team from following the rule book!

Don't worry, you'll get used to us in time!

Martin

From: Martin Lukes
To: Keri Tartt

Keri – how are you finding sales? Assume you're sitting there twiddling your thumbs. Can I ask a tiny favour? Don't dare ask Thelma . . . could you cash in my return air ticket from Orlando, for a ticket that stops off in Augusta?

My golf kit is also in need of upgrading . . . Basically what I need is a Callaway ERC II driver, some Callaway Hawkeye irons and the new Odyssey broom-handle putter. Two-tone Footjoys size 10 $\frac{1}{2}$. Some Hugo Boss golf-range shirts (size M) would be nice if you can find anything on special. Can you see if the UK websites can deliver them in two days, or buy from a US site, and get them delivered to my hotel?

Ta muchly M.

August 9

From: Pandora@CoachworX
To: Martin Lukes

Hi Martin – Challenging news, I'm afraid. I've just got back the feedback from your StressBusta! Tests showing your stress levels are dangerously high.

Before I feedback the results to you, I should say that I am not surprised. This sort of result is not unusual for my high-flying coachees.

Your score shows you are someone who has trouble coping with the demands of daily life, feels overwhelmed and has trouble sleeping. You are unable to relax and enjoy your non-working time.

People who score in this range cannot typically control and recognize their feelings or act on them appropriately. They can become bitter, angry and resentful.

Don't worry, Martin. There is hope!! You can decrease your level of burnout by rebalancing your life and following these tips.

1. Read books – try the classics – they're great!
2. Spend time loving your spouse.
3. Banish all negative thoughts.
4. Laugh!
5. Practice a random act of kindness every day
6. Slow down! Martin, you are a speed junky. Take some deep breaths. Relax!

Let's start with some easy wins. I want you to keep a stress diary. Recognizing your big stressors is the best way to overcome them. I also suggest you buy 200 Bio Dots. These are stick on spots (you can buy them from us at CoachworX.co.uk) that change colour to record your stress levels.

Strive and Thrive!
Pandora

August 10

From: Martin Lukes
To: Thelma Dowd

Hi – If we are going to work together successfully we need to agree on some basic parameters.

Where are all the papers that were on my desk? I'd appreciate it if you didn't move things around. Also why have you put all these internal meetings in my diary? My strategy is never to commit to any meeting unless I can see easy wins coming out of it.

Martin

From: Martin Lukes
To: Pandora@CoachworX

STRESS DIARY Day 1
Woke up to find that Svetlana had drunk the entire carton of blueberry and banana smoothies that I had bought to reduce stress. Comforted myself with the thought that she is sodding off back to Russia next week. Stress levels high. Got into work. Thelma starts talking to me about the weather.

The dot is dark purple, which is ominous.
Martin

From: Porky Perky
To: Kinky Pinky

I'm meant to be getting home at 7 this week as part of a new work–life balance jag that Pandora has me on . . . but if we're very quick, I think we could squeeze in a quick one. After all, now you are not my PA you count as 'life' not 'work'!
See you fire escape half an hour?? P xxx

From: Porky Perky
To: Kinky Pinky

Oh dear . . . that made my biodot go black – which is the highest stress you can have before you die! P xxx

From: Martin Lukes
To: Graham Wallace

I've just watched Thelma eating the large ham sandwich that she brings in every day. She opens her mouth very wide and leaves a rim of red lipstick on the white bread. Urgh. How are you getting on with Keri? Keeping your hands to yourself, I trust.
M

From: Jenny Withers
To: All Staff

I'm sure I don't need to remind you that this week is national Work–Life Balance Week! This year we are going to celebrate in style. Special features will include

• Breakfast at 7.00 am on Tuesday with the UK's number one stress guru, Professor Gary Copper. He is going to tell us how stress is this country's biggest killer, and share with us his 101 hottest stress-busting tips.

• On Wednesday we are also going to repeat last year's enormously successful Go Home On Time Day. However, we plan to make it even better by rolling it out across all departments, and posting a blacklist of co-workers who do not leave on time!

• I am also delighted to say that we shall be offering all co-workers an online grocery service. This will remove one of life's great stressors by allowing you to shop from your desk (outside normal working hours, please!!) Anyone willing to road-test the service plse message me or Faith!

Jenny

From: Martin Lukes
To: Jenny Withers

Darling – Great memo! Well done!

Would be delighted to do my bit for the WLB agenda. Why don't I share the platform with Copper and talk about my learnings? I think so often these things are women's ghettos, it would be refreshing to see a senior alpha male taking it seriously . . . Also count me in as a shopping guinea-pig . . . what groceries do we need?

Best, Martin

August 11

From: Roger Wright
To: All Staff
I am pleased to inform all staff that a-b glöbâl (UK) has been short-listed for the BT Work–Life Balance Award. This highly prestigious award is granted every year to the company with the most uniquely creative approach to Work–Life Balance. On Thursday we will have a team of judges from BT watching our work. For that day it is imperative that all staff arrive and leave promptly.
Roger Wright,
Acting Chairman.

From: Jenny Withers
To: All Staff

Hi!
There are two minor amendments to our plans for this week. Gary Copper informs me that due to excessive work pressures next week he is not going to be able to make the breakfast. However Martin Lukes has kindly agreed to step in and talk to us about 'Work–Life Balance – The Holistic Viewpoint'. I have also been informed that many of you have evening team-building workshops next week, and so will not be able to leave work on time. You will be exempted from leaving on time, and will NOT get black marks!
Cheers, Jenny

From: Martin Lukes
To: Keri Tartt

Pinky – sorry can't do tonight . . . am working on my breakfast presentation for tomorrow.
Perky

August 12

From: Martin Lukes
To: Faith Preston

Glad you enjoyed the talk!! As you know these are issues that are very close to my heart!
Martin

From: Martin Lukes
To: Help Desk

Urgent! Can somebody come down NOW and help me get my computer linked up to this supermarket thing. The screen keeps freezing. Urgent.

From: Martin Lukes
To: Help Desk

WHAT THE BLOODY HELL DO YOU MEAN – YOU'RE GOING HOME??? I WAS UNDER THE IMPRESSION THAT YOU WERE THE HELP DESK. I DON'T CARE IF IT'S 5.30. I'M A DIRECTOR OF THIS COMPANY SO GET DOWN HERE AT ONCE!!!!

August 13

From: Martin Lukes
To: Jenny Withers

For Godssakes, Jens, calm down! I've no idea why they've deliv-ered 8 six-packs of Grand Marnier chocolate mousse – I only meant to buy one. The reason I ordered 6 packets of anti-fungal shower cream was that it was on special – three for two. Great value! And the Orion DVD player was a sensational deal at only £49.95 – it's got the functionality and convenience of two

products for the price of one! And you should be delighted that I bought the Nutool cordless drill. You're always moaning that I never do any DIY. Sorry about forgetting your Cranks sunflower seed bread and the Olivio low fat spread.
Love you M xx

From: Roger Wright
To: All Staff

I'm delighted to say that a-b glöbâl (UK) is the gold medallist in the BT Work–Life Balance Day award. The judges were impressed by our 'passionate commitment to balancing work and life at every point along the value chain'.

Congratulations to all staff who facilitated the attainment of this prestigious award. Additionally, Martin Lukes was runner-up in the Individual Contribution to Work–Life Balance category. The judges found his approach an 'original contribution towards a wider understanding of where WLB fits into a global HR footprint'.
Roger Wright
Acting Chairman

From: Martin Lukes
To: Pandora@CoachworX

Fantastic news – yours truly has won an individual WLB award! Will supply details later, but thought you'd appreciate a heads-up.
22.5 per cent better than my bestest
Martin
PS Will do the stress diary when time permits.

From: Martin Lukes
To: All Staff

I just wanted to say a sincere 'thank you' to everyone who has congratulated me on my award. It is, of course a great honour.

Work–life balance is no longer an add-on to our raft of HR policies. It is the beating heart and soul of how we do things around here!

However I do feel uncomfortable at being singled out for an individual award. I feel that it was very much a team effort, and so I'd like to thank my team for the fantastic back-up they've given me. And I'd like to thank my ladywife, Jens, who, as well as masterminding our brilliant WLB day, is the 'balance' in my life!

All my very bestest

Martin Lukes

BT Outstanding Individual Contribution to Work–Life Balance (Runner Up)

From: Martin Lukes
To: Jenny Withers

Oh for Godssakes! What is wrong with the term 'ladywife'??? I just can't get it right, can I? If I mention you, you get cross, but if I didn't you'd be even crosser. It would have been nice if you had congratulated me on my award.

I've got lots of stuff to sort before we go. Would you mind taking my Paul Smith chinos to the dry cleaners, and going to the bookshop to pick me out a couple of the classics.

Pandora has prescribed it as beach reading.

Martin x

BT Outstanding Individual Contribution to Work–Life Balance (Runner Up)

From: Martin Lukes
To: Thelma Dowd

Hi Thelma – There is no need to keep sharpening my pencils nor to tidy my pens. I'm more creovative™ when the arrangement of my stationery is spontaneous.

Martin

BT Outstanding Individual Contribution to Work–Life Balance (Runner Up)

From: Porky Perky
To: Kinky Pinky

My dearest slinky pinky
I've bought you a necklace. Pandora says I must practise a random act of kindness every day.
P xx

From: Porky Perky
To: Kinky Pinky

Silly Pinky, of course it wasn't random . . . I didn't mean it like that! And yes, I did put it on my credit card, but don't worry, Jens is far too busy with her mid-life crisis and with her Professional/Personal Integration to be going through my things . . . though now I think of it, I think the receipt may be in my trouser pocket.
Pxx

From: Martin Lukes
To: Jenny Lukes

Darling – forget about the dry cleaning! In my new role as work–life balance supremo, I'll do it myself!!
Love you
M
BT Outstanding Individual Contribution to Work–Life Balance (Runner Up)

From: Martin Lukes
To: Katherine Lukes

Hi Katherine
Great to get your email! If I am 110 per cent honest I had given up hope of hearing from you. Still – better late than never!

Glad to hear that life is treating you well. Sounds like being a social worker suits you down to the ground! You don't say what's happening to you relationship-wise. It's been years since you split with Geoff?/Gregg? . . . what's been happening since then?

I wonder if you are having issues with the old biological clock? I suppose at 41 it's a bit late now for sprogglets . . . though in my experience they are a whole load of trouble!!

You suggest I come down to meet you in Brighton. Unfortunately I'm a tad tied up before we go on hols (we're off wakeboarding in Florida!) – so let's be in touch again in September
Bestest
Martin

From: Martin Lukes
To: Katherine Lukes

I see!! When you mentioned your friend Fiona, I didn't realize she was that sort of 'friend'! I don't know why you thought I'd react badly . . . I'm very open minded about these things. I've got a guy on my team who is as gay as they come, but is very good at his job.

Maybe you and Fiona would both like to come up to London for a drink when we're back from hols. We could have a 4-some with Jens – who I sometimes think has some dyky tendencies herself!!!
Martin

From: Martin Lukes
To: Phyllis Lukes
Dearest Mum
Sorry I didn't make it last night. I was involved in some grocery scheme at work (don't ask!!!) now looks like I won't see you till we're back.

I've just had a really odd email from Katherine. Did you know about 'Fiona'?? Why didn't you tell me?? It's all a bit of a shock, though I suppose fits in with the rest of her life.

Sorry this is so brief . . . you'll be proud to hear that I've won an award for my work–life balance!

Your loving son,

Martie

From: Martin Lukes
To: Phyllis Lukes

No, it doesn't mean that I am doing the housework – don't worry! It just means that I'm concentrating on all parts of my life. Prioritizing the bits that matter. I'm going to make much more time to see you, Mummy. Will come as soon as I'm back from Augusta, where I'll be teeing off with our CEO!!

Martie

From: Martin Lukes
To: Jake Lukes

Jake – just seen your message. No you can't go to Reading pop festival. You are going on holiday with us. Frankly I don't care what Tarquin or anyone else is doing. I've spent an arm and a leg on this wakeboarding holiday and you are coming for the duration. I have hardly seen you this summer, and you are spending quality time with me whether you like it or not.

Dad

From: Martin Lukes
To: Pandora@CoachworX

Stress diary 2

Sorry I haven't been keeping the diary properly. I've been totally up against it workwise. The weird thing is that I'm finding the home section of my life very stressful at present. Jake is being impossible, threatening not to come on holiday. Jens is getting more difficult by the day. And I just discovered that my sister is a dyke. Which explains a lot about her attitude to yours truly.

The only part of my life that is not stressful is golf. I played at the weekend. My biodots stayed yellow throughout.
22.5 per cent better than my bestest
Martin

BT Outstanding Individual Contribution to Work–Life Balance (Runner Up)

From: Pandora@CoachworX
To: Martin Lukes

Hi Martin
Remember I told you about words that drain your energy? Dyke is one of those. It is a negative judgment on the core values of others. You should welcome your sister's life choices, which are equally as valid as your own.

Can I also suggest a different way of communicating with your son? Often we are in too much of a hurry to realize the impact our words have upon children. Instead of blurting out, 'You're so clumsy!' or 'Why can't you be quiet?' – remarks that can powerfully undermine a child's sense of self-worth – try using humor to break his or her pattern. For example, you could say, 'If you continue on this track, I might start getting a smidge cranky,' with a smiling face.
Strive and Thrive!
Pandora

From: Martin Lukes
To: Pandora@CoachworX

Hi Pandora
I'm not sure you understand. Jake's self-worth is if anything too

high. Last time I tried the softy approach he asked if I was gay. Do you have any children yourself?

And on the subject of being gay, you get me wrong if you think I have any negative baggage on that score. Whatever turns you on!

22.5 per cent better than my bestest

Martin

BT Outstanding Individual Contribution to Work–Life Balance (Runner Up)

From: Porky Perky
To: Kinky Pinky

Pinky – we're off at lunchtime . . . I'll email, when I get a chance, I've got my BlackBerry. Make sure you take yours to Ibiza. I'm totally dreading it and being away from you. But at least it'll be our last family holiday. Porky promise.

Porky xxx

From: Martin Lukes
To: Christo Weinberg

Hi Christo

Arrived safely. Anxious to know what's going on? Can you send me a daily bulletin? Has there been any follow-up to my award?

Chrs Martin

August 17

From: Porky Perky
To: Kinky Pinky

Darling Pinky

Hotel noisy, food ropey, and I'm already missing you horribly . . . I've tried wakeboarding with the boys, and I'm pleased to say I'm better than Max, but not as good as Jake. Though I've hardly seen him since the first day . . . he's found some gorgeous little French number. She looks 18, but turns out to be 13. Jake – like his father – turns out to have a penchant for the younger woman!!

love you, miss you . . . P xxx

August 25

From: Martin Lukes
To: Pandora@CoachworX

I'm afraid the dots have been dark purple or black solidly since arrival. Jens is working flat out on a paper on our Personal/Professional Integration policy, so I've been doing more child-care than ideal. In the same hotel is the head of global market-ing at L'Oreal – who might have become a very useful contact, only Jake has ruined everything by shagging his 13-year-old daughter.

Max has started beating me at tennis, and J is so angry about my flying off to Atlanta she has stopped talking to me.

And Christo sends me almost hourly emails telling me how brilliantly he is coping in my absence.

Martin

August 26

From: Martin Lukes
To: Jenny Withers

Darling – Arrived safely in Augusta . . . all tickety boo here, though left my washbag with you, which is a nightmare as can't shave with a disposable . . . Hope you all get back to London safely. Email me news on Jake's GCSEs.

Love you, M XXX

From: Martin Lukes
To: Thelma Dowd

Hi Thelma – Am attaching all contact details, though please only use them if urgent. Can you do me a small favour? Unfortunately my washbag went back to the UK with my wife today. Could you send a cab around to my house to get it and then DHL to me asap?
Ta muchly, M

From: Martin Lukes
To: Graham Wallace

Augusta is UNBELIEVABLE – the course exquisite, most manicured in the world! I'm staying in the Log Cabin – my room is right next door to BSM and the others are all in an annexe. Cindy C is here too – strutting her stuff disgustingly. I didn't even realize she played golf – turns out she's a single handicap!!!!
M

August 27

From: Martin Lukes
To: Jenny Withers

CHRIST! Didn't that bloody school teach him ANYTHING? I've spent an arm and a leg on his education. And WHY the HELL did you phone the headmaster without consulting me? It is much better that these approaches come from me. I'll email him now.

From: Martin Lukes
To: Headmaster@MillgateSchool

Dear Mr Pitman
I understand that my son Jake has achieved only two Bs and two Cs at GCSE. I also understand that you spoke with my wife this

morning and informed her that you would not be able to offer the lad a place in the sixth form.

I believe that the boy has considerable creovative™ talents, and his poor results do not reflect a lack of ability, but issues with concentration.

He has grown up a lot over this summer, and I anticipate that these issues are now in the past. Going forward, I see Jake being a member of your school community who would excel in all areas.

I therefore believe it would be in the interests not just of my son, but of the school, for the lad to be given a place in the sixth form.

I am currently in the US, at a top level meeting with our CEO. However I would be happy to meet with you on my return to discuss how we progress this.

Yours sincerely
Martin Lukes
Marketing Director
a-b glöbâl (UK)
BT Outstanding Individual Contribution to Work–Life Balance (Runner Up)

From: Martin Lukes
To: Thelma Dowd

FRANKLY THELMA I AM NOT INTERESTED IN WHO AUTHORIZES THE EXPENSE. I AM A DIRECTOR OF THIS COMPANY AND I NEED MY SPONGE BAG. WOULD BE GRATEFUL IF YOU GOT IT SORTED ASAP.

From: Martin Lukes
To: Graham Wallace

Hi Graham – How goes it?
Yours truly has just played the game of a lifetime. The 12th hole is unbelievably tricky – and I got a birdie! And as if that wasn't enough, Cindy totally screwed up Amen Corner – topped the

tee shot on the 12th and then sliced her second on the 13th into the trees!!! BSM obviously impressed – put his arm around my shoulders practically crushing me to death and said: 'I just love this guy.' You should have seen the look Keith gave me. I think we've got it wrong about Barry. He's tough when he has to be but he's actually very sincere and has even got a wicked sense of humour!

Janine – that Fortune journalist – was there too. She's rather sexy in that scrawny American way. She's working on another article – in which yours truly may figure!

Mart

From: Martin Lukes
To: Jenny Withers

Jens –
Pitman isn't playing ball and had the cheek to suggest that the reason Jake didn't do better in his GCSEs is that he doesn't have the support at home. I said that I didn't pay £13,000 a year to educate him myself. Everything great here. It was definitely a good call to come. Sat next to BSM in his private plane on the way back to Atlanta, had a fascinating chat about a-b glöbâl, the world, the universe, everything. I never realized what a really nice guy he is –
Love M xx

August 29

From: Martin Lukes
To: Jenny Withers

Jens – Have been trying to work out what job Barry has in mind for me, and am left with the distinct idea that he doesn't see me as UK chairman at all. I think he's got something bigger up his sleeve here in Atlanta. Possibly Keith's job, which explains why Keith has been so short with me. It'd be brilliant for the whole

family to move here. It'd solve Jake's schooling issue. Max would come to visit us for the hols, and I'm sure you could always do something in the HQ press office. Whaddya think?
Love you, M XX

From: Martin Lukes
To: Keri Tartt

Your Porky is on his way home!!! Am coming straight in off the red-eye tomorrow. Can you book the Novotel for tomorrow pm? Corporal salutes you etc.
Perky xx

August 30

From: Martin Lukes
To: Barry S. Malone

Hi Barry, Just to say the last few days have been a ball for me! I am now back in London incredibly energized and am already setting up a scheme to roll out our blueprint for personal and organization consciousness across the UK company. Will keep you in the loop!
Cheers, Martin

From: Martin Lukes
To: All Directors

I have just spent a fascinating four days with our CEO and would like to debrief you on the essence of the many conversations we shared. Top of Barry's mind right now is the issue of how to drive value creation in the 21st C while unleashing our spiritual mission. I have attached a memo outlining our thinking and would be happy to discuss how we make it actionable.
Martin

From: Martin Lukes
To: Jenny Withers

Oh Jesus. That's all we need. Has his passport gone too? I bet the randy little sod has gone off in search of Solange. Perhaps you'd better email her father. On second thoughts, I'll do it. It'll look better coming from me, and my French is better than yours. M

From: Martin Lukes
To: Thelma Dowd

Have you got a French dictionary to hand?

From: Martin Lukes
To: Jean-MichelBon@loreal

Salut Jean-Michel!
    Nous avons passe un trés bon vacances avec votre famille. J'espere que vous etes en bon sante. Si vous avez aucunes questions sur les 'marketing breakthroughs' n'hesitez pas de demander a moi! Je suis toujours heureux de vous aider.
    J'ai un petit question pour vous. Avez vous aucune idee ou est mon fils? Il est disparu, et ma femme et moi-meme sont un peu inquietes. A-t-il dit quelquechose a Solange?
    Mille mille mercis, Martin

From: Martin Lukes
To: Jenny Withers

Just got an answer (in JM's pathetic English) saying he has absolutely no idea about Jake's whereabouts, and that Solange is forbidden from having any contact with him. M

From: Martin Lukes
To: Roger Wright

Roger – Yes, the £129 on my expenses was for a courier to deliver a vital package to myself in Atlanta. Given the work I did as ambassador for a-b glöbâl UK, I have issues around such small-mindedness. As Barry said to me, our purpose is to co-create a company where breakthrough experiences happen every day! You can't achieve this if you are flapping about minor expense items.
Martin

From: Martin Lukes
To: Jenny Withers

Well at least he's safe. Where did he get the money from??

From: Martin Lukes
To: Jake Lukes

JAKE – I AM BEYOND ANGRY. YOU HAVE STOLEN MONEY, DISOBEYED ORDERS AND CAUSED YOUR MOTHER AND MYSELF SERIOUS WORRY. YOU ARE GROUNDED AND YOUR ALLOWANCE IS STOPPED UNTIL FURTHER NOTICE.

YOU MAY BE INTERESTED TO KNOW THAT AS A RESULT OF YOUR PATHETIC EXAM RESULTS YOUR SCHOOL DOES NOT WANT YOU BACK. YOUR YOUNGER BROTHER FACES A BRILLIANT FUTURE AT ETON. YOU WILL DO WELL TO GET INTO TOOTING SIXTH FORM COLLEGE. I HAVE FOUGHT FOR YOU UNTIL NOW, BUT NOW FRANKLY YOU'VE GOT WHAT YOU DESERVE.
DAD

August 31

From: Martin Lukes
To: Pandora@CoachworX

Hi Pandora
It's been a very odd month. Some humungous wins, and some challenges. Basically I believe that I am now better placed than at any point in my career to date – I think a huge job is in the offing for me. Not Roger's job, but something bigger.

My stress levels have been high, but I've reached the conclusion that I am the kind of guy who likes stress. It just isn't a stressor for me.

We have had issues at home, but I think we have come through them and learnt something along the way! I feel I have shared some of my experience with Jake and that he will grow from it going forward.

A reflection, if you will. Golf is the perfect form of work–life balance. It is half work and half life, and very balanced.

At the end of the day, I don't think your biodots have anything to bring to the party. I am going to give them to Jens so that she can monitor her anger going forward.
22.5 per cent better than my bestest
Martin

Chapter Nine

September
My Development Opportunities

September 1

From: Pandora@CoachworX
To: Martin Lukes

Hi Martin!
When I spoke to you on the telephone just now I thought –
wow! This is a guy who is really going places! I can almost
smell your self-belief. And you know what, Martin? It is that
self-belief that is making everyone love you right now. It is
what is going to make your CEO want you at the very heart
of his top team.

But we're not there yet! So far we have worked hard on
your values, your dreams, your body, your heart. Now we are
going to peep onto the other half of the balance sheet and
meditate on your Less Strong Strengths. Martin, what do you
think they are? Are they holding you back?

I would like today to contact some of the people who know
you really well, and ask them where they think your
Development Opportunities lie. Then we'll have a baseline,
and can move forward from there.
Strive and thrive!
Pandora

From: Martin Lukes
To: Pandora@CoachworX

Hi Pandora

Absolutely no problem at all, only I'm not sure who you planned on asking. I don't think Roger has the emotional intelligence to be able to read other people. And Thelma hasn't had time to get to know me yet. If you want someone who really understands what makes yours truly tick, then Graham Wallace is your man.

Re my own take on my Development Opportunities – can I mull over for a day or two and get back to you?
22.5 per cent better than my bestest
Martin

From: Martin Lukes
To: Jenny Withers

Darling –
I know you're up against it . . . you seem to be working on 5 million different projects . . . Why don't I take Max down to Eton for his first day of term?
Martin xx
PS If Pandora contacts you about my weaknesses, can you try to be a tiny bit nice??

September 2

From: Martin Lukes
To: Phyllis Lukes

Dearest Mum,
Thanks for your message . . . yes it was lovely to see you on Saturday. Hope the curtain rail is still up . . . as I said, I think your curtains are a touch on the heavy side, and the wall is a bit soft, but fingers crossed!

Took Max off to Eton yesterday. He looked great in his black tail-coat. Totally confident, as if he owned the place. And guess who we bumped into? The man who does one of those decorating programmes on the telly that you like so much! He's got a son who was also starting – which was a surprise because I had him down as a shirtlifter! Max is also in the same house as some member of the Saudi royal family as well as the son of the head of Goldman Sachs in London – so a pretty diverse crowd!

Jake starts tomorrow at Tooting sixth-form college, and seems fairly positive about it. He's got some working out to do about who he is and where he's going, though that's not unusual for a lad that age. He finds his mother quite difficult, at the moment, but our relationship is quite strong . . . he just needs some space.
Your loving son
Martie

September 3

From: Martin Lukes
To: Provost@EtonCollege

Dear Provost
I'm so sorry our conversation got interrupted yesterday – it was all a bit of a scrum. As I explained, I'm Martin Lukes, Marketing Director of a-b glöbâl (UK), father of Max, one of your scholars.

Following on from what we were saying, I'm a great believer in partnership between business and education. We should join hands to pool best practice and enjoy the synergies, if you will. From your brochure, I see that last term you attracted speakers from the 'Arts World' including Jonathan Miller and Judi Dench, and on the sciences side you had Richard Dawkins (I have issues with his take on genetics, but that's another story). However, you do not appear to have any individuals from the business arena talking to the boys. This is a shame, not just for the boys themselves but for the world at large. We hope most of these boys will be adding value for UK plc (or Saudi Arabia plc) going forward!!

I would be delighted to assist by throwing some names into

the ring – John Browne, CEO of BP, happens to be a personal friend, or my own esteemed CEO, Barry S. Malone, would be only too delighted to help. Alternatively, if you did not want a 'Big Name' I myself would be honoured to offer the boys break-out workshops on creovation™.

As you know, most business people today are on the go 24/7/365, but I'm sure I could sort something out!

Your sincerely

Martin Lukes

From: Martin Lukes
To: Provost@EtonCollege

Dear Provost

Thanks for getting back to me so quickly. Further to your inquiry, the reason you could not find the word creovation™ in the Longer Oxford Dictionary is that it is a new concept. It is a unique blend of creativity and innovation and, since being developed by myself, it has been taken up by many leading-edge companies where it has found a growing resonance. I'd be happy to take the time to talk you through the concepts behind it, as it has implications for your own institution.

Best wishes, Martin

September 5

From: Martin Lukes
To: Pandora@CoachworX

Hi Pandora

Sorry for the delay. I always find it challenging thinking about my weaknesses – but I've tried to be very honest, and really dish the dirt!

1. I have an issue around not tolerating fools gladly. If I sense some-one is a lot less perceptive or forward-thinking than myself, I can seem a tad dismissive. Example? I suggested to the Provost of Eton

College that the lads should be taught creovation™. He had some difficulty grasping the concept. Although I was very polite to him, I could feel inside that I was withholding my approval.

2. I have a low boredom threshold. Because I am interested in driving change, I can get bored and frustrated when change is too slow. Basically that's my issue with Roger. He's a boring guy. End of story.

3. Because I set the bar very high for myself, I can sometimes get a bit frustrated if other people don't live up to the same standards. This is an issue in my relationship with Jake – it also may be a problem with Thelma going forward.

That's all for now. If I think of any others, I'll let you know!
22.5 per cent better than my bestest
Martin

From: Porky Perky
To: Kinky Pinky

Pinky . . . please don't put pressure on me. I WILL tell her. I'll do it when the time is right. I know I said as soon as Max had started at Eton, but I didn't mean immediately. I'll try to leave at 6 tonite and we can have a couple of hours before I go home
Kisses and more
Porky

From: Pandora@CoachworX
To: Martin Lukes

Hi Martin!
Before I feedback the – fascinating – results from the little exercise you've done, I want to share with you my disappointment.

Martin, you know what I feel about the negative. It has no place in Executive Bronze! We are NOT talking about your weaknesses. I never allow my coachees to say the w-word. It is banned on this program! All your characteristics are strengths, but some of them are less strong than some of the others! Once we get rid of the idea that we are discussing something negative, you'll be amazed at how much progress we can make to living your dream of being 22.5 per cent better than the very best you can be!

Now the feedback. I've kept the responses anonymous because people were more prepared to be completely frank on a no-names basis.

One less strong strength that various people flagged up was listening. It seems that you have serious issues in listening to what other people are saying. Don't worry Martin. We can fix that!

Another issue is around anger. My feedback suggests that you can have a short fuse!

It was also suggested that there were other issues – around snobbery, envy, ego, cynicism, lack of attention to detail, laziness, status anxiety – however I think we will leave those for another day and zero in on anger for now.

Anger is something we feel when our values have been violated. Mostly, when we get angry, the cause is not what we think it is. So next time you feel angry, Martin, get a little curious, and ask yourself: Why do I feel this? Which of my values has just been violated?

Then I want you to close your eyes and breathe. In – out – in – out – in – out. Ten times. When you have done that, you are ready to draw your anger. This can help let the toxins out of your brain. Once the toxins are out, you can start to deal with it in a more positive way!
Strive and Thrive!
Pandora

From: Martin Lukes
To: Pandora@CoachworX

Who said all that??? Have you been talking to my wife, by any chance? Completely fucking typical (if you'll pardon my French) that she would bad mouth me. You have probably sussed out

that we aren't exactly getting on like a house on fire at the present moment in time. Who else has been slagging me off?
Martin

From: Pandora@CoachworX
To: Martin Lukes
Remember, Martin . . . positive words only!! Expletives drain your energy source. As I said these are NOT negatives, and I don't feel it would be fair to name the people. They are all close to you, and all want to help you be better than your best! Strive and thrive!
Pandora

September 8

From: Barry S. Malone
To: All Staff

Howdy!
Over the past months we have taken many big steps towards our goal of Phenomenal Performance – Permanently. The biggest of these is viewing ourselves as a global family that is truly world class. That does not just mean picking players from Atlanta, or London or Tokyo. It means picking peak-performing players from every geography – in particular it means searching countries such as India for members to join our family. Many companies have taken the route of offshoring parts of their business. But that is not what we are doing. We are rightshoring. We are looking for the right shore to base certain business functions. We are looking for the right home for new members of our family.

We will approach this as creovatively as possible. This represents a phenomenal opportunity for us, and I know all of you will be as excited about this as I am.

I shall be leading a small team to India next week to visit various sites, and will keep you notified of all developments going forward.
I love you all
Barry

From: Martin Lukes
To: Graham Wallace

Sounds ominous – though marketing isn't something that you can expect cheap labour in India to get their heads around. Sales much more vulnerable . . . last two months' figures totally tanking, so if I were you I'd be very afraid. We work our arses off here in marketing, but where does it get us if you guys don't get out and sell???

Btw did you tell a whole bunch of evil lies to Pandora re yours truly??
Martin
PS Drink?

From: Martin Lukes
To: Barry S. Malone

Hi Barry
Many thanks for your message! I would be delighted to take part in the Indian trip. The subcontinent has always been close to my heart, and I am strongly in favour of offshoring as much as economically feasible. Diversity is one of our greatest challenges, and obviously in India the entire population is diverse! All my very bestest, Martin
PS Please onpass my best wishes to the charming Randee.

From: Martin Lukes
To: Jenny Withers

Jens – very exciting . . . I've just been asked to go on Barry's road show to India next week!! Basically, this is the most important project that the company has undertaken since ABC, and he wants me at the heart of it! This is going to broaden and deepen my relationship with him. Neither Keith nor Cindy are going . . . feels like I'm cruising past them on the inside lane . . .
Martin

From: Martin Lukes
To: Jenny Withers

How was I supposed to know you were going to the Diverse
High Potentials symposium in Dortmund? I don't remember that
being in the diary. In any case it's only Jake at home, and he'll
be fine with Svetlana.
M

September 9

From: Martin Lukes
To: Thelma Dowd

Hi Thelma – Can you Google 'India' and 'outsourcing' and get
me some facts and figures? I want to be able to blind BSM with
science! Also can you sort jabs and flights, visa, security situation, etc.
Ta muchly,
Martin

From: Martin Lukes
To: Thelma Dowd

WHY IN GOD'S NAME HAVE I BEEN SENT ECONOMY
TICKETS??? Can you get them changed asap?
Martin
PS I'm nearly out of business cards – will need more by tomor-
row . . .

From: Martin Lukes
To: Pandora@CoachworX

Hi Pandora – Potential anger situation over the air tickets. I've
meditated on the cause of my anger and you're wrong – I AM
angry over what I think I am angry over: travelling fucking econ-

omy. And the value that's been violated is: Thou shalt not travel economy on business. Anyway, I've taken a deep breath and drawn a picture of myself cooped up all night in economy, which if anything has made me ever crosser. Now I am going to send a cool logical email to Roger.
Martin

From: Martin Lukes
To: Roger Wright

Hi Roger
As you will be aware, I am participating in the top-level team travelling to Bangalore next week to investigate offshoring opportunities. I have been informed that for this trip, which will require my energy levels and my thinking capacity to be in excess of 110 per cent, I will have to travel economy. I believe this to be a short-sighted saving. I request you to authorize club class tickets.
Best, Martin

September 10

From: Martin Lukes
To: Katherine Lukes

Hi Katherine
Thanks for your email. Sorry to hear you've lost your job. Is the council cutting back generally? Fraid I can't do the 12th for our grand reunion . . . I'm off on a trip to India with our CEO. It's all very hush hush, but as you're not likely to be meeting anyone in the know, I can tell you that basically we are going to fire all our call centre and other non-core workers and employ cheap Indian labour instead. All v sensitive, and calls for a lot of tact in handling.

    Will be in touch on my return.
Martin
PS rgds to Fiona!

From: Martin Lukes
To: Thelma Dowd

WHAT'S WITH THESE NEW BUSINESS CARDS??? MINE IS
COMPLETELY USELESS BECAUSE IT HASN'T GOT MY
BLOODY TITLE ON IT. CALL STATIONARY AND GET
THEM TO SORT IT OUT ASAP. M

From: Martin Lukes
To: Thelma Dowd

I don't believe I'm hearing this! They're MEANT to be like that?
M

From: *Jenny Withers*
To: *All Staff*

*I would like to explain the thinking behind our exciting new business
cards, which you should be receiving today. You will notice that the
section that used to bear a title is now left blank. This is because each
individual member of the a-b glöbâl family is an ambassador for our
company.*

*One of the building blocks of our new culture is respect. Having
titles on cards is not aligned with that value.*
Jenny

From: Martin Lukes
To: Jenny Withers

I DO NOT FUCKING BELIEVE THIS. NOT ONLY IS THIS
MILES OUTSIDE YOUR REMIT . . . IT'S TOTALLY FUCKING
LOONEY TUNES. YOU DON'T SERIOUSLY BELIEVE ANY
OF THAT TWADDLE DO YOU????

IS THIS ANOTHER MAD AND DEMENTED ATTEMPT
OF YOURS TO SCUPPER MY CAREER OR WHAT??

From: Martin Lukes
To: Keith Buxton

Hi Keith –
Long time, no hear. Hope all is well in Atlanta. As you know
I'm pretty snowed under ahead of the Bangalore trip, which
promises to be interesting!

I wanted to contact you re the plan to remove titles from business cards, which my wife informs me she and your good self
have been working on co-jointly.

As you know, I am one of the least hierarchical directors on
this board. I passionately believe the flatter the structure, the
better. However, our business cards are tools for the outside
world. The people we meet need to know in functional terms
who it is they are dealing with. Withholding that information
makes it harder for us to do our jobs effectively.
Martin

From: Martin Lukes
To: Pandora@CoachworX

Pandora –
I'm totally fucking FURIOUS! I've drawn a picture of my
feelings which was a great big scribble. It didn't make me feel
any better, and all I've done is ruin the nib on my Mont Blanc
pen. I've lost two battles today, one over my economy ticket
and one over business cards. It makes me UNBELIEVABLY
hacked off to know that I give my all to this fucking place and
I get rewarded by meanness and some of the worst decision
making in the world . . .

I'm trying to be better than my best, but it's bloody hard.
Martin

From: Martin Lukes
To: Keri Tartt

Keri – fraid can't have our meeting tonight. I've got too much to do . . . will touch base tomorrow.
Martin

From: Porky Perky
To: Kinky Pinky

Dinky Pinky – Don't be like that . . . the reason I sent you a cold email was that I was using work email. We need to be unbelievably careful. Please understand – this trip is make or break for me with BSM. I really need my beauty sleep tonight. Will bring you back a lovely pressie from India.
Porky xxx

September 12

From: Martin Lukes
To: Graham Wallace

Hi Graham
Greetings from sunny Bangalore! Guess what I can see from my bedroom??? A beautiful golf course!! Sky is blue and it's 79 degrees. Barry was on the same flight from London – just as well I went economy – because he was in economy too. I didn't even see he was on the plane until I was well into my third g+t, a bit embarrassing as he was on the water. He's brought that Fortune journalist Janine with him. Apparently she's writing an article about this, too!
Cheers, M

From: Porky Perky
To: Kinky Pinky

Darling Pinky – Arrived safely, though knackered after the flight.
For now it's the minibar and Terminator 3. Will msg tomorrow.
Please don't be cross with me . . . Love you, M xx

From: Martin Lukes
To: Jenny Withers

Darling Jens – Arrived safely, though knackered after the flight.
For now it's the minibar and Terminator 3. Will msg tomorrow.
Please don't be cross with me . . . Love you, M xx

September 13

From: Martin Lukes
To: Barry S. Malone

Hi Barry,
Great meeting just now with Sanjay Balasubramanian. I'm
confident that by going the captive route we can ensure we get
210 per cent buy-in to our core values. However, I do feel there
are some communication issues and we need to be proactive in
addressing these.

   Suggestion. I feel it would be helpful if I sent a daily debrief
to the folks at home – something quite chatty in style, a bit like
a letter, to be posted on the intranet. This would facilitate wider
ownership/comprehension of the global process.

   Are you eating in the pavilion dining room later?
Bestest, Martin
btw, I see there is no meeting tomorrow am, so how about a
round of golf? Shall I ask some of the GE guys to join us?

From: Martin Lukes
To: Pandora@CoachworX

Hi Pandora
Incredibly embarrassing thing happened last night. I was sitting
on the edge of my bed with my eyes shut and chanting 'I feel
calm, I feel fabulous, I feel marvellous, I can do anything, I can
be anything' – exactly as you told me, when Barry came in. As
I had my eyes closed I didn't realize he was standing there.

At first I thought that was me done for. But it turns out that
he does the same thing himself! He says that he started working with his coach on his own self-esteem 20 years ago, so he's
a shining example of where it gets you!!
22.5 per cent better than my bestest
Martin

From: Martin Lukes
To: Graham Wallace

Stop press! Barry and Janine definitely an item. They keep disap-
pearing together . . . he turns off his mobile . . . supposedly to
conduct in-depth interviews . . .
Mart

From: Martin Lukes
To: Barry S. Malone

Hi Barry, just seen your message. Never mind about supper
tonight. That's fine for a 5.30 am breakfast tomorrow. See you
then – if I don't run into you in the gym beforehand!
Bestest, Martin

From: Martin Lukes
To: All Staff

Namaste! (as they say in these parts!)

This is Day Two of the rightshoring fact-finding mission fronted by Barry Malone and my good self. We felt it would be helpful to keep you in the loop with a daily email. This morning we visited the captive operations of GE. The place was incredible – really quiet, really clean. The Indian can-do headset is totally mind-boggling. These people smile all the time, nothing's too much trouble.

They have no issues around pay, as low salaries are part of the unique culture. I have attached a paper from McKinsey on the economics of BPO showing that this really is win-win. Namaste!
Martin

September 14

From: Porky Perky
To: Kinky Pinky

Dearest Pinky
Still no emails from you. And when I tried to call on your mobile it was turned off. Please don't sulk at me.

Sky is blue here, and everything fine, except that I am lonely in my big hotel bed. I've bought you a beautiful sari at the hotel shop (cost an arm and a leg) and a Nehru suit for myself, so we can play dressing-up when you get home. I thought you could wear it with no knickers and I'll unwrap you.
Love you, Perky

From: Porky Perky
To: Kinky Pinky

That's not very grateful! It's a lovely turquoise colour, which I thought would be nice with your eyes. Actually, the Nehru suit is a great hit – plenty of positive feedback from the shop assistants! Perky xx

September 15

From: Martin Lukes
To: All Staff

Subject: Banglore briefing note 2
Namaste!!

As I get to know this place better, I'm aware of how many profound misunderstandings there are about the Indian culture.

The first is about skillsets. These people are actually highly intelligent and educated! I had dinner last night with an Indian guy who was fascinated by my take on viral marketing. Not only did he speak really good English but has an MBA from Harvard!

The level of passion for work is really energizing.

The other observation is about corner shops – paradoxically there aren't any here at all. It's totally ironic that Indians have cornered (!) the market in corner shops in Britain, while the market here is wide open. An opportunity for some creovative [34] entrepreneur! Please don't hesitate to message Barry or myself if you have any questions.

Namaste!
Martin Lukes

From: Martin Lukes
To: Graham Wallace

Hi Graham
Thanks for your message. You're quite right – basically thousands of jobs will go in the US and UK, but only at junior level. For you and me, it'll be fine.

You'd love it here. Some of the girls are gorgeous though not very available. The cute little thing who cleans my room gave me a meaningful smile last night, but when I reciprocated she didn't want to know. Ironic she should be so uptight when this is the home of the Kama Sutra! Believe me, it's a land of paradoxes.
Martin

From: Martin Lukes
To: Thelma Dowd

Hi Thelma, Got back last night totally shattered. I'm off the caffeine, but a mint tea would be great if you can find such a thing . . .
Martin
PS I've got a gift for you – it's by your desk.

From: Martin Lukes
To: Thelma Dowd

Oh dear, you weren't meant to see the card! You're right, I did buy it originally for someone else but decided to give it to you instead! Actually she's smaller than you – but the good thing about saris is it's one size fits all!
Martin

From: Martin Lukes
To: Thelma Dowd

Goodness gracious me (as they say in India!) I didn't mean to be size-ist. Though as a matter of fact I noticed many Indian matrons – much larger than you! – who looked very good in saris. Where's that tea?
Martin

From: Porky Perky
To: Kinky Pinky

Please, my lovely kinkypinky. Let me take you out to supper somewhere nice tonight? Jens has her reading group. They are reading this book called The Closed Circle, all about couples splitting up, and last night she read me out this bit where this successful man, who has a beautiful wife, starts shagging his sexy

young assistant. She was looking for my response, but I made a big point of putting the plates in the dishwasher (big brownie marks, there) and said he sounded a cad . . .
Perky x

September 20

From: Barry S. Malone
To: All Staff

Hi Co-Leaders!
Following the hugely successful visit last week to Bangalore, we now have a road map in place for rightshoring as many of our functionalities as practicable. The intention is to aggressively realign our resources by opening two offshore satellite centres each of which will help deliver our goal of insane profitability.

By moving non-core and low-risk tasks to Indian developers we will be able to focus on maintaining edge across the board. It will also make us more flexible: we can add and subtract resources for ramp-ups and ramp-downs.

I have tasked Martin Lukes with feeding back more detail from the trip.
I love you all
Barry

From: Martin Lukes
To: Barry S. Malone

Hi Barry
Can I just say what a highly inspirational memo that was! You said some things that badly needed saying. The tone was 140 per cent spot-on! I believe there is now a window we can leverage to facilitate buy-in from those who have issues around rightshoring. I plan to hold a creovative™ series of lunchtime master-classes with video conferencing links to other geographies so that all our co-colleagues can share the learnings.
My bestest, Martin

September 21

From: Martin Lukes
To: Faith Preston

Hi Faith
Thanks for your message. Yes, I can see you are worried about HR being outsourced lock, stock and barrel. However, what I'm saying to all co-colleagues who are asking me is that I suggest a shift in the mindset from 'I' to 'we'. So you shouldn't ask what this means for you as an individual, but for the company as a whole. Viewed like that, rightshoring is very much the right option!
Martin
PS What's the name of that young Indian woman who has just joined HR?

From: Martin Lukes
To: Christo Weinberg

Hi Christo
I've got a great opportunity for you! Would you like to take my place at the annual Maverick Marketing conference in Milton Keynes and give a paper on Customer Relationship Marketing? I can email you the presentation I gave last year. It was way ahead of the curve then, so if you tweak it a bit, it should still be pretty leading edge this year.
Cheers, Martin

From: Martin Lukes
To: All Staff

Hi!
There has been a phenomenal level of interest in the trip fronted by myself and Barry to Bangalore. To enable everyone to take ownership of the process I shall be leading a series of five lunchtime

masterclasses. These are entitled, Believe in Bangalore! Bangalore Buy-In! Benchmark Bangalore! Breakthrough Bangalore! I believe they will address all key issues in a compelling and thought-provoking way. The first one is scheduled for Wednesday. There will be a live link to other geographies, featuring a guest appearance from Barry. Book early to avoid disappointment!
My best, Martin Lukes

From: Martin Lukes
To: Ameera Ali

Hi Ameera
As you may know, I've have just returned from a trip to Bangalore with our CEO. I wondered if you'd like to come along as a guest speaker at my first masterclass? It'll be really informal – I'd just like you to share your personal experience of India and talk about your nation's unique headset and so on. It'd be your chance for fame and stardom as the CEO himself will be joining in, hopefully!
Best, Martin

From: Martin Lukes
To: Ameera Ali

I see. Of course I realize you are British, but I didn't know your family originally hailed from Pakistan. Still I hope you'll come along and enjoy a samosa!
Martin

From: Martin Lukes
To: Keri Tartt

In haste – Corporal has got a plan . . . he could spend the whole night training with his Private on Tues . . .

From: Martin Lukes
To: Jenny Withers

Darling – I'm going to be away from home for one night on Tuesday at the Milton Keynes conference. It'll be v boring but I'm obliged to show my face.
Love you M xx

September 22

From: Martin Lukes
To: Jake Lukes

Jake – I understand that while I have been away you have failed to show up at college at all. Starting today, I am implementing the following remedial four-prong action plan.
1. You are grounded until further notice.
2. I have spoken with the principal of yr college. He will notify myself of your attendance daily.
3. Your allowance is cut to zero.
4. Your mobile phone is confiscated.
5. We will review the above on a weekly timeframe going forward.
Dad

From: Martin Lukes
To: Jenny Withers

Jens – I've dealt with Jake. In situations like these I find hard cop works much better than soft cop.

Have you seen my BlackBerry anywhere? I seem to have lost it. I am supposed to be going to McKinsey today for a mega session to kick around some ideas with their top guys on offshoring . . . I can't be out of touch for the whole afternoon.
M xx

From: Martin Lukes
To: Thelma Dowd

Hi Thelma – Has anyone been trying to contact me apart from this Bupa guy? If he calls again, can you say I'm still out of the country?

Fascinating session at McKinsey – I've left their reports on your desk. Can you turn some of the data into nice colour slides for my masterclass – I want a few charts, broken up with a few pics of smiling Indian people.
Martin
Could you nip up to the vending machine and get me some curry-flavoured Doritos?

From: Martin Lukes
To: Thelma Dowd

moron
Sent from my BlackBerry Wireless Handheld

From: Martin Lukes
To: Thelma Dowd

Frankly, Thelma, you've lost me this time. Industrial tribunal? What are you talking about? If you feel that strongly about it, I'll get the crisps myself. Martin

From: Martin Lukes
To: Keri Tartt

You sexy bitch. I want to fuck you right now!
Sent from my BlackBerry Wireless Handheld

From: Martin Lukes
To: Keri Tartt

Pinky, darling, you know I love it when you talk dirty like that
. . . but what brought that on? . . . Actually not really feeling like
it now as the coporal is a bit under the weather and I'm snowed
under with this McKinsey outsourcing report. Tomorrow or day
after?
Perky xx

From: Martin Lukes
To: Graham Wallace

Hi Graham – It's hormone city here. The women in this place
are losing it. First Thelma flies off the handle about a bland
memo I sent her. She's threatening me with legal action . . . and
something's up with Keri. Does she seem normal to you today?
M

From: Martin Lukes
To: Roger Wright

dickhead
Sent from my BlackBerry Wireless Handheld

From: Martin Lukes
To: Roger Wright

Hi Roger, Sure, I'll come up now. What did you want to see me
about? I hope it's not the India expenses? Barry has signed off
on them, so they are all on HQ's budget.

From: Martin Lukes
To: Jenny Withers

I've got a wicked little secret that you don't know about. Would
you like to know it?
Sent from my BlackBerry Wireless Handheld

From: Martin Lukes
To: Jenny Withers

Jens, can you help me here? You have ignored me since I got back from India, and now you send me a message saying 'not particularly'? Not particularly what??
Martin

From: Martin Lukes
To: Martin Lukes

Liar, wanker, plonker
Sent from my BlackBerry Wireless Handheld

From: Martin Lukes
To: Martin Lukes

JAKE DID YOU JUST SEND ME A MESSAGE FROM MY BLACKBERRY?? FEAR FOR YOUR LIFE IF YOU DID.

From: Martin Lukes
To: Systems

Can you disable my BlackBerry now??? Urgent.

From: Martin Lukes
To: Jenny Withers

DISASTER . . . JAKE'S GOT MY BLACKBERRY . . . HELP!!!!

From: Martin Lukes
To: All Staff

Some individuals have been receiving bogus messages apparently from myself sent on my BlackBerry hand-held device, which was stolen this morning. The thief has gained access to the security

code and has been sending prankster emails. If you receive any such messages please ignore. I apologize for any confusion caused.
Martin Lukes

From: Martin Lukes
To: Jake Lukes

JAKE – I AM BEYOND FURY – SUGGEST YOU DO NOT ATTEMPT TO COME HOME UNLESS YOU ARE PREPARED TO UNDERGO A ROOT AND BRANCH PERSONAL REBRANDING. I HAVE ALERTED EVERYONE IN MY ADDRESS BOOK TO IGNORE ANY 'JOKE' MESSAGES FROM YOU SO THERE IS NO POINT IN SEND-ING ANY FURTHER. SHOULD YOU DO SO, HOWEVER, I SHALL CONSIDER THIS TO BE FRAUD AND ALERT THE POLICE.
DAD

From: Martin Lukes
To: Martin Lukes

Wow . . . like I'm like so scared. Not. Though you should be, coz I'm just about to forward an interesting message out of your in box to mum . . . something about pinky? Sounds a bit fishy to me, dad. J
Sent from my BlackBerry Wireless Handheld

From: Martin Lukes
To: Systems

I DON'T FUCKING CARE IF YOU ARE SHORT-STAFFED TODAY. DISABLE MY BLACKBERRY NOW.

From: Martin Lukes
To: Jenny Withers

Here's a message from someone called 'pinky' sent to someone called 'perky'. I think you might find it interesting

From: Kinky Pinky
To: Porky Perky

My cutey, chunky, porky Perky
Pinky's feeling happy again!! Cool to spend the whole nite with u on wed. Sorry I gave u such a hard time . . . it's just I love u and want us to be together – which I no we will be 1 day!! It's hard for little Pinky going to bed on her own every night, knowing u are in bed with Jenny. Private P gets lonely . . . But I am going to be a big brave patient piggie. Loveya loveya loveya loads!!
Pinky xxxx

Fishy, huh?
Sent from my BlackBerry Wireless Handheld

From: Martin Lukes
To: Jenny Withers

Darling, This isn't what you think. We need to talk now. M xx

From: Martin Lukes
To: Thelma Dowd

Thelma – something has come up. I need to go home for a bit. Can you cancel the Bangalore masterclass?
Martin

From: Martin Lukes
To: Graham Wallace

Catastrophe – I've just been chucked out by the wife. Can I kip down with you tonight?

From: Martin Lukes
To: Jenny Withers

Darling . . . Please, can we just talk about it? I can really explain everything. Please. I'm sorry.
Love you
Martin

From: Martin Lukes
To: Graham Wallace

OK, quite understand. But I thought Lynne quite liked me. I suppose it reminds her of your scene with Lucinda . . . are you sure you can't talk her round? I suppose I'll have to move in with Keri, not sure I'm ready for anything so heavy. I need a drink. NOW.

From: Martin Lukes
To: Pandora@CoachworX

Pandora. Something really terrible has happened. I would rather not discuss on email or phone. Can I come and see you?
Martin

From: Porky Perky
To: Kinky Pinky

Pinky darling – Jens has kicked me out. I'll bring my stuff round to you tonight as an interim arrangement, and then we can see how things go. Perky xx

From: Martin Lukes
To: Keri Tartt

Of course I love you and want to marry you, you know that. I just didn't want it to happen like this. Please give me a break. This is the worst day of my life.

September 23

From: Pandora@CoachworX
To: Martin Lukes

Hi Martin
Sorry it took a while for me to get back to you. I'm so in demand at the moment! I'm afraid Executive Bronze Program is only email, so it would be irresponsible of me, under the terms of the contract, to allow personal visits. But please email me the issues, and I, as your greatest fan, will help you be better than your best!
Strive and Thrive!
Pandora

From: Martin Lukes
To: Pandora@CoachworX

Pandora,
Yes I know Executive Bronze is only email, but I thought you might have made an exception for an emergency.

Long story short? Basically I have been going on seeing Keri on an occasional basis. I feel she has been very helpful with New Me, beneficial to my self-image, to my body and also to my work–life balance. It has been a good arrangement, with no one getting hurt. Between you and me and the gatepost, Jens hasn't been that interested in the bedroom department for some time. Unfortunately my son Jake has issues with myself at present, has got hold of my BlackBerry and forwarded one of Keri's messages to Jens – who has totally flipped and chucked me out.

Obviously this is not what I need. I need to have the whole family behind me at the moment.

I'm moving in with Keri for now, but as I said, not ideal.
Martin

From: Pandora@CoachworX
To: Martin Lukes

Hi Martin
You may feel pain now, because whenever you violate your core values the result is pain. I also sense a lot of confusion in your account – I think you are losing sight of your goals. It would do you a lot of good right now to do a GROW model.

It is time to re-visit your core values Martin. Say them out loud to yourself. Ask yourself: Which values have I violated? And how do I repair and renew?
Strive and thrive!
Pandora

From: Martin Lukes
To: Pandora@CoachworX

Frankly, Pandora, I don't give a shit about my values right now. If you had ANY IDEA how bad I'm feeling right now you would not have dared suggest I do a FUCKING GROW model. My whole life is crashing around my ears. I am not in the mood for any of your other quick fixes.

I am going to see my mother (who is my genuine greatest fan), and I'm going to get some work done.
Martin

September 24

From: Martin Lukes
To: All Staff

Hi!

I know that many of you were disappointed at the cancellation of the Bangalore Brainstorm on Wednesday. I thought it might be helpful to do an FAQ to answer some of your issues.

Q: How can we be sure that people in India will have the same passion for our company as we do?

A: That's a great question! Basically we are not going to do ANYTHING that dilutes passion levels! We will be training every Indian co-worker to live our values, principles and goals.

Q: What is the time frame?

A: Basically we're still pushing the envelope on this one. We'll need to co-involve our Indian partners and get their valued contributions.

Q: What will this mean for jobs?

A: That's obviously another really key question! Basically, it's too early to say at this stage what the workforce impact will be. However we will ensure maximum dignity, compassion and respect for the impactees!

Q: When will the next Bangalore Brainstorm be?

A: Next week!

Martin Lukes

September 27

From: Martin Lukes
To: Phyllis Lukes

Dear Mum

Can I come and see you on Saturday morning?

Love Martin

From: Martin Lukes
To: Phyllis Lukes

Dear Mum
You ask if anything is up. I was going to wait until I saw you, but maybe I should tell you now. I know you never thought Jens was right for me, and maybe you were right. The bottom line is that she has chucked me out.

There is someone else, mum. I think you'd like her. She's very down to earth, calls a spade a spade. She's not the brightest cookie on the beach, but she's very intuitive and has been very good for me. She's called Keri and she's 29 and a New Zealander. Started to train as a physio, so she's very caring. A good-time girl. But it's all too soon for me to get serious, especially as the situation with Jens is all rather up in the air. I need to talk to Jens about it, but she's being totally unreasonable – listening, not a strong point of hers, to put it mildly!!
Much love
Martie

From: Martin Lukes
To: Phyllis Lukes

Yes of course I'm thinking about the boys. But Max is at Eton, and Jake has basically done something that I find hard to forgive. And don't forget, this wasn't my choice. I'm not leaving. I've been chucked out. I had hoped you'd see this from my point of view.
See you tomorrow
Martie

September 29

From: Martin Lukes
To: Barry S. Malone

Sure! Lets talk 11 am your time. Sounds exciting!
Bestest
Martin

From: Martin Lukes
To: Barry S. Malone

Hi Barry
I just wanted to say again how incredibly excited I am about
your offer. I feel this is just the right opening for me – and hopefully for yourself, as well. Truly win-win!

I love this company as much as you do. I am thrilled at this
opportunity to serve it in a more pivotal role. I will send you
soonest a memo detailing what should be front of mind for me
as your chief of staff.

You mentioned relocation of my wife and children. I just
wanted to flag up at this stage that my domestic situation is a
bit fluid. So I am not sure that the whole family will be coming
with me. All my very bestest
Martin
PS Give my best to the lovely Janine.

From: Martin Lukes
To Keri Tartt

Sorry darling, going to be back late tonight. Got an important
memo to write to Barry. Something vv exciting has happened.
Will tell you later.
M x

Chapter Ten

October
My Money

October 1

From: Martin Lukes
To: Jenny Withers

Jens –
I know you said no messages. But I've got such BRILLIANT news, it puts our difficulties into perspective. I'm going to Atlanta as BSM's Chief of Staff!! This is my DREAM JOB – it's got power, it's got profile AND it's going to be intellectually stimulating . . . I've been catapulted into the hot seat right in the heart of the control room!

But this isn't just win-win for me – if you approach this with a more positive headset it'd be great for you and the boys too. I'd be well placed to get you whatever job you fancy – within reason! Lunch today to discuss? Or I could come round to my own home this evening?
Love you,
M xxx

From: Martin Lukes
To: Jenny Withers

Did you get my message? What do you think?

From: Martin Lukes
To: Jenny Withers

Would a reply be too much to ask for?

From: Barry S. Malone
To: All Staff

Howdy!
I am today announcing some exciting changes to our corporate
structure that will position us ahead of the curve in our goal of
Phenomenal Performance – Permanently! To support my leadership
platform and facilitate execution of new policy initiatives I shall
be establishing an Office of the Chairman in Atlanta. The office
will be headed up by Martin Lukes, currently Marketing Director of
a-b glöbâl UK.

To those of you who do not know Martin, he has an unrivalled
track record in creovation. He has a results-driven headset and a very
British sense of humour! I know he is going to be a genius in his new
role, and a best-in-class addition to our top team!
I love you all
Barry

October 4

From: Pandora@CoachworX
To: Martin Lukes

Hi Martin – Do you know what singles out the best from the
rest? The best have an insatiable appetite for lifelong learning. Every day is a journey towards greater self-belief and
self-improvement.

This month we are going to focus in on some more
Development Opportunities. The biggest issues for you are
listening, and the giving of positive feedback! I am going to
send you How to Give Positive Strokes, by Dr Tony Covey.

Try to find time to read it over the weekend.
Strive and thrive!
Pandora

From: Martin Lukes
To: Pandora@CoachworX

Hi Pandora
In all honesty, I don't think it's fair to say that I have an issue around giving positive strokes. To prove it, Pandora, I'd like to recognize your role in my success to date. When historians come to write the book of my career, they will undoubtedly agree that you should play a supporting role as the midwife, if you will, to New Me. Although some might argue I would have got here eventually on my own – I think it's fair to say you've been a terrific catalyst.

That said, I wondered if we could be a little creovative™ about this module of the programme and home in on money instead? Basically, I need some expert advice on maximizing my package. On merit grounds alone, I should be paid more than anyone in the UK, and more than Keith. And given my present domestic situation (don't ask!!) I may be running two homes . . . which is obviously going to cost me an arm and a leg. However, given the current cost environment, I fear that getting the right package is going to be tough.
22.5 per cent better than my bestest
Martin

From: Pandora@CoachworX
To: Martin Lukes

Hi Martin!
Sure! I have no problem coaching you on wealth! It is something I have helped literally thousands of coachees on in the past, with phenomenal success! The first step is to understand true wealth isn't about money. It is about the joy you

feel seeing the face of a laughing child. Or the beauty of a turquoise ocean.

But money can be an aspect of wealth – and that is what we are going to work on now. Martin, this month I am going to help you develop the millionaire's mindset. Already in your mind, you have a collection of beliefs and emotions around money. We need to look at these before we can start increasing your wealth. If you believe that money is negative in some way – 'Money is the root of all evil' – you will struggle to acquire it.

Ask yourself: What does money mean to me? What would having more money give me that I don't already have?
Strive and Thrive!
Pandora
PS Given your new responsibilities, now would be a great time to upgrade to the Executive Gold or Executive Platinum Coaching Program. Not only would this be more in keeping with your status, it would free up more of my time to help you be even better than your best!

From: Martin Lukes
To: Thelma Dowd

Hi Thelma – I've got a lot to do trying to sort my package today. Various members of my team want to talk to me . . . can you keep them all away?
Martin

October 5

From: Martin Lukes
To: Pandora@CoachworX

Hi Pandora
You ask what would money give me that I don't have already? Easy! I'd like an Aston Martin DB9. I'd also like to upscale my

real estate. A substantial residence in Atlanta, with smaller pads in London, Antigua and Aspen Colorado. I am not into being flash with money – I certainly would never want my own plane. But I think I would like my own art collection, or something classy like that, which was as much about taste as money.

22.5 per cent better than my bestest

Martin

PS Re Executive Platinum, I strongly agree, though I think the best strategy is to get my package sorted first, and then to ask for extras. Sure it won't be a problemo.

From: Pandora@CoachworX
To: Martin Lukes

Martin –
I'm a teensy bit disappointed that you haven't grasped what this exercise is all about. I was asking what emotions – happiness, security, freedom, you thought money would get you?

Think again: Why do you want more money?

The reason Martin, has got to be: BECAUSE YOU'RE WORTH IT!!

If you don't believe that, you can throw away all your hopes of getting the package of your dreams. What is money? Money is a symbol of someone's confidence in you! If you want more money you are going to have to have Extraordinary Confidence in yourself, so that others will have Extraordinary Confidence in you!

Strive and thrive!

Pandora

From: Martin Lukes
To: Keri Tartt

Keri darling
I've been thinking about this, and I know I said I wanted us to be together. I do, obviously. But I don't think it would be a good idea

if you come to Atlanta with me unless you have a job. Not earning would be bad for your self-esteem. And if you had a job, if anything happened between us, you'd still have an income.

My plan is to import you as my PA. I'm sure I could wangle you more money and a grand title – something like – Senior Administrative Assistant to Chief of Staff, Office of the Chairman. Please say Yes: I'm going to need some people on my side, it's a vipers' nest out there. And we're a great team!
Love you M xxx

October 6

From: Martin Lukes
To: Max Lukes

Max old man,
I hope school is going well – well done for coming top in the Latin test!

I don't know if mum has said anything to you about me, but I thought you had a right to know that she's a tad miffed with me at the moment. To be perfectly honest, she has gone on a bit of a bender and chucked me out (!), so I'm presently living with a friend. I do hope that this is a temporary situation and that she'll come to her senses and won't break up our fantastic family. Might help if you put in a word for your old dad next time you talk to her?

The other big news item is that I've been offered a really wicked job in the US with loads of money – I'll have a ginormous house with pool and private golf course. I hope you'll spend your Christmas holidays with me. We'll definitely have all the burgers and skateboards and ipods you could ever want. Totally the American dream.
Love, Dad

From: Martin Lukes
To: Max Lukes

Hi Max – Yes, I'm sure it's possible for your pet rats to come.
No prob.
Love Dad
PS If you do talk to mum, could you let me know what she said?

From: Martin Lukes
To: Barry S. Malone

Hi, Barry –
As you know I am blown away with excitement about my
new position. I can't get started soon enough!

However, there are just a couple of details that I think we
should iron out re package.

We haven't talked numbers, but I'm assuming that my pay
would be in line with comparable senior executives. I would see
myself coming in slightly north of Keith and Cindy, but not out
of the ball park. In addition, 100 per cent housing allowance,
school fees, cars for myself, my ladywife and my older son and
all the other usual perks.

I understand that the job will not initially be a main board
position, but that this would happen in the fullness of time.
Could we nail down when that would be? I am also assuming
that I can bring my PA, Keri Tartt, with me. She is an exceptional administrator and has the key skillset to enable her to fully
support me in my new function. A small pay rise for her would
send a highly motivational message.

As I think I may have told you, there are some issues around
the relocation of my spouse. At present she is in External
Relations in London. To facilitate her transition I would like
some career coaching and psychological counselling. Can we
discuss these matters soonest?
My best, Martin

From: Martin Lukes
To: Keri Tartt

Keri – Sorry darling, I'm going to be late back – am working flat out on package negotiations.

I'm absolutely starving. Can you order a takeaway curry for about 9.30 – and I'd also like some Ben and Jerrys (Cherry Garcia if poss, otherwise The Full Vermonty) for afters.
Love P xx
PS Should be no prob at all getting you a great new job in Atlanta . . . but I'm insisting on monster rise for you.

October 7

From: Martin Lukes
To: Thelma Dowd

Hi Thelma
Have just drafted an email for all my external contacts. Can you make sure it goes out to everyone I've had any dealings with in the past three years? Ta muchly, M

From: Martin Lukes
To: All Contacts

Hi everyone!
Apologies for not reaching out to each of you personally, but I wanted to tell everyone who I have had the pleasure of working in partnership with these last few years that I am moving on to pastures new! From October 15 I shall be transferring to Atlanta to become Chief of Staff, Office of the Chairman. This is obviously a pivotal position, and I will be working directly with the legendary Barry S. Malone, who was recently named by Fortune as the 7th most respected business leader in the world. I will be tasked with assisting in the formulation of policy and heading up execution. I would like to say what a pleasure it has been

working with you in the past, and thank you for the deep interest you have always shown in my career. I hope you will feel able to continue your relationship with a-b glöbâl (UK) going forward.

My best regards
Martin Lukes
Marketing Director a-b glöbâl (UK)
Chief of Staff, Chairman's Office (designate)

From: Martin Lukes
To: Jenny Withers

Jens darling
I didn't appreciate it at all just now when I came to talk to you in your office and you went on talking to Suzanna as if I wasn't there. I know that you are upset. Rightly so, as I'd be the first to admit! But this is going too far.

I've been doing some digging about possible jobs for you in Atlanta, and there are two suitable openings in the press office – none with a grand title, but you'd be a small fish in a big pond!

I'm playing hardball re money, and looks like we'll be able to afford whatever we want accommodation-wise – I'm thinking enormous house, obviously with pool, in a gated community with its own golf course.

We must talk about this . . . time is running out
Martin

From: Martin Lukes
To: Jenny Withers

Yes I know you don't play golf. And please don't accuse me of going behind your back with Max . . . I simply told him what his life would be like with me in Atlanta. He's asked me to take his rats, and I've said fine. Actually it's a bit of a nuisance, but at the end of the day it's important that we are both prepared to walk the extra mile for the kids. M

From: Martin Lukes
To: Jake Lukes

Jake – I think it is time for you and I to be highly honest with each other. I am still very angry at what you did. You are presently living with the consequences of your actions, and I hope you have come to experience some serious regrets.

That said, I am aware that you are going through a difficult patch in your life, and that you need the support of your father. How about a drink before I go to the US? I shall come and pick you up from the house at 7 pm Thursday night.
Dad

October 8

From: Martin Lukes
To: Jenny Withers

Jens – Before you bite my head off for contacting you again, this is a legit business email! I've decided to write a light-hearted Q&A press release that could work as a diary piece – Brit Hits the Big Time in the US. The business pages are always looking for something a bit different, a bit humorous!
M
PS I'm planning to take Jake out for a drink next week. He hasn't honoured me with a reply. Can you make sure he is in, and ready on time?

MARTIN LUKES IS APPOINTED TO THE NEW POSITION OF CHIEF OF STAFF, OFFICE OF THE CHAIRMAN, A-B GLOBAL, MAKING HIM THE MOST SENIOR BRITISH EXECUTIVE IN THE COMPANY GLOBALLY.
With which historical figure do you identify most closely?
Einstein. He was the original creovative™ guy!
Which living person do you most admire?
My mum, who taught me to appreciate the little things in life!

And Barry S. Malone for teaching me not to understand the word 'impossible'.

What was your biggest break?

Getting this job. Oh, and meeting my wife, Jens.

What or who is the greatest love of your life?

That'd be telling! Seriously, after my own family, I love the extended family that is a-b glöbâl.

What is your greatest weakness?

Bounty bars!!!

What keeps you awake at night?

Nothing! I believe in work hard, play hard. I don't take my worries to bed with me!

What was your proudest moment?

Leading the award-winning a-b glöbâl rebranding initiative. And getting a birdie on the famous 12th at Augusta.

What is your most unappealing habit?

You'd have to ask my wife. She might mention something I do with the toothpaste tube!!!

How would you like to die?

As I have lived – giving 110 per cent.

What would be your epitaph?

A creovative™ talent who never stopped pushing the envelope!

From: Martin Lukes
To: Jenny Withers

What do you mean it's naff?? It's actually really funny and it helps people get to know me quickly. And what do you expect me to say: that my wife has kicked me out and is refusing to come to Atlanta with me??? And Keith isn't a more senior Brit. Although he's on the board, which arguably makes him ahead of yours truly on paper, but he doesn't have Barry's ear. Ergo, no power.

M.

October 11

From: Martin Lukes
To: Barry S. Malone

Barry – I've just had a message from a Kimberly Warp in HR outlining my package. I have serious issues with some of the detail. She says the only benefit I am entitled to is healthcare insurance, and that I cannot bring my PA with me. I guess I can train up a local hire as a PA, but I need confirmation that she has made an error over the benefits question.
All my bestest, Martin

From: Martin Lukes
To: Pandora@CoachworX

Hi, Pandora
Alas, the millionaire mindset isn't delivering the desired package. This isn't a confidence issue – I've got loads of that! The problem is that some idiot in HR begs to differ. Any advice?
Martin

**From: Pandora@CoachworX
To: Martin Lukes**

**Hi Martin
Can I share with you a little story about myself? When I was in my 30s, I was in debt, I was living in one room, and my self-worth was so low I could hardly get up in the mornings.**

A few months later I began creating money everywhere I looked! Within a few years I had become a millionaire. Because I had changed myself and my perception of the world, money came flowing to me!

Your mind is like a magnet, Martin. You must create the millionaire's mindset. Make a scrapbook and stick in it all the things you would like to own.

Imagine you own them already and one day you will!
Strive and thrive!
Pandora

From: Martin Lukes
To: Thelma Dowd

Hi Thelma – can you organize my leaving drinx for Thurs? Find out what Rog will swallow expense-wise – I don't want to be left with a sodding great bill!

Could you also reduce these Aston Martin pictures on the colour printer so that they'll fit into this notebook. Then cut them out and stick them in.
Martin

From: Martin Lukes
To: Keith Buxton

Hi Keith – Just seen yr message. No, I think you've got the wrong end of the stick – I certainly haven't been telling people I'm the most senior Brit in the US – I may have said 'one of' – I really can't remember. The basic point is that I'm much looking forward to joining you and other members of the top team in Atlanta.
My very bestest, as ever
Martin
PS Someone in HR tells me none of the US directors have company cars. Didn't sound right to me. Can you confirm?

From: Martin Lukes
To: Keri Tartt

Darling Pinky – going to be v late home – problems on the package front. Atlanta's playing silly buggers. There's been a hitch re yr job, but I'm fighting your corner – worry not! M

October 12

From: Martin Lukes
To: Kimberly Warp

Hi Kimberly – Thanks for your email re my package. Seems like we're approaching closure at last! I'm prepared to have a local hire as PA, though I want to clarify a small point on the share options. I understand that the package is meant to be highly leveraged to results. It is therefore imperative that my existing options are repriced, as they are underwater and are not providing any incentive to deliver. Cheers, Martin

From: Martin Lukes
To: Graham Wallace

Yes to drink, though it'll have to be a swift one as Keri is now getting funny about me staying late. Had a massive row with her last night about the US – she seems to think she can come as my partner, and live the life of Riley without lifting a finger. All v awkward, esp. as I think Jens will eventually back down and come.

Only good news is that I'm getting all my options repriced and the way the share price is tanking, it means a nominal additional £358,796.32, which can't be bad. Also planning to get an Aston Martin DB9 . . . eat yr heart out.
Martin

From: Martin Lukes
To: Phyllis Lukes
Dearest Mum – just a quick message to say I'm definitely coming on Saturday, and will bring Keri. She is very young, mum, and she's also a bit nervous about meeting you, as I've built you up into a bit of a wonderwoman! We'll try to arrive in good time for pre-prandial drinkies. Fraid she's a vegetarian, but don't go to any trouble
Your loving son,
Martie

October 13

From: Martin Lukes
To: Barry S. Malone

Hi Barry
I wanted to share with you some creovative™ thinking I've been doing around Monday's Q4 results. My idea is a live webcam for staff and investors featuring you talking through the figures. But instead of seeing you in your office – been there, done that, got the T-shirt! – we could have you playing a few holes at your club. This would be visually sensational and the message would be unforgettable!

As you introduce yourself, you could be teeing off – you could then talk about the importance of winning, of playing the game, and having fun! As you discuss the hostile economic landscape, we could see the ball going into the sand. When you talk about overcoming challenges ahead, we'd see you finding the green on that tricky 16th dog-leg. I feel there are many exciting pictorial opportunities here that we could explore. What do you think?
Cheers, Martin

From: Martin Lukes
To: Jake Lukes

Hi Jake – really good to catch up with you last night. A man-2-man chat like that was really useful for both of us. As I said, do hope you and Max will come out at Christmas – there's lots of young female talent – I think you'll like the look of my boss's daughters!!
Dad
PS – That was a joke, btw, I don't want you to get any ideas!!

From: Martin Lukes
To: Keri Tartt

Pinky Darling
Bad news . . . those idiots in Atlanta have said no to your transfer
for now, but I'm still working on them. What I suggest is that I go
over without you initially, and that you can always come out later
and join me when I've sorted something. I know it's a blow, but I
think we should look at it positively. We both need some space.

Don't wait for me this evening . . . I'm going to be a tiny bit
late . . .

Would you mind taking all my suits to the cleaners and make
sure they're ready tomorrow, as it now looks like I'm going to
be off on Friday night, a couple of days earlier than we thought?
Love you
Martin

From: Martin Lukes
To: Keri Tartt

Pinky, please don't be like that. Of course I still love you. You'll
always be my dinky winky kinky pinky! I know the corporal has
been a bit tired recently. It's so stressful trying to get this package
right. I only have one shot at it. I'll take you out to dinner tomorrow nite. Porky promise. xx
Love you Perky xxx

From: Martin Lukes
To: Thelma Dowd

Hi Thelma
Can you email a list of all the things you do for me to my new
PA – she's called Sherry Zook(!). Ta muchly. Can't believe Rog
is being so tight about the party – no way I'm paying for a big
bash out of my own pocket . . . I'll buy the team a round at the
local after work tomorrow. M

From: Martin Lukes
To: Sherry Zook

Hi Sherry
This is Martin Lukes in London. I'm delighted that you're going to be working with me as my assistant – I am sure we're going to be an unbeatable team! I'll be flying in on Saturday night at 22.45 EST. Can you arrange a car to pick me up from the airport, and reserve a suite at the W? I have asked my PA Thelma Dowd to email you a list of tasks – which hopefully will make your learning curve less steep! Can you also find out about quarantine arrangements for rats? I am planning to bring over six of them, though the way they are breeding, numbers are a moveable feast!
All the bestest
Martin

October 14

From: Martin Lukes
To: All Marketing

Team!
A reminder: everyone's invited for drinx tonite at the Dog and Duck to celebrate my departure Stateside! Let's make it a night to remember!
Martin

October 15

From: Martin Lukes
To: All Marketing

Team!
Thanks for the great send-off last night. I've certainly got a thick head this morning! I just wanted to say that you have

been a terrific load of people to work with these last few years, and together we've been producing some of the best marketing projects the company has ever seen – the Bay City Roller campaign was the stuff of legends – AND we've had a load of fun on the journey! I'll miss you, but obviously we'll keep in touch, and I'll take a keen interest in your work from afar.

All my very bestest

Martin Lukes

PS Many thanks for the book of golfing jokes. I'll never be at a loss for a way to begin a speech!

From: Martin Lukes
To: Christo Weinberg

Hi Christo

I just wanted to put on the record how very much I think you've grown into your role in the last ten months, since being my mentee. You've shown that with the right leadership you have genuine creovative™ promise.

Although obviously I won't be able to mentor you from Atlanta, I'll always be happy to help on an informal basis!

Cheers, Martin

PS It was good to meet Sven last night. Hope I didn't say anything out of line. He obviously doesn't realize what a joker I am . . .

From: Martin Lukes
To: Katherine Lukes

Hi Katherine

Really sorry but I'm afraid I'm going to have to cancel on you again tomorrow. My news – I'm moving to Atlanta to be the Numero Duo in the whole company, globally!!!

I don't know if mum mentioned to you that there are also some issues in my marriage, though I hope not too serious! Let's keep in email touch. It's always good to hear what you're up to

(or not up to!!) and we can see each other on one of my visits back to these shores.
Best
Martin

From: Martin Lukes
To: Phyllis Lukes

Dearest Mum
Thank you for saying that! You'll find this hard to believe, but no one else has had the decency to say that they'll miss me. In fact everyone seems to be against me at the moment. Jens is, obviously. And she's being very unfair with the boys and trying to talk them round to her point of view.

Most of my colleagues are so jealous of my new job they are being really weird – even my mates can't be happy for me.

And things with Keri are pretty difficult. I'm sorry you and she didn't hit it off a bit better, I think she was a bit nervous meeting you. That was why she was doing that silly laugh all the time. She isn't like that normally. She's actually a very sweet person, but I've decided that for now it's best if I go to Atlanta on my tod.

In spite of it all, I'm feeling pretty robust – the new job is going to be just brilliant. I'm off this evening, so all v chaotic.
Your loving son,
Martie
PS I was meant to be seeing Katherine tomorrow, but have had to cancel, and have even had a huffy message from her – so she's cross with me, too! Btw what do you think about her news on the adoption front? I'm pretty sceptical, though obviously I tried to put it very positively to her, as you know how touchy she can be. But the bottom line is that it's not really fair on the kid to be raised by two lessies. Try explaining that in the playground!

October 16

From: Martin Lukes
To: Jenny Withers

Jens – Arrived safely. Have attached all my contact numbers in case you felt an urge to speak to your husband.
M

October 17

From: Martin Lukes
To: Graham Wallace

Graham – Just spent the day at the Malone mansion. Totally amazing – really vast, luxurious and even quite tasteful. I didn't realize how cultured Barry is. He's passionate about art, and has got a Picasso drawing and two Matisses! He gave me a tour of all his pictures, and told me how much everything cost. I kept a running total, and I think I got up to $96m!

Randee was really friendly – all over me, in fact. She's in amazing shape given that she must be in her late 40s. Don't think she has any idea her husband is humping a tasty young journalist . . .

Must go to bed now to be fresh for the filming tomorrow. Barry gets into the office before dawn, and I think I should try to get in first. M

From: Martin Lukes
To: Barry S. Malone

Hi Barry, I just wanted to thank you and Randee for a really wonderful day. It was great for me to feel so welcomed into your family, and to get to know your beautiful daughters. I felt particularly privileged to see your sensational art collection. Like you, I've always been a huge fan of the 'art world'. My favourite artist is probably Jack Vettriano – have you thought of buying any of his? I'm told they're a great investment at the moment.

Have arranged for the camera crew to meet us at the golf club at 8.30 am for a run through. See you in the office before that. I normally get in at about 5.30 am.
Martin

October 18

From: Barry S. Malone
To: All Staff

Howdy!
I would like to welcome to Atlanta Martin Lukes, who today commences his new job heading up my 35-strong personal office.

His first task here will be spearheading the roll-out of our PPP programme, and masterminding our annual conference in Paradise Island, Bahamas next month, the very first under the new a-b glöbâl brand.

This is obviously a hyper-challenging operating environment, but we have plenty to celebrate and feel proud of. My gratitude to every one of you for the excitement and the love you commit to our business gets stronger every day.
I love you all
Barry

From: Martin Lukes
To: All Staff

Hi!
First up I would like to say a humungous thank you to Barry for making me feel so welcome here. The task is a big one, but people who know me well are kind enough to say that I have always embraced a challenge! Being a-b glöbâl's first chief of staff is a huge privilege. This is only Day One for myself, but

301

already, thanks to the sheer drive of our CEO I feel as if I've been here forever. I mean that in a good way, obviously!

All my very bestest

Martin Lukes

Chief of Staff, Office of the Chairman

From: Martin Lukes
To: Sherry Zook

Hi Sherry

Great to meet with you just now. If you'll forgive a personal remark, that green colour really goes with your eyes!

I'm confident that we can sort out any issues around the nature of your role. You may be used to a different way of working, but if you are prepared to fasten your seatbelt, working for me is going to be really stimulating and a load of fun!

Question. Do you have issues around getting coffee for your boss? I realize that this is something many PAs are concerned about, and if you do, no problem. However if you are comfortable with this, mine's a tall latte with soya – I'm on a dairy-free diet at the moment, and am finding it very beneficial.

Martin

From: Martin Lukes
To: Sherry Zook

Seems we're both on a steep learning curve! With all due respect, I just meant to be pleasant. I complimented my former PA Keri on her outfits all the time, and she loved it. She really is a great dresser, and she was very supportive about my health issues.

Can you help me on another small matter? I wanted to find out how to get Georgia customized licence plates for my car, which I shall be importing from the UK. I would like the plates to say CREOV8

Best, Martin

PS So where is the nearest Starbucks?

From: Martin Lukes
To: Sales@AstonMartin

Re my order.
Dear Sir
Thank you for your email confirming the order of my Aston
Martin DB9. I would like to confirm that the customized plaques
on the sills read: Driving Performance with Martin Lukes. Also
I have sent a swatch taken from the inside of my favourite Paul
Smith leather jacket. I would like the seat upholstery to be
matched exactly.

I note that the delivery is September next year, which I assume
is an error. I require the car asap. I understand that these highly
individualized cars are not built overnight, but I would like to
remind you that we live in a Just in Time marketplace. In my
business if we do not deliver extraordinary service with extraordinary speed, we'd go out of business.
Martin Lukes

October 20

From: Martin Lukes
To: All Staff

Hi everyone,
This morning at 10 am EST we will be broadcasting a live
webcast with our chairman and CEO, Barry S. Malone, who will
be taking us through the background to our Q4 figures. It is
essential that every co-colleague takes the time to watch it. Not
only is it humungous fun, it contains some very powerful and
uniquely motivational messages for the future of the company.
We are one family, one brand, united behind the a-b glöbâl
behaviours!
Bestest,
Martin Lukes
Chief of Staff, Office of the Chairman

From: Martin Lukes
To: Barry S. Malone

Hi Barry – That went brilliantly! You delivered the lines perfectly!
Total triumph!
Martin

From: Martin Lukes
To: Graham Wallace

Graham – Did you see it? What did you think?? That bit where
Barry deliberately topped the ball on the fairway while talking
about the one-off costs of Project ABC was really inspired. I
wrote the entire script myself – Barry might be a business genius
but he's not much of a wordsmith. Shares seem to be down
quite a lot. Which shows the market doesn't understand these
results. Good for my options though . . .
Mart
PS How's Keri behaving? I think she's sulking at me again, but
I don't have the mental capacity to deal with it right now.

October 21

From: Martin Lukes
To: Graham Wallace

This was in the Financial Times this morning. Journalists are
such bloody idiots. They know bugger all about the real world.

A-B GLOBAL SHARES TUMBLE ON RESULT
a-b glôbâl, the US-based multinational, yesterday disappointed
markets with a 35 per cent drop in revenues and a 42 per cent
fall in operating profits for the year to September. The figures
come just a month after a-b glôbâl and its chief executive, Barry
S. Malone, was named among the most highly respected in the
world by Fortune magazine.

In a broadcast to staff and investors, Mr Malone said yesterday that this was a temporary setback and that the earnings outlook was strong: 'We are taking the economic medicine today to oil the wheels for a blue-sky tomorrow,' he said. The broadcast, in which he was seen playing a round of golf, was yesterday criticized as 'inappropriate' by Wall Street analysts. 'What the hell was he doing playing golf while Rome burns?' said one.

A spokesman for a-b glöbâl said: 'This broadcast was concrete evidence of our creovation. It has had huge impact as a communications tool and proves we are never scared of pushing the envelope.'

From: Martin Lukes
To: Barry S. Malone

Hi Barry – Can I offer my perspective on this morning's press coverage? I think there are two key learnings we can take out from this. It is vital to bear in mind that the market and the media are incredibly conservative, and they take a long time to recognize a phenomenally effective new way of communicating.

I think the second message is that we are becoming victims of our own success. This is just a case of build 'em up, and knock 'em down. The market had decided that you can walk on water. That means if our numbers come in slightly below analysts' figures, they totally overreact.

I think you are 210 per cent right to keep a steady hand on the tiller. Shares have already bounced back a bit this am. This is just a blip.
All my very bestest,
Martin

October 24

From: Matin Lukes
To: Cindy Czarnikow

Hi Cindy! Thanks for your offer. A pot luck brunch next Sunday

would be great. I'm hoping that Jens will be over at the week-end. She'd love to see you too!
Best, Martin

From: Martin Lukes
To: Pandora@CoachworX

Hi Pandora
Sorry I haven't touched base until now. I've been so in demand, you wouldn't believe it. The job is a blast. Totally energizing – I'm still not over the jet lag, and am only sleeping about four hours a night, but I've never felt better. Will email properly when I get a window.
22.5 per cent better than my bestest
Martin

From: Martin Lukes
To Barry S. Malone

Hi Barry
I've been working on the schedule for the PPP conference. I've been thinking outside the square about the name for our conference and I think we need to brand it so that people will realize that we haven't simply changed our name to a-b glöbâl, but we are embracing change across the spectrum. I suggest we call it One Family! What do you think?

I've also contacted all the speakers agencies to find out who we can get.

Unfortunately Tiger Woods, who would obviously be a first choice is tied up. OJ Simpson is available, but I think there are other issues there.

I am adding the following internal speakers to the schedule.

'Storytelling – Sharing tales around the corporate campfire' – Jenny Withers

Great news is that we've got Tom Peters. I felt he hit a stale

patch a couple of years back, but his !Reimagine! stuff is extra-ordinary!
Bestest
Martin

From: Martin Lukes
To: Jenny Withers

Darling – I have personally argued the case for you to give a plenary address at our conference on Storytelling – Barry's very excited about it! This is going to be a mega opportunity for you to make your name.

In return, why don't you come out for the weekend – Cindy is giving a brunch for me, and it'd give you the chance to get to know Barry and Randee?
Martin
PS Give my love to the boys and tell Max I'll get him a top of the range iPod for his b'day.

From: Martin Lukes
To: Jenny Withers

I have been trying so incredibly hard to be nice to you. In return you are cold and sarcastic. If I wasn't such a basically decent guy I would can your speech.
Martin

From: Martin Lukes
To: Keri Tartt

Hi Pinky darling
Sorry I haven't emailed for a day or two. The pace is crazy here! Haven't had time to job hunt for you properly, but I've got an idea. Why not come out for a long weekend next weekend? There's a lot happening here . . . I'd show you a great time!
Love Perky xx

October 27

From: Martin Lukes
To: Cindy Czarnikow

Hi Cindy
Much looking forward to Sunday. What's your address?
Unfortunately Jens isn't going to be able to make it. A young
former colleague of mine might be passing through Atlanta, so
I might bring her.
Martin

From: Martin Lukes
To: Graham Wallace

Hi Graham – Big article in NY Times about Barry's affair with Janine,
implying that his Number 7 position in Fortune rankings was a
stitch-up, and that Randee is going to take him to the cleaners.
I told you something was up.
M

October 28

From: Martin Lukes
To: Barry S Malone

Hi Barry
First up can I offer my sincere condolences at all this recent
publicity. I strongly believe that your private life concerns only
your good self (and Randee and Janine, of course!). I know you
to be a man of the highest integrity, and if these stories persist,
I suggest we retaliate with stories about all your charity work.
    On a more personal level, can I say how strongly I empathize
with your position, being personally embroiled in something
similar myself! Sometimes it's tough being an alpha male!!
Bestest, Martin

October 31

From: Martin Lukes
To: Keri Tartt

Dearest Pinky
Did you get back home safely? I realize the weekend was a bit difficult for us both, and sorry if I was a tad distracted.
Perky

From: Martin Lukes
To: Keri Tartt

Pinky – yes of course I want us to carry on! I do love you a lot Pinky. And of course I want you to move here. I do, you know I do. I just need a bit of space at the moment. Sorry I didn't tell Cindy and everyone that we were an item. I was waiting for the right time. But then you got so pissed . . . it was all highly unfortunate.
P

From: Martin Lukes
To: Keri Tartt

Keri – Please don't! Please give me another chance . . . I really don't see why we can't carry on . . . you've totally got the wrong end of the stick in thinking that this is just a sex thing for me. Obviously the corporal appreciates you (!!) but I really love you as a holistic person. Going back to Kiwiland is way too extreme.
   Think about it Pinky.
From your busy but very loving Porky

From: Martin Lukes
To: Barry S. Malone

Do you ever think women are more trouble than they're worth?

From: Martin Lukes
To: Barry S. Malone

No, I don't either! I agree they are beautiful too – some more than others! And yes, I'm getting on with the synopsis for the One Family! conference, which I'll have with you shortly!
Bestest Martin

From: Martin Lukes
To: Jenny Withers

Dear Jenny
When we talked on the phone just now, I felt that you had no interest in hearing my side of the story. So I have decided to write this email to share my feelings with you. I wanted to put down on paper how things look from where I'm standing. You say you want a divorce. You've known me long enough to know that I am a highly reasonable individual, and I am not going to stand in your way.

However I think that before we go down that road, you should think about what this would do to the boys. You should also meditate on where you are now, and how you got there.

You seem to think that somehow I'm in the wrong. But it does take two. Deep down, I think you know that.

As I have decided to be totally honest, I should also say how angry I am with you. Relationships are hard work, Jens, and it deeply saddens me that you are not prepared to put that work in. I've been thinking outside the square on this one, and it seems to me that marriage involves give and take. And frankly at the moment you only seem interested in taking.

I made a mistake. Not only have I put my hand up and said sorry, from the bottom of my heart. I have also grown from my mistake. I have a saying that has helped me a lot in the past 10 months: No failure, only feedback. Neither of us has failed. We need to concentrate on the learnings out of this, and see if we can grow as people from them.

I have also decided that there is no place for Keri in my life. I doubt if she and I will ever speak to each other again. It never meant anything, Jens. She was my mid-life crisis, if you will, and I'm now ready to move onto the next level.

No need to reply at once. I want you to read this message and think deeply about it. Read it again. Sleep on it. And then tell me – are you prepared to walk the extra mile?

Jens – I've talked the talk. But now I am going to walk the walk. You must believe me.

Your husband

Martin

From: Martin Lukes
To: Pandora@CoachworX

Pandora

A lot has happened in the last two weeks that I should debrief you on. Basically, first and foremost, the job is all I wanted and more. Totally pivotal, totally powerful, and Barry and I make a perfect partnership. I'm the Yin to his Yang, if you will.

I've got the Aston Martin DB9! Since I put one in that scrap book, and focused on how much I really did want one, it's come true. (Or rather, it will come true when the guys at the AM factory move their lazy arses and make it for me!)

I think the car will be well aligned with my leadership brand . . . Already Barry sees me very much as the creative Brit maverick. The DB9 is the perfect car for that. On the domestic front, I am a bit miffed with Jens. I feel that she hasn't tried to save our marriage at all. Relationships need working at. But you'd be very proud of me – I have sent her a long email putting down all my feelings, and encouraging her to challenge her own. No reply as yet, but I told her to take her time.

22.5 per cent better than my bestest

Martin

Chapter Eleven

November

My Relationships

November 1

From: Barry S. Malone
To: All Staff

Howdy!
Next week our 300 most senior leaders will assemble in the beautiful
location of Paradise Island for this company's 16th annual manage-
ment conference.

This year is going to be uniquely special. For the first time we are
gathering under our new a-b glöbâl identity. It is the first year that we
have been united as One Global Family with One Prayer, One Mission
and One set of Behaviors. It is the first year that we have committed
to our goal of Phenomenal Performance – Permanently.

We have traveled a very long way in the past year. We have a lot to
celebrate.

If I had one wish, it would be that all of our 30,000 leaders could
join hands and celebrate together. And so for the first time I have
arranged to have my plenary address at Paradise Island beamed by
satellite to every location globally, so that we will all be able to share
the moment and rejoice together.

I have tasked Martin Lukes and Cindy Czarnikow with sending out
a schedule for the conference. Please reach out to them or to me if there
are any issues, any questions or any thoughts to share!
I love you all
Barry

From: Pandora@CoachworX
To: Martin Lukes

Hi Martin –
This morning as I went through my WakeUp! exercise regime
I meditated on how far we have journeyed together since this
program began. You have reclaimed your birthright, and are
already better than the very best you can be. You are in touch
with your body. You have re-dreamed your entire self. You
have embraced the idea that you cannot fail! You are ready
to binge on life!

Welcome to the top, Martin! There is one more thing to
do. We need to think about your personal brand, and how
this impacts on your relationships with other people.

Do your relationships help support your personal brand –
or do they undermine it?
Strive and Thrive!
Pandora

From: Martin Lukes
To: Pandora@CoachworX

Hi Pandora
Everything 120 per cent on track. Paradise Island is going to be
the perfect platform for marketing my own brand. The sky's the
limit!

My relationship with Barry is going from strength to strength
– today he sent out a memo to the whole company containing
many ML concepts (obviously presented as his own, but that's
the name of the game!) AND putting my name ahead of
Cindy's!

As for my other professional relationships, they're mostly
excellent – everyone in London seems to think I'm their new
best friend. Unfortunately I still have issues with both Jens and
Keri, neither of whom is presently speaking to myself.

Only other issue is that I've stopped sleeping. Basically I go to sleep fine – a couple of glasses of whisky do the trick – and then wake up around 3 am and can't get back. Went to the doctor last week who gave me some pills, but they don't make much difference, so I'm going back today for something stronger.

As I said, mostly I feel really energized and really good. Maybe my body is just adapting to my turbo-charged lifestyle. Margaret Thatcher was also on the go 24/7/365 and she only slept four hours a night. And she thrived on it!

22.5 per cent better than my very bestest

Martin

From: Pandora@CoachworX
To: Martin Lukes

Hi Martin
Alcohol and drugs are a no-no!! When you have true self-belief, you do not need crutches that give you a chemical high. Your brain is a powerful tool, Martin. You should be able to use it to make you feel deep profound relaxation. I am going to give you a little exercise that I hope will help your sleep patterns forever. Before you go to bed, dim the lights, sit on the side of your bed and close your eyes. I want you to imagine a sword of white light slowly penetrating your body from the top of your head, running down to the base of your spine. I want you to start chanting your core values to yourself, over and over again, until you feel a deep sense of peace and well being and are ready to lie down and to sleep.
Strive and thrive!
Pandora

November 2

From: Martin Lukes
To: Keri Tartt

Pinky – I do wish you wouldn't sulk – I have enough of that

with the wife. Please send me a message and tell me when you're going to come and see Perky. He misses you.
xxxx

From: Martin Lukes
To: Graham Wallace

Sorry I didn't reply to your message about your career hopes. I've been totally snowed under. But basically, yes, I am lobbying hard for you as UK chairman. The difficulty I'm bumping up against is that Barry is so totally focused on the conference that it's hard to get any other issues front of mind . . .
Martin
PS How's Keri? She's ignoring me.

From: Martin Lukes
To: Barry S. Malone

Hi Barry,
I think we need to do some thinking on the new chairman for the UK operation. My instinct is that we've let this one drift for too long, that as soon as the conference is over we should sort it soonest. I'm obviously very up to speed on what's happening there, and would be delighted to feed in . . . Can we brainstorm?
M

From: Martin Lukes
To: Barry S. Malone

Fine. I'll talk to Keith about it. And yes, I'm getting on very well with your speech for Paradise Island. I'll have something to show you tomorrow.
Best, Martin

November 3

From: Martin Lukes
To: Pandora@CoachworX

Hi Pandora

Alas, still no sleep. I did try the white sword but nothing doing. I know you don't like them, but the new pills the doctor gave me are brilliant.

You ask about worries. Obviously there are issues on relationships side of things presently, but frankly I'm more concerned about getting Barry's speech written – it has to be 140 per cent perfect or he's going to go ballistic . . .
22.5 per cent better than my bestest
Martin

**From: Pandora@CoachworX
To: Martin Lukes**

**Martin
With respect, I wonder if you are in denial about how your relationships are affecting your health? I'm going to help you look at them in a more holistic way. Ask yourself: are my relationships aligned with New Me? If not, it may be time to let them go.**

Martin, you won't get to the top of the game of life without other people! Relationships will help you be better than your best – but you have to choose them well. Some people may have been in your life a long time but they are not contributing.

**In essence there are three sorts of relationship –
• The energy draining relationship – you do not want these people in your life!
• The energy dependent relationship – there is balance here but it's not extraordinary.
• The energy exchange relationship – this works like a rocket,**

where the other person's energy will help catapult you to being better than your best.

You must make some choices Martin. I want you to be really honest and think of your relationships. Which ones hold you back, and which ones blast you into space?
Strive and thrive!
Pandora

From: Martin Lukes
To: Pandora@CoachworX

Hi Pandora
Hard one this. Off the top of my head, I'd say my relationship with Barry is definitely a rocket. We both give the other something – together we are much stronger than apart. My mum is probably a rocket, too. With her I feel I can go to the top. Pandora, although we've never shared face time, I'd say my relationship with you has some rocket-like qualities, too!! I hate to say it, but Jens does definitely sap my energy. But then she is my wife, so maybe that's different.

I think Keri is energy dependent. In the past I thought she might be a rocket, but now I'm not so sure.

It's all food for thought . . . must get on with the speech now.
22.5 per cent better than my very bestest
Martin

November 4

From: Martin Lukes
To: Barry S. Malone

Hi Barry, I've drafted your speech. I've made it as inclusive as I can, and I've put integrity centre stage. Hope you like it!
Bestest Martin

From: Martin Lukes
To: Barry S. Malone

Hi Barry
   Thanks for the honest feedback! I agree 230 per cent. I'll give it more thought and come back to you, soonest.
Martin

From: Faith Preston
To: All Staff

Hi – Keri Tartt is leaving our shores for NZ at the end of the week. If anyone would like to sign her card and contribute to her gift – it's on my desk.
Cheers, Faith

From: Martin Lukes
To: Keri Tartt

Keri – Frankly, I am surprised that I get to hear through Faith that you have decided to leave. You and I have always communicated very openly with each other, and so I thought you would have the decency to tell me yourself.
   However, it's all probably for the best, and I hope that we can remain friends. You may be interested to hear my news: all going exceedingly well here. I'm training up my new PA Sherry to sing from my hymn sheet – she seemed a bit slow at first but is getting up to speed nicely.
My best
Martin

From: Martin Lukes
To: Keri Tartt

I don't get it, Keri. I send you an extremely nice message, and you accuse me of being a cold selfish bastard only interested in

myself . . . blah, blah. Two can play at that game – I actually think it was extremely selfish of you to end our affair because you didn't think I was paying you enough attention. If you hadn't been so wrapped up in yourself you would have noticed that I have been given the job of a lifetime which is very stressful and is more than a 24/7 commitment. Frankly our relationship was an energy exchange – you didn't enhance my energy levels, and if I'm going to be totally honest, I should say I deserve a lot more.
Martin

From: Keri Tartt
To: All Staff

Hiya!
Thanx 2 everyone for the gr8 card and the generous M&S vouchers!!! I'm going to have loadsa fun spending them! It's been so cool working with ya! I'll take many happy memories back to NZ with me! And if u r ever in NZ come and c me!!
Cheers
Keri

November 5

From: Martin Lukes
To: Barry S. Malone

Hi Barry
I've re-dreamt your speech, and this time I hope you'll agree it's sensational! Question: what are the key wins we want to get out of this? We want to unite the company behind you – Barry Sylvester Malone, the phenomenal leader. We want everyone to come out of the session loving you. We don't want a Little Wow. We want a Massive Enormous Humungous WOW!

My Big Idea is to set up your address like a pop concert. There will be a flashing strobe and the Sister Sledge song 'We are family' will be playing very loudly. I shout over the PA – 'THE GUY YOU HAVE ALL BEEN WAITING FOR . . . BARRY MALONE!!' and you come running onto the stage and the crowd then gets up and whoops.

You march up and down on the stage shouting I LOVE THIS COMPANY!

WE ARE ONE FAMILY!! I'll get the crowd cheering, and then you ask: What are we? we'll shout back ONE FAMILY!! You'll say: WE ARE UNITED BY INTEGRITY.

WHAT ARE WE UNITED BY? We will shout back: INTEGRITY!!!

This will get everyone on their feet, and get the conference off to an exceptionally high-octane start.

If you think this is the way to go (and I hope you will!!) then I'll draft the rest of it tonight.

Bestest
Martin

From: Martin Lukes
To: Barry S. Malone

Hi – Thrilled you love it!! I am totally chuffed with it myself! Will have the rest of the address with you soonest!
Martin
PS Brunch on Sunday would be great. It's a bit lonely for me here with no family, so I much appreciate the hospitality!
Martin

November 7

From: Martin Lukes
To: Barry S. Malone

Hi Barry
Thank you for an energizing day! Can I congratulate you on the charm and beauty of your daughter? I'd lock her up if I were

you! Also congratulations on having found in Janine a woman who not only cooks the perfect eggs benedict but plays such excellent golf?

Martin

PS Sorry to bring up a work matter, but if there is a window tomorrow you and I and Keith should discuss the next chairman of the UK company.

November 8

From: Martin Lukes
To: Graham Wallace

Hi Graham

I've been fighting your corner here, though it's tough work. Barry unfortunately seems to have delegated it to Keith who is trying very hard to keep me out of the loop.

Went over to BSM's house again yesterday. Randee not there this time. Janine was there instead . . . v friendly to yours truly. Actually I've changed my mind on her – she's very bright, and we had some good intellectual discussions! Afterwards we played a fourball with his gorgeous daughter, who is 15 but looks 25. I played pretty well.

Barry has just bought a painting for $2.5m that he says is worth twice as much. Not sure how he managed that . . . and when I asked, he went all funny. Most of the time I know exactly what Barry's thinking, but sometimes he plays his cards v close to his chest.

Cheers, Mart

PS What's the London gossip? Feeling a tad out of the loop

From: Martin Lukes
To: Phyllis Lukes

Dearest Mum

So sorry not to have been in touch for yonks. Everything going mad here. Thanks for your message. Glad you went to have Sunday lunch with Jens and the boys.

Try not to worry too much about Jake – teenage boys always look pale and thin – they don't get out in the fresh air that much.

You didn't say anything about Jens. Did she mention the D word? She seems to have stopped talking about divorce, though if I'm totally honest, she's stopped talking about anything at all. Her coping strategy is to bury herself in her work – which worries me as it isn't the best thing for the boys.

Did I tell you that it's over with Keri? At the end of the day she decided she wanted something more serious than I was prepared to give at the present moment in time – I was upset for a bit, but then I figured that the two of us didn't have a lot in common – but I think you worked that out for yourself!

Work is fantastic, never been better, and all in all I'd say I'm having a great time here. Americans all really friendly and open, which suits me perfectly. Only slight trouble is that I can't sleep. Otherwise all ticketyboo. Will email or ring later in the week.

Yr loving son,

Martin x

From: Martin Lukes
To: Jenny Withers

Jens –

Mum says Jake's looking terrible. He doesn't reply to my messages, or speak on the phone. What's going on? Is he on drugs again? You really do need to keep me in the loop.

I hear you're working flat out, and frankly I worry that not only is that bad for the boys, it's not good for you.

Love, Martin x

From: Martin Lukes
To: Jenny Withers

J – No I can't possibly come back this w/end. In case you hadn't noticed, I'm doing the most important project this company has ever undertaken. I'm under a lot of pressure . . . and you aren't helping. In case you are interested, I'm not sleeping at all . . . M

From: Martin Lukes
To: Jenny Withers

Jens – thank you for your 'considerate' message. This is a very stressful time for me and I don't appreciate getting messages about my 'double standards' and 'dysfunctional behaviour'. I do NOT need therapy. If anyone needs it, it's you. By refusing to come and join me in Atlanta you are hurting yourself, myself and the boys. You are also draining our funds. I'm still in a hotel waiting on a decision from you on what sort of house to buy. The mini bar bill for a week alone is the same as our annual gas bill.

I know what you think of Pandora, but I've been doing some interesting work with her on my relationships, and looking at the ones that drain my energy compared to the ones that boost it. My relationship with you, regrettably, falls into the first camp. Pandora clearly thinks we should split up – you aren't bringing anything to my party, if you will. Frankly I'm beginning to see where she's coming from.
Martin

November 11

From: Martin Lukes
To: All Staff

Conference Update!
Attached is the schedule for Phenomenal Performance – Permanently at Paradise Island. This year the theme is One Global Family! Please note that the dress code is Smart Casual (no suits required). Evening events casual with a Bahamas theme. Feel free to dress colourful!

If you have any questions or issues or inspirations, please do not hesitate to touch base with myself.

Martin

AGENDA DAY ONE

Meeting Location: Ballroom

5.30 pm–7 pm CEO's Address: WE ARE FAMILY!

7 pm–8 pm Cocktails and canapes

8 pm Banquet – poolside

DAY TWO

7.30 Breakfast

8.30–9.30 Martin Lukes: THE ART OF CREOVATION™ – FROM LITTLE WOW TO BIG WOW

10.00 Keynote speaker – Tom Peters: !REIMAGINE!

11.00–1.00 BREAK-OUT WORKSHOPS LED BY A-B GLOBAL (UK)

These will be themed around a traditional Bahamas festival, Junkanoo, where the people get together and lose their inhibitions. At these workshops all co-colleagues will be invited to check their existing headsets at the door and free associate! It's going to be a ton of fun!

1. Christo Weinberg: BUSKING THE LGBT AGENDA – How lesbians, gays, bisexuals and transgenders grow the bottom line.

2. Jenny Withers: AROUND THE CORPORATE CAMPFIRE – The magical art of storytelling.

3. Roger Wright: DELIVERING ON BUDGET – Zero tolerance of cost overruns

4. Faith Preston: UNLEASHING THE HOLISTIC HEADSET – The HR/Business Strategy Partnership

1.00–2.30 LUNCH

2.30–4.00 Keith Buxton: RAISING THE TALENT BAR – Key learnings from ABC

4.00–6.00 Afternoon activities – Golf, Spa, Healing therapies.

6.00–7.30 Conference wrap up, Cindy Czarnikow: THE WEAKEST LINK VISION AND VALUES QUIZ!

From: Martin Lukes
To: Keith Buxton

Hi – yes I have scheduled your talk for the after-lunch slot. And no, it is not going to be possible to swap with mine. A huge amount of thought has gone into the logistics of this and I believe I have come up with a best-of-breed outcome.

I gave you the so-called 'graveyard slot' because I thought you'd deliver a presentation compelling enough so that people stay awake!!
Bestest
Martin

From: Martin Lukes
To: All Staff

Hi!
A reminder to all co-colleagues who will NOT be present at Paradise Island that Barry's speech will be broadcast live on the Web. Large screens will be erected in all geographies and co-colleagues are encouraged to watch it together in order to ensure maximum impact!
Bestest
Martin Lukes
Chief of Staff Office of the Chairman and CEO

November 12

From: Martin Lukes
To: All Paradise Island Delegates

Hi!
I'm very sorry to say that Tom Peters is not going to be able to make it to Paradise Island, but I'm delighted to announce that we have been lucky to get Bear Grylls, the famous mountaineer, to step into Tom's shoes at the last minute. He's going to talk

to us about how to climb to the top of our market space. I'm sure it is going to be a uniquely stimulating session!
Martin

November 13

From: Cindy Czarnikow
To: Paradise Island delegates

Welcome to this island paradise!! For the next few days we are going to bond, to brainstorm and to busk! Today everyone should swim, soak up the scene and enjoy a lite lunch in the Jungle Bar. I recommend the plantain-crusted Nassau grouper creole. Yum! Make sure you're well rested and refreshed ahead of Barry's extraordinary motivational plenary address at 5.30 pm. And sharpen your wits for the Vision and Values quiz tomorrow! I shall be testing everyone on our mission, our prayers, our behaviours and our dreams.

You don't want to be the Weakest Link!!!
Cheers, Cindy
Sent from my BlackBerry Wireless Handheld

From: Martin Lukes
To: Jake Lukes

Hi Jake – Just seen your message. No I don't know where your mother is, she hasn't arrived yet. And no, I can't send you more money. You get 200 quid at the beginning of the month. Would appreciate an email/phone call from you before then with some news in it, rather than just requests for dosh.
Dad
Sent from my BlackBerry Wireless Handheld

Text message to Jenny. Sent 14:23

Jens – are u here? Why haven't u checked in? M x

Why have you got a separate room??? I booked a double suite for both of us. M

From: Martin Lukes
To: Barry S. Malone

Hi Barry
Just wanted to say good luck, and put down a couple of pointers on run through. I think it's best if you let your natural warmth come through. Let your charisma fill the auditorium!

The sound system is brilliant so the music will be very, very loud. I've positioned a couple of cheer leaders in the audience who know when to clap, when to whoop, and when to stand up and stamp their feet. The rest of the audience will take their lead from them. Give it all you've got, and Good Luck!
Martin

From: Martin Lukes
To: All Staff

Welcome!
Everyone gather for Barry's address in the Ballroom now! Starting in 15 minutes!
Martin
Sent from my BlackBerry Wireless Handheld

From: Martin Lukes
To: Barry S. Malone

Hi Barry –
WHOOOOOAA!!! Your performance just now was amazing!! I haven't seen a crowd shout so much since I went to a Led

Zeppelin concert when I was 17! You have taken the family concept and breathed life into it. THEY ALL LOVED YOU!! After you bounded off stage there was a feeling of real passion in the audience. People were crying and hugging each other. Amazing. An example unto us all!! WE ARE FAMILY!!!
Martin
Sent from my BlackBerry Wireless Handheld

From: Martin Lukes
To: Graham Wallace

U not going to believe this . . . was coming out of the Bahama Boom Beach Club just now and saw Roger and Cindy snogging!!!! They saw me too – which is good as it means I have something on both of them. I'm in shock . . . I didn't think beancounters had sex! It would explain why Rog has been allowed to stay in that job for so long.

Bed now. I need my beauty sleep for tomorrow.

M
Sent from my BlackBerry Wireless Handheld

November 14

Text message to Jenny. Sent 07:57

Was upset u sat with Keith at breakfast. Can we have lunch? Am off to give my speech now. Fingers crossed. Best of British with yrs later. M xx

From: Martin Lukes
To: Barry S. Malone

Thank you very much! Yes, when I was standing on the podium I felt this terrific current of positive energy coming from the audience. I've had some fantastic feedback for my speech, but

to me it just proves that your strategy for uniting and re-energizing this company is delivering results already.
Bestest, Martin
Sent from my BlackBerry Wireless Handheld

From: Martin Lukes
To: Roger Wright

Thanks! Glad you enjoyed it! Sorry I couldn't make your budget workshop . . . hope it went well!
Cheers, Martin
PS btw, don't worry at all about the other night. I am a man of the world, and understand these things happen. Frankly, we've all been there!
Sent from my BlackBerry Wireless Handheld

From: Martin Lukes
To: Cindy Czarnikow

Thanks Cindy! Glad you found it so stimulating! I really enjoyed it myself!
Best Martin
PS btw, don't worry about the other night. Discretion is my middle name!!
Sent from my BlackBerry Wireless Handheld

From: Martin Lukes
To: Bear Grylls

Hi Bear,
Really great, hyper-motivational presentation on mountaineering just now!! Yr story about how you got up from that hospital bed and then climbed Everest, was incredibly moving. Personally, I've always believed that we all have the seed of something truly extraordinary inside us if only we know how to access

it. I will be propping up the bar in the Bahama Boom Beach Club tonight, and would be delighted to buy you a drink.
Martin
Sent from my BlackBerry Wireless Handheld

From: Cindy Czarnikow
To: Paradise Island delegates

Hi!
The Weakest Link quiz was a blast! Congratulations to Jenny Withers who knows all our visions and values down to the last letter! She was the fastest to name all our key behaviors, and to be able to list them in order. Well done Jenny!!! You win a free shiatsu massage in the health spa!!
Cheers, Cindy
Sent from my BlackBerry Wireless Handheld

Text message to Graham. Sent 23:57

Where r u? There's no one in the bar . . . can't find anyone to drink with. Don't feel like bed yet . . . am in the mood for some action. M

November 15

Text message to Graham. Sent 08:23

Arrgh. I'm so hungover. Can't face golf. C u later.

From: Martin Lukes
To: Jenny Withers

Jens – I'm very sorry about last night. I was very pissed – this insomnia thing is making me drink quite a lot. Anyway I didn't mean to barge into your room and force myself on you like that. Can we have a drink by the poolside tonight to make amends.

I'll have to be on call in case Barry needs me, but we should have a chance for a chat.
M xx
Sent from my BlackBerry Wireless Handheld

November 18

From: Barry S. Malone
To: All Staff

Howdy!
Last weekend every director of this company gathered in the Bahamas' beautiful Paradise Island for our annual conference. The theme was We are One Global Family, and we showed that we are stronger than ever, united by love, values and belief.

It would be unfair to single out any individual co-leader for such an exceptional event. However I would like to thank Martin Lukes, whose passion and dedication to making it the weekend of a lifetime knew no bounds.

Also Jenny Withers in London, whose speech Storytelling – Around the Corporate Campfire gave us all so much to think about. It's a long time since I read the classics, but her speech has inspired me to go back and take a peek!

It is these stories, not just in books, but by word of mouth that we pass down to each other that bind us together, to our past and our future. We are great apart. Together we are unbeatable.
I love you all
Barry

From: Martin Lukes
To: Jenny Withers

Sorry you dashed off to get your plane without saying goodbye. You see what an amazing couple we are – both singled out. Great apart – together unbeatable?
M xx

From: Martin Lukes
To: Pandora@CoachworX

Hi Pandora
It was an incredible four days, I feel that my personal/leadership brand is looking very good indeed. It was by far the most successful conference we've ever had, and everyone has congratulated me on it.

I tried for a reconciliation with Jens, but it didn't really work. I am coming around to your way of thinking – I can't afford the energy drain any more.

Still can't sleep, and although my brain is producing as many creovative™ ideas as before, it's beginning to get to me. When I was in the Bahamas I managed to see a holistic healer in the hotel who said I'm predominantly kinesthetic and that it's important to be in an environment where I feel comfortable, which made a lot of sense to me.
22.5 per cent better than my bestest
Martin

November 22

From: Martin Lukes
To: Barry S. Malone

Hi Barry
I see there have been a few more muck-raking stories in the papers while we have been in the Bahamas. Can I make a suggestion? This is the moment to put out an internal announcement relating to your integrity, something that will reinforce your brand values. I have in mind something that is totally authentic to your character, but will distract attention from any further press reports on your divorce and Janine.
Bestest, Martin

From: Barry S. Malone
To: All Staff

Howdy!
As everybody close to me knows, I do not rest easy knowing that
there is injustice in this world. Every day I try to fight for compassion,
against greed. It is for that reason, that I have decided to give a signif-
icant percentage of my bonus this year to the Boy Scouts League of
America. The gift means some personal hardship for my family, but
they understand that in tough times those at the top must make hard
choices and hard sacrifices.
I love you all
Barry S. Malone

From: Martin Lukes
To: Barry S. Malone

Hi Barry
Another Big Wow! That was just right. M

From: Martin Lukes
To: Graham Wallace

Graham – Frankly your carping pisses me off. Contrary to what
you say, Barry does deserve his bonus. It's particularly generous
of him to be giving money away when his wife Randee is suing
him for $98m . . . Cheers M

From: Martin Lukes
To: Pandora@CoachworX

Pandora
You know what you said last month about the millionaire's
mindset? Barry's definitely got it – money just seems to flow to
him . . . he's just bought a new Picasso, it's a very good one. I'm
no great connoisseur but I know what I like. Barry was impressed

333

by my commentary on the pictures because he's offered to put me in touch with his art dealer!

22.5 per cent better than my bestest

Martin

November 23

From: Keith Buxton
To: All Staff

Hi

I am delighted to announce that Christo Weinberg has been appointed Marketing Director in London. Christo has an exceptional creative talent, and I'm sure will breathe new life into this most important department.

An announcement on a new chairman of a-b glöbâl (UK) will be made shortly.

Keith Buxton
Global Chief Talent Officer

From: Martin Lukes
To: Keith Buxton

Keith –

Why wasn't I consulted about this??? Christo Weinberg is a very bright lad who has hugely benefited from my mentoring over the past year. But no way is he ready to head up such an important department. And when you say 'breathe new life' into the department what exactly are you driving at?

Re the UK chairman: I'm glad a decision is imminent though sad you did not see fit to consult myself. With respect, I should be kept in the loop.

Martin

From: Martin Lukes
To: Roger Wright

Hi Roger – Who told you that? I don't believe it. I've just been talking to Barry and if there was anything odd going on re insider trading he definitely would have told me.

Yes, obviously I'm rooting for you. An announcement is going to be made very soon, but I think you understand it wouldn't be fair if I dropped any hints. We need to make sure the playing field is level!
Martin

November 24

From: Barry S. Malone
To: All Staff

Howdy!
This morning I received notification from the SEC that it is investigating movements in the a-b glöbâl share price in the period leading up to Q2 and Q3 results. However, I have no reason to believe that this is any more than routine. There is no question of any wrongdoing by anybody inside this company.
I love you all.
Barry S. Malone

From: Martin Lukes
To: Graham Wallace

Hi Graham
What are people saying in London about the insider trading story? I think it's definitely a storm in a teacup – though BSM seems a bit paranoid about it all. I caught him shrieking at his PA just now, an attractive little number called Stacey.
Mart

November 25

From: Martin Lukes
To: Barry S. Malone

Hi Barry,
I suggest we do something to take people's minds off the insider trading story. Just been looking at the outsourcing figures. Looks like we'll be cutting 6,000 jobs globally. Do you think now might be a time to get some of that bad news into the open to detract attention, if you will? You suggest I send out a message to put an end to the rumours. I've thought hard about this and wonder if we might do better to sit tight and wait for it to blow over?
My best, Martin

From: Martin Lukes
To: Barry S. Malone

Sure, on second thoughts I think you're 250 per cent right. Will do soonest.
Martin

From: Martin Lukes
To: All Staff

Hi!
Our CEO, Barry S. Malone, has asked myself to touch base re the stories in the press relating to insider trading. Most of these bear little relation to the facts, which are as follows. An individual has been taken in for questioning for alleged insider trading in a-b glöbâl shares. We believe her to be a Manhattan-based art dealer. She has a large portfolio of stocks which she trades actively. Barry is a renowned art collector but has never met this individual. There is no link between the two whatsoever.
Martin Lukes
Chief of Staff, Office of the Chairman and CEO

From: Martin Lukes
To Pandora@CoachworX

Hi Pandora
Sorry I haven't been in touch – huge drama here on insider trading. Could be very serious, but I think we are controlling the agenda skilfully, and it'll probably blow over.
22.5 per cent better than my bestest
Martin

November 26

From: Martin Lukes
To: Stacey Stone

Oh my God I don't believe it. Where is he now?

From: Martin Lukes
To: Keith Buxton

Keith – have you heard anything?

From: Martin Lukes
To: Graham Wallace

Fucketyfuckingfuck – Barry's been taken in for questioning. I just don't bloody believe it. The total complete and utter idiot. This is a personal CATASTROPHE for me – I need a drink NOW. Wish u were here . . . M

From: Martin Lukes
To: Keith Buxton

As bad as that? I must say I'm not altogether surprised. As I got closer to Barry I realized something was up. I never really bought into the integrity thing. In fact I was so suspicious about his art

dealer person I had planned to check her out. Let's meet soonest to limit damage.
Martin

From: Martin Lukes
To: Keith Buxton

KEITH – I CAN'T BELIEVE YOU JUST SENT ME THAT. WHAT DO YOU MEAN – I'M PART OF THE PROBLEM NOT THE SOLUTION????

From: Martin Lukes
To: Katherine Lukes

Hi Katherine
Got your SOS. Sorry you have split with your partner. But really I can't help you. I'm in a worse crisis of my own. Might message when things get calmer.
Martin

From: Martin Lukes
To: Pandora@CoachworX

Pandora –
Malone has quit. He's been feeding insider information to this art dealer.
   Fucking Keith Buxton has dared suggest I should resign too. Fuckfuckfuck . . . I've been much too close to him . . . what shall I do? Help help M

From: Pandora@CoachworX
To: Martin Lukes

Martin – Can I remind you that crisis management is a coaching service only offered with the Executive Gold Program. Unfortunately as you have not upscaled from Executive

Bronze that means that I am not able to offer you in-depth coaching through this.

However, I can suggest as a start that you try to make a paradigm shift in your mindset. Take some deep breaths. Put your hands in front of your mouth, or find a bag and breath into it. This will stop you from hyperventilating. When the going gets tough, the tough get tougher . . .
Strive and thrive!
Pandora

From: Martin Lukes
To: Pandora@CoachworX

For fuck's sake Pandora – I may be about to lose my job. Now is NOT the time to start breathing into a paper bag. Do you have any USEFUL advice on what I should do now??
Martin

From: Pandora@CoachworX
To: Martin Lukes

As I said Martin, I shouldn't really be offering you this, but I do it out of the goodness of my heart.

Ask yourself some questions. Is my relationship with Barry really a rocket? How do I protect my personal brand? The GROW model will help you, Martin. Remember, this is a time to make sure that whatever you do is aligned with your values. If you ignore your values, you will damage your brand.
Strive and thrive!
Pandora

From: Martin Lukes
To: Lucy Kellaway@ft

Hi Lucy,
Long time no speak. Trust all is well with you and yours. We

spoke back in February when I was doing a project giving back to the homeless. I remember the Financial Times was the only newspaper that handled the story responsibly.

I wanted to touch base to offer an exclusive on the a-b glôbâl story. You'll have seen on the wire that our CEO Barry S. Malone resigned this morning. Many newspapers will be running with the story that a-b glôbâl had not kept proper checks and balances on him. This actually is not the case. It was becoming clear to myself, as Malone's chief of staff, that he did not meet my own, or the company's, exceptionally high standards of ethics. In particular my suspicions had been aroused by his art dealing. The day before he was taken in for questioning, I challenged him personally. He did not give me a satisfactory answer, and I had that day considered contacting a support group for whistle-blowers. I can offer you an exclusive interview.

All my very bestest
Martin Lukes

November 29

From: Christo Weinberg
To: All Marketing

Hi!
Day One for me as Marketing Director has certainly been exciting! In case anybody has not yet seen it, the following story appeared in the London Financial Times this morning. Particularly direct your attention to my predecessor's angle on page 17.

A-B GLOBAL CHIEF QUITS IN SHARE SCANDAL
By Lucy Kellaway
a-b glôbâl, the beleaguered Atlanta-based multinational, was plunged into crisis last night following the forced resignation of CEO Barry S. Malone after allegations of insider trading. Mr Malone, who is a renowned art collector, is alleged to have passed insider information

to his art dealer in return for works of art. Mr Keith Buxton, chief talent officer, takes over as CEO pending the announcement of a permanent replacement. Earlier this year Mr Malone was named by Fortune magazine the seventh most respected global leader. Last month Randee Malone, Mr Malone's fourth wife, filed for divorce, following allegations of her husband's affair with Janine Rozenholtz, a Fortune journalist.

Full Story page 2.
'My agony as whistle-blower', page 17

From: Martin Lukes
To: Keith Buxton

Keith – How DARE you accuse me of lying??? I was simply protecting the company, and correcting a few misconceptions about myself being a BSM groupie. Yes, I did send an email out defending Barry before the shit hit the proverbial. But the thinking behind that was complex, and this has been a fast-moving situation.
Martin

From: Martin Lukes
To: Janine Rozenholtz

Hi Janine
Just seen your messages. I realize you are upset by the article in today's newspaper, yet I fail to grasp your meaning when you compare myself with Judas. I hope in the fullness of time you will understand that, as a champion of the highest ethical standards, my first duty is to do what is right.
All my very bestest
Martin Lukes

November 30

From: Keith Buxton
To: All Staff

Hi everyone,
First up I would like to say how honoured I am to be given the oppor-
tunity to lead this company until the board has finalized a permanent
CEO appointment. This is a time for firm leadership, and I would like
to make two things very clear. It is imperative that no member of staff
speaks to the press without prior authorization from myself and from
our legal team. I cannot stress how essential this is. There have been
some unfortunate incidents in the past few days, which we do not want
repeated. I would like to reassure everyone that the company's strategy
of delivering astounding value to all our stakeholder groups remains
as strong as ever. The only short-term policy shift is to abandon the
roll-out for the new office of the CEO. In the current climate we do not
feel such extra resources to be justified. Individuals already recruited
to this team will be encouraged to apply for jobs elsewhere in the group.
All my very bestest, Keith Buxton

From: Martin Lukes
To: Keith Buxton

KEITH – DID NO ONE EVER TELL YOU IT IS NOT A GOOD
IDEA TO SACK PEOPLE BY PUBLIC EMAIL??? AND WHAT
THE HELL JOB AM I MEANT TO BE APPLYING FOR????????
MARTIN

From: Martin Lukes
To: Jenny Withers

Jens – Don't you start, as well. I gave that interview for good
reasons. I might have hoped you, as supposed media maestro,
would understand that. My position here is untenable. I'm on the
plane home tomorrow, and my first call will be to our solicitor.

This is a cut and dried case for constructive dismissal. Keith hates me, and frankly the feeling is mutual. He's not going to get away with this. Would appreciate if you came to meet me at Heathrow.

From: Martin Lukes
To: Sherry Zook

Sherry – I'll be out for the rest of the day, and I don't think I'll return tomorrow. If anyone wants me, tell them whatever you like. It's been great working with you, and if we had had the chance of working together for longer, I'm sure a greater understanding would have grown up between us. Next time you're in London do look me up.
Best, Martin
PS When my crates arrive from London, please send them back again.

From: Martin Lukes
To: Jenny Withers

You can't keep this up. I've had a very very serious blow. This is the biggest disaster that has ever happened to me in my life. It is so unfair . . . Let me home now. Please.
Love you M x

Chapter Twelve

December
Welcome Home

December 1

From: Pandora@CoachworX
To: Martin Lukes

Hi Martin
Congratulations, Martin, you have almost finished
Executive Bronze! The You that is reading this email has true
and amazing abilities, talent and potential. You are a human
BEING. So just . . . Be! Be you. You are a wonderful person,
with incredible gifts, talents and strengths beyond your
wildest dreams. Take that thought and feel its warmth. Now
double it. Double it again. And again. And smile. Because you
know, deep down inside it is time to reclaim your birthright.
It is time to return to your true self. WELCOME HOME!
Strive and thrive!
Pandora

From: Martin Lukes
To: Pandora@CoachworX

Pandora –
Can I be totally honest with you? I read your message with a
growing sense of disconnect. Has it escaped your notice that I
am NOT home?? I am actually staying at the Novotel Canning
Town for the foreseeable future and am living out of a suitcase.

Neither am I 'home' career-wise. At the moment it is not clear whether I have a job at all. I came into the office this morning, expecting to return to my position as Director of Marketing, to find Christo Weinberg at my desk. I have nowhere to sit. I have no PA. I have no idea what I am supposed to do. Not only is my wife ignoring me, everyone is ignoring me. I might have gifts and talents beyond my wildest dreams, but no one gives a monkeys. If this is New Me, frankly I would like to reconnect with Old Me.
Martin

From: Pandora@CoachworX
To: Martin Lukes

Hi Martin!
Whooaa! Looks like you need a refresher on some of the key learnings to date! I know that there have been some issues around your departure from Atlanta. But Martin, you must not take these personally. Have you forgotten the mantra, No Failure, Only Feedback? You haven't failed. You are the same You who was Chief of Staff. Martin, I want you to think about the events of the last week. What happened? Why did it happen? What are the learnings you can take out from it? Strive and thrive!
Pandora

From: Martin Lukes
To: Pandora@CoachworX

Pandora – There are no learnings in this. I backed the wrong horse, and now I'm paying for it, big time. The only issue for myself is what next?

Basically, there is one thing that I want now and that is to be made Chairman of a-b glöbâl (UK). There is a humungous problem – and that is Keith Buxton. He has issues around envy re yours truly, and frankly, it's going to be hard for me to persuade

him to appoint me. If you have any concrete suggestions on this I'm in the market for them.
Martin

December 2

From: Martin Lukes
To: Graham Wallace

Hi Graham, thanks for the invite, but no thanks. I think I'll just take it easy this weekend.

In any case my clubs are in my luggage which is in storage.
Cheers, Mart

From: Martin Lukes
To: Graham Wallace

Yes, I'm feeling fine. Just because I don't feel like playing golf doesn't mean that I'm heading for a nervous breakdown. On Sunday, I'll probably be seeing the family.
Cheers, Mart

From: Martin Lukes
To: Keith Buxton

Hi Keith –
Did you get my voicemail messages? I appreciate you're busy, but we really need to discuss my position as a matter of some urgency.

Basically, in a nutshell, there are two scenarios.

Scenario 1: I become Chariman of a-b glöbâl (UK). My previous position as chief of staff has established my proven track record for playing at the top of my game. This would be the preferred scenario for myself, and I hope you will agree that I am the strongest internal candidate in terms of skillsets and reach.

Scenario 2: I return to my old job in marketing, but give it a broader focus in line with my additional status and knowledge resource. I would be called Director of Marketing and Strategy, and would be tasked with broader strategic thinking around the company and its road map moving forward.

I appreciate there have been some issues between us of late, but I trust they will not get in the way of getting the right bod into the right job!
All my very bestest,
Martin

From: Martin Lukes
To: Jenny Withers

Dear estranged wife
I know you are beyond such normal emotions as human sympathy but you may be interested to know that I have this morning started bleeding from my arse.

You might also like to know that I am planning to go to Eton this weekend to see Max, who is now the only member of my family who responds to my messages.
Your husband
Martin

December 3

From: Cindy Czarnikow
To: All Staff

Hi, friends!
The holiday season is a time for giving and at a-b glöbâl, where compassion is built into our corporate DNA, giving has always been top of mind. The past year has shown us that life's journey can sometimes be tough, and this year more than ever, we feel the need to reach out and touch the souls of fellow humans. I am delighted to unveil a scheme to empower each and every one of you to make your own donations. Our charity this year is going to be Champ!

Carrying Hope to All Mothers on our Planet. Champ! has an unrivalled track record in delivering funds and solutions to families throughout the global community. We're committed to all the communities we serve. Because we live here too, and we believe . . . good works.
I'm smiling at you
Cindy

From: Keith Buxton
To: All Staff

Hi,
Thank you Cindy for that. I personally will be among the first to sign up. However, it is imperative that we are not deflected from our task of lifting performance onto the next level. We have some very stretching financial targets for Q4. I know that together we can meet and exceed them, but to do this we must rely on the 3Fs which lately we have lost sight of. Focus. Focus. Focus.
Best, Keith

From: Jenny Withers
To: All Staff

Hello everyone!
Let me just say how strongly I agree that our giving should not distract us from the task ahead. At a-b glöbâl (UK) we are making it as easy as possible to give, all you need do is click the Champ! icon on our intranet site. This will record your name as a donor. The good news is that 174 of you here in the UK have already given. The bad news is that 400 have yet to do so – if your name is not yet on the list please give money today. Champ! needs you!!
Jenny

From: Martin Lukes
To: Jenny Withers

Jens

As you don't reply to my personal messages, here is a professional one.

I'm a tad surprised that you think it's a good idea to publish
names of those who have given money. As you know, I've never
liked making a song and dance about my charitable donations.
It's a highly private matter – it is the giving that matters, not the
publicizing of it. That said, my name does not appear on your
list, despite the fact that I was one of the first to pledge my
money. Could you check and correct it?

Martin

From: Jenny Withers
To: All Staff

*I feel it might be helpful to spell out the thinking behind our decision
to collect the names of those who have given to Champ! The reason is
not to point the finger at any individual, but to ensure that those who
have given do not get pestered with further reminders. I omitted to
mention that the scheme has a £10 lower limit. Individuals donating
less than this amount do not become registered donors. Thank you for
giving!*

Jenny

December 6

From: Martin Lukes
To: Christo Weinberg

Hi Christo

Obviously I don't want to interfere, but I see you have cancelled
the Bay City Rollers campaign. That advertisement would have
scooped up all the creative awards. It was both ironic and iconic.
Very creovative™, very now. I'm just curious to know the
thought process that led up to it.

Cheers, Martin

From: Martin Lukes
To: Aston Martin

Dear Sir
Re: order 245
Due to an unforeseen change in my circumstances I no longer require my car to be assembled as per the US market. I will take delivery of it in London, and require the steering wheel on the right.

All the other customized details remain unchanged, except that I would like the customized plaques on the sills inscribed 'Driving Performance with Martin Lukes' on pewter rather than brass. I have ordered British customized number plates CREOV8, which was fortunately also available, which I will deliver to you closer to the time.
Yours sincerely
Martin Lukes

From: Martin Lukes
To: Graham Wallace

Graham
I don't know how much more can go wrong in my life . . . Christo is undoing all my good work in marketing and bloody Aston Martin say it's too late to put the steering wheel on the left hand side, so I'm going to have to drive around in a car that will be a daily reminder of the job I don't have . . . When you're shelling out £103,000 you expect a bit more in terms of customer service . . . and I've had to cough up nearly £20,000 for mum's op, as our bloody health insurance is totally pathetic.

Am just composing a missive to one of my headhunter friends, and then can we have the largest drink you've ever had?
Cheers, Mart

From: Martin Lukes
To: SebastianFforbesHever@HeidrickFerry

Hi Sebastian!
Long time no hear! I expect you will have been following the shenanigans at a-b glöbâl in the media, and will know that yours truly has been a key player!

Just to keep you in the loop, since we spoke I was appointed as Barry Malone's chief of staff in Atlanta, basically the second most powerful job in the company.

However following the recent upheaval, I'm back in London considering various challenging openings here. Could we have lunch/coffee soonest to kick around some ideas on what's happening in the 'outside world'?
All my very bestest,
Martin

December 7

From: Martin Lukes
To: SebastianFforbesHever@HeidrickFerry

Hi Sebastian
Did you get my message? Don't know if you've been trying to reach me on my office phone. My extension has changed, it's now x4096.
Cheers, Martin

From: Martin Lukes
To: Scott@Bupa

Dear Mr Scott
I have just received your letter, and I note with surprise that you are threatening to take legal action re the claim for my mother's knee replacement operation. I realize that you have been trying to contact myself for some time. I have been out of

the country, and hence the delay. I am sending a cheque for £19,763.27 to cover the cost of the operation which took place earlier this year. I regret that there has been so much confusion over this, and trust the matter is now resolved.

Your truly

Martin Lukes

From: Martin Lukes
To: Jenny Withers

Hi Jens – Just seen yr message. Why do you need to go to Atlanta at such short notice?

And why do you think I can just drop everything and help out??

You say you want a divorce because I'm 'totally obsessed with myself'. Then you turn around and ask me to move back in as a babysitter. Can I point out that YOU are the one who is selfish – your career obsession knows no bounds. You may despise Pandora, but she has taught me a lot about myself, and how I tick. I now understand that there is no point in playing silly games, what counts is for me to align my behaviours with my values. And that is why I am going to help you, not because you deserve my help, but because I miss the boys, and I actually care about their welfare. I am their father and they are badly in need of my input.

Martin

From: Martin Lukes
To: Jake Lukes

Jake

I'm moving back in for the weekend when mum's away. Would be good to have some quality time together. We could hire the new Star Wars movie, have a takeaway curry and a couple of beers? What do you think??

Dad

From: Martin Lukes
To: Max Lukes

Max old man
Mum's off to Atlanta on some job jaunt this weekend, and I'll be holding the fort chez nous. Your house master has given special permission for you to come back for the weekend – Let's do something really wicked!!
Dad

From: Martin Lukes
To: Max Lukes

You want to go to CHURCH? Why???

December 10

Text message to Jenny. Sent at 22.14

Jens – Can u call me NOW??? Jake's been picked up by the police for possession of 10 Ecstasy. Am heading down to Wimbledon police station. M

Text message to Max. Sent at 23:35

Max – am still at the station. Has mum called? tell her to get on the first plane. Dad

December 11

From: Martin Lukes
To: Jenny Withers

Jens –
We're back home, all in one piece. I've sorted everything on my own, so there's no need for you to come back early. They've

released Jake, who is presently sitting in front of the TV. He's very quiet and sullen. Still half off his head, I suppose.

The policeman was unusually bright and was pretty impressed when I told him about my job and I said I personally would be responsible for Jake's future good behaviour. I explained that the lad had been under a lot of pressure because you were working flat out and because of issues between us.

Looks like they're not going to press charges – worst case, I think he'll get away with a caution.

M

From: Martin Lukes
To: Jake Lukes

Dear Jake

The reason I'm putting this in an email rather than waiting until you get up and saying it face to face is because I often find it easier to express myself in writing than verbally. Basically, you deserve the biggest bollocking of your life. By being such an idiot and taking those drugs you have not just let yourself down, but you've let your mother and myself down. If it wasn't for me, you might be facing a 7-year prison sentence – which frankly would be the wake-up call you need.

However, I've been thinking outside the square and have decided not to punish you.

When you were in the police station last night I had one of those eureka moments of self-knowledge. I realized that at the end of the day what really counts is family. You, Max and, obviously, your mother.

I'd like to share something with you that you may find surprising. When I was your age, I got into a spot of trouble, too. One day a gang of mates and myself got pissed on a bottle of Armagnac (I still can't drink it to this day!) and then we went into an Ann Summers shop and yours truly nicked a lacy bra! I got caught, and the store detective threatened me with the police but then let me go. I was terrified he would tell granny, though luckily he didn't. So I totally understand what you're going through, and I hope that you will confide in me going forward.

Jake, I know we've had issues in the past. It's true that you've been a disappointing son in many regards. You did something very, very wrong with my BlackBerry. You've performed exceptionally poorly academically, you've been lazy and you've not chosen friends of your own calibre. And now you are taking Class A drugs and getting caught. It doesn't look very good on paper does it??

But I want to say that I'm your father, and I'm 110 per cent here for you. You are my oldest son. You are like myself (for your sins!!) in many regards. Moving forward, if you put your creovative™ streak to work, you won't go far wrong.
Your loving Dad

December 13

From: Martin Lukes
To: Graham Wallace

Who told you that?!!? Yes, Jens has gone to Atlanta. I just spoke to her 5 minutes ago and she didn't say anything about being offered a job. I know that Keith has always had a thing about her, but even he wouldn't do that . . .
M

From: Martin Lukes
To: Jenny Withers

Thanks for your message. Glad you are impressed. Jake much better this morning. He grunted at me in a slightly less hostile way. I've also sent him a long email establishing some new ground rules. There is going to be one big win out of this – my relationship with Jake is going to be a lot stronger.

Btw Graham has heard a rumour that you're in the frame for Roger's job!!!???
M

From: Martin Lukes
To: Jenny Withers

WHAT??? That is the most stupid thing I've ever heard . . . You do realize I couldn't possibly work under you, don't you??
　　When u coming back? We must talk about this NOW!
M

From: Martin Lukes
To: Jenny Withers

Jens, sorry if my message just then sounded a bit negative. I've thought about it some more, in a very logical way, and reached the conclusion that this is a lose-lose situation. You lose because you would be doing a job that is not well aligned with your skillsets. Being chairman would make you totally stressed and miserable. The company would lose because you would not be the right person and might start making sub-optimal decisions. I would lose because it is very unhealthy working for one's wife – or ex-wife, as you certainly would be if you took the job – and I would be left with no choice but to leave the company. Ergo, the company would lose again.

　　Most important, the boys would lose, especially Jake. If he had a mother who was around more, he would be much less interested in drugs. Max needs you around too. I was really shocked over the weekend at the change in him. He spent most of Sunday morning in church, did the washing up, took all the skate-boarding posters down in his bedroom, and has stuck up some nightmare Alpha course poster with a mobile phone saying 'Is there more to life than this?' He's clearly in a bad way.

　　Mull it over, and you'll see I'm right. Please don't think I'm making these points out of self-interest. I'm not. I'm just standing back and looking at all the issues in the round.
Martin

From: Martin Lukes
To: Jenny Withers

No Jens, I'm not trying to blame you for the boys. As their father I realize that I'm responsible too. It's just that until now you have been closer to them. Yes of course I realize that at the end of the day, it's your call.

Well at least can you promise me one thing . . . that you'll think about it for a few days before deciding? Talk about it when you're home tomorrow. When's your flight?
Martin

From: Martin Lukes
To: Keith Buxton

Hi Keith
I am somewhat surprised to learn that you have offered the job of Chairman (Chairperson, I should say!) of a-b glöbâl (UK) to my ladywife. You will appreciate that this puts me in an extremely awkward position.

Jenny, as you know, is a highly talented, capable person. She is a good communicator, and outstanding at networking within a small group of successful women. She is hard-working, and in a function like External Relations could add useful value. Question. Can she see the big picture? Can she think strategically? Her record in these areas is totally unproven, which would make the appointment a risk. At this present moment in time, a risk is a luxury we cannot afford. It is painful for me to have to write something that could be misinterpreted. However I am frank with you out of love for this company. As somebody who knows Jenny better than anyone else, I do not believe it would be in her best interests to take on a job that is beyond the level of her skills and experience. I shall be counselling her to say no.

We still need to discuss my position soonest.
All my very bestest
Martin

From: Martin Lukes
To: SebastianFforbesHever@HeidrickFerry

Hi Sebastian
Don't know if you got my email of last week. I'm attaching a copy of it in case not. Would be good to meet up soonest to kick around a couple of ideas.
Martin

From: Martin Lukes
To: Stewart@harleystreetclinic

Dear Dr Stewart
As I told your secretary on the telephone, I have been finding traces of blood in my stool. Obviously this is a serious matter and tends to confirm – what I suspected at the time – that the bowel cancer man you sent me to didn't know his arse from a hole in the ground, if you'll pardon my French.

I also have many other symptoms – a fast-beating heart, sometimes leading to palpitations. I have chronic insomnia. I am tending to sweat more than usual, and am tired all the time, and sometimes irritable. This is not at all like myself, as I am usually very controlled.

Would appreciate an appointment at the earliest opportunity.
Yours sincerely
Martin Lukes

From: Martin Lukes
To: Stewart@harleystreetclinic

Dear Dr Stewart
You ask if the blood was on the toilet tissue or in the stool itself. The answer is certainly the former, and possibly the latter, though this is harder to confirm. You also ask if I am depressed. No I am not depressed, though events in my life presently are less than perfect. Yes, I have been drinking a tad more than usual,

though I actually think my psyche is bearing up extremely well under adverse circumstances. I only wish I could say the same for my bowel and my body in the round. I will see you at 9.45 tomorrow.

Yours sincerely
Martin Lukes

From: Martin Lukes
To: Max Lukes

Dear Max,
Thanks for your message. It's kind of you to pray for me, but really old man, quite unnecessary. It was good to see you at the weekend, and so sorry that thanks to Jake's theatricals we didn't have much in the way of quality time.

Though if I'm being completely honest with you I'm a bit worried about this Alpha course malarky. It just doesn't seem very you.
Love Dad

From: Martin Lukes
To: Max Lukes

Dear Max
I didn't mean to be dismissive! I quite agree with Jesus re tolerance and belief. Of course, at the end of the day we all have to do what's right for us as individuals. Thanks also for sending me the material Alpha course in the workplace, all looks v interesting, but I'm not sure that a-b glöbâl (UK) is quite ready for it at the present moment in time!!
Love Dad

December 14

From: Martin Lukes
To: Phyllis Lukes

Dearest Mum
Thanks for your message, and sorry I haven't been able to nail down Christmas plans . . .

To be perfectly frank, you and I might be spending it on our own at your place. Things with Jens are beyond bad – you were so right when you said it was a disastrous idea for her to work at the same place as me. You're not going to believe this but it looks like she's going to wind up as my boss.

It's all taking its toll on me physically. I went to see the doctor this morning, and it turns out I have piles. He says I'm depressed, which frankly I don't accept, but I've decided to take the pills anyway – which means I'm now on Temazepam, Prozac and Anusol.

Don't worry about the boys. They are both fine.

Can I come down and stay with you this weekend?
Martie

From: Pandora@CoachworX
To: Martin Lukes

Hi Martin
I haven't heard from you for a couple of weeks, and wanted to check that you are connecting with the amazing possibilities in your life.

I would also like to make a suggestion. Although Executive Bronze usually only runs for one year, there is no reason why in your case we shouldn't extend into next year. I feel this could be helpful as there are some outstanding issues we could address. Frankly I would feel more comfortable if you did this. I do not feel happy signing off on my coachees until they are at least 10 per cent better than the best they can be.

And with you, Martin, it hasn't really worked out like that.

I am, as you know, your greatest and sincerest fan. It deeply pains me to know that you are letting your self-belief slip. Martin, please let me help you get to the top and stay there! Strive and Thrive!
Pandora

From: Suzanna Elliott
To: All Staff

Hiya!
This year at the Christmas party we are all going to play Secret Santa!

Pick a name out of the hat, and you get to buy a present for this person! All gifts must be under a fiver! It's going to be a load of fun!!
Suze

From: Roger Wright
To: All Staff

A reminder to all staff that in this challenging operating environment expenditure on the Xmas festivities has been capped at £20 per head. Any expenditure over and above this level must be met by the individual. It is most important that all departments observe this.
Roger Wright
Acting Chairman

From: Martin Lukes
To: Graham Wallace

Guess who I've picked out? Jens! Nightmare. She always hates my presents. I don't think secret santa really expects that you will be getting gifts for your wife who wants to divorce you . . .

December 15

From the Financial Times

BELEAGUERED A-B GLOBAL APPOINTS WOMAN IN
NUMBER ONE JOB

a-b glöbâl, the troubled Atlanta-based multinational, which was
last month rocked by allegations of insider dealing, yesterday
appointed Cindy Czarnikow (48) as its new chief executive.

Ms Czarnikow, who currently holds the position of Chief
Morale Champion has worked with the company for 10 years.
She takes over from Mr Keith Buxton who was appointed only
two weeks ago as acting CEO.

'I am humbled at the humungous responsibility that has been
placed on me,' she said yesterday. 'This is a much storied
company with a fine history, and I have pledged to return it to
profitability within 12 months.'

Asked if this would mean further job cuts, she said: 'I am not
frightened of tough choices. The only choices that scare me are
the wrong ones.'

Last month a-b glöbâl announced a loss of $4.6bn, the biggest
in its history.

Asked if there would be a role for Keith Buxton Ms
Czarnikow said: 'Keith Buxton has many wonderful talents, and
I will be speaking with him to see how best they can be leveraged going forward.' Analysts yesterday questioned whether Ms
Czarnikow would be tough enough to make the mass redun-
dancies needed to return the company to profitability. However
one source close to her said 'Underneath the sweet manner is
one tough cookie.'

Cindy Czarnikow is the second woman to run a Fortune 500
company after Carly Fiorina of Hewlett Packard.

From: Martin Lukes
To: Graham Wallace

Graham – have you seen this in the FT today??? I knew that Cindy and Keith didn't get on, but didn't realize it was that bad. My sources say that Keith's blunt manner got up the shareholders' noses. Cindy probably got the job because she's a woman . . . She's an idiot, but it's still good news for us – Keith had it in for me, and Cindy has to be nice to me, or I'll tell about Rog. And as a woman there's no way Cindy is going to promote Jens, she'd be too much like competition.
Martin

From: Cindy Czarnikow
To: All Staff

Hi
First up, thank you for your trust. It means a lot to me.

At the press conference yesterday a journalist asked how I will do things differently. I said I am different because I believe. I believe that miracles are within our grasp. I want each one of you to come into work every day believing you are about to do something miraculous. If you do that, we will exceed our goals within months! Can I ask you all to join hands on this holiday season and take a minute to think about the journey we are going to travel together.

I have two announcements to make on my top team. Keith will sadly be leaving us and I'd like to take this opportunity to thank him for the love and passion he has devoted to this company, and wish him the best on his travels, wherever they may lead him!

Roger Wright, who has done a best-of-breed job in leading the UK company through turbulent times, is appointed to be chairman of a-b glôbâl UK on a permanent basis.

We have a long way to go, but I am confident that we have the winning team in place to transition us to the very top of the league!
I'm smiling at you
Cindy

From: Keith Buxton
To: All Staff

Hi everyone
It is with mixed emotions that I announce my resignation from a-b
glöbâl. It has been a tough decision, but I have decided to pursue other
options and spend more time with my wife and family. I would like to
thank everyone here for making the last few years so enjoyable. This
is a company where an incredibly talented community of colleagues
work with energy and creativity to make a real difference in the lives
of our customers. I feel privileged to have worked with you and wish
you everything good in continuing a-b glöbâl's proud legacy.
Very truly yours
Keith

From: Martin Lukes
To: Jenny Withers

Jens,
We are quits now. I've lost my protector and you've lost yours.
Don't feel badly about the job. It's all for the best. M

From: Martin Lukes
To: Jenny Withers

You had already turned it down??? Why??

From: Martin Lukes
To: Jenny Withers

THAT'S FANTASTIC NEWS!!!!!!!!! When were you planning to
tell me??? Did it happen that night in the hotel in Paradise Island?
Can we have supper tonight to celebrate a new start?
M xx

From: Martin Lukes
To: Jenny Withers

PS Just reassure me – it is mine, isn't it?

December 16

From: Martin Lukes
To: Cindy Czarnikow

Hi Cindy

Can I be the first to say congratulations?? As you know, I have always had the greatest respect for your work and have always got a terrific buzz out of working with you. I'd also like to say that I share your respect for Roger, and have every confidence that he is the right man to lead us into calmer waters! He has kept a steady hand on the tiller these last six months, and deserves reward.

However his skills are more on the finance/cost side and would be complemented by someone who is more on the vision/strategy side. I am proposing myself in the new role of Director of Marketing and Strategy. Can we talk about this?

All my very bestest

Martin

From: Martin Lukes
To: Roger Wright

Hi Roger, many congratulations on your appointment. Very well deserved, if I might venture so bold.

Can we have some face time re my position? I am prepared to move back to Marketing, but would like some additional scope to deploy my big-picture creovative™ skills.

Best, Martin

From: Martin Lukes
To: Roger Wright

Hi Roger
Director of Special Projects??? Not sure I like the sound of
that. How many people would be on my team? Unless the job
is clearly senior to Marketing Director, I don't feel at all inclined
to accept it. In fact if that's all you can offer myself, you leave
me no choice but to pursue options in the 'outside world'.
Martin

From: Martin Lukes
To: Jenny Withers

Darling –
How are you feeling? Hope you're not tiring yourself.
    I'm being offered Director of Special Projects, but I've turned
it down. I've said that if they call it Director of Special Projects
and Strategy I might consider it. Team is minimal, but I would
be allowed to do almost unlimited blue-sky thinking. Rog says
that the position has been created specially for me, and it would
be up to me to make my mark on it. What bothers me is that
Christo may think he's senior to me. I couldn't take that.
Martin

From: Martin Lukes
To: Phyllis Lukes

Dearest Mum
I've got some very big news for you. Jens is pregnant . . . I am
totally over the moon, obviously. I think it means that I'll be
moving back home soon, though Jens wants to take it very slowly.
We are going to see a counsellor next week to sort out a couple
of issues, but should be for the best.
    Job-wise, things are also looking up. I've been offered the job
of Director of Special Projects and Strategy, which in a way is

better than Marketing Director as it's a broader sweep intellectually. If I take it, I would be a bit less frantic, so I'll be able to devote more time to the family. Not sure what to do.
Your loving son
Martie

From: Faith Preston
To: All Directors

Everyone congregate in reception at 6.45 in your best 70s fancy dress, and we'll go together to the London Dungeons!!

December 17

From: Martin Lukes
To: Graham Wallace

Great party last nite! I saw you snogging that new trainee on your team – she can't be more than 21!!!

Odd turn-up for yours truly – this must be the first Christmas party on record where I spent the evening trying to get off with my ladywife. Didn't altogether succeed, she said that my vintage 1970s lilac ruched shirt and brown velvet jacket made her feel sick. But at least she is talking to me again.
Martin
Hair of the dog later?

From: Martin Lukes
To: Jenny Withers

Jens, darling – I've been thinking . . . let's have our usual Yule party. It's been an amazing year, and we've got a lot to celebrate. What do you think? It needn't be that much work. In view of your condition, let's push the boat out and get caterers in. I'll look after the booze, but they could do a seasonal finger buffet. How about doing it on the 22nd? Love both of you (!) M x

From: Martin Lukes
To: Pandora@CoachworX

Hi Pandora
First up, I wanted to say sorry its taken me a while to get back to you re the suggestion of prolonging Executive Bronze. I'm happy to say that won't be necessary as things have taken a turn for the better chez nous – most surprising turn up is that we're having another baby!

I've also been offered a job here which I think I'm going to accept. I've been thinking about my core values, and I think it plays to all of them.

As a combined 'thank you' and a 'meet and greet' I wondered if you'd be able to attend our annual Christmas Party on Wednesday night? For obvious reasons it's all very last minute, but I do hope you can make it. It'll be very informal – just a few really close friends. 37 The Avenue, Wimbledon. Finger buffet, champers and Martin Lukes' famous lethal mulled wine! Any time from 7 pm – hope to see you then!
Cheers, Martin

From: Martin Lukes
To: Katherine Lukes

Hi Katherine
Thanks for your message, and apologies not to have got back sooner. Sorry to hear that you're still feeling so low after the break-up with Fiona. It's been quite a year for that sort of thing. Are you sure it's wise to go ahead with the adoption on your own?

Looks like Jens and I are back together, and we're having a party to celebrate. Do hope you can come. You'll meet the whole family in one go. Details and map attached. Hope to see you then!
Best, Martin

From: Martin Lukes
To: Graham Wallace

Very short notice, but we've decided to have our traditional Xmas knees-up after all this year. 22nd. Hope you and Lynne can make it.
Mart

From: Keri Tartt
To: All Staff

Hiya!
I just wanted to send Yule greetings to all my mates, and say I haven't forgotten you! I've been back in Kiwi for just 4 weeks, and loads has happened! My old boyfriend met me off the plane, and within a week he got down on one knee and popped the question!!
And I said YES!!!!!
I've enrolled to finish my physio course! I'll think of you as I have my turkey on the beach!!
Cheers Keri x

December 23

From: Martin Lukes
To: Graham Wallace

Glad you enjoyed it! Am feeling v rough this am, but I think everyone had a good time.
Was it the hallucinatory effects of my punch, or did you disappear upstairs at one point with Svetlana? She certainly doesn't believe in playing hard to get!!! Even Jake had a go at her at one point . . .
Cheers, Martin
PS What did you think of my speech? Went down like a lead balloon with Jens, but I was pretty chuffed with it.

From: Martin Lukes
To: Graham Wallace

Thanks, yes I thought you'd get the joke! Jens has been giving me a v hard time about it – when everyone had finally gone home last night she went ballistic that I had announced the impending birth of our little one – she says that she hasn't told anyone at work yet, that it's all early days etc. etc. She also didn't think my comparisons with the virgin birth were at all funny.

Btw I think it's a great idea for Pandora to coach you next year. Did I overhear her saying that she's your #1 fan?? I should warn you she says that to all her coachees!!

You'll find that although some of what she says is bullshit, basically she's very sound. On balance, she's been cathartic for myself over the past year but now is the right time for me to move on. I've signed up with Steven Roberts from 4-Dimensional Leadership, who specializes in coaching people at the chief exec level. He's a bit more expensive than Pandora, but hopefully worth it to me at this juncture in my career.

Have a good one.

Mart

From: Martin Lukes
To: Katherine Lukes

Hi Katherine

It was great to see you last night after all this time. You haven't changed a bit. Once I got used to your new hair-do I could see you are just the same little sis! Obviously there's a bit more of you than there used to be, but then I'm spreading out a bit myself!

It was good of you to spend so much of the evening chatting to Jake. Most adults have difficulty in seeing the positive side of him. Not sure you should have been encouraging him with the wacky backy though!!

Great that you got on so well with Pandora. Did I ever tell you that it was she who suggested that I make contact with you, as she said you'd benefit from closure with me? Hope you don't mind, but I took the liberty of telling her that you had just come out of a long-term relationship, and that she might be able to help you work through some issues on rejection. I've found her very useful on matters personal.

Actually, it was very weird for me meeting her, as until last night I had never clapped eyes on her. I've been emailing her all my innermost thoughts for the past year so there's very little about yours truly that she doesn't know intimately!!!! I couldn't get over her appearance – I was expecting her to be petite and forceful and sexy. So you can imagine how shocked I was at the reality!

Have a triffic Crimble. Let's meet up in the new year a deux to have a natter about old times.

Cheers, Martin

From: Martin Lukes
To: Phyllis Lukes

Dearest Mum

Sorry you couldn't make it to the party. It was a huge success. Weird seeing Katherine after all this time. At first I didn't recognize her at all. She's aged a lot and put on weight. The red spiky hair is a mistake.

It was also very odd meeting Pandora. She's hugely fat and was wearing a pink shell suit, and kept on nipping out onto loggia for a fag. It's very hard to believe that she was ever a ballerina . . . She was all over Katherine, and the two of them shared a cab home afterwards. The thought occurred to me that she may be that way inclined too. Which would make a lot of sense. I suppose neither of them, for different reasons, ever met the right man.

It's funny to think that although Pandora has obviously cocked up her own relationships she has this weird talent for helping other people. That line from Wordsworth came to me: Physician heal thyself.

Jake and Katherine really bonded, and as I said to Jens afterwards, there are a lot of similarities between them. Both of them have been damaged by having brilliant siblings. It's definitely left scars on both of them. K's asked Jake to go and stay in Brighton in the New Year at her place and experience some of the counter-culture there, which was nice of her.

This new religious jag of Max's is really getting to me. He stood on the sidelines looking disapproving as we all got merry. Drinking is what Crimble is all about. I'll drive down and pick you up tomorrow morning. Really looking forward to a lovely family Christmas xx

Your loving son

Martie

From: Martin Lukes
To: Katherine Lukes

I didn't mean to be critical of Pandora – really glad you liked her so much!!! Don't take seriously what I said about her appearance – I've never believed in a one-size-fits-all mentality! My watchword is: different strokes for different folks.

So on that philosophical note, Happy Crimble.

M

December 27

From: Martin Lukes
To: Graham Wallace

Hi Graham

How was yours?? Ours pretty good, though Jens feeling sick and very bad-tempered. Jake and I went for a long Boxing Day walk, and although he's still monosyllabic I think relations between us are pretty good. Max spent most of the morning at church, and the afternoon doling out soup in some hostel. And Mum was happy as Jens let her cook the turkey. Slight friction when Mum said Jens should stop work and 43 was an unnatural age to have a baby. I could see where she was coming from, but it wasn't exactly tactful. Still I was allowed back into the marital bed – though no hanky panky as yet due to the nausea. Jens gave me the South Beach Diet for Crimble, and I've said I'll start in the New Year. I think it allows me to drink, but only red wine. Pint of Guinness in an hour?

Martin

PS Did you read in the papers over Christmas that it looks like BSM may get locked up for some time? Serves him right.

December 31

From: Roger Wright
To: All Staff

Re: Staff changes
Martin Lukes is to become Director of Special Projects and Strategy, effective immediately. This is a main board position, reporting to myself. Martin will be in charge of a broad range of projects and will work closely with other directors and members of staff. He will continue to be responsible for our Rightshoring Project. I wish him every success in his new role.

Thelma Dowd has been appointed his assistant.

Roger Wright
Chairman

From: Pandora@CoachworX
To: Martin Lukes

Hi Martin
This is the last day of Executive Bronze and the last day of our journey. I have said many words to you over the year, and I have only two left.

Martin, I want to say: Thank you. Thank you for making the journey. Thank you for growing. It's been an incredible year. Thank you for sharing it with me. You have come a long,

long way and I now can officially declare you to be 22.5 per cent better than your best! As your Number One fan I would like to say:

Martin, keep striving and keep thriving!
Pandora

From: Martin Lukes
To: All Staff

Dear friends, co-colleagues, mentors and mentees,
After some gut-wrenching soul-searching with family and friends, I have come to an important decision re my career at a-b glöbâl. Over the holiday season I have pondered whether to pursue some exceedingly interesting opportunities in the 'outside world', or whether to stay here at a-b glöbâl.

You will have seen from Roger's announcement what my decision has been. However I'm sure that you will all be curious about the thinking that went into this decision, and so I have decided to share it with you.

I'm staying because I've been given the freedom to be the creovative™ genius I aspire to be.

I'm staying because the people I work with are brilliant and uniquely talented.

I'm staying because I never have to say, 'Can I be frank?' or, 'Can I be honest?' I just always am.

I'm staying because I believe in our behaviours.

I'm staying because I continuously want to see 'what's around the corner'.

I'm staying because I think we can make this company a better place to work, and I want to be part of that.

I'm staying because coming to work is a load of fun.

I'm staying for these reasons and many more. But, most importantly, I'm staying because when I meet someone on an aeroplane or at a dinner party or at a convention and they ask me what I do for a living, I'm extremely proud to tell them that I am Director of Special Projects and Strategy at a-b glöbâl.

All my very bestest
Martin Lukes

From: Cindy Czarnikow
To: All Staff

Hi everyone!
Wow! Thank you Martin for your honesty in sharing something so
personal with us. I know that many hundreds of a-b glöbâl employees
will be so grateful to you for expressing – so eloquently – exactly what
each of them was feeling.
*   Next year is going to be a great one for all of us. I can just feel it.*
I'm smiling at all of you.
Cindy

From: Martin Lukes
To: Graham Wallace

Meet you downstairs now. I've got a raging thirst. M

From: Martin Lukes
To: Thelma Dowd

Hi Thelma
Off for a drink with Graham. Happy New Year. Have a good
one.
Martin
PS What's this urgent message from Sebastian Fforbes Hever?
Did he say what he wanted?

From: Martin Lukes
To: Thelma Dowd

Wow! Sounds intriguing. If he calls back, I've got my mobile,
pager and BlackBerry with me.
Martin

Authors' Acknowledgements

At the end of the day, a book is basically all about team work. *Who Moved My BlackBerry?* was no exception.

First up, we would like to celebrate the contribution of Jasper McMahon who brainstormed, thought outside the box and sweated the small stuff. Kathryn Davies and Sathnam Sanghera had many key inputs to bring to the party, as did Edward Lucas.

Juliet Annan and Clare Alexander gave 120 per cent all the way.

And above all, sincerest gratitude to my coach, friend and mentor, Michael Skapinker, for his unstinting creovative assistance each week for my column in the *Financial Times*. Credit is also due to Richard Lambert, who had the guts and vision to see that *FT* readers would be interested in the weekly antics of one Martin Lukes! It is no exaggeration to say we could not have done this without any of you. Cheers.

Last but not least, we would like to thank our loving better halves, Jenny Withers and David Goodhart, who helped by reading the chapters, and for being there for us 24/7. Thanks to our children Jake, Max, Rosie, Maud, Arthur and Stan, for sharing in the tears and the laughter, and for pushing the envelope until it almost fell off the table.

Martin Lukes and Lucy Kellaway

Pandora's Acknowledgements

I would like to celebrate the work of my friends and mentors from the coaching community who have taught me so much, and whose teachings I have passed on to Martin and to many coachees down the years.

Above all I would like to mention Steve Covey, whose funeral exercise is one of the most profoundly moving and revealing lessons of all. I would also like to thank David Taylor, Laura Berman Fortgang, Paul McKenna, Pam Richardson, Antony Robbins and Arielle Essex for the inspiration I have garnered from you and your books. I have learned more about life from you than you will ever know.

LUCY KELLAWAY

IN OFFICE HOURS

A Masterclass in Office Love…

Stella Bradberry and Bella Chambers work for Atlantic Energy, a global oil company in London. Bella is a pretty single mother who dropped out of college and is doomed to work as an invisible assistant to a series of men of half her intelligence. Stella is twenty years older, about to get a seat on the board, and is the original no-glass-ceiling, high-achieving, multi-tasking mother of two. Everyone admires her; she's so straightforward and sensible. So what possesses both women to embark on pole-axing, heart-wrenching affairs with men they wouldn't have looked twice at outside the office?

Smart, funny, moving and agonizing, In Office Hours holds up a mirror to modern corporate life. It's all here - the lies and sabotage, the strutting lunacy of CEOs, men's choice of sandwiches, women's choice of affair underwear, taking credit for others' ideas, the building and crashing of egos. And the obsessive, dangerous conduct of work colleagues who, in the grip of passion, break all the rules.

'A fast-moving novel about office affairs. The unusual feature of Kellaway's writing is the witty way in which she challenges established mores'
Daily Telegraph